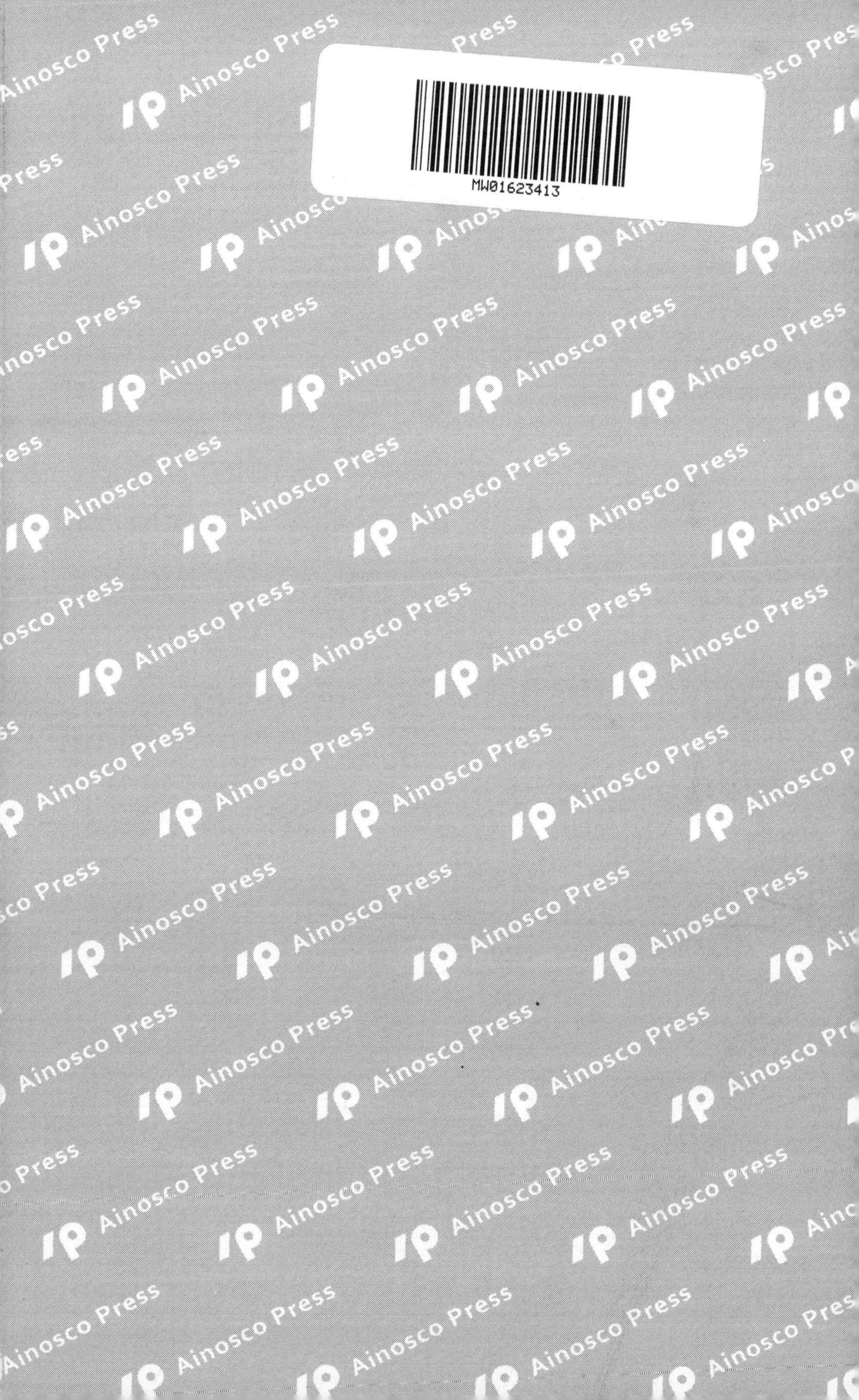
MW01623413

Heavenly Empress: The Age of Wu Zetian

A Novel of Tang and Wu Zhou China

Victor Cunrui Xiong

Ainosco Press

Heavenly Empress: The Age of Wu Zetian

Table of Contents

Part I. Ascent

Part II. Sole Sovereign

Part III. Sunset Years

Author's Note

This book is a "faction," that is, a hybrid of fiction and fact. Strictly speaking, it is more like a history in the guise of a historical novel. All the named characters and major events are based on historical records. As a rule, I do not indulge in much creative license when it comes to characterization. One notable exception is Yidu Neiren. I give her a larger role to play than what the only surviving record of her activity by the Tang man of letters Li Shangyin would suggest.

To the largest extent possible, I use historical place names in the main text, placing their modern equivalents in the notes. Occasionally, I use modern place names in the main text as well (for example, "Central Asia," "West Asia," "Manchuria," and others) for areas where historical place names either do not exist or do not make a lot of sense to modern readers.

In Tang and Wu-Zhou times, China used a solar-lunar calendar that was quite incompatible with the Julian Calendar. Oftentimes, but not always, the Chinese month was about one month behind. Under Wu Zetian, however, for some time, the Chinese month was about one month ahead. Nor do the Chinese days of the month match their Western counterparts. For these and other reasons, I use English months (e.g., January, February, etc.) to indicate months in the Julian Calendar, but numbered months (e.g., the first month, the second month, etc.) to indicate Chinese months. In most cases I follow the Julian Calendar when denoting years instead of the regnal system of dating (e.g., Yonghui 1).

In a related issue, traditional China and the modern West are quite different in the ways they divide time. In Tang China a month was divided into three ten-day weeks; and a day was divided into twelve double-hours (*shichen*).[1] In this book, I use modern units of time in most cases for the benefit of readers.

In the long span of human history to the twentieth century, government politics was almost always considered the exclusive domain of men with few exceptions. One of them was Tianhou, Heavenly Empress Wu Zetian. She was among the few Chinese

---

[1] The seven-day week existed in Chinese astrology.

female rulers who could stand alongside a handful of truly powerful female sovereigns in history—Hatshepset of the Egyptian Middle Kingdom, Cleopatra of the Ptolemaic Dynasty, Theodora of Byzantium, Irene of Athens, Maria Theresa of the Habsburg Empire, and Catherine the Great of Russia, among others. But Tianhou is the only female ruler in history to have overthrown a powerful dynasty in a major country and the only female emperor in Chinese history who ruled in her own right.[2]

In writing this novel I benefitted from the great literary works of the Western writers in the last two centuries and took particular inspiration from *Tales of the Alhambra*, a bilingual version of which I picked up at the bus station of Granada, Andalucía. While my plan to use it as a tool to study Spanish didn't pan out, I ended up imbibing this famous work by Washington Irving, with its blend of history, myth, and fantastic tales.

In the last place, I wish to acknowledge my debts to Hannah R. Keller, now a Ph.D. candidate at Ohio State University, for her helpful suggestions; to the Department of History, Western Michigan University, for providing a supportive work environment; and to my wife, Li Xiaoqing, for her constant support. In addition, I would like to express my sincere thanks to the Timothy Light Center for Chinese Studies, Western Michigan University, for a generous grant that made the publication of this book possible.

Victor Cunrui Xiong

March 2023

Kalamazoo, MI

---

[2] Irene of Athens (r. 797–802), the Byzantine ruler, may be considered a female emperor, even though some scholars prefer to call her "empress regnant." There are also those who argue that Wu Zetian (Tianhou) should be referred to by the same title, which has not been widely accepted at all.

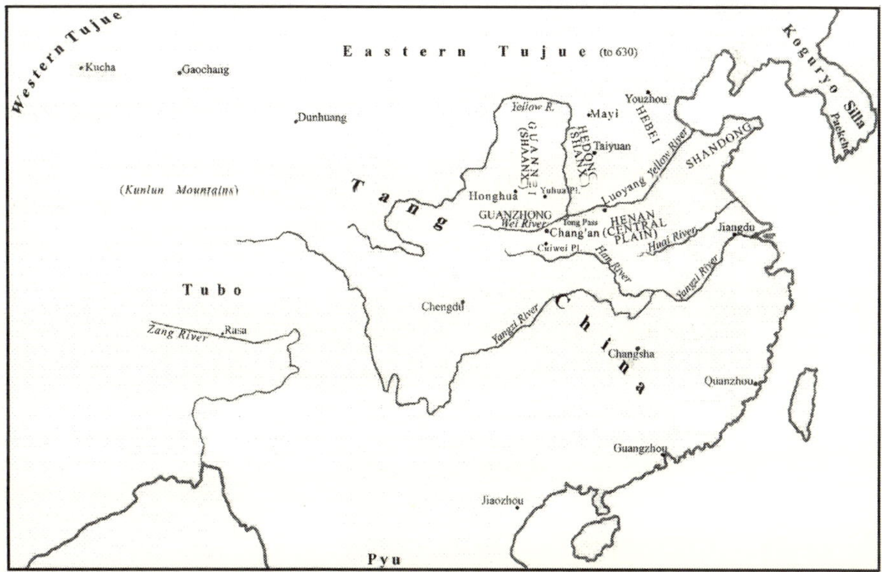

Figure 1. Tang China in the Early Seventh Century

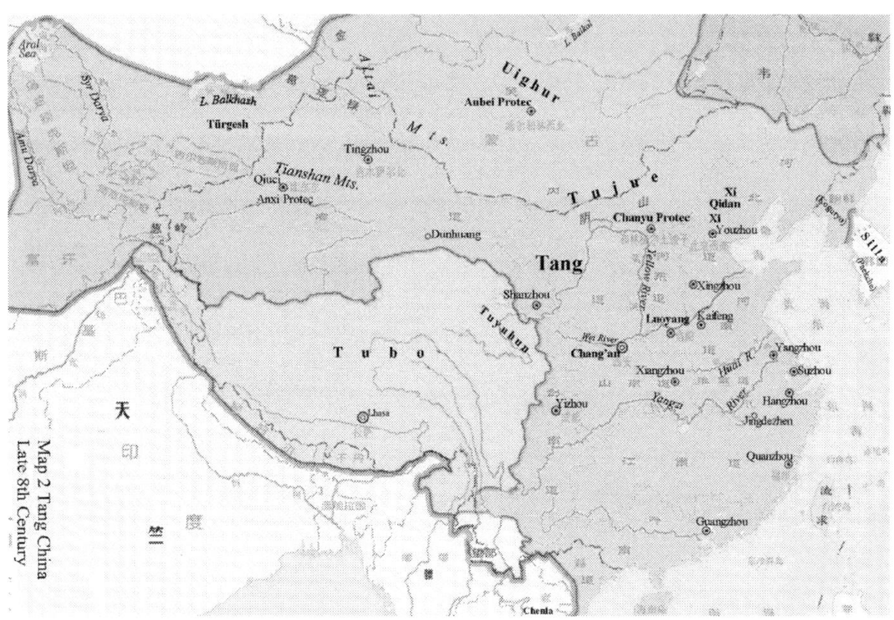

Figure 2. Tang China in the Late Eighth Century

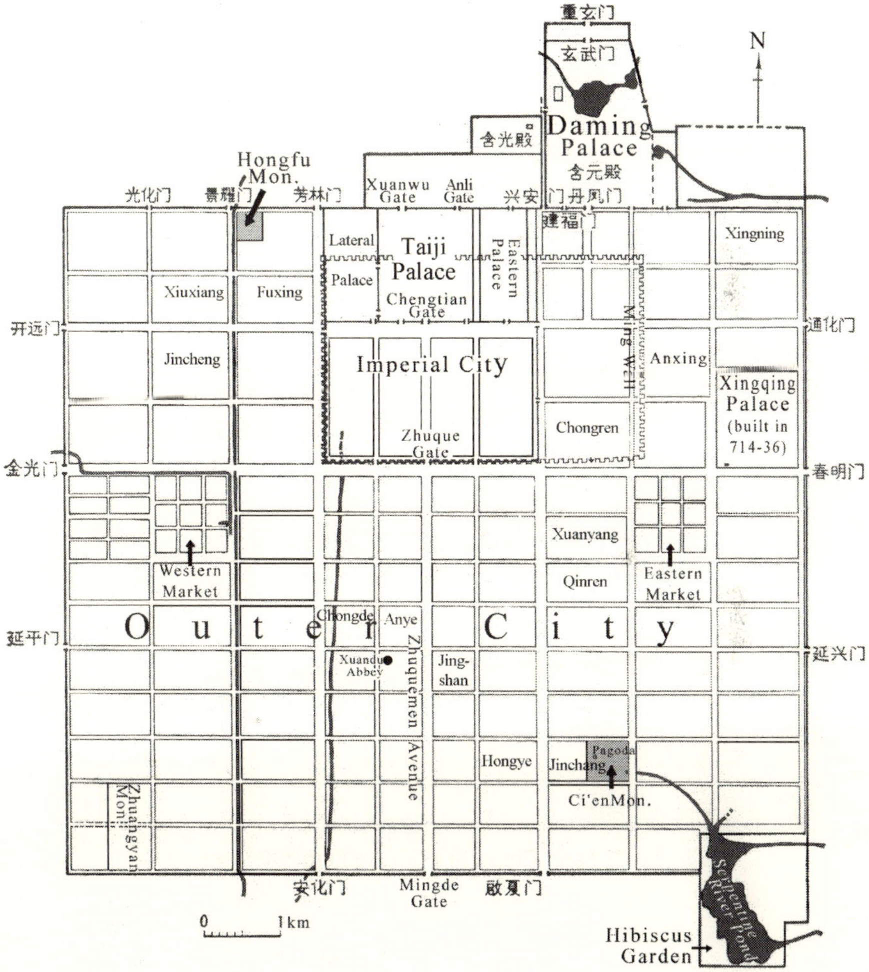

Figure 3. Tang Chang'an

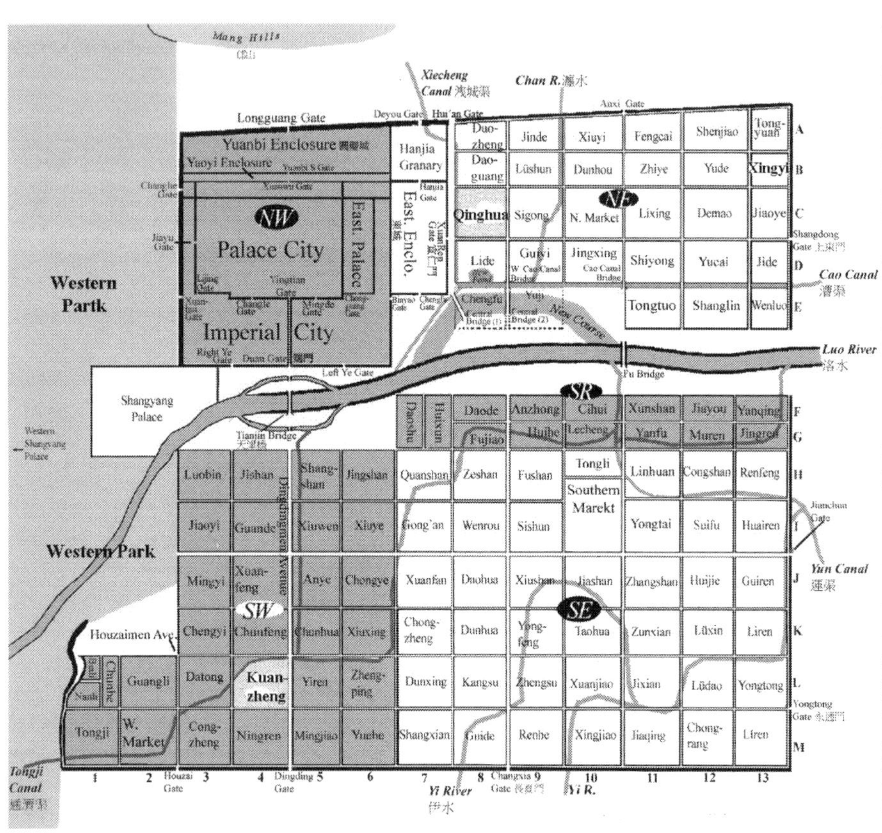

Figure 4. Tang Luoyang

Figure 5. Tianhou's Gold Tablet of 700 CE
(Collection of Henan Museum; size: 36.2 × 8.0 × 0.1 cm)

Figure 6. Inscription in Tianhou's Calligraphy
(from the "Stela of the Immortal Crown Prince")

Chronology

21st–17th c. BCE: Xia dynasty

17th–11th c. BCE: Shang dynasty

11th c.–3th c. BCE: Zhou dynasty

- 722–481 BCE: Spring and Autumn
- 403–221 BCE: Warring States

221–206 BCE: Qin dynasty

206 BCE–9 CE: Western Han dynasty

9–23 CE: Xin dynasty

25–220 CE: Eastern Han dynasty

220–266: Three Kingdoms

266–316: Western Jin dynasty

317–420: Eastern Jin dynasty

420–589: Southern Dynasties

- 420–479: Song
- 479–502: Qi
- 502–557: Liang
- 557–589: Chen

439–581: Northern Dynasties

- 386–534: Northern Wei
  - 439: unifier of the north
- 534–550: Eastern Wei
- 535–557: Western Wei
- 550–577: Northern Qi
- 557–581: Northern Zhou

581–618: Sui dynasty

618–907: Tang dynasty

618–712:	**Early Tang**
618–626:	Reign of Gaozu (Li Yuan).
624:	Birth of Wu Zetian (Tianhou).
626–649:	Reign of Taizong (Li Shimin).
637:	Wu Zetian admitted into the palace.
649:	Wu Zetian's affair with Li Zhi (Gaozong).
	Taizong passes away.
	Wu Zetian sent to Gan'ye Nunnery.
649–683:	Reign of Gaozong (Li Zhi).
651:	Wu Zetian readmitted into the palace.
652:	Birth of Li Hong.
653:	Fang Yi'ai incident.
654:	Birth and death of Wu Zetian's baby daughter.
655:	Wu Zetian's ascension as empress.
	Torture and death of former Empress Wang and Consort Xiao.
657:	Fall of the Western Tujue Khanate.
658:	Death of Chu Suiliang.
659:	Death of Zhangsun Wuji.
660:	Conquest of Paekche by Su Dingfang.
663:	Penglai (Daming) Palace completed.
665:	Shangguan Yi killed for drafting an edict to dethrone Wu Zetian.
665–666:	*Fengshan* trip to Mount Tai.
666:	Death of the state mistress of Wei, Wu Weiliang, Wu Huaiyun, and Li Yifu.
	Banishment and death (666 or later) of Wu Yuanqing and Wu Yuanshuang.
668:	Conquest of Koguryŏ by Li Ji.

669:	Death of Li Ji.
670:	Loss of the Four Garrisons to Tubo.
671:	Death of Helan Minzhi.
672:	Death of Xu Jingzong.
674:	Wu Zetian given the title Tianhou (Heavenly Empress).
675:	Death of Crown Prince Li Hong.
676:	Ashina Duzhi declares himself khan of the Ten Tribes.
	Annotated edition of the *Book of the Later Han* edited by Li Xián.
679:	Death of the magician Ming Chongyan.
	Pei Xingjian defeats Ashina Duzhi.
	Prince Narsieh attempts to return to Persia without success.
	Suiye (Tokmak) built by Wang Fangyi.
679–681:	Tujue rebellion in former Eastern Tujue.
	Tujue defeated by Pei Xingjian and Cheng Wuting (681).
680:	Crown Prince Li Xián deposed.
682:	Tujue rebellion in former Western Tujue.
682–745:	Later Tujue Khanate.
682–694:	Reign of Ashina Gudulu of Later Tujue.
683:	Death of Gaozong.
684:	First reign of Zhongzong (Li Zhe).
	First reign of Ruizong (Li Dan).
	Li Jingye rebellion in Yangzhou suppressed.
	Court leader Pei Yan executed.
684–705:	Reign of Tianhou (Wu Zetian).
685:	Xue Huaiyi becomes Tianhou's favorite.
686:	The Bronze Chest installed.
686–697:	Legalist law officers—Hou Sizhi, Wang Hongyi, Zhou

	Xing, Lai Junchen, and others—work for Tianhou to go after royals and her opponents.
688:	Li Chong-Li Zhen rebellion.
Early 689:	Mingtang and the Hall of Heaven set up in the Palace City, Luoyang.
689:	Heichi Changzhi dies of suicide.
690–705:	**Wu-Zhou dynasty**
690	Basilica Examination (*dianshi*) introduced.
691:	Death of Zhou Xing.
692:	The chief ministers' clique.
	Di Renjie's confession.
	Chief Minister Li Zhaode at the height of his power.
	Wang Xiaojie reestablishes control over the Four Garrisons.
	Li Dan's two wives (Consorts Liu and Dou) killed for practicing witchcraft.
693:	Death of Legalist officers Hou Sizhi and Wan Guojun.
694:	Death of Legalist officer Wang Hongyi.
	Legalist officer Lai Junchen's fall from grace.
	Chief Minister Li Zhaode's fall from grace.
	Hall of Heaven set on fire by Xue Huaiyi.
694–716:	Reign of Mochuo of Later Tujue.
695:	Xue Huaiyi killed.
	Heavenly Pivot set up in Luoyang.
696:	Tianhou's *fengshan* trip to Mount Song.
	Qidan rebellion suppressed in 697.
	Tubo's mission with a request for *heqin*.
	Di Renjie and Xu Yougong in favor with Tianhou.

697:	Zhang Changzong and Zhang Yizhi (the Zhang brothers) now Tianhou's favorite gigolos.
	Yan Zhiwei turns traitor in favor of Mochuo of Tujue.
	Execution of Lai Junchen and Li Zhaode.
698:	Directorate of Crane-Riders (later renamed Palace Office) founded.
699:	Civil war in Tubo; Lun Qinling dies; his brother Lun Zanpo flees to Wu Zhou.
	Death of the court leader Lou Shide.
700:	*Sanjiao zhuying* project begins and ends a few years later.
	Chief Minister Ji Xu demoted.
701:	Li Chongrun (Prince Yide), Li Xianhui (Princess Yongtai), and Wu Yanji killed for gossiping about the Zhang brothers.
702:	Martial Skills Examination (*wuju*) introduced.
703:	Trial of Chief Minister Wei Yuanzhong.
	Mochuo sends emissaries with a proposal to marry his daughter to a son of Tianhou's crown prince.
704:	Death of Tubo Zanpu Chidu Songzan.
	Death of the court leader Di Renjie (State Elder).
705:	"Five Princes" headed by Zhang Jianzhi launch a coup, in which they kill the Two Zhangs and topple Tianhou's rule.
	Tianhou passes away by year-end.
	Empress Wei, Wu Sansi, and Princess Anle form a powerful clique.
705–710:	Second reign of Zhongzong (Li Zhe).

706:	Wang Tongjiao incident. Tianhou buried in the Qianling Tomb Park near Chang'an.
707:	Li Chongjun incident; Wu Sansi, Wu Chongxun, and Li himself killed.
710:	Zhongzong poisoned to death by Empress Wei. Li Longji supported by Princess Taiping starts the Xuanwu Gate incident and seizes power; Empress Wei, Princess Anle, and their supporters killed.
710–712:	Second reign of Ruizong (Li Dan).
712–756:	**High Tang**
712–756:	Reign of Xuanzong (Li Longji).
755–763:	An Lushan rebellion.
756–820:	**Middle Tang**
820–907:	**Late Tang**
907:	Fall of the Tang dynasty.
907–979:	Five Dynasties
960–1279:	Song dynasty
1271–1368:	Yuan dynasty
1368–1644:	Ming dynasty
1644–1912:	Qing dynasty

Part I.

Ascent

1. Prince Li Sujie (649–651)

In the Middle East, the Muslims had been engaged in an aggressive expansion out of the Arabian Peninsula since 632. Under Caliph Uthman, they captured the island of Cyprus (649) and trounced the Persians.
In 651, Yazdegerd III, king of Sassanian Persia, fled east and was killed. The Sassanian Empire fell.

THE WHITE-HEADED Zhangsun Wuji made the announcement: "Today, in my capacity as regent of the Tang Empire, I hereby declare Prince Li Zhi as our new emperor." His booming voice echoed through the cavernous main hall of the Taiji Basilica in Chang'an's Taiji Palace.[1]

On this hot summer day in July 649, a young man in a hemp mourning vestment, stepped up a short flight of stairs onto the dais and seated himself in the embroidered yellow silk throne. He cast a fleeting glance at the crowd below—senior officials and officers. With traces of tears still visible on their faces, they made their way forward by turns to offer felicitations to the newly enthroned sovereign.

A large black lacquer coffin draped with white silk hangings was looming in the background. Inside lay the body of the late emperor Li Shimin (temple name:[2] Taizong). The new emperor Li Zhi (temple name: Gaozong) rose from the throne, turned around, and dropped on his knees in front of the coffin and touched the floor with his forehead again and again until Zhangsun Wuji came over and stopped him before helping him to his feet. Guided by the chief ritualist of the palace, the emperor concluded his inauguration without a major faux pas.

As he was being carried in his imperial palanquin, the emperor contemplated the majestic presence of Uncle Zhangsun, a constant reminder that, had it not been for his backing, all this—heirship and succession to the throne—would have been impossible. While Father was alive and well, no one in his right mind would have thought of Li Zhi as a serious contender for the throne. At least not until his two elder brothers were disgraced and punished, and an opportunity opened up for him. His father Taizong, on the advice of Zhangsun, then made him the crown prince. But he changed his mind a few months later after Li Zhi had failed to shake off his reputation as a milksop. For a time Taizong seriously considered replacing him with his half-brother Li Ke, who, although born to a lowly concubine, took after Taizong more than any of his sons. Eventually, however, the replacement did not happen, thanks to the stubborn opposition of Uncle Zhangsun Wuji.

For months after the double event of the funeral and coronation, the emperor Li Zhi had lived in mourning, wearing a mourning hemp vestment in public and doing his best to avoid wine, meat, intimacy with women, and even bathing. On his orders, key structures in the palace were draped in white, and all entertainment activities at court were suspended.

On the first day of the first month of the New Year (in early 650), half a year after the funeral, the emperor opened a grand ceremony in the Gatetower of the Chengtianmen[3] (the southern main entrance to the Taiji Palace, which occupied the central and main part of the Palace City) and proclaimed a new reign period—Yonghui or "Eternal Beauty." With that, the pall of grief that had descended upon the palace was finally lifted. An extravaganza lasting three days followed as the entire city celebrated the new beginning.

***

"Your Majesty," Zhangsun Wuji said, "since enthronement in July, the transition of power has gone much, much better than expected."

The emperor, who was having an audience with the regent in the Ganlu Basilica,[4] remained quiet as he listened with rapt attention.

"Well, all the chief ministers," Zhangsun continued, "are loyal supporters. The Three Departments, the Six Boards, the Nine Courts, and the Sixteen Guards are in safe hands. Now, as I am approaching the age of sixty, I often feel washed out. And I do hope I can step down before long. Don't worry, if Your Majesty needs advice, I will always be there. For now, there is one important matter that needs to be addressed—the naming of the empress."

"How soon, Uncle?" The emperor knitted his brows.

"Your Majesty," said Zhangsun as he lifted a celadon bowl from the small table and took a sip of his Mengding green tea.[5] "It should take place as soon as the New Year celebration is over."

"But my wife is not ready yet, I'm afraid."

"What does Your Majesty mean?"

"She has been having trouble getting pregnant."

"That should not make her ineligible."

"But I'm still worried."

"About what, Your Majesty?"

"Who is going to be my heir?"

"Well, there is still hope that your young wife may give birth to a boy before long. In the worst case, we can choose someone from your four sons born by the other consorts."

"Are you sure it does not break any rules?"

"Rules? Rules are made to be broken. Moreover, you are the emperor and what you say can trump whatever rules on the books!"

"Seriously?" The emperor looked astonished.

"Yes, Your Majesty."

"Then I shall see to it, Uncle."

"Excellent, Your Majesty." With a light smile on his face, Zhangsun took another sip of his tea.

***

In the second week of the New Year, an edict went forth to appoint Lady Wang, the emperor's principal wife, as empress and create her father Wang Renyou the state duke of Wei and her mother Lady Liǔ the state mistress of Wei. More festivities followed to celebrate the propitious occasion.

On the day of her coronation in the audience hall of the Taiji Basilica, a palanquin borne by eight eunuchs was carried across the hall. At the flight of stairs leading to the dais, the palanquin came to a stop. Out came a young woman, who, guided by two court ladies, mounted the dais to settle herself on the throne beside the emperor seated on his own throne.

The vision of his wife decked out in the empress's regalia brought back to the emperor past memories. It was Grand Princess Tong'an[6] who had proposed the marriage. Father was favorably inclined towards it, in part because of the young lady's remarkable beauty. The fact that the go-between herself was a grandaunt to both bridegroom and bride made the proposal even more appealing. The proposed union avoided violating the incest taboo by the fact that the prince and his bride-to-be bore different surnames. Since all marriages were arranged by parents, Li Zhi had no say in the matter, but he was pleased with his father's decision. After the marriage, he took in more women, legally, of course, under the polygamy system of Tang China, but she remained his one and only principal wife.

***

"The emperor has not paid me a visit for almost two weeks, Uncle," Empress Wang said to a middle-aged man in his purple official robes. She was having an audience in the reception room of her own basilica.

"Because of her, Your Majesty?"

"Yes, I think so. The vixen is casting a spell on him. I'm in trouble."

"I would not think so, Your Majesty. Consort Xiao[7] was already His Majesty's favorite when he made you his empress. At least for a while, the emperor will not change his mind. But . . ." Uncle Liǔ Shi dithered as he glanced at the two court ladies in attendance.

"What?" said the empress, who gestured the ladies away.

"Well," Liǔ Shi said in a low voice, "to be frank, you have to take measures to protect yourself sooner or later, Your Majesty. And the best protection is—a son."

The young empress sighed and said with resignation, "Where can I get a son? In the last six years, I haven't had a single pregnancy."

"Now is different. As empress, you have access to the best physicians in the palace. I know for a fact that they have secret nostrums for infertility."

"Do they? I'll summon one tomorrow."

"Sooner the better, Your Majesty," Liǔ Shi said. A long pause followed, as his face darkened. "Meanwhile," he resumed, "you have to 'hedge your bets,' as they say in gambling, and play a hand in the selection of the crown prince."

"To set up one of those boys by others?"

"Exactly," Liǔ Shi said. "You have to do it."

"What if I give birth to a boy later?"

"No worries, Your Majesty. The crown prince is made and unmade by man. So long as you are the empress, you can depose him any time."

"The emperor has four sons, aged five to nine. Sujie, the youngest, is his favorite."

"Your Majesty has to do everything in your power to prevent *him* from becoming crown prince."

"I know. His mother Consort Xiao wants to replace me even in her dreams. Who then would *you* pick, Uncle?"

"The oldest, Li Zhong."

"Prince Li Zhong? He doesn't look too bright. In fact, he is kind of dumb, isn't he?"

"That doesn't matter."

"But his mother is so boorish."

"Well, she comes from a low-ranking official's family. So much the better. Because of her humble birth, she is unlikely to cause trouble in the future."

"But who can persuade the emperor to pass over his favorite son Sujie?"

"As president of the Secretariat,[8] I have daily contact with His Majesty. I think I may have an influence on him. At any rate, leave that to me, Your Majesty," said Liǔ Shi with confidence.

***

At the annual gathering of prefectural representatives[9] from all over the country in the Liangyi Basilica[10] of the Taiji Palace in early 651, the emperor Li Zhi announced the appointment of two senior officials to de facto chief ministers.[11] One of them was the empress's uncle Liǔ Shi, president of the Secretariat. The emperor made the "de facto" appointment on purpose, because, unlike the "formal" appointment, it did not require a complex procedure. With that appointment, the emperor made him a member of his inner circle.

The cooperation between the chief ministers under Zhangsun Wuji and Chu Suiliang had worked so well in the first year of the

Yonghui reign (650) that it invites favorable comparison with Taizong's Zhenguan reign (627–649), a golden age that deserves to be called a *Pax Sinica*.

Then something took place that could shift the balance of power at the top. First, Regent Chu Suiliang was transferred out of the capital by way of demotion, after he was impeached for purchasing a plot of land at an unfair price. Then, the top military officer General Li Ji (Li Shiji) was divested of his substantive post as vice premier of the Department of State Affairs[12] at his own insistence but was then appointed de facto chief minister.

Defender-in-Chief (*taiwei*)[13] Zhangsun Wuji was now the indisputable leader of the court. But as such he could not avoid arousing jealousy and suspicion. And there were no lack of people who wished to see him fall from grace.

A certain Li Hongtai[14] from Luoyang, probably speaking on behalf of people in high places, accused him of plotting rebellion. The emperor felt violated and ordered the accuser's summary execution. The malicious attempt achieved the opposite effect and the bond between uncle and nephew strengthened. But doubt in the leadership lingered on.

***

One afternoon in early winter, the emperor withdrew into the Rear Palace,[15] where he entered the courtyard of a small basilica shaded with juniper and cedar trees. His face beamed as he saw a little boy holding the hand of his mother, walking towards him, patches of sunlight falling on them. The emperor hoisted him up in his arms and asked, "What have you been doing, my precious?"

The woman said to her son, “Sujie, tell His Majesty what you have learned?”

The child stared at the emperor without saying a word.

“Never mind, if he doesn’t want to,” the emperor said.

“Could your humble servant tell Your Majesty about it?”

“Go ahead, Consort Xiao.”

“Sujie has learned to recite poems.”

“Really?” asked the emperor, his eyes open in disbelief.

“Yes, Your Majesty.”

“Amazing!” Staring down at the boy, the emperor demanded, “Recite one for me!”

“Fireflies,” the child murmured.

“What?”

“He wants to catch fireflies, Your Majesty.” Xiao then said to her son, “Don’t be so rude, Sujie.”

“That’s fine,” the emperor said as he put him down. A lady attendant took him away.

With his eyes on Xiao, the emperor asked, “How are you, my darling?”

“What should I say,” she answered with a sigh as tears began to brim in her dark almond eyes.

“Not again! I can’t demote Empress Wang now. She was chosen by Grand Princess Tong’an with Taizong’s approval.”

“That is not what I am worried about. It is this hatred she has for me. After Sujie’s birthday, I took him to see her, and that was required by ritual. After we sat for a long time in the waiting area, the head eunuch came out and told us that the empress was not in a mood to receive visitors. I cannot imagine what is going to happen to Sujie once . . ."

"Don't you worry, my dear. I'm still young and will be the guardian of you and your child forever."

"Mom!" Sujie shouted with excitement. He was running towards her with the lady attendant chasing after him.

"Look at what I caught." As he said so, he held up his little fist and opened it. A small firefly took off as it glowed intermittently.

"Nice kid!" the emperor said. "He even knows not to harm life."

"I know this poem about fireflies too," Sujie said.

"Can you recite it for His Majesty?" the mother prompted.

A loud voice began to speak:

It emits a light bright but tiny,
Floating on wings weak and dainty.
Afraid no one should take notice,
It glows by itself in darkness.[16]

"My goodness!" shouted the emperor in amazement. "The poem by Yu Shinan, one of the poetic greats."

The emperor picked Sujie up, held him in his arms, and continued, "My son, you are a genius. I have to reward you. Let me see . . . The Capital Prefecture of Yong[17] needs a top leader. How about you? Can you do it?"

Sujie nodded his head.

"Your Majesty cannot be serious," the mother hastened to say.

"Of course, I am. Since antiquity, the sovereign is never allowed to joke about such matters. I'll see to it that Sujie be appointed prince of Yong and governor of Yong."[18]

Notes

1 The Taiji Palace 太極宮 was the Palace City (*gongcheng* 宮城) in Chang'an and occupied the north-central part of the city. The Taiji Basilica 太極殿 was its principal structure and the venue for formal court assemblies and major ritual activities.

2 Traditionally, a deceased emperor is referred to by his temple name (*miaohao* 廟號) or posthumous title (*sihao* 諡號). The Tang emperors are all referred to by their temple name in the sources.

3 The Chengtianmen 承天門: here *men* means "gate." The "gatetower" of Chengtianmen functioned like a basilica and served as a venue for court gatherings and ritual activities.

4 The Ganlu Basilica 甘露殿: a key palatial building located at the center of the Taiji Palace on its central axis and north of the Liangyi Basilica 兩儀殿.

5 Mengding 蒙頂 tea: a highly prized green tea grown in the Mengding Mountains in Sichuan.

6 Grand Princess Tong'an 同安長公主: younger sister of Tang Gaozu Li Yuan 唐高祖李淵 (Li Zhi's grandfather). The title "grand princess" was usually conferred upon the emperor's sister or aunt.

7 She was also known as Xiao Shufei 淑妃. *Shufei* (Pure Consort) was a title for a high-ranking imperial consort next to *guifei* 貴妃 (Noble Consort) in rank.

8 The Secretariat (*zhongshu sheng* 中書省), also known *xitai* 西臺 (Western Terrace), *fengge* 鳳閣 (Phoenix Pavilion), and *ziwei sheng* 紫微省 (Department of Purple Tenuity), was one of the three top-echelon government agencies known as the "Three Departments."

9 Prefectural representatives (*chaoji shi* 朝集使): high-level representatives sent to the court annually by various prefectures (*zhou* 州) to report on their administrative and financial activities.

10 The Liangyi Basilica 兩儀殿: a key palatial building located at the center of the Taiji Palace on the central axis and south of the Ganlu Basilica 甘露殿.

11 Chief minister: designation for a chief policymaker at the center. In the Tang, de facto chief ministers were often appointed with such status indicators as *tong zhongshu-menxia sanpin* 同中書門下三品 (equal in status with the Secretariat-Chancellery officials of the third rank), *tong zhongshu-menxia pingzhang shi* 平章事 (policy adviser), or simply, *pingzhang shi*.

[12] *Puye* 僕射 (vice premier; vice president of the Department of State Affairs): one of the two co-presidents of the Department. The post of president (*shangshu ling* 尚書令) existed in name only in most of the Tang.

[13] Defender-in-chief (*taiwei* 太尉): one of the three highest prestige titles known as the Three Dukes (*sangong* 三公).

[14] Li Hongtai 李宏泰: not to be confused with the occultist Li Hongtai 李弘泰.

[15] The Rear Palace (*hougong* 後宮): the part of the palace where the empress and imperial consorts and concubines resided, similar to a harem.

[16] *Quan Tang shi* 36, "Yongying" 咏螢 by Yu Shinan 虞世南.

[17] Yongzhou 雍州.

[18] Prince of Yong (*Yongwang* 雍王) and governor of Yong (*Yongzhou mu* 雍州牧): Yong was the Wei River valley area (in present-day southern Shaanxi) where Chang'an was. Prince of Yong was a most prestigious title.

2. Gan'ye Nunnery

IN CHANG'AN'S GAN'YE Nunnery,[1] Lady Wu was fetching water from a deep stone well. She lowered a well bucket on a rope to let it hit the water surface, swung the rope a couple of times until a splashing sound was heard and the bucket was filled. She then pulled it up hand over hand. After she moved in two years before, she had fetched water almost every day, and come to enjoy the work, especially during summer. The sound of water somehow helped break the monotony of her daily routine and refreshed her.

But to bring water home from the well was always a challenge. She had to place two heavy wood buckets on the two ends of a balancing pole and carry the pole on her slender shoulder. She would then lumber all the way to the dorm house, up a long flight of steps. She had to take care of other chores as well: cooking meals, doing laundry, washing crockery, and cleaning. During the farming seasons she even had to work in the fields.

Luckily, her life as *bhikṣunī* (Buddhist nun) did not consist entirely of physical labor. She spent much of her time reading and reciting the sutras and meditating while facing a wall. Brought up as a Buddhist, she was an ardent believer of the religion. That somehow eased her transition to monastic life. Her only regret now was the loss of her femininity: the shaved head, the absence of make-up, drab-color clothing, and of course, no more contact with men.[2]

At night, she would reminisce ruefully about her past lay life. One of her most cherished memories was about Yuan Tiangang's visit when she was still a toddler in diapers. After the white-bearded physiognomist in a white Daoist robe examined her much older siblings, he told Father that all of them would end up with high social status, but none of them would come to a good end. Just as Yuan was about to make for the door, he saw this beautiful baby in the crib. Dumbfounded, he shouted to Father, "This child is Heaven's favorite! If you don't mind showing me his Eight Characters (*bazi*), I can give you a firm prediction." Father gladly wrote down the four pairs of *jiazi* characters, indicating the double-hour, day, month, and year of her birth, on a piece of paper.

Also known as the Four Pillars of Destiny, the Eight Characters, it is believed, contain a secret message about a person's entire life. Yuan Tiangang studied the child's Eight Characters for only a few brief minutes before he announced, "My first impression is right. This boy is one in a million. No, one in one hundred million. His birth year, birthday, and birth double-hour pillars are all headed by the character *jia*, the first of the Heavenly Stems.[3] That suggests extreme *yang* power. I can assure you, Shiyue, this boy is destined to be the one to rule over the entire realm."[4]

Father would have believed in such an auspicious prophecy, had it not been for the physiognomist's error in identifying the baby as a boy. It was a great pity, because Yuan was the most famed diviner in the nation at that time.

Of course, Lady Wu did not have a meaningful recollection of the event. It was from her father Wu Shiyue that she learned about it much later. And the prophecy left in her mind a lasting impression and instilled in her a strong sense of destiny.

As she grew up, she found herself in a highly competitive family environment. She lived under the same roof with her father and his two wives—Lady Xiangli the principal wife and Lady Wu's own mother Lady Yang the concubine, in addition to two half-brothers and two sisters. All her siblings were older than she except for one sister. She fought against her sisters for parental favor, but measured herself to her much older half-brothers, Wu Yuanqing and Wu Yuanshuang (the Yuan brothers), and to her paternal cousins, Wu Huailiang, Wu Weiliang, and Wu Huaiyun. She easily got bored with domestic tasks such as needlework, weaving, and cooking, but could spend hours reading the classics, history, and literature, having learned how to read at a young age.

Her father, a merchant by trade, was among the earliest to join Emperor Li Yuan's (temple name: Gaozu) rebellion towards the end of the Sui dynasty. With the founding of the Tang, her father was rewarded with senior government posts, which brought power and wealth.

After her father's death in 635, the family wealth of the Wus went into a marked decline. The tensions between the two broods of children that Lady Wu had hardly noticed before now bubbled up to the surface.

Having dismissed their domestics, Lady Xiangli the principal wife and Lady Yang the concubine now took turns to cook for the family.

Once at an evening meal, Yuanqing complained about not having enough to eat and got into a row with Lady Yang, brandishing his chopsticks in a threatening way. It soon degenerated into name-calling. Yuanshuang joined his brother in heaping abuse on the middle-aged woman. Lady Xiangli tried to pull them apart, but in vain.

Lady Yang's children were scared stiff except for Lady Wu of eleven *sui*, now seething with anger. When she heard Yuanqing utter the word "whore," she plunged herself at him, sinking her young teeth into his hand. Yuanqing, raging mad, seized the little girl by the hair, and hurled her several feet away.

Lady Wu found herself in trouble with her cousins as well—Wu Huailiang, Wu Weiliang, and Wu Huaiyun, sons of her father Wu Shiyue's elder brother. By tradition, they were considered members of the same Wu family. They often dropped by and rubbed shoulders with the young Lady Wu and her sisters and the Yuan brothers. Whenever there was a squabble between the Yuan brothers and the Wu sisters, the three cousins almost always sided with the former.

Cousin Weiliang once shouted out to the Wu sisters, in an attempt to put them in their place, his favorite Confucian saying, " 'Women and petty men are hard to deal with.' "

Her face turning red with fury, Lady Wu shot back, "Baloney!"

"How dare you?" Weiliang went for her, and she bolted away.

Weiliang gave chase around the courtyard garden until he caught hold of the girl behind a clump of bushes about five minutes later. He pinned her down on the ground. With his right hand clasping her slender right wrist, he twisted it behind her back no less than half a dozen times. Each time she grunted with pain. All the while, he screeched something about "insulting the Sage."

***

For Lady Wu and her two sisters, life without Father was becoming more and more unbearable. They were now second-class members in their own family. Lady Wu began to pin her hope on marriage as a way to get away from the bullying of her brothers and cousins.

An opportunity came when a eunuch envoy arrived in Bingzhou[5] where the Wus called home, looking for a young lady of marriageable age to serve as the emperor's concubine. Out of hundreds of qualified candidates, he selected Lady Wu at fourteen *sui*.

When she was leaving for Chang'an, her mother Lady Yang, holding her hand through the carriage window, began to tear up.

Lady Wu, much annoyed, shouted, "Stop it, Mother! Attending on the Son of Heaven—how does one know it is not good luck? To me, it is far, far better than becoming the wife of a middle-ranking official in the middle of nowhere. Don't be so worked up. I will be fine."

Upon her arrival in the Rear Palace in the Palace City, a palanquin picked her up and took her to the Ganlu Basilica for an audience with the emperor Li Shimin (temple name: Taizong). The meeting went well. Not long afterwards, a eunuch came to her dorm and read an edict that granted her the title "Talented Lady" (*cairen*) and the nickname "Charming Girl" (*meiniang*).[6] She was thrilled—His Majesty must have been impressed with her beauty.

In the following month, she was summoned into the imperial residence to attend on His Majesty no less than five times. Then for two months thereafter, she received no summons at all. *Probably not because I have done anything wrong*, she figured, *but there are simply too many consorts, concubines, and court ladies around the emperor; all are eager to please him.*

Later she learned from a eunuch that, after the death of Empress Zhangsun,[7] the emperor had not felt passionate about any woman yet.

By and by, the monotonous palace life settled into a pattern. Lady Wu became accustomed to it. Still, she would not miss an opportunity to stand out from the crowd.

One afternoon, as she was on duty at the Wude Basilica, a wild horse called "the Lion" was brought into its courtyard.[8] Five eunuch officers had tried but failed to tame it. That piqued the emperor's interest. He shed his imperial robes and put on his caftan and boots. Like an experienced trainer, he chirruped to the horse and it plodded over. He petted it gently on the head, and then, picking up a brush from a eunuch, started grooming its rump, back, all the way to the neck. The horse seemed to like the friendly gesture and stood still as the emperor climbed onto the saddle. He squeezed its girth with his legs ever so slightly and the Lion broke into a canter. A few paces on, it came to a halt and then started rearing its haunches, before, without warning, springing into the air, forcing the rider to vault off the saddle.

As the emperor was wiping off sweat on his face with a silk towel, Lady Wu got closer and said, "I, your humble servant, would like to help Your Majesty tame the animal."

"What would you do, Charming Girl?" the emperor asked, sizing up this young woman of slender build.

"It is simple. I only need three instruments: an iron whip, an iron stick, and a dagger."

"Yes?" The emperor was intrigued.

"I will first use the whip to lash it; if it fails to subdue the horse, I will then use the stick to strike its head; if the stick still fails, I will then use the dagger to cut its throat."

"As simple as that," the emperor said with a smile and went inside. Later, she was told by the eunuchs that she had won high praise from His Majesty. But for some reasons, her candid advice seemed to have estranged herself from him. In fact, for twelve years, she remained at the middling rank of "Talented Lady."

***

When Emperor Taizong grew old and sick, his heir, Prince Li Zhi, came to be with him every night, rain or shine. That gave her a chance to see him often. And she came to like this weakling of a prince, who was filial but without his father's martial skills at all. One night she caught sight of him stealing a look at her with a stupid expression on his face. She turned to stare at him. Their gazes froze and they fell for each other. From then on, despite the danger involved, they managed to have a tryst almost every day without being detected.

Soon they began to address each other by their pet names, Zhinu[9] for him and Huagu[10] for her, and exchange gifts. The most memorable one she received was a light-colored frock with pomegranate patterns. When she rendezvoused with him in that outfit, he seemed to have a hard time taking his eyes off her.

As the emperor's illness took a turn for the worse, the intimacy between Lady Wu and the crown prince deepened. Then, the emperor passed away. Although it was not unexpected, it caught the lovers unawares. All of a sudden, they no longer had the pretext to see each other. Worse, after the burial, they were forced to part their ways, apparently for good. He became the emperor, and she, a nun in the Gan'ye Nunnery.

By the time she left the palace, most of her worldly possessions had been taken away, except for a few undergarments and her pomegranate frock, which she had managed to hide in the bottom of her clothes chest. When alone, she would take out the frock, hold it to her chest, and caress it as she cried her heart out. One night, with tears streaming down her cheeks, she wrote on a white silk handkerchief a poem for her lover. She slipped it into the front pocket of the frock and drifted to sleep.

***

After Li Sujie was confirmed as the prince of Yong, rivalry between Empress Wang and Consort Xiao grew more and more intense. It was true that the emperor took more pleasure in Xiao's company. She was younger, better looking, and more cultivated; and her son was such a joy. But Wang was his only principal wife and enjoyed widespread support at court. Besides, she had done nothing wrong to deserve a reprimand, much less a demotion, which Xiao wanted. The emperor was conflicted.

One morning, as the emperor was getting dressed with the assistance of two palace maids, a trusted old eunuch came in with a silk bundle, something sent from a Buddhist institution. With a wave of his hand to dismiss the maids and the eunuch, he opened the bundle and found a frock with pomegranate patterns. From its front pocket he pulled out a crumpled silk handkerchief. He smoothed it flat and saw a poem brushed by his beloved Huagu. It read:

In my confused state of mind, I see red as blue,

Frazzled and haggard I've been thinking of you.
If you don't believe the tears I've shed for you daily,
See the pomegranate frock in this bundle.

The emperor glanced at the frock one more time. His face turned scarlet with shame and remorse, as a deluge of tears poured down his cheeks. His thoughts flew back to that fateful summer month he had spent in the Cuiwei Palace[11] south of Chang'an in 649. It was a weird time: as his heart was torn by the declining health of his father, he lived through the happiest moment of his life in the company of his father's concubine. He found it almost impossible to put it into words. Certainly, there was physical attraction. She was a legendary beauty. But in his eyes, there was something more, something magical about her that was irresistible and led to the belief that they were fated for each other by the will of Heaven. He recalled with great clarity the secret oath they had taken together never to be separated from each other no matter what. Oh, he so wanted to have her back in the palace. But how? What would Uncle Zhangsun Wuji, General Li Ji, and other senior advisers say about it? How would Empress Wang react to it? He balked at the idea and put the pomegranate frock away.

***

In July 651, on the second anniversary of Emperor Taizong's death, the emperor Li Zhi with a massive entourage visited the Zhaoling Tomb Park to pay homage to the joint tomb of his parents, Emperor Taizong and Empress Zhangsun, in the northwestern suburb of Chang'an. On his way back, the emperor, along with Empress Wang, stopped at the Gan'ye Nunnery to take part in a religious rite. Accompanied by the abbess and a small group of nuns, the imperial couple walked the whole length of the pine-covered central pathway in the courtyard to the Grand Basilica.

Inside, facing south was the central statue of Sakyamuni flanked by two smaller attendant bodhisattvas. In front of them was a long table on which was placed an incense burner filled with sand. The emperor lit a set of joss sticks, stuck them in the sand, knelt down on a round yellow cushion, and prayed quietly. With the help of a eunuch, he rose to leave. The empress got on her knees to do her offering. At the heavy basilica door, the emperor noticed one of the nuns with a thin face, a freshly tonsured head, and dark eyes, staring at him. The emperor asked, "Is that you, Huagu?"

"Yes, Zhinu." The nun made an obeisance, with tears on the brink of bursting out.

"How have you been?" asked the emperor, struggling to hold back his own tears.

"I am fine, Your Majesty."

"I'll make sure they will take care of you," the emperor said as he stepped over the threshold.

He walked to the imperial carriage and found that Empress Wang was already inside. He climbed into it and seated himself by her side. Tears flooded his eyes as the carriage drove off.

After a while, the empress broke the silence by asking, "Isn't that Lay Wu, Your Majesty?"

"Yes," he answered.

"Almost unrecognizable."

"Her condition is much worse than I thought."

"Your Majesty will do something about it?"

"What can I do?"

"Recall her."

"You are not afraid she'll compete with you for imperial favor?"

The empress chuckled and said, "Well, the daughter of a merchant and his concubine approaching thirty—why should I be afraid?"

"You really think there is no need to worry?"

"Not at all."

"Well, I'll see what I can do," he answered.

***

As Lady Wu was toting two buckets of water on a shoulder pole along the footpath strewn with fallen leaves, she was stopped by two nuns. One took from her the heavy buckets and the other led her away to the abbess's office. A eunuch officer rose to greet her and announced an imperial edict whereby Lady Wu would stop doing physical labor, live in her own dorm room, grow hair, wear lay clothes, and be attended on by two palace maids. He then handed her a silk bundle from His Majesty, in which she found the pomegranate frock.

Three months later one morning, with her hair fully grown, Lady Wu re-entered the Palace City and was settled in the Rear Palace.

Soon Lady Wu received her first key visitor, Empress Wang, bringing with her a small retinue of palace maids and eunuchs. As soon as she settled herself in a seat, a palace maid came around, holding a lacquer tray with two bowls of freshly brewed green tea, and set the tea bowls on the small table. The empress motioned to send all the maids and eunuchs away.

With a flustered look on her face, Lady Wu asked, "How can I be of service to Your Majesty?"

"Relax, Lady Wu," said the empress, her voice reassuring. "I just want to see how you are settling in."

During the casual chat with no special purpose that followed, the empress sized up the emperor's new woman in her head. *Obviously, age is creeping up on her. And her humble demeanor suggests she is obedient by nature. Yes, my early judgment was right: she is someone I can trust.*

When the time came for her to leave, the empress decided to let her into a secret and said, "One person bothers me though. You probably can guess who she is."

Lady Wu paused to think for a while, blinking her large dark eyes, shook her head, and said, "No, I cannot, Your Majesty."

"Consort Xiao."

"What has she done, Your Majesty?" Lady Wu was taken aback.

"She beguiles the emperor with her foxy charm and bad-mouths me at every turn."

"With your power and might, could you not just bring her down, Your Majesty?"

"No, so long as she keeps the emperor under her spell. That's why I need *your* help."

"Me, an unranked concubine?" Lady Wu asked in bewilderment.

"If you help me keep her away from the throne, I'll promote you. I promise."

"I will be thrilled to render any kind of service to Your Majesty. Just tell me what to do."

"Tomorrow, when the emperor pays you a visit, I want you to put on your most attractive dress." She opened a jewel box she had placed on a dresser nearby to show what was inside: several gold and silver hairpins with bird and floral patterns, and a pearl necklace. "These are my gifts to you for tomorrow."

Lady Wu thanked the empress with an obeisance. The empress got to her feet, saying, "Before I forget, take a fragrance bath as well."

"Yes, Your Majesty." Lady Wu inclined her head in a demure pose as the empress made for the door.

***

The emperor came the following afternoon. The moment he set his eyes on Lady Wu, he fell under her charm. She was wearing her pomegranate frock, with two floral hair pins, one gold and one silver, tucked in her hair, and a pearl necklace hanging on her neck.

As his nose took in her fragrant scent, his eyes bore deep into hers and his hands pulled her body close to him.

"I was afraid," Lady Wu said as she began to sob softly, "I would never see Your Majesty again."

"No one will ever separate us ever again," said the emperor, with tears rolling in his eyes, his hands busy taking off her jewels and dress.

She gulped down her sobs as the emperor hugged her tight.

They took in each other's essence, mouths pressed against skin, body against body.

Hours went by and it was getting dark. The emperor freed his hands and clapped them. A eunuch rushed in to receive his order: to cancel all of the emperor's nightly appointments, including the one with Consort Xiao. That had happened for the first time since her admittance into the palace. The eunuch made an obeisance and quietly left the room. The emperor returned to the embrace of his lover.

***

While visiting his niece in her basilica, Liŭ Shi, clad in his purple official attire, asked, "Your Majesty, how is Consort Xiao doing?"

"Well, Uncle," Empress Wang replied, "it seems that the emperor is losing interest in her. In fact, in the last two months, His Majesty has not paid her a single visit." She sounded almost gleeful.

"So His Majesty has been busy doing what?"

"He is smitten with love for that nun."

"Is he? But as an unranked concubine, Wu's position is not secure. When his passion for her cools, and I am sure it will, the emperor may return to the arms of Consort Xiao. Don't forget, Xiao is the mother of Sujie, his favorite son, after all."

"I wonder why Wu hasn't received a promotion yet."

"As Taizong's woman, she should remain in the nunnery. That is an age-old convention. Many top court officials do not like her recall to the palace at all. But without their approval, her promotion is difficult."

"She's stuck at the bottom?"

"Unless Your Majesty speaks out on her behalf. In this matter, your opinion carries great weight."

"I see . . . But I heard an unflattering whisper about her."

"What kind of whisper, Your Majesty?"

"She has a cruel streak."

"I think the opposite is true, Your Majesty. Actually, the first thing that strikes me about her is humility."

"I've got the same impression. But one of my eunuch officers warns me that she'll become a rival."

"Not a chance, Your Majesty. She will be thirty in a few months and start losing her physical charm in a couple of years. The only way for her to challenge you at all is to give birth to a boy. At her age, it will be nigh impossible to get pregnant, much less have a healthy boy baby. Besides, I suspect she won't pose a threat to you if even she has a son."

"What should be done, then, Uncle?"

"Well, I think we should *promote* her."

"How?"

"I just prepared a memorial." Liǔ Shi produced a silk scroll covered with fine characters.

After a quick browse, the empress called in a lady-in-waiting. With her assistance, the empress affixed her seal to the document.

The next morning, Liǔ Shi submitted the memorial to the court. To his total astonishment, it caused an uproar among the court leaders. Led by Zhangsun Wuji, they opposed, almost in one voice, the idea of raising Lady Wu to a high rank on grounds of tradition and lack of precedent. Li Ji was the only top leader who gave his assent to the memorial, since he regarded the promotion of an imperial concubine as the "family business of the emperor." In the end, it was the empress's endorsement that persuaded the emperor to go ahead with the motion to promote Lady Wu to Lady of Majestic Bearing (*zhaoyi*).[12]

***

With the passage of time, the empress's interest in promoting the emperor's eldest son Li Zhong had grown. But it was two years now since she had recommended him as crown prince and the emperor seemed to have ignored the recommendation altogether. That kept her on edge.

One day in the summer of 652, she summoned Uncle Liŭ Shi for consultation.

"Just look at Sujie." the empress said. "He was made the prince of Yong when he was barely five *sui*."

"Your Majesty, it is not unusual for an emperor to enfeoff five-year-olds."

"But his fiefdom is in Yong, the area where Chang'an is." A brief silence followed.

Before Liŭ Shi opened his mouth again the empress said abruptly, "How long again do I have to wait for Li Zhong's appointment? It is driving me crazy."

"Well, it is not as easy as I thought, Your Majesty. I cannot do it alone. So far, I have not been able to persuade His Majesty. If I try too hard, it may backfire. I need support from the Regents Zhangsun Wuji and Chu Suiliang. Zhangsun is inclined to side with me, but Chu is no longer in the capital."

"Chu Suiliang is now a local prefect. Does his opinion still count?"

"It does. As far as I can tell, his punishment is only temporary."

"So we do nothing now?"

"Well, Your Majesty, being patient is the best course of action."

In less than three months, Chu Suiliang was recalled to the capital. Liŭ Shi lost no time in paying him a visit in his Chang'an home and getting his approval.

Soon a joint memorial bearing the seals of Zhangsun Wuji, Chu Suiliang, and Liŭ Shi was delivered to the emperor's table. It recommended that Li Zhong be named crown prince. It filled the emperor with anger because it would prevent him from considering Sujie as heir. But when three of his most powerful court leaders spoke in one voice, the emperor had to listen. With great reluctance, he issued an edict appointing his none-too-bright eldest son to the post.

***

Following her promotion to Lady of Majestic Bearing, Wu became pregnant in 652 at a time when she was well past what was considered the "normal" child-bearing age. Staring at her growing belly, Lady Wu asked herself in ecstasy, "Isn't this a sign that I am favored by Heaven after all?" Ever since her return to the palace, she had been looking forward to the day when Yuan Tiangang's prophecy would come true. With this pregnancy, that day was getting closer.

The emperor, elated beyond words, had a team of palace physicians take turns to attend to the expectant mother day and night. At the end of a nine-month period, Lady Wu gave birth to a chubby boy without much pain at all. "Heaven be thanked!" she murmured and broke down crying.

To mark the birth of the new prince (later known as Li Hong), the emperor granted a three-day national holiday, and held lavish banquets at court to share his joy with senior officials and foreign dignitaries.

***

The empress welcomed the news of Lady Wu's pregnancy. She knew that by tradition the emperor was required to stay away from the expectant mother during the pregnancy to avoid premature birth, and not to share bed with her at least in the first month after birth. Thus, the empress had reason to believe that this would afford *her* a window of opportunity to get pregnant.

During Lady Wu's pregnancy, the empress had received the emperor in the Rear Palace a few times. But nothing came out of it. Starting in the second month of the baby's life, the emperor had stopped coming altogether. Instead, her sources told her, he went to see the baby boy every day and often spent the night with his mother.

The empress was not too concerned with Lady Wu getting intimate with the emperor every night until she was informed of her new plan: she had urged His Majesty to set up her own son Li Hong, still in swaddling clothes, as crown prince! It did not work, but was alarming enough for Empress Wang to ask herself, "What if she wants to do it again?"

After a long talk with Uncle Liǔ Shi behind closed doors, she made up her mind to redirect her energies to a new goal—to stop the nun in her tracks. She enlisted the help of her usual supporters at court such as Zhangsun Wuji, and offered to bury the hatchet with her rival Consort Xiao, who had been likewise neglected by the emperor since the nun's arrival. Faced with a common threat, they made an alliance of convenience and did everything they could to unmask the nun for who she really was—a lowborn, immoral woman who had intentionally broken the incest taboo of the Great Tang and was now out there to lead the emperor astray.

The emperor, for his part, had fallen completely under her sway. Lady Wu had become not only his bedmate, but his confidante, constant companion, and soul mate. Because of her, he had gone through a change in persona to become more sure-footed than ever before. Gone were the days when he would dilly-dally on important issues or defer decision-making to the chief ministers. Nor did he feel alone any longer in confronting his senior advisers, now that he could count on the firm support of this strong-willed woman.

Notes

1 The Gan'ye (Thaumaturge) Nunnery 感業尼寺 is traditionally identified as the Jidu Nunnery 濟度尼寺 in Anye Ward 安業坊, south of the Imperial City. See Zhang Yonglu 1990, 380, 368. Another view believes that the institution in question is the Lingbao Monastery 靈寶寺 in Chongde Ward 崇德坊 instead. See Li Jianchao 2006, 170, 181.

2 According to the sources (*Xing Tang shu*, *Jiu Tang shu*, *Tang huiyao*, and *Zizhi tongjian*), after Taizong's death, Wu Zetian was ordained as a nun. Some challenge this record. But most scholars accept it as believable.

3 *Jia* 甲 represents the first sign in the Heavenly Stems of ten, which are combined with the Earthly Branches of twelve to form the Sexagenary Cycle or the *jiazi* system.

4 Some believe that the Eight-Characters (*bazi* 八字) divination system debuted in the Mid-Tang period. Others, however, trace it to the Period of Division (220–589).

5 Bingzhou 并州 (Bing Prefecture) refers both to the prefecture (*zhou*) and its seat (capital), which was located southwest of present-day Taiyuan, Shanxi. Here it refers to the latter.

6 "Talented Lady" (*cairen* 才人) was the title for a middle-ranking concubine. "Charming Girl" (*meiniang* 媚娘): Wu Zetian is referred to as Wu Meiniang as well.

7 Empress Zhangsun 長孫皇后: Taizong's principal wife and younger sister of Zhangsun Wuji.

[8] The Wude Basilica 武德殿 was east of the Liangyi Basilica in the east-central part of the Taiji Palace.

[9] Zhinu 雉奴, lit., "pheasant slave." The graph *zhi* (pheasant) is a gender-neutral name. The graph *nu* (lit., "slave") here is used as a diminutive in reference to a boy or man. This usage was not uncommon. For example, Liu Yu 劉裕 (founder of the Liu Song dynasty) is also known as Jinu 寄奴; and Chen Shubao 陳叔寶 (last emperor of the Chen) as Huangnu 黃奴.

[10] Huagu 華姑, lit., "lass in blossom." Some suspect that here Wu Zetian's pet name was recorded in error, since her grandfather Wu Hua 武華 has *hua* as his given name, which should be tabooed within the lineage.

[11] The Cuiwei Palace 翠微宮 was a touring palace on the northern slopes of the Qinling Mountains south of Xi'an, Shaanxi.

[12] The Lady of Majestic Bearing (*zhaoyi* 昭儀) was a title for a high-ranking imperial consort. It had existed since the Western Han.

3. Lady Wu (652–654)

Japan sent its second mission to Tang China (kentōshi) in 652 and its third mission in 654.

THE PEACE OF the Yonghui reign came under serious threat because of an incident that happened close to the palace grounds in late 652. The emperor was greatly upset when he learned about it through Zhangsun Wuji's memorial.

Lady Wu, out of curiosity, read all the files. She noticed that everything stemmed from a squabble between the princess of Gaoyang (Fang Yi'ai's consort) and her brother-in-law Fang Yizhi (Yi'ai's elder brother). Conflict arose when the princess accused Yizhi of treating her with disrespect. Rumor had it that what she was aiming at was the duke's title which Yizhi had inherited from his father Fang Xuanling. But up to then the contention was only over relatively minor issues.

Then Fang Yizhi made his counter-allegation that exposed unflattering and reckless whispers by the rival camp headed by Gaoyang and her husband Fang Yi'ai. The quarrel now took on a new level of seriousness.

An investigation headed by Zhangsun Wuji then uncovered a conspiracy to usurp the throne with Prince Li Yuanjing (Taizong's brother) as the ringleader. It also dragged through the mud Prince Li Ke, the princess of Baling (Taizong's daughter), several imperial in-laws, and a group of high-powered officials.

However, Lady Wu suspected that many of the charges were on shaky grounds, especially those directed against Li Ke. She reminded the emperor that the late Emperor Taizong had seriously considered Li Ke as heir. It was Zhangsun Wuji's objection that had prevented it from happening. She argued that if the emperor now pardoned Brother Li Ke, it would go a long way in enhancing his image as a fair-minded, magnanimous sovereign without weakening the throne in the slightest.

The emperor agreed. At a court meeting the next morning he went one step further, offering to spare the lives of both Brother Li Ke and Uncle Li Yuanjing. But, to his dismay, it met with strong opposition from a host of top leaders, especially President of the Board of War[1] Cui Dunli. "Both princes have to be made an example of," he argued, "because the authority of the throne is at stake." In the end, this argument gave the emperor pause.

In early 653, the emperor gave his begrudging approval to the penalties recommended by Zhangsun Wuji. All the imperial in-laws implicated in the Fang Yi'ai treason case, including Fang himself,[2] would be decapitated in the Western Market; all the royals involved including the two princes and the two princesses would die in a more dignified manner—by suicide.

With a sword in hand, Prince Li Ke blurted out his last words, "Zhangsun Wuji, I condemn your entire clan to extirpation in five years!" He heaved a long sigh and struck his neck with the sword and fell.

Court officials who were close to Fang Yi'ai were all banished to the far south, including Prince Li Daozong (Emperor Gaozu Li Yuan's nephew), who had been a powerful general and a serious adversary at court to both Zhangsun Wuji and Chu Suiliang.

***

In early 654, to everyone's amazement, Lady Wu gave birth to a healthy, pretty girl while she was well into her thirties! This seemed to have a magical effect on all parties involved. The emperor was transformed into an adoring father who frequented the baby's chamber several times a day. Lady Wu insisted on breastfeeding her, turning down all wet nurses provided by the Rear Palace. The empress suspended the war of words with Wu and dropped in from time to time to play with the cute baby.

About sixth months after birth, the girl was dead. On that sad day, all the palace maids on duty were arrested by the Board of Justice.[3] Their confessions extracted under torture pointed to one suspect, the empress. That morning, they claimed, while Lady Wu was away, the empress had come to see the baby and left after she had fallen asleep. By the time Lady Wu returned in the afternoon, the baby was no longer breathing.

The emperor was grief-stricken beyond measure. Giving in to the belief that Empress Wang was behind the death of his daughter, he now found the very sight of her unbearable and stopped visiting her basilica altogether. Some court officials, worried over the long-term separation of the imperial couple, attempted to mend the bond between them. But the emperor was in no mood to follow their suggestions. Instead, he increasingly looked upon her a source of trouble and began to consider setting up Lady Wu as her replacement in earnest, something that had crossed his mind before, but he had never thought possible. By and by, he came to accept Lady Wu's desire to become empress as a reasonable measure to protect herself and her son from the machinations of Empress Wang. Furthermore, to place Wu on the throne of empress would silence once and for all her opponents—Empress Wang herself and Consort Xiao and their supporters at court. Naturally, it would also force Li Zhong, Empress Wang's "adopted son," to yield the title of crown prince to Li Hong. However, before making the move, the emperor, in keeping with convention, had to raise the issue with the two regents and other old court leaders.

***

On a late autumn afternoon, in his spacious mansion in the southeast quadrant of Chongren Ward,[4] Zhangsun Wuji was making preparations for a grand night party.

By then, with hundreds of Left Guard[5] troops standing guard, the city street running from the Yanxi Gate (the northernmost one of the three eastern entrances to the Imperial City) down to Chongren Ward (northwest of the Eastern Market) to the south was closed off to pedestrian and cart traffic.

The imperial procession was moving through the city street from north to south at full pelt. The main passenger, the emperor, kept this trip "incognito" on purpose, with a cavalcade much shorter than usual. Nonetheless, it consisted of dozens of horse-drawn carriages. He brought along with him Lady Wu and ten oxcarts loaded silk, gold and silver objects, and precious jewels, in addition to several jars of aged vintage wine from the palace.

Zhangsun Wuji, at the advanced age of sixty *sui*, came out to greet the arrival of the emperor and Lady Wu at the entrance to his home. When he saw the cavalcade, he felt overwhelmed by the show of imperial favor. He was glad that his family chefs had prepared an exquisite banquet. With roast piglets, pita breads stuffed with sliced donkey meat, and a variety of other dishes, it did not disappoint. His long-aged homebrew they served matched the emperor's palace wine in flavor. Both host and guests delighted in partaking of the fragrant drinks in an ambiance that was at once pleasant and relaxing.

The emperor, now semi-tipsy, rose to make an announcement, "Hereupon I am granting the Rank-5 prestige title of 'counselor for closing court'[6] to the three youngest sons of Uncle Zhangsun, all born to his favorite concubine."

Zhangsun knelt down to show his profound gratitude, despite his stiff back; the emperor hastened to help him to his feet.

After they both sat down again, the emperor added, "One more thing: about Empress Wang. Clearly, she is barren. I have been thinking of replacing her."

With a flushed face and neck, Zhangsun arched his eyebrows and said, raising his goblet, "This palace wine is exce- . . . excellent! Could I have some more, Your Majesty?"

"Of course," said the emperor as he picked up the silver ewer and filled up Zhangsun's goblet. He then repeated the proposal.

Zhangsun wagged his head, smiling, as he sipped his wine but did not seem to understand the issue.

After the emperor and Lady Wu stayed on at the Zhangsun mansion for two more hours, they left empty-handed.

A few days later, at Lady Wu's request, her mother Lady Yang and President of the Board of Rites[7] Xu Jingzong (now the leader of the pro-Wu party) each paid a visit to Zhangsun Wuji at his Chongren home to plead with him while he was sober, but he flatly rejected both.

***

Lady Wu was sitting in front of a bronze mirror placed on top of a dressing table. A maid was fixing her hair. Lady Wu noticed a small lock of silver hair on her forehead and sighed.

The maid asked, "Is there anything the matter, My Lady?"

"I am aging fast, all because of her."

"The empress?"

"Who else?"

"I heard she is very cocky. Not only that. She is rude and stingy to her housemaids. Her mother and uncle are like that as well."

"How do you know?"

"One of my fellow villagers works there."

"Oh? Is she also from Wenshui, Bingzhou?"[8]

"Yes, like myself, she also comes from My Lady's native place."

"Can you absolutely trust her?"

"I swear to Buddha, I can."

"Does she want to work somewhere else?"

"Yes. Every single day."

"Wait a moment," said Lady Wu as she pulled out a pouch from under her seat and poured a handful of silver pieces into the maid's hand. "I want you to have half of these and give the rest to her."

"Thank you, My Lady. But what do you want her to do?"

"I'll let her know later. You can also tell her, if she does as she's told, a much bigger reward is waiting for her."

"Yes, My Lady."

"You do know the rule, don't you?"

"Yes, I know, My Lady. We must never tell it to another soul," said the maid as she inserted a long silver hairpin into the back of Wu's lush hair.

Notes

1 The Board of War (*bingbu* 兵部): one of the Six Boards (*liubu* 六部), which were the executive agencies under the Department of State Affairs (*shangshu sheng* 尚書省).

2 Fang Yi'ai was the second son of Fang Xuanling 房玄齡, Taizong's most trusted senior official.

3 The Board of Justice (*xingbu* 刑部): one of the Six Boards under the Department of State Affairs.

4 In Tang China, cities were divided into a number of gated, walled neighborhoods known as "wards" (*fang* 坊). In Chang'an, the largest city, there were more than 100 wards. Chongren 崇仁 was one of them.

5 The Left Guard (*zuowei* 左衛) was one of the Sixteen Guards. Its headquarters was in Chang'an.

[6] The counselor for closing court (*chaosan dafu* 朝散大夫) was an upper-middle level prestige title.

[7] The Board of Rites (*libu* 禮部): one of the Six Boards under the Department of State Affairs.

[8] Wenshui 文水: county east of present-day Wenshui, Shanxi. Bingzhou 并州: prefecture in Shanxi with its seat southwest of present-day Taiyuan, Shanxi.

4. Ascension (655)

In the West, Pope Martin I died. During his pontificate, he had condemned Monothelitism.

IN THE SIXTH month of 655, acting on a tip, court investigators raided the main residential basilica of the Rear Palace. In the backyard they unearthed five cloth dolls a few paces away from a stone wellhead. With needles pierced through the heart, each bore the character *wu* on its back. This piece of evidence and a barrage of interrogations that followed linked the empress and her mother to black magic activities.

The emperor, livid with anger, ordered to banish Empress Wang's mother Lady Liŭ from the palace for good and demote Liŭ Shi, the empress' uncle, to a provincial post in Sichuan. His original post of president of the Secretariat now went to Cui Dunli, one of Lady Wu's allies at court. The maid of Wenshui in the service of the empress received under the table 200 ounces of silver from Lady Wu for her help in discovering the crucial evidence.

***

In the pecking order of the Rear Palace, the empress was at the top as the leader of female officers. Immediately below her were the Noble Consort (*guifei*), Pure Consort (*shufei*), Virtuous Consort (*defei*), and Worthy Consort (*xianfei*),[1] all belonging to the first equivalency rank (*shi yipin*).[2]

Since Empress Wang was still backed by the key officials at court, it was hard at this stage to replace her. The emperor decided to create a new title especially for Lady Wu with a rank just below the empress. He called it "Imperial Consort" (*chenfei*).[3] To his annoyance, two junior chief ministers, Hann Yuan and Lai Ji, stepped forward to oppose it with the stubbornness of a mule. The other leaders were lukewarm to the new title. Not a single one of them offered to write a memorial in support of Wu. And the emperor had no choice but to shelve the plan. He did not want to get into an argument with the top court leaders but was nonetheless disheartened by the lack of enthusiasm.

While the emperor was at a loss for how to promote his favorite woman, he received a memorial from Zhangsun Wuji to banish a middle-ranking official in the Secretariat, named Li Yifu. The emperor recognized the name: Li had served as his secretary during Taizong's reign when he was crown prince.

"Li Yifu seems like a soft-spoken gentleman, very nice and always smiling. What has he done wrong?" the emperor asked.

"Your Majesty," Zhangsun Wuji answered, "he has a kindly façade all right, but he is a treacherous schemer at heart. That is why his nickname is 'Man Cat.' "

"Oh?" The emperor was intrigued.

"He was caught lying multiple times and convicted of selling offices."

"In that case, I will issue the edict to transfer him out of Chang'an right away," the emperor said.

***

The emperor spent the whole afternoon browsing through more than a hundred memorials. They bored him except for the one about Lady Wu. It made an eloquent argument that she had won the hearts and minds of the people and the court should promote her to empress instead of creating a new title for her. Delighted, the emperor shifted his eyes to the name of the memorialist and his seal at the bottom—Li Yifu.

"What a pity! Li Yifu would have made a great advocate," the emperor commented to Lady Wu. "But it is too late, I've already banished him."

"Why?"

"On Zhangsun Wuji's advice."

"But you are the emperor, aren't you? You are supposed to call the shots."

"I do call the shots. But my edict has gone out."

"When did you issue it?"

"Early this afternoon."

"It has not left the Secretariat yet. You can cancel it."

"How?"

"Let me handle that, all right?"

The emperor nodded his head.

Forthwith a rescript, marked "urgent," was issued to countermand the earlier edict regarding the banishment of Li Yifu. Meanwhile, a peck of pearls was sent to Li's home courtesy of the emperor.

With Lady Wu's backing and the emperor's approval, Li Yifu was soon appointed vice president of the Secretariat and de facto chief minister. Now at the top of officialdom, Li and Cui Dunli joined forces to form the core of the pro-Wu party. Gathered around them were a number of key officials, including Xu Jingzong (chamberlain of the Court of the Imperial Regalia), Cui Yixuan (censor-in-chief), and Yuan Gongyu (vice censor-in-chief).[4]

***

In the ninth month, the emperor, with the strong support of the pro-Wu party, felt confident enough to revisit the issue of Wu's promotion at a special meeting in the interior hall of the Ganlu Basilica. Only four individuals were invited: Zhangsun Wuji, Chu Suiliang, Yu Zhining, and Li Ji—the chief ministers with the greatest seniority. As such they constituted the surviving members of Taizong's inner circle. All were present except for Li Ji, who was excused for health reasons.

The emperor was seated on the dais at the furthest end of the hall with his back to a light-colored bamboo screen. Across the dais, the background was hidden behind thick dark embroidered curtains. A short flight of stairs led down to the main floor, where the chief ministers, each carrying a ceremonial ritual tablet (*hu*)[5] in his hands indicating rank and wearing purple robes, took their seats facing the emperor.

"Last time," the emperor said, "I proposed to create the title of

'Imperial Consort' for Lady Wu but came across strenuous opposition from Hann Yuan and Lai Ji. I had to shelve the issue. Recently, I received a memorial from Li Yifu. It proposes that Lady Wu be set up as empress, replacing Empress Wang. This time, I am going to see it through. Here it is." The emperor handed a silk scroll to a eunuch, who then took it to Zhangsun Wuji.

"As you know," the emperor continued, "Empress Wang has committed several serious transgressions. And that makes her unworthy of the throne."

"Your Majesty," Zhangsun Wuji said, his voice raspy. "I certainly do not want to exonerate the empress. However, there are doubts concerning her role in those unfortunate events. If she wanted to harm the little princess, she had plenty of opportunities. Why did she choose to do it at a time when she could be easily caught?"

"Are you intimating that Lady Wu caused the death of her own daughter?" The emperor was very displeased.

"No, Your Majesty . . ."

"The palace maids' testimonies all point to Wang as the culprit. Furthermore, there is irrefutable evidence that she engaged in black magic, which is her second transgression. That alone warrants forfeiture of life under normal circumstances."

"Your Majesty, but the empress was never known to have practiced black magic before. If she did it at all, she should have hidden the effigies in a most secret place. How could a lowly maid from Wenshui know everything about them?"

"What's wrong with a maid exposing her master? Besides, the Board of Justice did a thorough investigation. Do you want to call *their* reports into question?"

"No, Your Majesty. But I find the results hard to believe. To this day, the empress has not confessed."

"That is true, Uncle. But the main problem is something else: she has been unable to bear me a son. Don't you think she should be replaced?"

"Assuming what Your Majesty says is right, Lady Wu, I am afraid, is not the most appropriate choice."

"Why not, Uncle? She is the mother of Prince Li Hong!"

"Could I say a few words, Your Majesty." Chu Suiliang could no longer keep his silence.

"Yes, go ahead, Suiliang."

"Before his passing, the late Emperor Taizong entrusted the matter of succession to Zhangsun and me. My view should at least carry some weight."

"Sure! Speak up, Suiliang."

"The empress is a descendent of a great noble family and was personally selected by Emperor Taizong for both looks and character. Your Majesty certainly remembers, before his death, the late emperor, while holding your hands, said to me, 'Take care of my good son and my good daughter-in-law.' If I give in to Your Majesty's demand, I will have to disobey the late emperor's order. Moreover, if Your Majesty insists on replacing Empress Wang, please choose someone from an upper-class noble family, not from the Wus of Wenshui. What is more, it is widely known that Lady Wu once was a concubine of the late emperor. If she becomes the empress of Your Majesty, how can it be explained to the masses and posterity?"

"How dare you?" shouted the emperor, standing up, his face turning purple. "I reprimand you for your insolence!"

An agitated Chu stepped forward, saying, "My sincerest apologies." Lowering his body to place his jade tablet on the dais, he prostrated himself, knocked his forehead forcefully against the marble floor several times, and shouted in an emotional tone, "It is obvious that I am no longer worthy of being Your Majesty's servant and I beg for permission to retire in the countryside." He then rose to his feet, his head stained with blood, and took his leave.

Lady Wu's sharp voice burst out from behind the bamboo screen, "Bastard! Why don't we bump him off?"

An infuriated emperor was left wordless.

"Your Majesty," Zhangsun Wuji said, "Suiliang is a regent appointed by the late Emperor Taizong. He cannot be punished unless he commits a crime."

"He will be all right. But what exactly is your opinion?" the emperor asked.

"Your Majesty, I really do not know what to say right now."

All this while, Yu Zhining had not said a word. He had been known for his courage and integrity under Taizong. It was obvious that age was getting the best of him.

***

The two junior chief ministers Hann Yuan and Lai Ji were alarmed when they heard what had happened at the Ganlu Basilica meeting. They submitted more memorials to the throne. Hann Yuan warned the emperor against making a laughingstock of himself by following in the footsteps of the Western Zhou, brought down by the femme fatale Si of Bao, for whom King You fell.[6] Lai Ji cited the example of Emperor Cheng of Western Han, who was infatuated with a lewd dancer called Flying Swallow Zhao[7] and named her his empress.

The emperor was so shocked by the candid language that he suffered a severe headache. Lady Wu lost her temper and demanded that the memorialists be taken to task. But the emperor held up his hand and shook his head hard. He did not want to punish his officials for giving loyal advice.

When the emperor was somewhat recovered from his ailment a few days later, he summoned Li Ji (Li Shiji), a heavyweight at Taizong's court and the most decorated military officer alive, to the palace and said, "I want to promote Lady Wu to empress, but Chu Suiliang is against it. As a regent, his opinion is important. But am I obligated to listen to him in this matter?"

"Of course not, Your Majesty," replied Li Ji without a moment's hesitation. "This is Your Majesty's family business. Why ask the opinion of an outsider?"

In the meantime, Zhangsun Wuji, for his part, stopped fighting. He did not alter his view on Lady Wu's promotion. But confrontations with the pro-Wu gang and repeated requests from the emperor had worn him down.

With Li Ji on his side and with the support the newly-formed pro-Wu party, including Li Yifu, Cui Dunli, Xu Jingzong, Cui Yixuan, and Yuan Gongyu,[8] the emperor pushed ahead with his plan.

A few days later, Chu Suiliang received an edict that demoted him to a much lower post in a miasma-infested remote town in the far south.

Later, when Xu Jingzong, one of Lady Wu's most devoted fans, was asked about his thought on the promotion controversy, he said, "Those busybodies! Why did they make a fuss about who should be empress? A country bumpkin who has harvested an extra ten bushels of wheat will consider replacing his wife. To speak nothing of the emperor wanting to set up an empress! Don't forget, His Majesty owns all under Heaven." This comment indicated a new way of thinking about the throne. Lady Wu liked it so much that she had multiple copies of it made for circulation at court.

***

On the morning of December 4, 655, a propitious day selected by the diviners of the Board of Rites, a grand ceremony was taking place on the front terrace of the Taiji Basilica, marking the coronation of Lady Wu as empress. The emperor in his ceremonial yellow robes was seated under a vast yellow canopy beneath overhanging eaves of the building. In the spacious square below, thousands of court officials, clerks, and military officers stood in formation.

Clad in a dark-colored damask robe with a pheasant pattern in front and matching black shoes and socks, her head bedecked with twelve floral-patterned silver hairpins, Lady Wu looked stunning and majestic. She stepped forward to receive from Master of Ceremony Li Ji the empress's gold seal in a gilded box tied with yellow ribbons and the imperial edict of appointment.

In the afternoon, she in full regalia mounted the gatetower of the Suzhangmen[9] west of the Taiji Basilica, where she gave her first audience as empress to the Hundred Officials,[10] who had arrived to offer felicitations. Notably among them were Hann Yuan and Lai Ji, the two junior chief ministers who had, just a short while before, argued against her promotion.

As the rise of Wu had become unstoppable, both Hann and Lai had handed in their resignations. But at her insistence, they had stayed on in their posts and even received accolades from her for their loyal service to the throne.

To mark this memorable occasion, a general amnesty had been declared, whereby prison inmates were all set free except for those who had committed the Ten Abominations[11]—unpardonable crimes such as sedition, rebellion, *lèse majesté*, extreme unfilial behavior, incest, and others.

The new empress's son of four *sui* Li Hong was now the new crown prince, replacing his half-brother Li Zhong.

Empress Wu 's political enemies—former Empress Wang and former Consort Xiao—were taken into custody. Taking their cue from Empress Wu, some court prosecutors known as censors[12] accused both women of making attempts on Wu's life with poisoned wine, a capital crime. For now, as their punishment, both were disenrolled[13] from the official register and reduced to commoner status. Their brothers and Wang's mother were banished to the far south, never allowed to return to the capital. Wang's father, Wang Renyou, now dead, was posthumously disenrolled. Well, this was not just an effort to add insult to injury, but a standard practice. High-ranking officials, even in death, kept certain privileges that could benefit their offspring. Those privileges were, of course, revoked with posthumous disenrollment.

Notes

1 Noble Consort (*guifei* 貴妃), Pure Consort (*shufei* 淑妃), Virtuous Consort (*defei* 德妃), and Worthy Consort (*xianfei* 賢妃) were titles for the highest-ranking imperial consorts.

2 *Shi yipin* 視一品 (the first equivalency rank): the character *shi* 視 (equivalent to) was usually prefixed to honorific titles.

3 Imperial Consort (*chenfei* 宸妃) was a new title.

4 The chamberlain of the Court of the Imperial Regalia (*weiwei qing* 衛尉卿): head of a third-tier central agency (*si* 寺 or Court) in charge of weaponry and regalia. The censor-in-chief (*yushi dafu* 御史大夫): head of the Censorate. The vice censor-in-chief (*yushi zhongcheng* 御史中丞): his lieutenant.

5 *Hu* 笏.

6 According to a traditional account, to make his unhappy concubine Si of Bao (or Bao Si 褒姒) laugh, King You of Western Zhou 周幽王 had beacon fires north of the capital lit up, which suggested that barbarian attacks were imminent. The local lords sent their troops to defend the king, only to find him having fun with his woman. Later, when a real invasion came, the king had the beacon fires lit up again. Nobody came to his rescue. And the Western Zhou fell.

7 Flying Swallow Zhao (Zhao Feiyan 趙飛燕) was a legendary beauty and great dancer with a slender waist.

8 Cui Yixuan崔義玄 was censor-in-chief. Yuan Gongyu 袁公瑜 was vice censor-in-chief.

9 Suzhangmen 肅章門 or Suzhang Gate: an "inner gate" located to the west of the Taiji and Liangyi Basilicas in the western part of the Taiji Palace. Inner gates were those within the palace grounds. Outer gates were entrances leading from the outside to the palace.

10 The Hundred Officials (*baiguan* 百官): various officials and officers.

11 The Ten Abominations (*shi'e* 十惡): ten egregious crimes deemed unpardonable in the *Tang Code*.

12 Censor (*yushi* 御使): a middle-ranking central government official from the Censorate responsible for maintaining discipline among officials and impeaching them.

13 To be disenrolled (*chuming* 除名): to have one's name struck from the official registry; to lose one's official status.

5. Wang and Xiao (655)

THE LATERAL PALACE (Yeting)[1] in the western part of the Palace City housed court ladies and palace maids. Following a Han convention, a forbidden area was set aside for women from the Taiji Palace who had fallen from grace. It was here that former Empress Wang and former Consort Xiao were imprisoned in an unmarked house.

As the two disgraced women were clinging to hope that His Majesty would come to their rescue, a eunuch officer in gray arrived to visit them. He sniffed his nose in the dank air, waved his flywhisk to chase away a swarm of flies, unrolled a silk scroll, and read out an edict of condemnation while standing.

Holding back tears, Empress Wang made an obeisance and murmured, "I know it! I know it! With her in power, I must die." After a pause, she shouted in a raised voice, "Long live His Majesty!"

Consort Xiao lost her composure and blustered, "It is all the work of Foxy Demon Wu! I swear, in the next world, I'll become a cat and she, a mouse. This cat will seize the mouse by the throat and choke her! Mark my words!"

***

When informants reported the former empress's and consort's remarks, Empress Wu felt as if she had been punched in the solar plexus. She especially abhorred the cat-and-mouse metaphor. In no small part because she was a Buddhist *and* a strong believer in karma. Soon thereafter she began to have nightly dreams in which she was haunted by a large cat with sharp fangs. To counter that, she conducted a campaign to eliminate all cats in the palace grounds and any references to cats in speeches and writings at court. After a while, the haunting died down, but there was a significant increase of rat infestation. To her, however, this was a minor nuisance, a small price she had to pay as she fought her way to the top.

As the empress continued to hold sway over the emperor, the emperor came to rely on her in making decisions, big and small, political or domestic. But deep down he did not exactly like his role as an uxorious husband. In fact, he hated himself for not being able to stand up and say no. He often waxed nostalgic for the good old days before her re-entry into the palace. True, it was a time when Empress Wang and Consort Xiao were constantly backbiting each other, but it was also a time when he called the shots at court and served as the arbiter between them. The thought of it made him wonder what had happened to the two women.

With the help of his most trusted eunuchs, the emperor made a secret visit to the forbidden area. A shadow swept across his face as he was led to a run-down house through a yard denuded of trees but overgrown with brambles and weeds. A mixture of anger and sadness rose up in his chest the moment he caught sight of the battered door and windows, all boarded up. He then shifted his gaze to a round hole about a foot across in the thick wall and became teary-eyed when a eunuch told him that food trays and chamber pots were passed in and out through the hole. Kneeling down close to the hole on a cushion placed by the eunuch, he peeped inside but could not make out anything.

"Are you there?" asked he in a shivering voice. "My Empress? My Pure Consort?"

"Your Majesty! Your Majesty!" The two women shouted in ecstatic astonishment.

"I know Your Majesty has not forgotten us!" said Consort Xiao on the verge of tears. "The other night, I had a dream. Your Majesty, Sujie, and your humble servant were strolling along the bank of the Kunming Pond."

"Yes, yes. I miss you, Pure Consort. And you, Empress? How are you doing?"

"I am doing fine, Your Majesty." Empress Wang was sobbing.

"Is there anything I can do for both of you? Anything you want?"

"No! Nothing!" Empress Wang said. "I feel overwhelmed by Your Majesty's visit."

"I do not need anything either," Consort Xiao said. "But I do have a humble wish, if Your Majesty does not mind."

"Yes?"

"Could Your Majesty look after Sujie for me? And keep that woman away from him?"

"Pure Consort Xiao, I will do my best to keep our son Sujie safe," said the emperor chokingly.

"I have got a humble wish too. Could I say it?" Empress Wang resumed.

"Of course."

"For old times' sake, could Your Majesty allow me your humble concubine to see the sun and moon once more before I vanish? Could Your Majesty have this place renamed the 'Heart-Changing Yard?' "

"Yes, yes, I promise," the emperor said.

When the kneeling proved too much for him, the emperor, with the help of a eunuch, got to his feet and took leave of the two women, tears rolling down his cheeks.

***

In her struggle to rise to the top, Empress Wu became painfully aware of the importance of clan status. She was mortified when Chu Suiliang intimated that she came from a lowborn family, and resented the snobbery of the gentry aristocracy comprised of a select number of noble clans, such as the Wangs of Taiyuan of Empress Wang, and the Xiaos of Lanling of Consort Xiao. Using family pedigree, social prestige, and public opinion as criteria, they made admittance by the likes of the Wus to this highly exclusive club almost impossible. After her return to the palace, one of the first things she did was to elevate her father's status through the granting of prestigious posthumous titles. At the time of her ascension, at her insistence, the imperial edict on her appointment made a point of stressing the extraordinary merit of the Wu clan.

Now, as the legal spouse of the emperor, the empress was expected to epitomize the best virtues of a wife: submission, obedience, solicitousness, chastity, and fecundity. As the ultimate yin of the world, she was supposed to complement the ultimate yang, her husband, and was prohibited from meddling in court affairs, because of the underlying fear that her yin might eclipse the yang of the emperor. But Empress Wu was not interested in wifely virtues at all. Considering herself the equal of any man, she took an active part in what was considered man's business—court politics. And her forceful character allowed her to dominate her husband and his court without much effort. By sitting behind the bamboo screen, she got around the age-old rule excluding females from men's gatherings and was able to attend court sessions and Chief Ministers' Council meetings whenever the emperor was present. In truth, she had become an overmighty sovereign in her own right.

One unpleasant encounter with her husband one evening, however, reminded her that all she had achieved could be taken away in an instant. On that occasion, the emperor was benighted enough to suggest freeing her political rivals Wang and Xiao, both of whom possessed much greater legitimacy and much higher family status.

It triggered an explosive outburst from the empress that cowed the emperor into inaction. She then lost no time in transferring the two hated women in the Lateral Palace to a secret location. As her husband's passion to free them finally died down, she handed down their ultimate punishment and sent her minions to carry it out. After they gave each woman a flogging of 100 blows, they had their arms and legs lopped off and their mutilated bodies thrown into two wine-filled vats for the purpose of making their "bones intoxicated." The ex-empress and ex-consort expired soon afterwards. She then issued an empress's decree that revoked the aristocratic status of both and converted the surnames of the Wang and Xiao clans to Cobra and Owl.[2]

Notes

[1] The Lateral Palace (*Yeting gong* 掖庭宮) housed disgraced court ladies and palace maids. It derived from the Eternal Lane (Yongxiang 永巷) in the Western Han dynasty.

[2] Cobra (*mang* 蟒) and Owl (*xiao* 梟): cf. Wang 王 and Xiao 蕭.

6. Chu Suiliang and Zhangsun Wuji (656–659)

In the Middle East, Uthman was assassinated in Medina. Ali, cousin and son-in-law of the Prophet, rose to power (656).

CHU SUILIANG HAD spent his entire official career at court. He found it hard to get adjusted to provincial life south of the Yangzi River, first in Changsha (in Hunan), then further down south in Guizhou[1] (in Guangxi; 656). But thanks to the help of his former colleagues Hann Yuan and Lai Ji, he was allowed to hold a relatively high post as area commander.[2]

It was only natural that, before long, he started looking for ways to return to the capital. Hann Yuan again lent a helping hand, writing a memorial that requested Chu's recall. He argued that Chu had been Taizong's trusted adviser for years and committed no crime during the current reign; and that, although his candid remarks were sometimes unpalatable, he remained loyal to the throne. The emperor responded, "Perhaps, but what he has committed is *lèse majesté*, and that is unpardonable."

And that would have been that. Except that it caught the empress's attention. She summoned Xu Jingzong and Li Yifu to her basilica for a late afternoon meeting.

Two young palace maids in red served the guests with a kind of "fruit wine" from the Western Regions.

Li Yifu lifted his silver goblet to have a taste. With his face beaming, he uttered his surprise at the beverage. "The flavor changes as one swallows the wine. It is simply wonderful."

Xu Jingzong took a sip of his wine and added in a pleasant voice, "It is creamier and fruitier than common grape wine. The taste is heavenly!"

"No doubt, you two are great connoisseurs," the empress said. Pointing to the lidded silver ewer on the table, she continued, "This is the royal wine of Gaochang,[3] produced for its royalty before the kingdom fell."

Li Yifu said, "The capture of Gaochang was one of the great exploits during the previous reign under Taizong." With a feline smile on his face from ear to ear, he made a subtle attempt to switch subjects and said, "I suppose that Your Majesty does not invite us just to taste wine."

"Well, there is nothing wrong with rewarding my most capable senior advisers this way. But I do want to know if you have heard anything about Chu Suiliang?"

"I was told that he is trying to return," Xu Jingzong said.

"With Hann Yuan's help," Li Yifu said.

"Bastard," said the Empress, her face darkening.

"He is an area commander in the far south, and cannot pose a threat now, Your Majesty."

"He couldn't threaten me when he was in power. But he has insulted my ancestors. For that, he has to pay."

After the meeting, Xu Jingzong and Li Yifu and their minions worked for days to come up with a solution until the ingenious mind of Xu Jingzong hit upon a brilliant idea, which then became the central theme of a joint memorial Xu and Li submitted to the court a few days later. It argued that Chu was actually the leader of a secret cabal that was bent on harming the empress. Other members of the clique included Hann Yuan, Lai Ji, and Liŭ Shi (Empress Wang's uncle). It was Hann and Lai who had placed Chu Suiliang in a strategic location in the far south so that he would be able to serve as an external force to support a future rebellion at the center.

For the emperor, the memorial brought back memories of Taizong lying in his deathbed. With the last bit of his strength, he begged a tearful Chu Suiliang to take good care of his heir. Clutching Taizong's hands, Chu Suiliang pledged his loyalty in a sobbing voice.

"Does Suiliang harbor malicious intent towards the empress?" the emperor asked himself. "And me? Does the cabal really exist?" The emperor shook his head in disbelief. In the end, however, to avoid crossing the empress, he approved some "light" measures of punishment anyway. Chu Suiliang was sent further down south to Aizhou (in northern Vietnam). Hann Yuan was banished to Zhenzhou (in Hainan); Lai Ji to Taizhou (in Zhejiang); and Liǔ Shi to Xiangzhou (in Guangxi).[4]

To Chu Suiliang, life in his new place of banishment was pure suffering. The locals spoke a language he could not understand; the weather was hot and humid for half of the year; and the whole landscape was shrouded in malaria-causing miasma. He made one more desperate appeal to the emperor, but got no answer.

***

When he succeeded to the throne in 649, the emperor Li Zhi had no military experience to fall back on. Fortunately for him, a generation of battle-hardened generals who had matured under Taizong continued to serve the court with loyalty.

General Su Dingfang was one of the most formidable generals of the previous reign. Under the command of the legendary Li Jing, Su had led a vanguard force of 200 in dislodging the doughty Xieli Khan (Qaghan)[5] from his camp (629). The following year, the mighty Eastern Tujue Khanate fell apart.

In 651, when Li Zhi was still fresh on the throne, his rule came under challenge by an overmighty figure, Shaboluo Khan of Western Tujue. Under the previous reign, Shaboluo had taken refuge at Emperor Taizong's court and been appointed to a high-ranking post with the authority to govern the Western Regions on behalf of the Tang court. Not long after Taizong's passing, he launched an open rebellion. General Su was charged with bringing him to heels.

In the Battle of the Irtysh River[6] (early 658),[7] Su, commanding 10,000 Tang-Uighur troops, trounced the main force of the Western Tujue army under Shaboluo Khan (Ashina Helu) ten times their size.

An ecstatic emperor appointed General Su commander-in-chief of Ili District,[8] an area comprised of the vast Western Regions.

In the wake of the battle, the mighty Western Tujue Khanate crumbled. The Tang went on to divide the Western Tujue territory—extending as far west as the border of Persia and encompassing entire Central Asia—into area commands (*dudu fu*) and prefectures (*zhou*) under the jurisdiction of the Anxi Protectorate (*duhu fu*).[9]

***

Shaboluo was on the run. In the oasis state of Shi (Chach) in Tashkent (in Uzbekistan), the khan, exhausted with thirst and hunger, decided to seek shelter. The locals put him up in a state guesthouse. In the dead of night, as he was deep in his slumber, a troop of riders stormed into his chamber, weapons in hand. They took him captive before he could make a move.

Trussed up and blind-folded, Shaboluo was brought into the presence of the Tang commanding officer in his campaign tent. With his blindfold taken off, the khan held his neck straight and said, "The late emperor Taizong took me in when I was in trouble. His Majesty treated me well, but I let him down. Now Heaven is punishing me."

He paused for a moment before he continued in a beseeching voice, "I know I committed an unpardonable crime and deserve to die one thousand times. And I understand that in your country, there is the custom of executing criminals in a marketplace. Before I die, I have only one wish. Please allow my beheading to take place in the Zhaoling Tomb Park as a way to show my gratitude to the late Emperor Taizong . . . one last time." Overcome with emotion, the khan began to sob. The Tang general gestured to have him taken away.

Months later, a parade of prisoners of war was held in Zhaoling, and Shaboluo Khan was among them. As his last moment approached, he was pushed out of his prison cart and dragged to a wooden platform along with a dozen or so his senior officers, where they were forced on their knees. Muscle-bound executors were standing by, each holding a broadsword. Below hundreds of spectators were watching.

With a sudden clatter of horse hooves, a eunuch officer arrived to announce an urgent edict that saved the Tujue leader and his men from the sword.

The khan would spend the rest of his days as the former leader of Western Tujue. After his passing, he would be buried in a secret cemetery where Xieli Khan's tomb was.

***

Now Zhangsun Wuji was the only leading member of the anti-Wu group with his reputation still intact. One reason for his survival so far was his close ties with the emperor. His younger sister Empress Zhangsun was Taizong's wife and the emperor Li Zhi's birthmother. In the succession struggle of Taizong's reign, Zhangsun Wuji was the only top leader who consistently rooted for Li Zhi. Upon Taizong's death, he was the stalwart of the country who played a vital role in making sure that his nephew Li Zhi ascended the throne without incident.

Moreover, Zhangsun Wuji was also much more elusive than his colleagues, for example, Chu Suiliang. And the fact that he had been in semi-retirement for quite some time made it difficult to pin a crime on him.

What was more, whenever he was under assault, the emperor would not hesitate to come to his defense.

Xu Jingzong, president of the Secretariat, had been looking for evidence he could use against Zhangsun for weeks, but in vain. Then the case of Wei Jifang came to his attention in the fourth month of 659. This senior attendant of the crown prince had been accused of having cliquish association with a censor, which was prohibited under the *Tang Code*. He was run in and subjected to insult and torture. When he could not take it anymore, he made an attempt on his own life, which failed.

While reviewing Wei's case, the innovative Xu Jingzong realized its potential in helping the empress's cause. He cobbled together an elaborate report in which he changed the verdict on Wei Jifang, making him a member of a cabal that had conspired to bring down the leading court officials and members of the royal family and to seize the throne! The leader of the cabal was none other than Zhangsun Wuji!

"What? Another cabal? I don't believe it for a second," the emperor said in a sharp voice, upon reading the report. "How can it be? The whole thing must have been a frame-up."

"I thought so too until I saw irrefutable evidence that he had plotted against the throne."

"Uncle Zhangsun is trying to harm me? No! No! It can't be true, Jingzong."

"In case Your Majesty forgets, Zhangsun Wuji killed Your Majesty's brother Li Ke, and banished Prince Li Daozong. Both he hates, and both are innocent. So, despite his façade as a benevolent uncle, he is a sinister schemer at heart. I understand that Your Majesty has close emotional and familial ties with him, but what he has done is of grave concern and requires your immediate attention. Indecision will put the country and the throne in danger."

"Heaven, have mercy!" the emperor exclaimed. "Why is my family so unfortunate? Sister Gaoyang and Fang Yi'ai plotted against me before; now Uncle Zhangsun wants to seize the throne?"

"I greatly respect Your Majesty's feelings," Xu Jingzong said. "But the stakes are too high, and the court cannot ignore the serious consequences. Gaoyang was a woman, and Fang Yi'ai was a playboy. Their rebellion had no chance of success. But Zhangsun Wuji is totally different. He helped Taizong seize the throne and has been chief minister on and off for thirty years. All under Heaven are impressed with his formidable intellect and ability. If he decides to rebel, who can stop him?"

"But Uncle Zhangsun is like a father to me. Without his help, I couldn't have ascended the throne. I don't understand: why does he wants to oppose me?"

"Your Majesty, when I asked Wei Jifang the same question, he told me that, after Crown Prince Li Zhong was deposed, Wuji, his supporter, started to worry about his own fate. Recently, two of his nephews were arrested, then banished from the capital. He almost panicked. He was afraid of losing favor with the throne and decided that the only way to survive was to seize power for himself."

The emperor remained quiet for a long while before saying, a stunned look on his face, "If Uncle is really like that, I can't bear to kill him. If I do, what will all under Heaven say about me? What will posterity say about me?"

"With due respect for Your Majesty's concerns, to prove my point, I need only to cite this saying from the *Book of the Han*:[10] 'If one is indecisive when it calls for a prompt decision, one will suffer the consequences.' It clearly applies to the situation in question. The fact of the matter is, the fate of the country is now hanging in the balance so long as Wuji is at large. He is an arch-villain in the same league with such notorious usurpers as Wang Mang and Sima Yi.[11] If Your Majesty hesitates, and something happens, it will be too late."

The emperor was silent.

Xu Jingzong continued. "At the minimum, for the sake of the country, could I, Your Majesty's servant, ask for permission to start an investigation?"

"Just an investigation?"

"Yes, Your Majesty."

"Request granted," the emperor said with resignation.

After Xu Jingzong left the hall, the emperor laid his head on the cold surface of the mahogany table and broke out crying.

***

Through probing the Zhangsun Wuji case, Xu Jingzong gathered more evidence that fingered Chu Suiliang, Liŭ Shi, and Hann Yuan as members of the cabal under his control. Xu then filed a request for a full prosecution. At the empress's urging, the emperor nodded his approval. In the end, all the conspirators, as expected, were found guilty.

For his punishment, Zhangsun was banished to Qianzhou in the southwest.[12] At the emperor's insistence, he was allowed to keep his privileges as a first-rank official. By then Chu Suiliang was already dead. His two sons were banished to Aizhou (in north Vietnam) and killed en route. Liŭ Shi and Hann Yuan suffered disenrollment and banishment to the far south. Yu Zhining, who was not nailed as a member of the clique but had been sitting on the fence, was dismissed from office.[13]

The empress was not pleased. She insisted that the conspirators had gotten off easy. She pressed the emperor for a retrial at a higher level. After he gave his nod with great reluctance, a panel of five top officials, including Li Ji and Xu Jingzong, was appointed to take charge. Unsurprisingly, they found the named conspirators guilty again and handed down the death penalty. The emperor wanted to intervene. But his close advisers all urged him not to, for fear his debilitating headaches would get worse. So in the end he did not.

***

In the seventh month of 659, Xu Jingzong's agents were tasked with carrying out the executions. One group traveled to Qianzhou. They sought out Zhangsun Wuji, old and frail, and put him through a round of torture before forcing him to take his own life.

Another group went down to the far south. They finished Liǔ Shi, the uncle of the former empress, in situ by decapitation.

Hann Yuan was the only one of the three spared the same fate, because he was already dead.

The family assets of the the conspirators were confiscated, and their close male relatives, banished to the far south.

***

One of the arguments against Lady Wu's ascension was her lowborn status. In the court-sanctioned *Treatise on Genealogy*,[14] the Wus of Wenshui were not even recorded. At the empress's urging, Xu Jingzong led a group of scholars to do a thorough overhaul of the *Treatise*. When the revised edition came out, it got a new title: *A Record of Clans and Lineages*.[15] The original ranking of noble lineages based on choronym was discarded. A new ranking system was created which placed the Wus of Wenshui at the top of the first class. All other lineages were arranged in nine classes according to the ranks of their most illustrious members in Tang officialdom. Of these, Ranks 1 through 5 counted as nobility.

Notes

1 Guizhou 桂州: prefecture (*zhou*) and its seat (in present-day Guilin, Guangxi).

2 Area commander (*dudu* 都督): commanding officer of an area command.

3 Gaochang 高昌: Central Asian oasis state with its capital at Turfan, Xinjiang. It was conquered by the Tang in 640.

[4] Aizhou 愛州: prefecture in north Vietnam. Zhenzhou 振州: prefecture with its seat northwest of Sanya, Hainan. Taizhou 台州: prefecture in Zhejiang with Linhai 臨海 as its seat. Xiangzhou 象州: prefecture in Guangxi with its seat northwest of present-day Xiangzhou.

[5] The head of a Turkic (Tujue) tribal confederation was known as *kehan* 可汗 (*qaghan*) or "khan."

[6] The Irtysh River (E'erqisi River 額爾齊斯河 or Yedie River 曳咥河): the battle took place in present-day Altay, north Xinjiang.

[7] The years in the Chinese lunar calendar roughly correspond with those in the Julian Calendar. There are some discrepancies. In the Xia Calendar used by the Tang, the standard month starts with the first month of the lunar calendar, which is roughly one month behind its Western counterpart. According to *Zizhi tongjian* (200.6306–7), the battle took place after the first day of the twelve month of Xianqing 顯慶 2, which is January 10, 658 in the Julian Calendar.

[8] Ili District 伊麗道: administrative area based in north Xinjiang.

[9] The Anxi 安西 Protectorate (*duhu fu* 都護府) covered Xinjiang and its neighboring areas to the west. A protectorate was a super-sized local administrative area in a border region with predominantly non-Han populations.

[10] The *Book of the Han* (*Hanshu* 漢書) is by Ban Gu 班固, the leading Eastern Han historian.

[11] Wang Mang 王莽 (45 BCE–23 CE; r. 9–23 CE) and Sima Yi 司馬懿 (179–251) were both notorious usurpers of power. Sima Yi himself never ascended the throne but laid the foundation for the Western Jin dynasty.

[12] Qianzhou 黔州: prefecture in southeast Chongqing and northeast Guizhou with its seat east of Pengshui.

[13] Later, Yu Zhining was appointed prefect of Rongzhou 榮州 (seat: Rongxian, Sichuan).

[14] The *Treatise on Genealogy* (*Shizu zhi* 氏族志) was compiled by Gao Shilian 高士廉 et al. under Taizong.

[15] *A Record of Clans and Lineages* (*Xingshi lu* 姓氏錄) was compiled by Kong Zhiyue 孔志約 et al.

7. Cockfight (661)

In the Middle East, following the assassination of Ali, the fourth caliph of the Rashidun Caliphate, Muawiyah I founded the Umayyad Caliphate.
In Persia, Prince Peroz, son of Yazdegerd III and the last Sasanian king, requested military assistance from Tang China against the Arabs, which was rejected.

ON AN AUTUMN day in 661, around half a dozen children were huddled around the gamecocks Duke and Warrior in a corner of the courtyard of a princely residence in the northeastern part of Chang'an. Duke was in full attack mode, as its beak snapped and stabbed at the neck, eyes, and crest of its rival Warrior with ferocity. Warrior was struggling with all its might to stand the ground, its white feathers stained with blood. A sudden peck on the eye sent it running, flapping wings, and cackling like crazy.

Wang Bo, a talented scholar in his early twenties and the only adult present, pronounced Duke the winner. The owners—Princes Li Xián (655–684) and Li Zhe (aka Li Xian; 656–710)[1] at seven and six *sui*, both clad in silk—picked up their gamecocks and left the scene with their young friends.

As Prince Li Xián's reader-companion,[2] Wang Bo was charged with coaching the prince on how to read and write. Despite his young age, Wang was already being compared to the three great poets of the day—Yang Jiong, Lu Zhaolin, and Luo Binwang.[3] Later when they were lumped together as the Four Eminences of the Early Tang, Wang was ranked at the top of the group. It was his duty as well to dissuade the prince from taking part in cockfights. With that in mind, he wrote a rhapsody[4] for the occasion. It was entitled "A Call to Arms against Prince of Ying Li Zhe's Warrior."[5] Written in a parallel style[6] in mock seriousness, the piece was replete with classical allusions. Initially, the author probably intended to lampoon the game, but the message was lost in the florid language. Nevertheless, rhapsody took on a life of its own. Its popularity grew, as it was copied, recopied, and circulated among court officials.

When the emperor read it, he was red with anger, thinking, *I have said time and again that cockfighting is evil. It is a cruel sport from the West and serves no purpose but to corrupt the young. How come my past orders against it are completely ignored? I need to make an example of the repeat offenders.* He then issued an edict to reiterate the ban on cockfighting, severely reprimand the princes, and condemned Wang Bo. For his neglect of duty, the reader-companion was disenrolled and banished from Chang'an to the far south.

Notes

1 Li Xián 李賢 (655–684) and Li Zhe 李哲 (aka Li Xian 李顯; 656–710): these two brothers should not be confused. The former was known posthumously as Prince Zhanghuai 章懷太子; the latter was to rule as emperor (temple name: Zhongzong). See *Zizhi tongjian* 200.6325 (*Jiu Tang shu* [198, 王勃傳] dates the event to 666 or later). The precise location of the event is unknown. The ward in the northeastern corner of the city (north of Xingning Ward 興寧坊) was converted into the exclusive neighborhood for the princes under Emperor Xuanzong (r. 712–756), sometimes called the Sixteen Princely Residences (Shiliuwang zhai 十六王宅). It was possible that Princes Li Xián and Li Zhe, who had been active earlier, lived in this area or its neighboring wards. See *Tang liangjing chengfang kao* 3.81–82.

2 The reader-companion (*bandu* 伴讀): a minor official in a princely establishment.

3 Yang Jiong 楊炯, Lu Zhaolin 盧照鄰, and Luo Binwang 駱賓王.

4 Rhapsody (*fu* 賦) or rhymed prose: a popular literary genre.

5 "Xi Yingwang ji" 檄英王雞, lit., "A Call to Arms against Prince of Ying's Rooster." The piece is collected in the *Jianhu ji buji* 堅瓠集補集 by Chu Renhuo 褚人獲 (Qing) as "Douji xi" 鬬雞檄.

6 Parallel style (*pianwen* 駢文): a *pianwen* piece consists of a series of paired sentences (couplets) that are rhymed and of identical syntactical structure.

8. Shangguan Yi (663–665)

Arab forces invaded the southern Punjab (in modern Pakistan). Muslims entered Afghanistan and captured the city of Kabul (664).

WHEN CHANG'AN WAS built in 583, the Sui architect Yuwen Kai situated different functional areas of the city in accord with some crude geomantic (*fengshui*) principles. He matched the six horizontal lines of the terrain with the six lines of the first hexagram (*qian*) in the *Book of Changes*.[1] The imperial abode known as the Palace City (commonly referred to as "the palace") was placed in the north-central part of the site, which was considered most auspicious for the throne based on the line-by-line interpretations of the hexagram. That placement, it was believed, would guarantee the longevity of the emperor and the continued prosperity of his progeny.

However, since the Palace City was located in a depression, it was hot and humid in summer, which made life miserable for its principal resident, the emperor Li Zhi, who suffered from headaches induced by hyperactive liver yang.[2]

Under the previous reign, his father Taizong had started building a suburban palace called "Penglai" north of the city on higher ground for his own father Gaozu after the latter had suffered a stroke. But Gaozu died soon afterwards, and the building project was halted. In 662, the emperor Li Zhi ordered its revival. As soon as the new suburban palace was completed in 663, the emperor moved in along with his empress and a large entourage.

The empress had her own reason to welcome the move. While living in the old palace, despite the cat eradication campaign, she had been haunted by the ghosts of Empress Wang and Consort Xiao at night. After their death their nocturnal visits had become more frequent.

Her new residential basilica in the Penglai (later known as Daming or Great Brilliance) Palace[3] was enveloped by greenery and lay close to the Taiye Pond[4] at the center of the northern area. In these pleasant, salubrious surroundings, she expected to have peaceful sleep at night.

One afternoon, having spent a long time sitting behind the bamboo screen and keeping a watch on the emperor, she withdrew into her bedchamber to have a rest and dozed off. Before mealtime, two maids on duty outside heard a sharp shriek. They rushed in to find a distraught empress sitting in bed propped by pillows with a macabre look on her face. She spluttered, "They . . . they came!" and gave an account of her encounter with two disheveled, blood-stained women.

A palace physician soon arrived. He checked her pulse rate, using his index and middle fingers, and examined her facial complexion and the color and thickness of her tongue coating. Without a word, he rose to his feet and left the room, and did not return until about forty minutes later with a bowl of freshly brewed herbal mix soup, which would help soothe the nerves and promote mental tranquility. After he made sure that she had drunk up the soup, he made for the door.

The ghostly apparitions disappeared for two months. Then they came back with a vengeance, and night after night left her helpless and desperate.

It was then that she heard from her head eunuch Wang Fusheng that a certain Master Guo Xingzhen could help. She summoned the man into the palace.

As abbot general of the Eastern Marchmount (Mount Tai),[5] this middle-aged man was a most renowned Daoist priest. When he came on his first visit, he was smuggled into the Rear Palace disguised as a eunuch. Upon a brief examination of the patient, he suggested performing an apotropaic ritual. "To exorcise the ghosts who dwell in Your Majesty's body," he reasoned.

"Please do," a desperate Empress Wu responded. "The ghosts are driving me to insanity."

When the time for the ritual arrived, the Daoist master came again at midnight on an autumn day. After he changed into shiny white silk robes, with his eyes half-closed, he began humming an incantation mantra. All of a sudden, his eyes wide open, he unsheathed a long sword that gave off a cold glint under the moonlight, and started a series of rhythmic, nimble movements up and down the front terrace of the residential basilica as he struck and parried, stabbed and jabbed, fighting in all seriousness against an invisible enemy. The ritual came to a close when the master thrust the sword into the sheath as he chanted, "Now I solemnly invite the six stars of the Southern Dipper and the seven stars of the Northern Dipper, as I pay homage to the Most High Lord Lao. Quickly, quickly as the laws and statutes command."

The eunuch officer Wang Fusheng came over and handed him a silver flask, saying, "Courtesy of the empress."

"Thank Her Majesty," Master Guo said as he took his first swig. "Excellent wine!" he exclaimed.

With the eunuch leading the way, the Daoist master entered the basilica to join the empress for a late-night meal.

The following day, the empress seemed to be on the mend. In the course of the next two months, more secret exorcising sessions were held at night at five-day intervals.

***

After her return to the palace, Empress Wu's rise to the pinnacle of power was relentless and unstoppable. The emperor had supported her every step of the way, but, over time, he began to have second thoughts. His tender feelings for the vulnerable concubine in her pomegranate frock had given way to a mixture of fear and remorse. Deep down, he knew that he himself was in part to blame for the making of the bossy empress. Polite and soft-hearted by nature and often plagued by a crippling headache, he had virtually made no attempt to restrain her domineering ways.

He then read a confidential report that claimed that the Daoist priest Guo Xingzhen had made several secret visits to the Rear Palace. *This was a gross violation of the Tang Code and Statutes!* the emperor thought. To make things still worse, the priest had performed reprehensible, black-magic-like rituals on the palace grounds. The informant, Wang Fusheng, head eunuch in the Rear Palace, fingered the empress as the chief offender.

Isn't this the opportunity afforded by Heaven to topple her? thought the emperor. *But how? I'm surrounded by her spies.* He had no choice but to approach this matter with secrecy and great caution. He called in his close adviser Shangguan Yi for a closed-door discussion.

Shangguan, in his mid-fifties, was one of those few officials who was blessed at home and in office. The recent birth of his first granddaughter Wan'er had coincided with his promotion to chief minister. Both the emperor and the empress had endorsed him. Widely known as a good administrator, he also enjoyed an excellent reputation in literary circles. His "Shangguan style" poetry had made its fame long before his rise to power.

To the emperor's inquiry Shangguan responded, "Your Majesty, in my humble opinion, the report is not groundless. In submitting it Wang Fusheng was actually risking his own neck. He would not do it if he did not have iron-clad evidence."

"You really think so?" asked the emperor, who was surprised by the chief minister's candor.

"Yes, Your Majesty. There is no reason for the eunuch to fabricate something so serious if he does not have something to back it up."

"Why then did Wang Fusheng tell on his master?"

"He is the empress's favorite all right, but he probably doesn't like it when the Daoist steals the thunder."

"But he should know the unwritten rule: 'Don't bite the hand that feeds you.' "

"It is an excellent point, Your Majesty. However, what usually happens is that, when a master is exposed and punished, his underlings are sacrificed as scapegoats. So, Wang may also worry about the egregious activities she engages in. And reporting them to the throne, it seems to me, is the only way to protect himself."

"Well," said the emperor, who paused to think for a few moments. Then, he continued, "I suppose that explains it. Does anyone else know this, Yi?"

"No, I do not think so, Your Majesty. The eunuch is scared to death that the empress would find out that he was the source of the leak."

"There is no need to worry. I'll make sure he is safe. But what kind of charges on the books can one bring?"

"At least two, Your Majesty," Shangguan answered. "First, bringing unauthorized adult males into the forbidden zone of the palace at night; and second, illegal communications with an occultist. Both can have serious consequences."

"Good! What happens next?"

"Based on the *Tang Code*, the empress can be deposed, if Your Majesty wishes."

The emperor closed his eyes to collect his thoughts, then said in a serious voice, "Are you willing to draft an edict to that effect?"

"Yes, Your Majesty," Shangguan answered.

***

With his promotion from de facto to formal chief minister, Li Yifu reached the peak of his career. At court, he was put in charge of the Board of Personnel,[6] with the power to recruit qualified people for officialdom. With the help of his sons and sons-in-law, he turned his office into a money-making enterprise. Numerous complaints were filed against his corrupt practice. But, because he seemed to enjoy unconditional support from the emperor and the empress, no censorial officers wanted to take up a case against him. However, as the number of unqualified officials continued to mount, the emperor began to take notice and said, "Don't try to deny it, Yifu. You and your family are running a secular simony business. Each time I hear a complaint against you, I always try to protect you. But you must quit that business as soon as you can."

"Who told Your Majesty so?" asked the chief minister, his face turning red and his carotid artery bulging.

"Does it matter?" asked a displeased emperor.

"I suppose not, Your Majesty."

"You have to bear in mind: it is entirely illegal."

"Yes, Your Majesty." Li Yifu left the emperor's study with a sullen face.

For months after that unpleasant meeting with Li Yifu, the emperor had not heard a whisper against him until one afternoon in the early summer of 663 when he read a report marked "top secret." It accused him of consulting an aeromancer, who, after a visual survey of Li's mansion, told him that it had an aura of imprisonment and that, to counteract its evil effect, 200,000 strings of cash were needed. To raise the money, Li resumed his money-making scheme. The report also claimed that, on a secret trip they took together to the eastern suburbs, they were seen scaling ancient tumuli and checking out their surroundings and speculated that Li Yifu had engaged in occult activities to divine future disasters. That was a crime on a par with high treason because of the threat it posed to the safety of the throne.

The emperor was scandalized and ordered the president of the Board of Justice to take charge of the case under the supervision of Li Ji. The investigation soon resulted in a guilty verdict. Due to the heinous nature of the crime, the empress did not come to Li Yifu's aid.

An edict then went forth whereby Li Yifu and his sons and sons-in-law were disenrolled and banished to the far south.

Li Yifu should count himself lucky because a typical punishment for a crime like this was the execution of the culprit and the extirpation of his Three Clans.[7] He was spared all that thanks to his meritorious service to the emperor and the empress in the past. He certainly fared better than most. Still, he found his punishment unbearable. He had fallen from the top to the bottom of society and was banished from the capital for good to a backwater place in the southwest.

***

In the summer of 663, it was unusually muggy and humid. The emperor was glad that he had moved out of the Palace City, where the conditions must be intolerable, and that he was now living in the Penglai Palace on higher ground in the northern suburbs. In its newly constructed Zichen Basilica,[8] some distance away from the Palace City, he was holding a discussion with senior court officials on the Tubo-Tuyuhun War in the west. Recently, both sides had sent emissaries to the court, each accusing the other of starting the conflict. And both were requesting military assistance.

"Last time when the Tuyuhun were attacked, was it in 660?" the emperor asked Shangguan Yi, now his go-to person after the ouster of Li Yifu.

"Yes, Your Majesty."

"The Tubo mounted an attack against Tuyuhun immediately after it had submitted to the Tang. This time the Tubo have launched a massive campaign with the aim of thorough subjugation."

"Tuyuhun is now in dire straits," Xu Jingzong said. "As a faithful tributary state, it deserves our protection. However, considering the recent expansion of the Anxi Protectorate, the war against Paekche,[9] and the plan to conquer Koguryŏ, I am afraid, our military is overstretched and won't be able to provide much aid at all."

"Can't we use our Western Regions forces to help them?" the emperor asked.

"It will be very difficult, Your Majesty," Shangguan Yi answered. "We have a small military presence in that vast area in the first place. Last year, General Su Haizheng was nearly killed by the Tubo in Shulê.[10] He managed to escape only after placing large bribes."

"What should I do then with their requests for assistance?" the emperor asked all present.

"Your Majesty should reject them," Xu Jingzong said. "We simply do not have the wherewithal to support both sides. But if we give aid to Tuyuhun only, we will risk war with Tubo."

"I concur," Shangguan Yi said.

In the end, the emperor and his senior advisers reached a consensus to refrain from involvement. An edict followed. It reprimanded both Tubo and Tuyuhun and urged restraint. However, not backed with military force, the edict had no teeth and both belligerents ignored it. In the course of a few months, the much more numerous Tubo army overran Tuyuhun territory south of Lake Qinghai. The Tuyuhun khan Nuohebo and his queen Princess Honghua, a Tang royal, crossed over the border into Liangzhou, a prefecture in Gansu, to take shelter.

***

One summer morning in 664, after holding court, the emperor withdrew into his study with Chief Minister Shangguan Yi.

"Your Majesty," Shangguan Yi said, after both had seated themselves, "I would like to continue our discussion on General Liu Rengui if I may."

"Fill me in on him, Yi."

"First, Liu is one of the top Tang generals alive. After Su Dingfang conquered the area, the formidable Paekche general Heichi Changzhi submitted, only to rebel a few months later, capturing more than 200 towns and cities. Not long afterwards, he surrendered again, this time to Liu Rengui. Liu allowed him to keep his own army and even supplied him with grain and *materiel* against the advice of his colleagues. As a result, Heichi stayed loyal to the Tang and that made it possible to pacify Paekche."

"That's excellent," the emperor said. "But if I remember correctly, on the previous campaign, Liu was disenrolled and reduced to commoner status for neglect of duty."

"Yes, Your Majesty. On the 659 campaign he was responsible for the shipment of grain by sea. His fleet was caught in a typhoon. A large number of ships capsized, and many laborers drowned. Li Yifu wanted him dead. Your Majesty punished him with disenrollment instead. Thanks to Your Majesty's leniency, he survived. And what happened next was nothing short of extraordinary."

"Oh?" The emperor raised an eyebrow.

"He did not return home in Chang'an but volunteered to rejoin the campaign as a common foot soldier. From then on, he began his ascent again all the way to commander-in-chief of the Paekche Garrison. By then Paekche had been thoroughly ravished by war. Houses were in ruin and corpses were scattered across the field."

Shangguan Yi pulled a scroll from his sleeve and continued, "Here is a list of his accomplishments I drew up. If I may, I would like to share some of them with Your Majesty."

"Go right ahead," said the emperor with a wave of his hand.

With his eyes on the unfolded scroll, Shangguan Yi continued, "First, Liu took a slew of positive measures: burying the dead, registering the locals, rebuilding villages and settlements, appointing local talents to fill official posts, restoring roads, setting up bridges, repairing dams, dredging ponds . . ."

"Well, what are you driving at, Yi?"

"What I mean is that, as a result, farming and sericulture were revived and became the main source of government revenue. In addition, he gave aids to the poor and provided for the widowed and the old. He also had the Tang Ancestral Temple and the Altars of Soil and Grain erected, the Tang Calendar adopted, and the Tang taboo characters[11] observed. The Paekche people were content with their new life under Liu Rengui and the whole country was at peace. It was on the basis of this that he set up military settlement farms, stored up grain, and drilled his troops in preparation for a war against Koguryŏ."

"What's your point then?"

"In view of the foregoing, I would like to recommend him for a promotion and reward."

"Let me see. How about promoting him by six steps to prefect of Daifang Prefecture (*zhou*)?"

"The highest post in Koguryŏ—that is excellent!"

"On top of that, have a class-A house built in a good neighborhood near the Eastern Market in Chang'an."

"For General Liu, Your Majesty?"

"Yes. Don't forget to send an envoy to his home with generous gifts to his wife and children."

"Yes, Your Majesty." Shangguan Yi bobbed his head with a grin.

***

A short while after the chief minister's departure, the emperor received an unexpected visitor.

"What's up, Empress?" He was taken aback by her ruffled looks. "You didn't have to barge in like that, did you?"

Without answering his question, she riffled through a pile of paper scrolls on a long low table to the emperor's right and picked out one of them. She unfurled it to read, as a look of alarm swept across her beautiful face. She asked, "What's this?"

With her eyes settled on the last two lines of the scroll, she read, "It is hereby ordered that Empress Wu be deposed from the throne and banished from the palace and the capital."

The room fell into silence for several minutes.

With tears pouring down her cheeks, the empress asked in a soft but tragic voice, "Zhinu, how can you do this to your Huagu?"

At the mention of the pet names, the emperor lowered his gaze to the floor in silence. She continued with passion, "Have you forgotten the Cuiwei Palace? The way you stared at me? The way we snuggled against each other for the first time?"

As the emperor listened, his face turned from red to purple.

"You loved me best when I was wearing the pomegranate frock, didn't you? And the secret oath? Don't you remember? We took it together in front of the Buddha and promised to belong to each other for ever and ever, didn't we?"

The emperor was reduced to tears of remorse and fear.

"How about the Gan'ye Nunnery? Our first meeting after the long separation? Zhinu, you do remember, don't you?"

"Yes, I do," the emperor said timidly. Looking at the scroll of paper the empress was holding in her hand, he stammered, "The e . . . e . . . edict was originally not my idea."

"Whose then?"

"It was written on the suggestion of a senior official."

"It can't be Xu Jingzong; and must have been the other chief minister in charge, Shangguan Yi. Am I right?"

The emperor said nothing.

"You still want to issue it, don't you?"

"Of course not."

"Then, I will dispose of it for you." The empress rolled up the scroll.

"But Shangguan Yi is innocent! He should not be punished for offering his honest opinion. Please don't hurt him, I beg you," the emperor implored.

"I won't," the empress said and walked out, the scroll in hand.

***

Early the next afternoon, Chief Minister Xu Jingzong visited the empress on summons. With Cui Dunli dead and Li Yifu in exile for the crime of selling offices, now Xu Jingzong was her most trusted adviser.

No sooner did he sit down than the empress informed him of his next secret mission.

Back at home alone, he mulled over the task at hand: to eliminate Shangguan Yi and Wang Fusheng. It took him three days before he came up with an ingenious way to link them to a serious crime. In the secret report Xu submitted, he claimed to have discovered a meaningful connection between the two. Both had once worked for the ex-crown prince Li Zhong, banished first to Liangzhou, then to Qianzhou.[12] All this suggested, Xu claimed, that an anti-emperor alliance among the three had been formed with the prince as its leader.

The emperor found Xu's reasoning far-fetched, but, at the empress's suggestion, granted him the permission to investigate the suspects. Xu Jingzong lost no time in taking Shangguan Yi and Wang Fusheng into custody. After a few secret trials, he found both of them guilty of high treason. Backed by the empress, he managed to have the emperor's seal affixed to the death writs of the two wretched men. Both were later beheaded in public in the Eastern Market of the capital. In accord with the law of guilt by association, Shangguan Yi's grownup son was dispatched as well. His female dependents, including his daughter-in-law Lady Zheng and her newborn daughter Shangguan Wan'er, were condemned to work as bondservants in the Lateral Palace for life.

Xu Jingzong then sent his agents to Qianzhou in the south to go after Li Zhong. When they located the prince in his home, they were surprised to see him cross-dressed as a woman. Out of curiosity, they asked what kind of game he was playing. Li Zhong chuckled and answered good-humoredly that he just wanted to confuse his would-be assassins. Thereupon, one of the agents whipped out an official document and announced his crime and punishment. It came as such a shock that the frightened prince fainted. When he regained consciousness a few moments later, they forced a goblet of poisoned wine down his throat, putting him out of his misery. This humble prince by a lowborn concubine, one-time heir to the throne, was twenty-two *sui*.[13]

In the end, when the dust had settled, hundreds of officials were demoted or banished for association with members of the clique. Now that the court was purged of all her potential opponents, the empress demanded and succeeded in obtaining absolute loyalty from the surviving senior officials and officers. People began to hold her in awe and speak of her and her husband together as the "Two Sages." Although Li Zhi was still the emperor, the empress was acting more and more like the real boss ruling over the country.

Notes

1 Geomancy (*fengshui* 風水) is an ancient occult practice. It believes that the positioning of tombs and buildings has an influence, auspicious or baleful, on related individuals and their families. In the *Book of Changes* (*Yijing* 易經), the basic symbols are the eight trigrams, which are matched to create the sixty-four hexagrams, each consisting of six lines, solid and/or broken. Each hexagram has its own line-by-line interpretations. The first hexagram is called *qian* 乾 consisting of six solid lines.

2 Hyperactive or rising liver yang is a condition that results when the yin and yang of the body are out of balance. Its typical symptom—throbbing headache—is likely related to high blood pressure.

3 The Penglai Palace 蓬萊宮 (Daming |dah-ming| Palace 大明宮), upon completion, became the favorite imperial residence.

4 The Taiye Pond 太液池: the central lake in the northern part of the Daming Palace.

[5] The Eastern Marchmount (*dongyue* 東嶽): "marchmount" is a neologism for one of the five famous mountains representing the five directions (east, west, south, north, and center). All are important to ritual and religion. The Eastern Marchmount (Mount Tai 泰山) is the most famous among them.

[6] The Board of Personnel (*libu* 吏部): the most important one of the Six Boards under the Department of State Affairs.

[7] The Three Clans (*sanzu* 三族) have several configurations and may refer to the clans of one's father, mother, and wife. The extermination of the Three Clans is based on the legal concept of culpability by association.

[8] The Zichen Basilica 紫宸殿: the third palatial building on the central axis of the Penglai/Daming Palace and north of the Xuanzheng Basilica 宣政殿.

[9] Paekche was defeated and annexed in 660.

[10] Shulê 疏勒 (Kashgar): one of the Four Garrisons of Anxi. It was in Kashi, west Xinjiang.

[11] Certain Chinese characters, especially those used in the given names of the emperor and his direct ancestors, were tabooed out of respect. To observe this custom was a sign of submission.

[12] Liangzhou 梁州: prefecture with its seat east of Hanzhong, Shaanxi. Qianzhou 黔州: prefecture with its seat east of Pengshui, Chongqing.

[13] According to *Zizhi tongjian* (201.6341), Shangguan Yi was arrested on the *bingxu* 丙戌 day of the twelfth month, which falls on January 4, 665. He was then executed with his son and the eunuch Wang Fusheng. Prince Li Zhong died on the *wuzi* 戊子 day (January 6, 665). See Lin Daoxin 2003, 455.

9. Li Ji (665–669)

A Tang-Koguryŏ War broke out in early 667. The Tang forces under Li Ji and Xue Rengui conquered Koguryŏ in 668.

THE 660S WAS an age of great prosperity. After several consecutive years of good harvest, rice was selling for as low as five cash per peck (*dou*). Wheat and soybeans were so abundant that they were no longer displayed in market bazaars.

At the beginning of the year Linde 2 (665), the emperor and the empress set off from Chang'an to embark on their one and only *fengshan* trip to Mount Tai. As the highest form of thanksgiving ritual, the *fengshan* mainly consisted of *feng* sacrifices to Heaven and *shan* sacrifices to Earth. In the past, only the most vainglorious rulers such as the First Emperor and Emperor Wu of Han had undertaken it.

General Li Ji, as *fengshan* commissioner, assumed overall leadership of the journey. After the death of Chu Suiliang and Zhangsun Wuji, and the banishment of Yu Zhining, Li Ji became the only remaining *senior* chief minister at court.

As he was riding along, the clip-clop of horse hooves took him back to his past existence during the founding years of the Tang. Known then as Xu Shiji, he had at first served General Li Mi, a main rival of the Tang, before switching sides and joining the Tang army. When his erstwhile master had died, Li Ji had given him an elaborate ritual burial, an act that had only served to enhance his reputation as a man of honor and loyalty in the eyes of the Tang.

Towards the end of Taizong's reign, he found himself in a bind as a succession struggle unfolded. He had to choose sides between Li Zhi, the future emperor, and his brother Li Tai. In the end, he did nothing. Upon Taizong's death and Li Zhi's accession, Li Ji was banished to a remote post by a death-bed order of Taizong to test his loyalty. But soon he was recalled by the new emperor to serve as the top general of the military. As such, Li Ji had shown unquestioned loyalty to the new sovereign and Empress Wu and won their complete trust.

A career army officer all his adult life, Li Ji often mused about the life he shared with his officers and men in battle and on the march and the great camaraderie he enjoyed with them. As a commanding officer, he had done extraordinarily well. One key reason for his success was his generosity. He had always given away war booty, including gold, silk, and precious objects, to his subaltern officers and soldiers. Thus, those serving under him followed his orders without hesitation and fought without fear.

In large part thanks to their support and backed by the emperor, Li Ji had risen to the top of officialdom as *puye* (vice premier or co-president) of the Department of State Affairs. Residing in a mansion in an upscale neighborhood of Chang'an where he had called home for decades, he had never forgotten about family. As the oldest of the Li/Xu brothers, he enjoyed a close bond with his siblings. When he heard that his widowed elder sister had come down with a long ailment, he made time to visit her in the country.

During his stay at her home, he insisted on cooking breakfast for her.

One morning, he rose early to boil millet porridge and got his beard seared. To this his elderly sister said, "Brother Ji, don't bother anymore, please. I can ask a maid to do it."

Li Ji replied, "How many times can I cook porridge for my big sister again?" So he continued to perform the morning ritual every day until the end of his long visit.

***

When the imperial procession was passing through Huazhou,[1] the empress, no less, broke her journey to pay the big sister a visit. She brought with her generous gifts, including many pieces of fine clothing, and granted her a noble title. It was obvious that this was her way of thanking Li Ji for his support and of encouraging his exemplary behavior.

A few days later, Tianhou rejoined the emperor. Soon the procession resumed the journey east. At head of thousands of officials and officers in the entourage was Li Ji. As the road ahead was approaching a narrow bridge, his bay horse shied, thrusting him onto the ground. The emperor swung off his horse and rushed over. Li Ji, despite his badly sprained ankle, struggled to his feet with the help of two eunuch officers. When they tried but failed to get Li Ji's horse to stand, the emperor gifted his own mount to the general.

***

The procession came to a halt in the Eastern Capital, where the emperor and the empress would sojourn until of the end of the year when they would embark on the last leg of the journey to Mount Tai to consummate the *fengshan* ceremonies.

Under the Sui and the Tang up to now, no emperor had attempted to take a *fengshan* trip. But the topic had been brought up from time to time at court meetings. As early as 632, when Li Zhi was just five *sui*, a heated debate had raged at Taizong's court on Zhangsun Wuji's proposal for the first *fengshan* trip under the Tang. Eventually, Taizong had turned it down thanks to the opposition of his confidant Wei Zheng on grounds of cost and lack of merit. Now thirty-three years later, that unpleasant episode had faded from memory. The country was doing much better, and for the court, cost was no longer an issue. What was more, senior remonstrators of Wei Zheng's caliber had entirely vanished from the scene.

In the eleventh month of 665, the imperial procession set off again towards the east, stretching several hundred *li* on the road.

Accompanying the Two Sages was a large following numbering in the hundreds of thousands, ranging from leading court officials and top military commanders to corvée laborers and foot soldiers. Dozens of foreign delegations with their tents, wigwams, long baggage trains, and herds of oxen, sheep, camels, and horses were converging on Mount Tai from as far west as Persia and as far east as Koguryŏ and Japan.

Prefect of Daifang Liu Rengui brought with him a most extraordinary delegation, consisting of leaders of four non-Sinitic states—Silla, Paekche, Tamna (Danluo),[2] and Yamato.[3] The empress was thrilled to see the scene of "10,000 nations coming to court bearing tribute"[4] playing out before her eyes. At her prompting, an equally impressed emperor appointed Liu to the prestigious post of censor-in-chief.[5]

Early on the morning of the Chinese New Year, 666, the emperor and the empress initiated a five-day ritual at Mount Tai. After they paid homage to the Lord on High[6] at an altar set up for the occasion, the emperor was carried in a palanquin to the top of the main peak. Here the ritual journey reached its apex when descending from his vehicle, the emperor made offerings of jade documents to the Lord on High and the Auxiliary Gods.

The next day the Two Sages were carried to a lower peak called Sheshou[7] to worship at an altar to Earth. The emperor came up first, accompanied by a large retinue of attendants, and offered the first libation of wine to the accompaniment of ritual music.

Then the empress's turn came. She made her way to the front of three rows of bronze ritual vessels against the backdrop of a damask curtain and offered the second libation, followed by a ritual dance put on by dozens of palace ladies.

On the last day of their stay, the emperor mounted another altar where he received felicitations from the officials and announced a general amnesty and a new reign title, Qianfeng or "Supernal Sacrifice," signifying the completion of the ceremonies and the dawn of a new era.

On the return journey, the emperor and the empress stopped at the city of Qufu[8] (in Shandong), the capital of the ancient state of Lu, where Confucius had called home. There they made sacrifices to the Sage at his eponymous temple and honored him with the august title of grand preceptor (*taishi*).[9]

In Bozhou (in northwest Anhui),[10] they paid homage to the Temple of Lord Lao and honored him with the grandiose title of Superior Mysterious and Primordial Emperor.[11]

***

As the Two Sages were still on the road, copies of the edict on amnesty began to circulate across China. In a few weeks' time, one copy reached Xizhou[12] as well, a remote prefecture in the southwest. It gave Ex-Chief Minister Li Yifu, aging and sick, a glimmer of hope. But when he learned that the amnesty did not apply to those sentenced to long-term banishment, including himself, he sank into a funk. Feeling abandoned by the court, he succumbed not long afterwards.

***

After Lady Wu became Empress Wu, her mother, Lady Yang, was granted a noble title, "the state mistress of Rong,"[13] and her other relatives in officialdom were promoted to high posts. Her two half-brothers Wu Yuanqing and Wu Yuanshuang and her paternal cousin Wu Weiliang were all transferred from insignificant provincial jobs to cushy positions in the capital. Wu Huaiyun, another cousin, was raised to prefect of Zizhou,[14] a key prefecture in present-day Shandong.

The surprising thing was that all this had happened without the empress lifting a finger and that she was not keen on promoting those male relatives of hers at all.

One autumn evening, the empress paid a routine visit to her mother, the state mistress of Rong. During the after-meal chitchat, her mother mentioned her recent encounter with the empress's cousins. "The other day at this drinking party, I saw Huaiyun and Weiliang. Huaiyun was in the capital on official business. I tried to put them at ease and said, 'Don't worry about what happened in the past. It wouldn't affect your career advancement at all.' Guess what? Cousin Weiliang turned defensive and said, 'Huaiyun and I are sons of a meritorious official. We joined officialdom when young and achieved promotion through our own efforts.' Huaiyun then said, 'I agree. We haven't taken advantage of our famous cousin's power and connections. And we never will.' "

"Bastards! What do they think they are!" the empress growled.

"I am surprised that these two are arrogant as ever."

"How about my half-brothers, Yuanqing and Yuanshuang."

"Like the two cousins, they too are full of themselves. They both believe their promotions have nothing to do with you."

"How are those two bullies doing nowadays anyway, Mother?"

"Yuanqing and Yuanshuang are doing extremely well after their transfers to high posts in the capital."

"Really?" the empress asked, unpleasant memories flooding her mind. Granted that the promotions of the four Wus had been arranged by courtiers who wanted to curry favor with the empress, but they did not please her in the least. Not that she opposed nepotism as a matter of principle, but that she could never forget the humiliation she and her mother and sisters had suffered at their hands following Father's passing.

A few days later, the male members of the Wu clan were in for an unpleasant surprise when they received an edict on their demotion transfers. Three of the four were now banished to provincial posts south of the capital. The only one who was untouched was Huaiyun, who had been in a provincial post already. In the same edict, the emperor stressed the importance of not giving preferential treatment to consort relatives[15] and praised the empress for being impartial when she proposed these transfers.

***

Wu Yuanqing and Wu Yuanshuang (the Yuan brothers), their arrogance deflated, sank into a chronic depression. They just could not comprehend what they had done to deserve banishment and never got over it. They both had a hard time getting used to the hardscrabble life on the frontier, and soon perished.[16]

As expected, the iron-hearted empress did not shed a single tear over the death of her two half-brothers. But she was worried about one unexpected outcome of their death. For the first time, she had to face the harsh reality that, according to the millennia-old patriarchal tradition, the Wu family was now officially without an heir to carry on the surname.

She set her sights on her nephew Helan Minzhi (her elder sister's son) now in his early twenties. She did not care that the young man took after his beautiful sister, the state mistress of Wei, and that his fine facial features gave him an air of feminine grace. But he was the only one who fit the bill: male, young, and closely related. She granted him the surname of Wu and made him the adopted heir of the late Wu Shiyue (her own father), which allowed him to inherit the title of the duke of Zhou. To add prestige to his status, she appointed him academician of the Institute for the Advancement of Literature,[17] a highly elitist school for sons of the high-ranking officials that doubled as a government agency for compiling and editing important literary anthologies and other types of lengthy books of great value.

***

Wu Weiliang, now in Shizhou,[18] was clinging to hope for rehabilitation and re-appointment to a capital post in the not-so-distant future. Empress Wu could make it happen with a nod of her head. He and his brother Huaiyun based in Shandong co-wrote humble memorials to beg the forgiveness of the empress but never received a response from her.

At the time of the *fengshan* trip, Weiliang and Huaiyun, both prefects, joined other prefectural leaders in traveling to Mount Tai to take part in the ceremonies. The pilgrimage over, they could have returned to their provincial posts in Sichuan and Shandong but did not. Instead, they joined the imperial procession to head for Chang'an. Bearing a special gift—a small red jar of homemade fish paste—they went straight to the palace to offer it to their paternal cousin. Although they did not get an audience, they received a decent enough welcome from one of her eunuch officers, who accepted the gift on her behalf and placed it in her study.

In truth, the empress was not interested in meeting Weiliang and Huaiyun at all, especially at a time when she was preoccupied with something else, the presence of her niece, the state mistress of Wei, in the palace. She was alarmed that the young woman, who had started attending on the emperor only recently, had already won his favor. Had it not been for the empress's opposition, he would have appointed the cousin consort.

***

One late afternoon, the empress was entertaining the emperor in her residential basilica. As usual, he was accompanied by her piece, the stunningly beautiful state mistress of Wei. The empress engaged them in a pleasant conversation for a while, then she brought up the subject of her mother Lady Yang.

To the emperor's inquiry after her health, the empress said, "My mother is doing fine, except for a cold."

"Oh? Is that serious?" The emperor sounded concerned.

"Not at all," the empress said, casting a glance at her niece. "But if Your Majesty pays her a visit, it will do her much good. She often talks about you."

"Yes, indeed."

Their conversation went on for a while until it was getting late. The emperor rose and said to the empress, "I'd better leave now if I want to see your mother tonight."

"In that case, I won't keep Your Majesty any longer," the empress said.

The state mistress of Wei got up as well.

"You don't have to go, Niece," the empress said to her. "We still have a lot to chat about. Your grandmother is doing just fine."

The empress walked the emperor to the gate, bid him good-bye, and turned on her heels. Before rejoining her niece, she stopped in her study to pick up the small red jar, and asked a eunuch on duty to give it to her niece when she left.

"Courtesy of the empress?" the eunuch asked.

"Yes, you can say that," she answered.

The empress then returned to the reception hall, and the casual chat continued until about an hour later when she allowed her niece to leave.

The empress saw her off at the basilica door and returned to her study.

A few moments later, the eunuch entered and reported: "She was absolutely delighted when I handed her the jar at the gate."

"Did she say something?"

"Yes. She said that she could not wait to taste it."

"Great job," the empress said as she handed him a few pieces of silver.

***

Late that night Empress Wu received the news of her niece's passing.

"How did His Majesty react to this?" the empress asked the eunuch who had brought the message.

"Thoroughly devastated. His Majesty said to her brother Helan Minzhi, 'When I saw her at the morning court assembly, she was alive and well; by evening, she was gone! How could life be snatched away so easily?' "

"What did Minzhi said?"

"He said nothing, Your Majesty. He just kept sobbing and wailing for his lost sister."

What's matter with Minzhi? thought the empress, a burst of anger rising in her chest. *He didn't shed a tear when his mother died. Is he suspecting I had anything to do with his sister's death?*

A subsequent investigation of the lamentable incident pointed to two culprits: Wu Weiliang and Wu Huaiyun, now in Sichuan and Shandong. They were the ones who had gifted the red jar to the empress after all. The two cousins were then arrested, tortured, convicted, and summarily executed. Their crimes: attempting to assassinate the empress and the murder of the state mistress of Wei. As an expression of her righteous indignation, the empress issued a decree to have the surname of the two dead criminals changed to "Viper."[19]

Wu Huailiang, the eldest brother of the two, had died early, and thus avoided the humiliation of public execution. But his wife was still alive. Because of the crimes of her brothers-in-law, she was condemned to work in the Lateral Palace as a bondwoman for life. Like her husband and brothers-in-law, she had acted superior to the empress's mother Lady Yang in the old days. And the empress had never forgiven her. Soon the empress found an excuse to further punish her. At her request, the poor widow was flogged with a spiked whip until her skin burst open and her flesh hung in shreds to reveal the white bones beneath. She succumbed soon afterwards.

***

In early 667, Li Ji was appointed commander-in-chief of the Liaodong[20] District Expeditionary Army to lead the fight against Koguryŏ. By then, Paekche, despite Yamato's assistance, had been annexed by the Tang general Su Dingfang in 660 and King Puyŏ P'ung had fled to Koguryŏ, the most powerful of the Three States on the Korean Peninsula.

In Koguryŏ, the power-holder Quan Gaisuwen had died. His heir apparent Quan Nansheng,[21] challenged by his two younger brothers Nanchan and Nanjian, turned to the Tang for help.

For his part, Li Ji was anxious to launch the last military campaign of his life in the midst of the Second Tang-Koguryŏ War. More than twenty years before, he had joined Emperor Taizong in the First Tang-Koguryŏ War (645), which had failed. Now was the time to erase the humiliation. What was more important, General Li wanted to use this opportunity to show his gratitude to Taizong's successor, the emperor Li Zhi, who had held him in high esteem.

***

As the Tang invading army was well inside the Koguryŏ territory, an astrological event caught the emperor Li Zhi's attention. On May 18, 668, a comet with a bright tail was sighted near the Northeast Star of the Five Chariots Constellation in the Bi Lunar Lodge.[22] The Five Chariots was the carriage house for the Five Emperors. According to *fenye* (allotted fields) theory,[23] the apparition of a comet did not bode well for the corresponding terrestrial regions, that was, the Yan and

Zhao areas in Hebei and south Manchuria. A ritual official made a few recommendations.

But Xu Jingzong begged to differ, saying, "The passage of the comet near the Northeast Star is disastrous for the enemy, not us. And it points to the destruction of Koguryŏ."

The emperor replied, "It is a warning from Heaven against my transgressions. How can you lay the blame on a barbarian people? Moreover, the Koguryŏ are my subjects too. I take no pleasure in their suffering." So he took the proposed measures—avoiding appearing in person in the main basilica, reducing the consumption of food, and cancelling musical performances at court.

While the emperor was doing what he could to mitigate the baleful impact of astral events, General Li Ji led a numerous invading army deep into Koguryŏ. By the autumn of 668, he had joined forces with other commanding officers on the campaign—Liu Rengui, Hao Chujun, Xue Rengui, and Qibi Heli—at Pyongyang.

On Li Ji's orders, the Tang troops began to lay siege to the Koguryŏ capital. But the city was well protected by strong fortifications and tall walls. And the defenders had turned down all Tang requests for battle.

But, one month into the siege, the situation inside the walls was getting desperate, with serious food and water shortages. Just when General Li Ji was about to mount a general assault, he received a ninety-eight-man delegation headed by Quan Nanchan on behalf of King Pojang, with their terms of surrender. The general accepted them. But Nanchan's brother Nanjian, who was in charge of defending the city, still offered resistance. In the end, the Tang attack troops, equipped with trebuchets, repeating crossbows, and battering rams, defeated him and his forces, after his top military adviser betrayed him and had a city gate secretly unlatched from the inside.

***

In the early winter of 668, Chang'an opened its arms to welcome State Duke of Ying Li Ji. His conquest of Koguryŏ was an extraordinary feat the two Sui emperors and Taizong had attempted but failed to accomplish. At a grand ceremony celebrating the victory he rode a tall bay stallion at a slow trot along the city's central north-south boulevard at the head of a long procession. It was a most gratifying way to end his long military career when he was at the peak of his glory and he and his subordinate officers received great honors and generous rewards.

Marking the height of the event was the presentation of the Koguryŏ royals and other high-ranking prisoners-of-war to the emperor and the empress in the Hanyuan Basilica,[24] the principal structure of the Penglai Palace. In a ceremonial speech, the emperor reproached them before issuing an edict to set them free and appoint them to high posts in the Tang government. There were two notable exceptions: Quan Nanjian, one of the Quan brothers, who had offered resistance even after the peace deal, and Puyŏ P'ung, the former king of Paekche, who had been working on the revival of his state with the help of Koguryŏ. The former was banished to Qianzhou,[25] and the latter to the far south.

***

Not long after the celebration, Li Ji's health went into an unexpected decline. Starting in mid-669, he began to go from bad to worse with each passing month. Life as a career soldier for five decades in a row, particularly the recent military campaign he had led at the age of seventy-five *sui*, had taken its toll. He was now losing his ability to fight off a serious ailment.

The emperor was distraught beyond measure. On the advice of the empress, he issued an urgent edict to Li Ji's close male relatives, requesting them to come to Chang'an posthaste to attend on the general by turns. The emperor, the empress, and the crown prince all gifted him with precious herbal blends. Li Ji, for his part, had them decocted before taking them dutifully. His close relatives also sent him healers and shamanists. But he kept all of them at the gate of his mansion. He saw no point in having some dubious human agents interfere with Heaven's plan.

"What a life I have led!" exclaimed Li Ji as he was surrounded by his two brothers, only surviving son, grandson Li Jingye, and other relatives.

"At twelve or thirteen *sui*, I ran away from home to start my career, as a bandit! I was then a vicious bandit, killing people at random. At fourteen or fifteen *sui*, I was out of control, killing whoever I disliked. At seventeen or eighteen *sui*, I turned over a new leaf after I joined Zhai Rang's army, killing people only in the battlefield. At twenty *sui*, I was a general-in-chief,[26] leading my troops to save people from death. When I got started, I was nothing but a country bumpkin from Shandong. Thanks to His Majesty's generosity, I have reached the rank of the Three Dukes[27] and lived to be seventy-six *sui*! Isn't that . . ." He coughed and wheezed.

His grandson Li Jingye held up a porcelain tea bowl to his lips. Li Ji took a gulp of the brown medicinal tea and continued, "Isn't that fate? The length of one's life is predetermined. How can one expect to extend it with the help of healers and shamans? No, one simply can't. In fact, in the last few months, my condition has gotten so bad that I am afraid

I won't be able to get up again. And I know I will end my journey on earth soon—that is inevitable."[28]

Addressing Li Bi,[29] the second oldest of the Li brothers, Li Ji asked, "What's the date today?"

"The day of *bingwu*, Elder Brother."

Li Ji closed his eyes for a few seconds, moving his lips as if he were counting. Opening his eyes again, he said, "Now I know, I shall depart on the day of *wushen*,[30] that is, the day after tomorrow."

"Elder Brother!" Li Bi sobbed.

"Grandpa! You won't!" Li Jingye was on the verge of tears.

"Before I go, I must share my thoughts on the future of the Li lineage. Listen well. This is important. I am sure you are familiar with Du Ruhui and Fang Xuanling. These were the greatest chief ministers under Taizong. They worked tirelessly their entire lives for the court. The late Emperor Taizong trusted them more than his closest relatives and married his favorite daughters to their sons. What happened after the death of Du and Fang? Their unfilial sons Du He and Fang Yi'ai conspired against the current emperor. In so doing, they destroyed the Du and Fang lineages."

He paused to stare down at his brothers and offspring and continued, "You must take the lesson of the Dus and Fangs to heart."

Fixing his gaze on his grandson, he said sternly, "Jingye, I am naming you as the heir of the Li lineage and the inheritor of my title—the state duke of Ying—after my death."

Li Jingye, a tall man in his early thirties, fell on his knees and kowtowed three times to his grandfather lying in his sickbed.

"Don't you ever," Li Ji said, gesturing him to stand up, "take this title of duke for granted. In fact, I, your grandfather, owe it to the throne. Not only that. I owe everything to His Majesty, including my rank, power, wealth, and even my surname Li. Whatever happens in the future, you must never, never do anything that may harm the emperor and the empress. Grandson, can you live up to my expectations?"

Li Jingye nodded his head forcibly, with tears streaming down his cheeks.

Patting him on the shoulder, Li Ji said, "Don't cry. Be a true soldier like your father and grandfather."

"Yes, Grandpa."

Addressing himself to all present, Li Ji said, "Listen, I want you to give Jingye as much support as you can so that the Li bloodline will continue for generations to come. Can you?"

They gave their tearful assent, then came forward one by one to express their best wishes and take their leave. Li Bi was the only one who remained.

"I am asking you, Younger Brother," Li Ji said solemnly, "to take over all family affairs. As soon as my funeral is over, move into this house. As the paterfamilias, you will hold the power of life and death over all other members of the Li household. Should anyone turn out to be unworthy, club him to death, and report it to the court later." Li Bi nodded his head.

Two days later, on a *wushen* day (December 31, 669), surrounded by his loved ones and with the emperor weeping by his side, Li Ji breathed his last in bed.

⁂

On the emperor's orders, court business was suspended for seven days while the country was in mourning. That was the greatest honor ever granted to a person, royal or nonroyal, in death.

Li Ji's remains were laid to rest in the Zhaoling Tomb Park,[31] where Taizong was buried. His tomb was fronted by a tall stela. The long epitaph on it was inscribed in the emperor's calligraphy.

Notes

1 Huazhou 滑州: prefecture in north Henan with its seat southeast of Huaxian.

2 Tamna (Danluo 耽羅): kingdom based on Chejudo (Jeju Island) 濟州島, off the south coast of South Korea.

3 Yamato 大和: kingdom based in Nara, Hongshu, Japan, during the Kofun 古墳 and Asuka 飛鳥 periods.

4 *Wanguo laichao* 王國來朝: an early reference to this idiom can be found in *Zuozhuan* (Ai 7).

5 *Da sixian* 大司憲: the same as *yushi dafu* 御史大夫.

6 The Lord on High (Haotian Shangdi 昊天上帝): the highest godhead in the traditional Chinese pantheon.

7 Mount Sheshou 社首 was a lower mountain next to Mount Tai. Traditionally, it was where Earth was worshipped. It was leveled in 1951.

8 Qufu 曲阜, Shandong, is home to the best-known Confucian Temple, the Kong Cemetery, and the Kong Residence.

9 Grand Preceptor (*taishi* 太師): normally, a highest prestige title and one of the Three Preceptors.

10 Bozhou 亳州 (prefecture with its seat in present-day Bozhou, northwest Anhui): Laozi is believed to have been born in Bozhou.

11 The Superior Mysterious and Primordial Emperor (*taishang xuanyuan huangdi* 太上玄元皇帝): an honorific title conferred on Laozi. It was more elevated than previous titles he had received.

[12] Xizhou 巂州: prefecture in west Sichuan with its seat in Xichang. It was in a peripheral area of the empire.

[13] The state mistress of Rong (Rongguo furen 榮國夫人): a *guo furen* (state mistress or state consort) was a title conferred upon the wife or mother of a high-ranking official.

[14] Zizhou 淄州: prefecture in Shandong with its seat southwest of Zibo.

[15] Consort relatives (*waiqi* 外戚): male relatives of an empress or imperial consort. Because their close relations to the empress or consort, they were often appointed to important posts at the center.

[16] *Zizhi tongjian* 201.6349–50.

[17] The Institute for the Advancement of Literature (Hongwen guan 弘文館): starting in 627, it was the new name for the Institute for the Cultivation of Literature (Xiuwen guan 修文館, founded in 621). It was in charge of editing and compiling literary and other works and of training sons of high-ranking officials.

[18] Shizhou 始州: prefecture in northeast Sichuan with its seat in present-day Jiange, Sichuan.

[19] *Fu* 蝮.

[20] Liaodong 遼東: area east of the Daling River in Liaoning.

[21] Quan Nansheng 泉男生 [Yŏn Namsaeng] (634–679): eldest son of Quan Gaisuwen.

[22] The Wuche 五車 (Five Chariots) is a constellation in Taurus and Auriga. Bi 畢 (Net) is one of the seven lunar lodges (*xiu* 宿) in the west. In Chinese astrology, the astral bodies along the ecliptic and celestial equator are divided into twenty-eight regions, known as the Twenty-Eight Lunar Lodges (*ershi ba xiu* 二十八宿).

[23] *Fenye* 分野 (allotted fields): an astrological system that matches the Twenty-Eight Lunar Lodges with corresponding regions on earth.

[24] The Hanyuan Basilica 含元殿: the largest palatial building of the Penglai/Daming Palace, Chang'an, and also the largest structure in China. Luoyang had a palatial building by the same name.

[25] Qianzhou 黔州: prefecture in Chongqing with its seat east of Pengshui. *See* note in Part I, Chapter 6.

[26] General-in-chief (*da jiangjun* 大將軍): senior officer, usually commander of one of the Sixteen Guards.

[27] The Three Dukes: the defender-in-chief (*taiwei* 太尉), the minister of the masses (*situ* 司徒), and the minister of works (*sikong* 司空). They were the highest prestige titles.

[28] After *Zizhi tongjian* 201.6360–61.

[29] Li Bi 李弼: prefect of Jinzhou 晉州 based in Shanxi.

[30] *Bingwu* 丙午, *wushen* 戊申: days in the Sexagenary Cycle.

[31] The Zhaoling 昭陵 Tomb Park is a super-sized Tang royal cemetery with Taizong and his wife Empress Zhangsun's joint burial as its main tomb. Located to the northwest of Xi'an, Shaanxi, it is home to more than 180 accompanying tombs. Its area is close to 50,000 acres.

10. Heavenly Empress (Tianhou) (667–674)

The first Arab siege of Constantinople began in 674.

FOR DECADES, THE true powerholder of the Tubo Empire on the Tibetan Plateau was Chancellor Lu Dongzan. On his watch, Tubo had grown into a formidable military power. It had challenged Tang authority in the Western Regions and dislodged Tuyuhun, a friendly power to the Tang, from its traditional habitat in Qinghai. Despite his success in enlarging Tubo's territory, Lu Dongzan remained cautious towards the Tang. In 667, he passed away. His son Lun Qinling took over the reins and threw caution to the wind. He seized a vast stretch of land from some Tang loose-rein prefectures,[1] areas governed by court-approved tribal leaders.

In the face of the Tubo menace, the emperor felt compelled to act. He had an edict drafted in 669, which would resettle the displaced Tuyuhun nomads in the South Mountains area[2] and send an expedition force to take on the Tubo.

But, when the emperor consulted his top advisers on these issues, Chief Minister Yan Liben voiced his concerns, saying, "In the last two years, there has not been enough rain in the north, especially in

Guanzhong. Grain prices have more than doubled. The urban and rural neighborhoods are packed with the starving masses. If we launch an expedition against Tubo, it will add a huge burden to the people. In my humble opinion, we should not do it now."

As he listened to the eloquent flow of words from Yan, the emperor was reminded of his background as an accomplished artist. In fact, before his promotion to chancellor, he had been the most celebrated painter bar none in the nation and a great architect to boot. But he had no battlefield experience at all.

The emperor shifted his gaze from Yan to the military leaders, asking, "What do you think?"

The Turkic Qibi Heli, one of Taizong's doughtiest generals, said, "In general, I support the expedition. It is obvious that the Tubo intend to go after the remnants of the Tuyuhun. But, at this stage, we do not have to make a move. Instead, we wait until they doubt our capabilities and become arrogant. We can then attack with Tuyuhun and crush them."

The battle-hardened Jiang Ke, the other chancellor, responded, "I have to disagree with General Qibi. Clearly, Tubo is on the rise while Tuyuhun is in decline. To meet the rising power with a declining army will result in total defeat. But if we do not aid them now, the Tuyuhun will be wiped out. In my opinion, our priority should be sending a relief army to make sure that Tuyuhun survives. That will in turn make it possible to deal with Tubo on a long-term basis."

"Yes, we must consider the long-term outcome," the emperor said, as a sudden throbbing pain in his temples caused him to lose his balance and fall back hard into his chair. With a flick of his hand, he dismissed the session. While the emperor continued to consider his options in the days that followed, he stopped short of issuing the edict.

***

The Tubo sensed the Tang's indecision and launched a massive assault in the Western Regions. Eighteen loose-rein prefectures fell into their hands. The Tang court was forced to give up the Four Garrisons—Qiuci, Yutian, Yanqi, and Shulê[3]—in 670. And Chang'an was shaken.

The emperor had no choice but to confront the Tubo aggression. He appointed the invincible General Xue Rengui as commander-in-chief of a 100,000-strong expeditionary army. Xue's task was to expel the Tubo forces from the Western Regions, seize back the Four Garrisons, and revive the Tuyuhun state in its former territory. General Guo Daifeng and General Ashina Daozhen served as Xue's lieutenants.

However, General Xue soon found himself in trouble with Guo Daifeng, the son of the famous General Guo Xiaoke. It was obvious that Guo Daifeng felt ashamed of being a subordinate to Xue Rengui, who was of the same rank. So he often ignored the commander-in-chief's orders. When his army was marching unaided with a large quantity of *matériel* through Wuhai,[4] it was set upon by a Tuobo army of 200,000 men under Chancellor Lun Qinling and suffered a disastrous defeat.

Xue Rengui led the main force of the Tang expeditionary army to retreat into the Dafei Plain,[5] an area with neither natural barriers nor access to grain supply. Soon Lun Qinling's much more numerous army of 400,000 men caught up with it, and attacked and trounced it.

Under the threat of knives, Xue Rengui and Guo Daifeng negotiated a humiliating peace treaty with Lun Qinling and were allowed to return. By then, they had lost all their men except for a few hundred. As soon as they were back in Chang'an, the top generals were taken in cangue to the court to face the imperial wrath. Xue Rengui accepted personal responsibility for the defeat, but also added, "In this year of *gengwu*,[6] it is inauspicious to start war in the west."

The emperor did not accept this argument. After giving them a severe chastisement, he disenrolled Xue and his lieutenants and reduced them to commoner status.

***

The spies the empress had deployed to keep a watch on her nephew Helan Minzhi had failed to find evidence of disloyalty as was previously suspected but uncovered something equally disturbing.

First, he had committed major acts of thieving. The most atrocious one involved a huge amount of fine silk Tianhou had put aside to fund the building of a Buddhist temple in honor of her mother.

Second, he had engaged in deliberate, flagrant violation of ritual. While in mourning for the passing of his grandmother, he had shed his mourning attire and put on colorful silk garments to watch musical performances by courtesans.

The most troubling of all was his total lack of moral restraint when it came to satisfying his appetite for women. In fact, he would bed any good-looking housemaid he could lay his hands on. As a young teenager living in the mansion of his maternal grandmother (the empress's mother), the state mistress of Rong (aka Lady Yang), he had routinely spent the night in her bedchamber!

What was the most repugnant was a recent act he committed in the palace right beneath the empress's nose.

Not long after Crown Prince Li Hong came of age, the empress led a nationwide search for a bride, and chose from hundreds of virgins of marriageable age an attractive young girl with good family background and upbringing.

After the day was set for the grand matrimonial ceremony, invitations went out to the royals, court nobles, and high-ranking officials and officers. As the auspicious event drew near, the distinguished guests received a notice of cancellation with an apology from the empress. It turned out that the bride-to-be had been deflowered while visiting the palace as the empress's guest. The lecher was none other than Helan Minzhi!

As the only legal heir of the Wu family, Helan (Wu) Minzhi so far had been able to avert prosecution. But his promiscuous and incestuous behavior had left the empress sad and angry. It had often brought back bad memories of men—the Wu boys who had abused Mother, Sisters, and herself with foul language; and the old codgers at court, who had insulted Mother as a concubine, but who themselves all kept multiple bedmates at home. Although Minzhi was adopted as the Wu heir, he was still one of those men with a beastly desire that required instant gratification, in total disregard for ritual, benevolence, and righteousness.

The pretty boy with no morals has to go, she thought and went on to issue an empress's decree that declared:

> *By dint of his criminal conduct, Wu (Helan) Minzhi has forfeited his Wu surname, which now reverts to Helan, and will be banished to the far south and barred from returning to Chang'an forever.*

While Minzhi the common criminal was in transit to the far south, the empress's men caught up with him and garroted him with horse reins (671).[7]

The death of Helan Minzhi almost coincided with the death of Chief Minister Xu Jingzong, another man of bad reputation (672). But Xu was different from Helan in that he had never lost his good standing with the empress, even though he was widely feared and detested. A debate raged over what his posthumous title, an official epithet for eternity, should be, involving officials from the Court of Imperial Sacrifices (*taichang*), the Board of Revenue (*hubu*), and the Board of Rites (*libu*).[8] Initially, a negative *miu* (erroneous)[9] was suggested based on the fact he had married off his daughter to a barbarian chieftain in exchange for monetary gains. In the *Law of Posthumous Titles* (*Shifa*),[10] *miu* implies "to be contrary to the truth." Eventually, however, they settled on a slightly positive one, *gong*.[11] It suggests that the person in question has committed errors but known how to rectify them.

***

A mourning ritual for Helan Minzhi was held; Empress Wu, his aunt, did not even bother to attend. She would never forgive him for sullying her mother's reputation. Nonetheless his death made her more aware of the deaths that had happened around her. Apart from this nephew of hers, there were her mother, two half-brothers, two cousins, and one niece (the state mistress of Wei). It seemed that too many of the Wu lineage and its close relatives had died too soon. The empress knew very well that she was responsible, directly or indirectly, for sending all these (except for her mother) and countless others to the netherworld. Sometimes, the mere thought of it gave her the jitters, because as a Buddhist she worried about retribution from Heaven.

***

Chief minister Hao Chujun, a holder of the *jinshi* degree, was more of an erudite scholar than a career bureaucrat, having committed the entire *Book of the Han*[12] to memory. He was surprised when the empress summoned him into her study to give an assessment of the Wu lineage.

"I am afraid I am not the right man to do it, Your Majesty," he said.

"Don't worry. Just tell me what you think."

"What exactly is on your mind, Your Majesty?"

"After the passing of Minzhi, the Wu lineage is without an heir again. I want to know which one of the Wus will fit the bill. Of the four surviving nephews, Wu Chengsi is the son of Wu Yuanshuang, my eldest half-brother; Wu Sansi is the son of Wu Yuanqing, Yuanshuang's younger brother. Then there are two more distant nephews: Wu Youxu, the son of Cousin Wu Weiliang; and Wu Yizong, the grandson of Uncle Wu Shiyi."[13]

"There is not much difference among the four. But if Your Majesty still wants me rank them, I will put Chengsi at the top."

"Oh?"

"Yes, Your Majesty. He is not only the oldest, but the most mature of the four. Furthermore, he grew up while living with his father Wu Yuanshuang in the far south, and experienced hardship. Thus he is more in touch with the downtrodden."

"He is still there," the empress said.

"So much the better. He knows what it is like to live at the bottom of society."

"Sounds good." The empress nodded her head.

About two months later, Wu Chengsi received a summons of recall and moved from his father's place of banishment to the capital. Now a middle-ranking official in the Court of the Imperial Clan[14]—one of the third-tier central agencies, he assumed a low profile at work and got along with his colleagues and bosses very well. By 674 he was promoted to lead the Court as its chamberlain.[15]

The empress had been observing Wu Chengsi to see if he had what it took to carry on the Wu surname. So far, he had exceeded her expectations and given her hope that he would be able to compete for heirship to the throne when the opportunity arose.

***

Of all the powerful women in history Tianhou admired, Empress Dowager Feng[16] inspired her the most. When her state of Northern Yan fell, she was taken to the Northern Wei as a bondmaid to work in the Lateral Palace. Through perseverance and good luck, she rose to Noble Lady,[17] empress, and regent of Emperors Xianwen and Xiaowen. And she deserved credit for making those epoch-making reforms possible, reforms carried out in the name of her grandson Xiaowen.

In a way, what Tianhou had accomplished so far had surpassed the work of the empress dowager. If Tianhou wanted to push for more change, she was in uncharted territory. Standing in her way now, first and foremost, was the emperor institution. As the Son of Heaven and a progeny of Lord Lao, the emperor had a divine right to govern the moment he ascended the throne. When he passed on, that divine right would go with him or to his male heir. As inheritor of his legacy, the empress would *not* be able to justify her right to rule by divine sanction in a conventional way. To get around it, she turned to Buddhism, of which she was a fervent believer.

In the Fengxian Monastery of Longmen in the southern suburbs of Luoyang,[18] a gigantic sitting statue of Vairocana Buddha had recently been erected (672). The largest donation to the project was made by the empress—20,000 cash of her own cosmetics money. As the primordial Buddha from whom all other Buddhas originated, Vairocana was a most revered god in Tang China. There was reason to believe that Tianhou had his statue at Fengxian created in her own image.[19] In so doing, she probably aspired to possess the powers of the Buddha.

She found inspiration in the history and lore of India, the homeland of the Buddha, where the Buddhist ruler Aśoka[20] took on celestial titles and came to be known as Chakravartin (the King of the Turning Wheel). According to a Buddhist tradition, when a world-unifier descends upon the earth, a golden turning wheel will reveal itself in heaven. The unifier will come into possession of this wheel and with it rule over the entire universe.

She would like to adopt for herself an appropriate celestial title that would give her the same power as the Turning Wheel and make her an equal of her husband in the eyes of the masses.

But the chief ministers—Hao Chujun, Liu Rengui, Li Jingxuan, and others—might stand in the way. She appealed directly to the emperor Li Zhi through a memorial, in which she proposed, among other things, to stop using the terms "late emperor" and "late empress" at court. These were the standard references to a recently deceased sovereign and his spouse. Empress Wu argued that they did not do justice to the deceased emperor and empress, nor would they do justice to the current emperor and herself in the future when they passed on.

Instead, each deceased emperor or empress should be given a specific designation. Thus she proposed to adopt a pair of eternal titles for this life and the hereafter: the "Heavenly Emperor" (Tianhuang) for him and "Heavenly Empress" (Tianhou) for herself.

The emperor appreciated his wife for her wisdom and foresight. Still, he asked, "In what way can the new titles be much better than the old?"

She answered, "Confucius says, 'If names are not correct, language is not in accordance with the truth of things. If language is not in accordance with the truth of things, affairs cannot be carried on with success.' The suggested new titles rectify the inadequacy of the old ones. Since they have never been used before, they will be the exclusive titles of Your Majesty and his spouse and assure their 'posthumous immortality.' "

The emperor closed his eyes to ponder for a few moments, then nodded his approval.

Thus, starting in the eighth month of 674, the emperor and the empress began to be known as "Heavenly Emperor" and "Heavenly Empress" (Tianhou). What was so amazing about this was the fact that Empress Wu had managed to deify herself without even taking the throne. And that in turn fulfilled what Yuan Tiangang had said in his prophecy: she "is Heaven's favorite."

***

Encouraged by her success, the empress submitted another memorial with twelve policy proposals, including promoting farming and sericulture; reducing tax and corvée burdens; desisting from military activities; and edifying all under Heaven with moral and virtue.

On the tricky issue of the Daoist religion, it said, "Since our emperor is a descendant of the Mysterious and Primordial Emperor (Laozi), members of the nobility from the princes and dukes down should read the *Daode jing* (Classic of the Way and Its Virtue).[21] Students for the classicist degree (*mingjing*) should devote themselves to the study of this Daoist scripture, and each year, the court should hold degree examinations based on Daoist topics." For court officials trained in the Confucian tradition, this was nothing short of subversive. Up to that time, it had been a given that students of classics only studied the *Confucian* classics.

In the realm of filial piety, the memorial proposed that the offspring of a deceased mother extend their mourning period from one to three years when the father was alive. In other words, it would place the mother in death on an equal footing with the father. That was a major departure from the teaching of the *Record of Rites*,[22] the canonical Confucian work that governs mourning ritual.

The memorial ended with the proposal that emoluments for officials of Rank 8 and above be raised across the board as a way to display the court's generosity.

The emperor praised the empress for her sagacity and gave his assent to all the proposals in the memorial, which forthwith went into effect.

In one master stroke, the empress helped bolster the imperial claim to rule by accentuating its Daoist connections; won the emperor's accolade; elevated the status of the female gender; and pleased the general officialdom.

Notes

[1] Loose-rein (*jimi* 羈縻): designation of non-Han territories and administrative areas (prefectures and counties) with loose, tributary relations with the court.

[2] The South Mountains (Nanshan 南山) were west of Bairi 天祝 County, east Gansu.

[3] The Four Garrisons made up the defense command that controlled the Western Regions. Of the four, Qiuci 龜茲, Yanqi 焉耆, and Shulê 疏勒 were on the middle route of the Silk Road, and Yutian 于闐, on the southern route.

[4] Wuhai 烏海: town northeast of Maduo 瑪多, Qinghai.

[5] The Dafei Plain 大非川: south of Lake Qinghai.

[6] *Gengwu* 庚午: one of the sixty combinations in the Sexagenary Cycle.

[7] Or alternatively, according to his epitaph, Helan Minzhi died in his place of banishment.

[8] The Court of Imperial Sacrifices (*taichang* 太常) was one of the Nine Courts (*jiusi* 九寺, third-tier central government agencies). The Board of Revenue (*hubu* 戶部) and the Board of Rites (*libu* 禮部) were two of the Six Boards under the Department of State Affairs.

[9] *Miu* 繆.

[10] The *Law of Posthumous Titles* (*Shifa* 謚法): ancient book that explains posthumous titles.

[11] *Gong* 恭.

[12] The *Book of the Han* (*Hanshu* 漢書) is known for using a large vocabulary.

[13] Wu Shiyi 武士逸 was a brother of Wu Shiyue 武士彠, Wu Zetian's father.

[14] The Court of the Imperial Clan (*zongzheng si* 宗正司): one of the Nine Courts.

[15] Chamberlain (*qing* 卿): head of one of the Nine Courts.

[16] Empress Dowager Feng 馮太后 (441–490) was the regent of Emperors Xianwen 獻文 and Xiaowen 孝文.

[17] Noble Lady (*guiren* 貴人): title for a high-ranking imperial consort.

[18] The Fengxian Monastery 奉先寺 of Longmen: Cave 19 of the Longmen Caves (one of the three largest Buddhist cave complexes in premodern China) south of Luoyang. The Fengxian is best known for its Vairocana statue. Some argue that the monastery is in a separate location facing Cave 19.

[19] This assertion is controversial. The Fengxian Vairocana 盧舍那 Buddha statue of 17 m in height is the tallest statue of the entire cave complex.

[20] Aśoka (Ayuwang 阿育王) (r. 268–232 BCE) was the most successful ruler of the Maurya dynasty of India. He was best known for his aggressive promotion of Buddhism.

[21] The *Daode jing* 道德經 (Classic of the Way and Its Virtue) was attributed to Laozi, but the claim is rejected by modern scholars.

[22] The *Record of Rites* (*Liji* 禮記) is a collection of explications on Zhou ritual by Confucius's disciples and scholars of the Warring States period, edited by Dai Sheng 戴勝 (Dai De's nephew) of the Western Han.

11. Li Hong and Li Xián (675–676)

AFTER ITS CONQUEST of Koguryŏ (668), the Tang Empire had annexed its territory on the Korean Peninsula and in Manchuria. Silla, the only surviving native power on the peninsula, had been the key ally in the wars against Paekche and Koguryŏ. Now, however, it had turned hostile. In a series of campaigns in the second month of 675, General Liu Rengui and others trounced the Silla forces, forcing their king to sue for peace. Consequently, a Silla emissary came with valuable gifts to offer apologies on behalf of his king.

At a court session in Luoyang, the emperor received the emissary. He pardoned the king and reconfirmed his Tang appointments. After the foreign guest and his men left the audience hall, the emperor rose to his feet to address the audience. Before he said a word, he keeled over, smashing his head against the top of a low table in front. He was having one of his dizzy spells brought on by hyperactive liver yang. Two eunuch officers rushed to lift him to a couch as the palace physician on duty checked his vital signs. Dazed but still conscious, the emperor requested through a eunuch officer that all officials present leave except for the chief ministers. He then gestured to the court leaders to move closer and held an emergency meeting lying down.

"My dear court leaders," the emperor spoke in a feeble voice, "as you've just witnessed, I'm in declining health. More and more I don't feel equal to the task of ruling over the realm. I'd like to have the empress take over *all* the day-to-day affairs of the court as regent. Do you agree?"

The five senior advisers present all fell silent for a while before a white-haired man in his late sixties stood up and said, "The Son of Heaven manages external affairs, and the empress manages domestic affairs. This has worked well. If Your Majesty passes on, the country founded by Gaozu and Taizong can be handed over to Crown Prince Li Hong. I, your humble servant, see no need for change."

The emperor swept his gaze at all present, and asked, "Do you agree with Hao Chujun?"

"Yes, Your Majesty," they all said in a timid tone.

"All right, I'll think about it," the emperor said.

***

In her initial struggle to gain power, the empress had appointed officials of dubious reputation, notably Li Yifu and Xu Jingzong, by choice and, more importantly, out of necessity. Their unquestioned loyalty was needed at a time when she had to face hostility in the Rear Palace and officialdom and around the throne. With their help, but mostly relying on her own effort and good luck, she had risen to the top to hold the power of a de facto sovereign.

After the death of Li Yifu and Xu Jingzong, the empress no longer staffed the leadership with sycophants on purpose. Instead, she made chief minister appointments mainly based on merit. Hao Chujun, for example, was promoted on account of his excellent track record as civil administrator and military commander. She was nonetheless displeased that, supported by his colleagues in the Chief Ministers' Council, Hao strenuously opposed her appointment as regent.

To work around the "old codgers," she recruited a body of middle-ranking advisers, all accomplished literati without much seniority. While their official duty was compiling voluminous works such as the *Biographies of Women* (*Lienü zhuan*),[1] they were also given power to make decisions on memorials submitted to the throne. They worked and waited for their summons by the emperor or the empress in an office area later known as the Hanlin Academy. The fact that the office area was located in the northwest part of the Daming Palace, and the palace itself was northeast of the Taiji Palace gave rise to the term the "Northern Gate." And the scholars associated with the area were known as the "Northern Gate Academicians."[2]

The purpose of employing these unofficially appointed young advisers, however, was not necessarily to undercut the leadership of the chief ministers, but to prevent them from blocking her political moves.

***

For now, far more worrisome than the chief ministers was her own son Crown Prince Li Hong.

In character, the prince at twenty-four *sui* took after his father and had the reputation of being benevolent, filial, and humble. He was popular with the chief ministers and the Northern Gate academicians alike. But, after him, Tianhou had given birth to three more boys, Li Xián (in early 655), Li Zhe (Li Xian; in 656), and Li Dan (in 662). All were alive and well. All she could count on as her successor. That meant that Li Hong was by no means indispensable.

At first, the empress did not think much of Li Hong, a weakling suffering from consumption since childhood. But her view changed after she returned from a long stay in Luoyang accompanying the emperor. The prince had done very well in Chang'an during their absence. As the emperor's headache continued to get worse, the clamor for the prince to take over grew louder and louder. Thus, the prince, perhaps despite himself, had become her main rival.

While the empress was keeping a close eye on him, the crown prince did something that seemed to have crossed the line.

It all started with a piece of gossip about two missing princesses. After he picked it up, the prince did a bit of digging and was flabbergasted to learn that the princesses of Yiyang and Xuancheng were incarcerated in the Lateral Palace (Yeting) with no contact from the outside world. He could not help commiserating with their wretched condition and wrote a passionate memorial to argue for their release so that they could get married. In a society where most women got married before twenty,[3] these two sisters, both in their thirties, were already very much over the hill.

Perhaps because the emperor had too many offspring, he had completely forgotten about Yiyang and Xuancheng. The prince's plea reminded him of their existence and moved him to tears. Without consulting the empress, he gave his assent to the request to set them free. But the emperor did not realize that the innocuous memorial touched a raw nerve in the empress. The princesses were the daughters of the hated Consort Xiao, whose ghost still haunted her. They would have perished together with their wretched mother years before, had it not been for the emperor's effort to shield them. To her chagrin, with the issuance of the edict, the empress could no longer block their release from custody. Once out, they could expect to marry an official of Rank 5 or above. Still, she went out of her way to make sure that their life after imprisonment would not be too comfy and chose two guardsmen as their husbands.[4]

Apart from the two princesses, the memorial also reminded the empress of Sujie, Consort Xiao's best-known child. That born pleaser used to be the emperor's apple of the eye. At the time of his mother's death, the emperor went out of his way to make sure that no harm would come to him and transferred him to the post of prefect of Qizhou,[5] a key prefecture near the capital in Guanzhong. Before his two sisters regained their freedom, the empress had him secretly banished to Shenzhou farther down south.[6]

For months afterwards, the empress heard nothing of Sujie and was ready to put him in the back of her mind. Then a report from her informants alarmed her. Sujie, it claimed, had expressed his wishes to pay homage to the Two Sages. She sent him an edict in the name of the emperor that said, "Because of his sickness, Sujie does not need to visit the court." Sujie responded with an emotion-laden long piece called "On Loyalty and Filiality" to pledge his obedience to his father and the empress.[7] For fear of irking the empress, no one was willing to deliver it until a low-ranking official called Zhang Jianzhi, sympathetic with the prince's plight, smuggled it into the palace.

The empress, upon reading the piece, was annoyed beyond belief at the brazenness of the prince. She sent her men to silence him.

Thereafter, news about Sujie stopped coming. But the empress still felt uneasy about him. After the release of his two sisters, she ordered her minions to make him vanish from view. They soon managed to demote and banish him to the far south on a trumped-up charge of embezzlement.

Through dealing with the offspring of Consort Xiao, the empress's dislike of Crown Prince Li Hong deepened. The way she saw it, all the trouble with them stemmed from his nosy memorial.

***

In the fourth month of 675, the emperor was holding court in Luoyang's Zhenguan Basilica.[8] A eunuch officer flitted across the dais to fall on his knees in front of His Majesty and muttered something under his breath.

"What? It can't be true!" shouted the emperor in a despairing voice, as he went limp with his head drooping. Four eunuchs rushed forward to carry him away. An attendant on duty announced the death of the crown prince and the suspension of the court session.

Crown Prince Li Hong had been visiting the Hebi Palace[9] in the westernmost part of the Western Park of Luoyang. He was taken ill after a drink served by a eunuch and lost consciousness. By the time the palace physicians arrived, his heart had stopped beating.

The death of the young prince was shrouded in mystery and suspicion. And that gave rise to the rumor that it was caused by the poisoned wine served by the empress's men. At his funeral, his mother's expressionless poker face seemed to prove that point.

The emperor was overcome with sorrow, clutching the edge of the black coffin and wailing without restraint until he was dragged away by two eunuchs on the empress's orders.

The edict that followed gave the late crown prince an *imperial* posthumous title and allowed him to be buried as a deceased *emperor* in the Gongling Tomb Park[10] in the eastern suburbs of Luoyang.

***

The cockfighting incident several years back gave the impression that Prince Li Xián cared more about fun and games than study. In reality, under the tutelage of Wang Bo and other mentors, he had become well-versed in the classics and literature.

The emperor had taken notice. He once commented to Li Ji about him, "I hate to brag about my sons, but this kid has what you may call a prodigious memory. At such a young age, he has already studied some of the toughest classics: the *Venerable Documents* (*Shangshu*), the *Record of Rites* (*Liji*), the *Confucian Analects*,[11] and others; he can recite from memory more than a dozen rhapsodies. He started reading the *Analects* when still a little boy and immediately got hooked. And he often recited his favorite passage: 'Respect men for their excellence and appreciate women *not* for their beauty.' I asked why. He said, 'I simply love it!' This kid *is* smart!"

All smiles, General Li responded, "I have heard a lot of great things about the prince. I have no doubt that he will grow up to be a proud son of Your Majesty."

Now Li Xián had matured into a handsome young man, with a noble bearing and urbane manners. Upon his brother Li Hong's death, he was appointed by default crown prince and prince-regent. That allowed him to exercise the power of the empire in Chang'an while his parents continued their sojourn in Luoyang.

Upon return in 676, the emperor was pleased with what the prince had accomplished and issued a rescript to express his appreciation:

During the short period when the crown prince was prince-

regent, he dealt with government affairs with competence. When pacifying the masses, he showed great empathy; when meting out justice and punishment, he exercised great caution. Apart from attending to government affairs, he made a point of studying the canonical writings of the ancients. He delved deep into the famous works of the sages and researched the books by the past sovereigns. Kind-hearted and loyal by nature, he represents the hope for the nation. It is hereby ordered that 500 bolts of silk be gifted to the prince as a reward.[12]

His emperor-father's praise inspired Prince Li Xián to do more. At that time, the four earliest Standard Histories, later known as the Four Early Histories, were widely accepted as the exemplary works of historiography. Serious scholarship had sprung up around them in the form of annotations.[13] Li Xián had the wisdom to notice that no serious effort had been made to annotate Fan Ye's *Book of the Later Han*,[14] the last one of the four.

The prince proposed to launch the undertaking. With the emperor's support, he soon had a team of senior officials and scholars working under him on the project. That afforded him a rare opportunity to form bonds with them and enhance his popularity.

Upon completion of the newly annotated edition of the book, the prince presented a copy to the court. An ecstatic emperor browsed through its entire ninety *juan* (scrolls).[15] After he had the book deposited in the Imperial Library, he ordered 30,000 bolts of silk as a reward to the prince.

The empress, however, did not share her husband's enthusiasm. Not that she was reluctant to give praise to her son's prodigious achievement, but that she could not help comparing him to Taizong and Prince Li

Tai.[16] With Gaozu's approval, then-Prince Li Shimin (Taizong) had founded the Institute for the Cultivation of Literature[17] in 621 and turned it into his think-tank over time. It was with the help of the Institute that Taizong had planned and staged the coup of 626 to seize power.[18]

As emperor, Taizong had granted Prince Li Tai (the current emperor's elder brother) the privilege to set up an Institute for Literature[19] in his residence. He too had headed a group of officials to compile a voluminous book called the *Comprehensive Gazetteer*,[20] an encyclopedic work on administrative geography. All those involved in the project had formed the core of a clique around him. In the end, they had all become supporters of Prince Li Tai in the succession struggle of 643, and almost succeeded.

Thus, from the vantage point of hindsight, the empress saw in what Li Xián had done an ominous pattern and looked upon his achievement not with joy but with suspicion.

Notes

1 The *Biographies of Women* (*Lienü zhuan* 列女傳): the best-known *Lienü zhuan* is the one compiled by Liu Xiang 劉向 (W. Han). The version compiled under Wu Zetian's auspices is no longer extant.

2 Following *Yonglu* 4.73–74.

3 According to *Tang huiyao* (83.1527–29), the marriageable age was twenty *sui* for men and fifteen for women in the Early Tang; it was later lowered to fifteen *sui* for men and thirteen for women.

4 The two guardsmen, Quan Yi 權毅 (husband of Yiyang) and Wang Xu 王勖 (husband of Xuancheng), would be later promoted to prefects (*cishi*).

5 Qizhou 岐州: prefecture with its seat in present-day Fengxiang, Shaanxi.

6 Shenzhou 申州: prefecture with its seat northwest of present-day Xinyang, south Henan.

[7] "Zhongxiao lun" 忠孝論.

[8] The Zhenguan Basilica 貞觀殿: a key palatial building located on the central axis of Luoyang's Palace City and north of the Hanyuan Basilica 含元殿.

[9] The Hebi Palace 合璧宮: suburban palace in the Western Park of Luoyang. It was close to the Palace City.

[10] The Gongling Tomb Park 恭陵: located in present-day Yanshishi, Henan, east of Luoyang.

[11] The *Venerable Documents* (*Shangshu* 尚書): the oldest work of history and a Confucian classic. The *Confucian Analects* or the *Analects* (*Lunyu* 論語): a collection of sayings by Confucius and his disciples and anecdotes about them, and a Confucian classic.

[12] *Jiu Tang shu* 90, 章懷太子傳.

[13] Sima Qian's 司馬遷 *Shiji* 史記 is annotated by Pei Yin 裴駰 (Liu Song); Ban Gu's 班固 *Hanshu* 漢書, by Yan Shigu 顏師古 (Tang); and Chen Shou's 陳壽 *Sanguo zhi* 三國志, by Pei Songzhi 裴松之 (Liu Song). These three annotators were great scholars in their own right.

[14] The *Book of the Later Han* (*Hou Han shu* 後漢書) by Fan Ye 范曄 (Liu Song).

[15] The received edition of the *Book of the Later Han* includes thirty treatise chapters from Sima Biao's 司馬彪 (W. Jin) *Xu Hanshu* 續漢書 as well.

[16] Li Tai 李泰 (618–652): favorite son of Taizong.

[17] The Institute for the Cultivation of Literature (Xiuwen guan 修文館): set up in 621 in the Chancellery.

[18] The coup refers to the Xuanwu Gate incident of 626, in which Li Shimin 李世民 (Taizong) and his supporters killed his elder brother Crown Prince Li Jiancheng 李建成. It paved the way for Li Shimin's rise to power.

[19] Wenxue guan 文學館.

[20] The *Comprehensive Gazetteer* (*Kuodi zhi* 括地志) consisted of 555 *juan* 卷 (scrolls or chapters).

12. Shangguan Wan'er (676–677)

IN THE NINTH month of 676, the emperor, while sojourning in the Jiucheng Palace[1] to the west of Chang'an, read a report on a crime committed by two officers. General-in-Chief Quan Shancai and Commandant Fan Huaiyi[2] had felled by accident a cypress tree in the grounds of the Zhaoling Tomb Park. The emperor felt violated by this act of *lèse majesté* that had taken place in the sacred burial place of his father Taizong and his mother Empress Zhangsun. With decision, he handed down the death sentence in an edict.

"But the two men do not deserve to die, Your Majesty," an average-looking man with sloping shoulders in his mid-forties argued at court. "It is true that they felled a tomb park cypress tree, and that is a terrible crime. But the punishment on the books is disenrollment."

"If I don't execute them," the emperor said, "I am not a filial son."

The man with sloping shoulders persisted. His throaty voice got on the emperor's nerves.

"Get out, you bookworm!" the emperor shouted.

The "bookworm" got down his knees and pleaded, "Your Majesty, the reason I keep on remonstrating with you is because I, your servant, regard you as a sage ruler like Yao or Shun,[3] not a tyrant like Jie or Zhòu.[4] But bending the law to execute the two officers will make a mockery of the law and confuse the people, and is not the way of the sages. If, in the end, the two wretched men lose their lives for a cypress tree, perhaps nobody will say anything against you right now. But it does not mean that posterity will do the same. Because I, as your humble servant, do not want to lead you down the wrong path, I refuse to accept this edict."

"I think he's got a point, Your Majesty," a female voice came over from behind the bamboo screen. "To judge a case like this requires one to keep one's emotion out and go strictly by the book. Otherwise, Taizong would not be pleased."

"All right, all right, Empress, I will reconsider," murmured the emperor with impatience.

That evening when the Two Sages were alone, the empress asked, "Are you going to reduce the sentence?"

"Yes, the two officers will be disenrolled and banished to the far south."

"That's good to know. You just avoided committing an act of injustice. You should thank that 'bookworm' for it. What is he called?"

"Di Renjie, a judge in the Court of Judicial Review."[5]

"He seems to be a smart person. I can use him to try high-profile cases."

"Where exactly do you want him to work?"

"The Censorate.[6] He will make an excellent investigative censor."[7]

"I suppose so," the emperor said.

***

One late morning in the spring of 677, a girl of fourteen *sui* was brought into the empress's residential basilica by a female officer of the Department of Domestic Service.[8] She had sparkling eyes that exuded intelligence and a shapely but young body that had yet to grow into maturity. Her brownish hemp garment gave her away as a bondmaid from the Lateral Palace.

"You know why you are here, Shangguan Wan'er?" the empress asked.

"Not quite, Your Majesty," answered the young girl in a reverent, girlish voice.

"You are spotted by one of our talent hunters. Well, why don't you write me something to demonstrate your talent?"

"Yes, Your Majesty." Wan'er genuflected.

"The topic is 'Plum Blossom.' "

The girl picked up the weasel hair writing brush from the jade brush holder on the small table, and adroitly dipped it in the black ink in the inkstone in front of her and started penning a piece on a sheet of rice paper. When she was done about ten minutes later, she put the writing brush back on the holder and sat straight on her seat, hands behind her back.

A female attendant came over and took the paper to the empress. The moment the empress glanced at it, she was fascinated by the dozen or so neatly arranged vertical rows of characters. The running hand calligraphy was reminiscent of Yu Shinan, the greatest Early Tang calligrapher. The succinctly structured short prose piece, written in graceful language, showed a precocious mastery of verbiage.

"Brilliant," the empress muttered under her breath. "From this day forward," she continued, addressing the young girl, "you will work for me at court. For now, your job will be drafting edicts. Naturally, you will shed your bondmaid status and become a court official."

The girl fell on both knees to do the kowtow ritual.

The empress ordered sharply, "On your feet, Wan'er!" and then asked, "Who teaches you to write like this?"

"My mother Lady Zheng,[9] Your Majesty."

"Where is she?"

"She also works in the Lateral Palace."

"As a bondwoman?"

"Yes, Your Majesty."

"I will then restore her Chang'an resident status." The empress gestured to a female attendant to take the girl away.

***

One autumn afternoon in 677, the empress was reading a book scroll in her study in the Ganlu Basilica in Chang'an. The emperor rushed in and spluttered, "The Tubo king is asking for . . . the hand of a Tang princess!"

"I know, Your Majesty," answered the empress, setting the scroll down on the low table.

"But the letter delivered by the Tubo emissary mentions Taiping by name."

"What? Our young daughter is only thirteen *sui*. I won't allow that to happen!" Of her five surviving offspring, the empress showed affection only for Taiping, probably because she was like her mother in looks and character.

"However, if we turn them down, the Tubo will not take it too well," the emperor said. "During the reign of Taizong, the Tubo started a war against us when we refused to send them a *heqin* bride. Things quieted down only after Princess Wencheng was married off to Songzan Ganbu.[10] Now they have massed an army of 200,000 men on our western border and may invade any moment."

"Can't we shore up the border defense first, Your Majesty? How about sending General Liu Rengui with a reinforcement army of 50,000?"

"Yes, we can do that. But it takes time. Besides, we still have to find a way to keep Taiping safe."

"Have you granted an audience to the emissary yet?"

"It will take place tomorrow."

"Good. We can say in the letter to the *zanpu*[11] that our daughter has been ordained as a Daoist nun and is no longer available."

"Are you trying to play games with the Tubo, Wife? They have eyes and ears in the capital and will find out what is going on before you know it."

"No, I am not playing games, Your Majesty. I am serious about putting Taiping up in a convent."

"Are you out of your mind?"

"What do you think I should do?"

The emperor fell silent for a long time, his brows knitted, as if looking for ways to keep his pampered little daughter in the palace. Then he shook his head in helplessness.

About two weeks later, Taiping was forced to doff her princess outfit—silk gown, silk sash, and head and waist ornaments in jade and silver—to don a child-sized greyish Daoist robe. She threw a hell of a tantrum as she was dragged into a closed carriage. Under the escort of a small troop of mounted guardsmen, it pulled off towards the south. By the time it arrived in her eponymous convent in Hongye Ward,[12] the little passenger was worn out by exhaustion. She was led to a spacious but sparsely furnished dorm room, crawled into the bed, and fell asleep.

Notes

[1] The Jiucheng Palace 九成宮 (Sui Renshou Palace 仁壽宮) was in Linyou, Shaanxi.

[2] Quan Shancai 權善才was general-in-chief (*da jiangjun* 大將軍) of the Left Awe-Inspiring Guard (*zuo weiwei* 左威衛). Fan Huaiyi 范懷義 was commandant (*zhong langjiang* 中郎將) of the Left Palace Gate Guard (*zuo jianmen wei* 左監門衛). They both belonged to the Sixteen Guards.

[3] Yao 堯 and Shun 舜 were two of the Five Lords (Five Emperors) in predynastic times. Both were considered exemplary sovereigns.

[4] Jie 傑 and Zhòu 紂 were the "last bad sovereigns" of the Xia and Shang, respectively, and were considered the paragons of evil.

[5] The judge of the Court of Judicial Review (*dali cheng* 大理丞): in the pecking order at the Court (*si*), a judge (*cheng*) was below the chamberlain (*qing* 卿), vice chamberlain (*shaoqing* 少卿), and chief judge (*zheng* 正).

[6] The Censorate (*yushi tai* 御史臺) was the central surveillance agency.

[7] The investigative censor (*jiancha yushi* 監察御史): member of the Censorate responsible for investigating and impeaching officials, especially those in the provinces.

[8] The Department of Domestic Service (*neishi sheng* 內侍省): central agency headed and staffed mainly by eunuchs to provide services to the emperor and imperial consorts and concubines.

[9] "Lady" denotes a woman of high social position as was the case with Lady Zheng when she was the daughter-in-law of a chief minister. Now, she was reduced to a bondservant. I continue to use the term for consistency.

[10] Princess Wencheng 文成公主 was married off to Songzan Ganbu 松贊干布 (Songtsen Gampo) in 640.

[11] *Zanpu* 贊普: Tubo king.

[12] The Taiping Convent 太平女冠觀 was located in the southeast corner of Hongye Ward 弘業坊 in the southernmost part of Chang'an. Later, the ward would be renamed Daye 大業. To its east was Jinchang Ward 晉昌坊, famous for its Greater Wild Goose Pagoda (Dayan ta 大雁塔) still standing today. See *Tang liangjing chengfang kao* 2.47.

13. Ming Chongyan (679)

Byzantium under Constantine IV using Greek fire repulsed Arabs attackers.
The first Arab siege of Constantinople was lifted (678).

THE EMPEROR VISITED Luoyang again in early 679. During his absence, three new palaces had risen near the city—Suyu, Gaoshan, and Shangyang[1]—all situated in the expansive Western Park. Of these the Shangyang Palace was by far the most important. Partially coterminous with the Imperial City,[2] it was more of an accretion to the city proper than a suburban palace. The emperor had personally selected the site when he stood on an eminence south of the Luo River, looking north, and was struck by the breath-taking scenery. Its design and construction were entrusted to one Wei Hongji, then chamberlain of the Court of Agriculture.[3] The palace layout reflected the fundamental concept of traditional city-planning, with a north-south main axis. On the axis were located the principal basilicas, which were flanked by secondary basilicas on both sides. With a long corridor stretching east-west along the Luo, the palace grounds were dotted with halls, loft-buildings, towers, pavilions, and kiosks. What made this palace different from all others was its luxurious design, with glazed yellow roof tiles and multiple arches and upturned eaves from different angles, and its elaborate ornamentation of lotus flowers and dragons and of numerous exotic plants and animals.

"Isn't that a spectacular sight?" asked the emperor as he was taking a stroll along the Long Corridor bedecked with paintings of stories from the classics and of auspicious plants and animals. The attendant officials in his entourage all echoed his sentiment. Later, when the emperor took a rest in one of the basilicas, he wrote an edict that heaped praise on Wei Hongji the chief architect.

The next afternoon, the emperor, having spent a peaceful night and a pleasant morning in the new palace, started browsing through dozens of memorials submitted by court officials. Most of them were panegyrics in florid language singing praise to the Shangyang and its builder. There were a few, however, that questioned the rationale for the palace. The one from Di Renjie was particularly disturbing: it called for the impeachment of Wei Hongji for leading the sovereign down the path of extravagance and grandeur. The emperor felt annoyed by the brusque tone of the memorialist but could not find a reason to counter his argument. The empress, however, upon reading the same memorial, insisted that Di Renjie was right. "Your Majesty must take action," she said. "The level of luxury is beyond imagination. We must do something to curb this trend."

With great reluctance, the emperor issued another edict to dismiss Wei Hongji from office. The lavishly built palace, however, was left untouched apart from a few minor alterations.

Soon the emperor received another memorial by Di Renjie that cried out for his attention. It demanded that Wang Benli, a bureau director in the Department of State Affairs, be impeached for bullying his colleagues. Although a middle-ranking official, Wang was one of the emperor's favorites.

As expected, the emperor came to his defense. That prompted an immediate response from Di at a court session. He said, "The country lacks talents, but does not lack the likes of Wang Benli. In sparing this guilty person, Your Majesty is doing an injustice to the law of the land. If Your Majesty insists on doing it, please banish me to a no-man's-land, as a warning to the loyal and honest remonstrators of the future."

"Enough of your impudence," shouted the emperor, livid with anger.

Two guardsmen rushed to seize Di Renjie by the arms and march him out of the hall.

"Calm down, calm down, Your Majesty," the empress said from behind the bamboo screen. "Di Renjie did not behave very well today. But don't you think we should launch an investigation on Wang anyway?"

The emperor did not say a word; he wobbled a couple of steps and collapsed onto the floor, his face flushing scarlet and the purple veins on his forehead bulging. Two eunuch officers rushed to lift him to the couch.

"Get the counselor of remonstrance, now!" shouted the empress, who had emerged from behind the bamboo screen.

A few moments later, Ming Chongyan arrived on the scene in haste. This handsome man in his early thirties with a bushy mustache carried with him a cloth bundle on a metal stick. He set the bundle down on the table and opened it to reveal two rows of silver needles of varying sizes. He selected seven of them; with three behind each ear, and one in his mouth, he squatted down by the side of the emperor, lying unconscious with foam coming from the corners of his mouth. After wetting the needles in his mouth, Ming inserted them, one by one, into a select number of acupoints in the patient's forehead, face, and hands. He then twisted the needle handles back and forth multiple times. Stepping aside, he picked up the metal stick—his magic silver wand—and brandished it above his head rhythmically while uttering a series of incantations, which sounded like Sanskrit. But nobody could tell.

Half an hour later, the emperor came to, his face looking pallid.

The empress engaged him in a simple conversation for about ten minutes, then asked, "An investigation on Wang, yes?"

"Well," the emperor answered, "if you think so, I have no objection."

Two weeks later, a report was filed by the Court of Judicial Review proving Di Renjie's accusation. Subsequently, Wang Benli was dismissed from office, and Di Renjie received an accolade from the throne.

***

"Had it not been for your magical power," the empress said to Ming Chongyan one afternoon, "His Majesty would have been in deep, deep trouble. We appreciate your service,"

"It is a great honor to serve His Majesty," said Ming, making a deep bow.

"Well, when I promoted you to counselor of remonstrance, I had great plans for you. Do you know who served in this position before?"

"No, Your Majesty."

"Chu Suiliang, one of the two regents. He was promoted to chief minister only a short while after he became a counselor."

Bowing again, Ming said, "I cannot thank Your Majesty enough for your patronage."

"So long as you stay loyal, I guarantee you'll get there."

Ming Chongyan dropped on his knees and said, "Seas may run dry and stones may decay, my loyalty to Your Majesty remains forever."

"Well then," said the empress as she motioned Ming to his seat. "I wonder if you have anything to report on the prince."

"Yes. Recently, I had occasion to examine his physiognomy closely. It tells me something very revealing."

"Oh?"

"Everybody knows Crown Prince Li Xián has a pointed chin. But few people know the shape of his ears because they are always covered by his long hair. The other day, I went swimming with him in the lake, and saw his ears in their entirety at close range. They look like..."

With a wave of her hand, the empress dismissed all the attendants present, and Ming continued, "Like a pair of withered flowers. And the earlobes hardly exist. Both signs indicate that succession to the throne is not in his destiny."

"How about Li Zhe and Li Dan?"

"His two younger brothers Zhe and Dan look quite different. Zhe, for example, resembles his grandfather, Taizong. That is a sign of great strength. However, Dan, the youngest, possesses the noblest physiognomy among the three brothers."

"How can you be sure that these readings are accurate?"

"Well, Your Majesty, they are corroborated by astrological signs. If you don't terribly mind, I can elaborate."

"Won't be necessary. But I want to remind you again: under no circumstances should you reveal the content of today's talk to anyone."

"Undoubtedly, Your Majesty."

"If you do, it is at your peril," the empress warned.

***

Before long, the content of the secret meeting leaked out, probably through Ming Chongyan himself. But no effort was made to prosecute him over the leak, and he continued to be in favor with the emperor and the empress.

One night in the sixth month of 679, Ming's life took an unexpected turn. In his Luoyang home in a ward south of the Imperial City, he was lying in bed in the torrid heat of summer, his magic wand by his side. He kept the door and windows of his bedchamber open. Still, there was no hint of a draft. He bounced out of bed, poured himself a half goblet of rice wine from a jar on a table, and tipped it down his throat before returning to bed. After much tossing and turning, he fell asleep. It was already well past midnight.

Moments later, he awoke to the flickering light of the oil lamp and felt some clammy hands like iron shackles holding down his arms and legs. He struggled to scream but could only spurt out a few muffled sounds through his gagged mouth. He closed his eyes as a raised broadsword was falling . . .

***

The emperor and especially the empress were visibly shaken by the horrible incident. They ordered an extensive search for the assassins. It led to the arrest of dozens of suspects, and all were subsequently dispatched. But nobody was sure whether they were the true culprits or not.

The slain magician was given a grand funeral on a scale befitting a chief minister and received the prestigious posthumous title of "president of the Chancellery."[4]

***

After the Western Tujue Khanate was crushed (657), the Tang court took over its territory and placed it under a network of area commands, garrisons, and protectorates.[5]

By 676, one surrendered Tujue chieftain named Ashina Duzhi had defied the central authority by declaring himself khan of the Ten Tribes.[6] He went on to join forces with Tubo and invaded the Anxi Protectorate.

The emperor wanted to put a stop to this ominous trend and was ready, at the suggestion of a chief minister, to launch an expedition. It was then that Vice President of the Board of Personnel[7] Pei Xingjian came up with a different solution:

> *In the wake of the fall of Sassanid Persia, Prince Peroz, son of Yazdegerd III (the last Sassanid king), took refuge in the Tang empire. After Peroz died in the 670s, his son Narsieh succeeded. I can lead a small troop of men west in the name of escorting Narsieh back to his own country. Once we arrive in Anxi, we can take action as we see fit.*[8]

Pei Xingjian was a resourceful officer with decades of experience in the border areas and an intimate knowledge of frontier affairs. It was obvious that in the plan he proposed, he knew what he was talking about. For sure, it was a bit adventurous but cost much less than the mobilization of a vast army. The emperor, after mulling it over at night, nodded his approval.

***

In the summer of 679, Pei Xingjian and his party reached Xizhou.[9] He recruited 1,000 cavalrymen from the households of local magnates and pushed further west. While passing through the Four Garrisons, he and his associates lured more people into their ranks. Sons of the local leaders fell over one another to sign up, for fear of missing out on a rare hunting expedition.

With a force swelling to close to 10,000, Pei Xingjian continued the trek west until he was less than 20 *li* from Ashina Duzhi's headquarters camp. On his orders, the troops pitched camp while a small group of men went to see Ashina with Pei's request for a meeting.

The massing of a large Tang army at his doorstep took Ashina by surprise. He rushed over with a small escort to meet with Pei's men, only to find himself surrounded by a much larger force and taken into custody.

General Pei proceeded to pacify the rest of the vast region under Ashina's control and went on his return journey to Luoyang, taking Ashina Duzhi and his associates as prisoners-of-war with him.

His lieutenant General Wang Fangyi stayed behind to build a Tang-style city called Suiye,[10] with a ring of city wall and twelve gates. It would be home to the headquarters of one of the Four Garrisons.

Under the escort of a small body of riders, Prince Narsieh resumed his journey west into the lands of former Sassanian Persia.

Notes

[1] The Suyu 宿羽, Gaoshan 高山, and Shangyang 上陽 Palaces. See *Zizhi tongjian* 202.6388. *Henan zhi* (唐城闕古蹟, 127), perhaps following *Xin Tang shu*, dates the building of the Shangyang to the Shangyuan period (674–676).

[2] The Imperial City (Huangcheng 皇城): in the traditional sources, the Palace City was located in the north-central part of Luoyang, and the Imperial City was to its south. What archaeology discovered is somewhat different. The Imperial City wrapped around the Palace City on three sides. See Li Jianchao 2006, 273–74.

[3] Chamberlain of the Court of Agriculture (*sinong qing* 司農卿): head of the Court, which was one of the Nine Courts.

[4] The Chancellery (*menxia sheng* 門下省) was a first-tier central government agency. Its president was *shizhong* 侍中.

[5] Area command (*dudu fu* 都督府): a military district with one or more prefectures/commanderies. Garrison (*zhen* 鎮): a territorial garrison at the prefectural, commandery, or county level. On the protectorate (*duhu fu* 都護府), *see* note in Part I, Chapter 6.

[6] The khan of the Ten Tribes (*shixing kehan* 十姓可汗).

[7] Vice President of the Board of Personnel (*libu shilang* 吏部侍郎).

[8] Prince Peroz (Bilusi 卑路斯) (636–ca. 679), son of Yazdegerd III of Sassanid Persia, took refuge in Chang'an after his country had been overrun by the Arabs. Narsieh (Ninieshi 泥涅師), son of Peroz, would fail in his mission and return to China. Anxi 安西 refers to the Anxi Protectorate based in present-day Xinjiang.

[9] Xizhou 西州: prefecture with its seat in Turfan, Xinjiang.

[10] Suiye 碎葉 (Suyab): town in Tokmak, Kirgizstan.

14. Central Marchmount (680)

In the Middle East, Caliph Muawiyah I died; his son Yazid I succeeded.

Husayn, son of Ali and Muhammad's daughter Fatimah, was killed at Karbala in Iraq. The split between Shiites and Sunnis deepened. Husayn's martyrdom is still celebrated by Shiites today.

IN THE SECOND month of 680, the emperor and the empress went on a trip to the Central Marchmount—Mount Song—consisting of the Taishi and Shaoshi Mountains,[1] where the world-renowned Shaolin Temple (Monastery) is.

On arrival, the Imperial Couple settled in a basilica at the Imperial Hot Spring on the southern slopes of the Taishi (Grand Chamber). At dawn, the emperor was carried in a palanquin to the gate of the Imperial Bathhouse for the morning ablution. With the help of two eunuch officers, the emperor undressed and descended into the steaming water of the marble pool. Having been soaked for about half an hour, he stepped out of the pool, his body red from head to toe. The eunuchs dried him up with silk towels and wrapped him in a silk imperial robe. After a bowl of thick green tea, he was carried into the palanquin waiting at the gate. With his lingering headache gone, he drifted off to slumber.

In the afternoon, the emperor and the empress went to see Tian Youyan, a famous recluse living in the mountains. At court, few people had ever seen him, but most were familiar with stories about him.

For instance, once on a nice winter day, a close friend of his saw him dressed in a peasant kirtle having a sunbath after washing his hair in a hot spring.

"We respect your old age," the friend said, "but that is no excuse to neglect clothing and manners."

Tian answered with a grin, "I don't care. With the sky as my comb and the sun as my hat, I am having the time of my life. What more can I ask for?"

When the emperor and the empress arrived at the gate to a cottage yard, they saw an old man in his seventies, wearing a farmer's outfit—complete with head kerchief, girdle, and dirt-stained sandals. The moment the Two Sages stepped down from their palanquin, assisted by eunuchs, the old man prostrated himself in obeisance. The emperor motioned to his attendants to stop the ritual greeting.

"I am awfully sorry," the old man said. "I am not wearing proper attire for the occasion, Your Majesty. I have been doing farm work."

"No standing on ceremony, Master Tian," the emperor said, full of respect. "How have you been, living in the mountains?"

"To answer Your Majesty's question, I am doing very well. Decades ago, I fell into the habit of visiting mountains and rivers. Thanks to Your Majesty's wise rulership, I still do it today. That does me a lot of good."

"Could you tell us what's so good about living in the mountains?" the empress asked.

"Yes, Your Majesty. Fresh air, serenity at night, greenery all over the place, farm work all year round, and, above all, being close to nature."

With a smile on his face, the emperor asked, "You will not be interested in coming out of seclusion for a change?"

"Well, it depends, Your Majesty, on what it is for."

"How about serving the court?" the empress asked.

"Your Majesty, I will be honored," Tian Youyan answered politely. "But in what area can I be of service?"

"For instance, you can enlighten the emperor and me with your knowledge of Dao, and most importantly, your way to preserve and prolong life."

"That I should be able to do, Your Majesties," the recluse answered.

"Excellent!" said the emperor, beaming. "It is as if the Four White-Haired Recluses of Mount Shang[2] decided to serve me."

***

The next day the emperor and the empress paid a visit to the Dell of Happy Excursion[3] nearby to see a Daoist adept, living in a thatch-roofed hut at the foot of the mountain.

"Master Pan, I am a great fan of yours," the emperor said.

"Me too," the empress said.

"It is a great honor to see both Your Majesties," answered the white-haired Pan Shizheng,[4] now in his nineties.

"I am curious," the emperor said, "about how to maintain good vision and hearing."

"Well," Pan said, "I have been taking a special kind of beverage, made with pine needles. I am not sure if this will work on Your Majesty. But it certainly works on me."

"This pine-needle tea is a secret to longevity?" the empress asked.

"Yes, Your Majesty. In addition, I also practice the art of *pigu*, 'avoidance of grains,' passed down from my mentor Master Wang Yuanzhi of Maoshan."[5]

"Father visited Master Wang before assuming the reins," the emperor said to the empress.

"What else should I know about the Maoshan School[6] of thinking on longevity?" the emperor asked the old man.

"There is a lot more, Your Majesty. For instance, every morning, I practice 'guiding and pulling.' "[7]

"A kind of breathing exercise?" the empress asked.

"Not exactly, Your Majesty. It is a combination of breath control, meditation, and physical exercise. The purpose is to cultivate one's pneuma so that it can have a nurturing effect on body and mind."

"It is a cure-all?" the empress asked.

Pan Shizheng thought a few moments, then said, "Yes, Your Majesty. It can act as a sort of panacea against all sorts of diseases."

"I often have this splitting headache," the emperor said, "that can leave me hopeless and depressed."

"Your Majesty, from the Maoshan's point of view, no disease is hopeless."

"Really?"

"I think so, Your Majesty."

"But how do you use the pneuma to deal with a headache?"

"Well, the first step is to discover the pneuma through meditative breathing."

"How long does it take before one discovers one's pneuma?"

"It depends. For some people it takes years. But, under the right guidance, one may be able to do it in a matter of months."

"Fascinating!" the empress uttered.

"What is that?" asked the emperor, pointing to a large, dried gourd with a golden color hanging on the wall.

"Your Majesty has sharp eyes. Inside this container is 'black rice.' A special kind of glutinous rice mixed with celestial bamboo slices and other ingredients cooked nine times."

"Oh?"

"It is then taken to prolong life."

"Isn't this a kind of grain as well?"

"Yes, Your Majesty. But it is so essentialized that it has become an elixir."

"Make sure you learn how to do it," the emperor said, addressing an attendant.

"Master Pan," the emperor continued, "would you pay me a visit in Luoyang before I leave? I want you to coach me on how to do 'guiding and pulling' and 'avoidance of grains.' "

"That will be a great honor indeed. For the moment, I am recovering from a cold. As soon as I am well enough to travel, I will go."

"Great!" the emperor exclaimed.

***

Ever since he learned of Ming Chongyan's prediction, Crown Prince Li Xián had been fearful that something bad would happen. He took refuge in sex and wine. In the Eastern Palace, he watched flimsily dressed court courtesans staging nightly performances. He would take one or two of them into his bedchamber to keep him company throughout the night and engage in indecent acts. His favorite, however, was not one of the girls invited to his parties *à trois*, but an effeminate male bondservant called Zhao Daosheng, upon whom he showered many expensive gifts.

The empress was scandalized by her son's immoral behavior. It had persisted despite repeated warnings by a remonstrator. On her orders, the Northern Gate academicians hurriedly put together two books, the *Proper Model for the Crown Prince* and the *Biographies of Filial Sons.*[8] She then had them gifted to the prince.

The crown prince canceled the performances. But his fear deepened when he was informed of a rumor circulating among palace servants that he was not the son of the empress, but of her elder sister, the late state mistress of Hann. He suspected, *the empress must have spread the rumor. She will dump me sooner or later.* Every night he lost himself in wine in the company of Zhao Daosheng.

The empress was not pleased. *I have long suspected Li Xián was behind the murder of Ming Chongyan*, she thought. *What matters more is that he has let me down. They say that he is Sister's son. Not true. But what difference does it make?*

"Nobody has dared to touch him because he was Daddy's darling son," she said to Chief Ministers Xue Yuanchao and Pei Yan, and Censor-in-Chief Gao Zhizhou. "But what this prince has done clearly shows that he is incorrigible. Listen well, I want you to go after him with the full force of the law."

The prosecutors with their henchmen raided the Eastern Palace. They did a thorough search and uncovered hundreds of black leather armor sets in the stable and had them hauled away. Before leaving, they took the prince's lover Zhao Daosheng into custody.

Under torture, the lover gave a damning confession: he had committed the murder of Ming Chongyan on orders from the crown prince!

"Li Xián has crossed the line," the empress said to the emperor. "He has to be deposed."

"But he is my favorite son. Among the princes, he is the only true scholar. His annotated edition of the *Book of the Later Han* really does me proud." With tears brimming in his eyes, the emperor asked imploringly, "Can I pardon him just this once?"

"He is my son too. But he has betrayed the trust of the court and must be punished for the sake of justice."

The broken-hearted emperor in the end yielded to the empress's request. In the eighth month of 680, by an imperial edict, Li Xián was deprived of his crown prince's title, reduced to commoner status, and transported under guard to Chang'an, where he was kept in custody in an undisclosed location. Dozens of his confederates, including Zhao Daosheng, were executed. The black armor sets, proof of the prince's sinister scheme, were piled up at the southern end of the Tianjin Bridge and put to the torch, as tens of thousands of Luoyang residents watched on with excitement.

Two princes, Li Ming and Li Hui,[9] both on intimate terms with Li Xián, and some of his mentors and attendant officials were punished with banishment. One of them, Gao Zheng,[10] was the grandson of Gao Shilian—one of the twenty-four hall-of-framers[11] under Taizong and adoptive father of the current emperor's mother. Out of respect for his grandfather, the court had Gao Zheng delivered to his father's home for punishment under the Family Law of the Gaos. As soon as he entered the mansion's gate, a servant shut it tight behind him. Gao Zheng's father, uncle, and cousin came up, tackled him onto the ground, stabbed him in the throat and belly, and lopped off his head. The only saving grace of this heinous incident was the fact they were motivated by their loyalty to the throne.

The emperor was horrified by the lynching and banished all three killers to provincial posts.

Notes

1 The Central Marchmount (*zhongyue* 中嶽)—Mount Song 嵩山: in west Henan; it consists of the Taishi 太室 and Shaoshi 少室 Mountains.

2 These were four virtuous elderly men who came out of seclusion to mentor Liu Bang's 劉邦 crown prince Liu Ying 劉盈.

3 The Dell of Happy Excursion (Xiaoyao gu 逍遙谷) is named after a chapter in the *Zhuangzi* 莊子.

4 As the Shangqing 上清 School patriarch, Pan Shizheng 潘師正 was the most revered Daoist master in the country. The Shangqing was the most influential Daoist school at that time. It was then based in Maoshan 茅山 (Mt. Mao) (east of Nanjing, Jiangsu).

5 *Pigu* 辟穀 (avoidance of grains): a Daoist technique aimed at prolonging life. It is believed that those who live on pneuma (*qi* 氣) instead of grains are divine and long-living. Wang Yuanzhi 王遠知 (510—635), while alive, was the patriarch of the Shangqing School.

6 The Maoshan 茅山 School is another name for the Shangqing School.

7 Guiding and pulling (*daoyin* 導引) is a kind of ancient body and mind exercise.

8 Both the *Proper Model for the Crown Prince* (*Shaoyang zhengfan* 少陽正範) and the *Biographies of Filial Sons* (*Xiaozi zhuan* 孝子傳) are no longer extant.

9 Li Hui 李煒 was the prince of Jiang 蔣王 and Taizong' grandson.

10 Gao Zheng 高政 (–680) was assistant manager of food in the Eastern Palace (*taizi dianshan cheng* 太子典膳丞). See *Zizhi tongjian* 202.6398.

11 The Hall of Fame was set up by Taizong in the Lingyan Pavilion 凌煙閣 where portraits of twenty-four meritorious officials were hung. See *Jiu Tang shu* 3, 貞觀十七年.

15. Later Tujue (679–682)

IN THE TENTH month of 679, the Tujue chieftains Ashide Wenfu and Ashide Fengzhi started an open rebellion in the southeast part of the Mongolian Plateau in the former Eastern Tujue territory. They chose as their khan Ashina Nishufu, a member of the former ruling tribe. The area was under the jurisdiction of the Chanyu Grand Protectorate with Grand Protector[1] Prince Li Dan as its titular leader. The man actually in charge was Chief Administrator[2] Xiao Siye. Tasked with rebellion suppression, General Xiao marched a large Tang army north to confront the newly assembled Tujue army allegedly 100,000 strong.

After winning an easy victory, the Tang army pushed on with gusto until it was pummeled by a snowstorm that seriously degraded its combat-effectiveness. A few days later, when it camped out somewhere north of the Protectorate's seat, the headquarters camp was caught in a stealth attack at night. The commanding officers' decision to strike camp in a hurry caused much confusion and panic, leaving countless officers and men killed or captured.

When General Xiao Siye led what was left of his army back to Chang'an, he was tried, convicted, and banished to the far south.

To check the alarming rise of the Tujue, the court appointed General Pei Xingjian as commander-in-chief of the Dingxiang District Expeditionary Army,[3] with General Cheng Wuting as his lieutenant. General Pei, who had been mentored by the legendary Su Dingfang, had under his command a total of 300,000 men.

In early 680, as General Pei Xingjian, a wiry man over sixty, was marching his army on the Shuo Plain,[4] he came across a mountain pass. He alighted from his horse and crawled over cool rocks and stones to reach a hilltop. From there he looked down into the valley and saw his army winding through like a serpent. He scanned the terrain around him for a while before issuing orders to his adjutants: two bands of commandos would take up position behind bushes in the mountains flanking the pass; and three hundred baggage wagons would proceed at a slow pace a long distance ahead of the combat troops.

Soon the baggage train came under assault and the Tang escort soldiers vanished without a trace. The Tujue men brought the newly captured wagons to the bank of the river close by. As they were watering the draft animals, they were set upon by Tang commandos who had hidden themselves in hay inside the wagons, and many got slain. The survivors galloped away, only to be ambushed along the narrow pass as the Tang troops descended from the mountain slopes and made short work of them.

In the third month, General Pei Xingjian thrashed the main force of the Tujue in the Black Mountains.[5] In the process, his generals had taken the Tujue chieftain Ashide Fengzhi captive.

As the rebellion was falling apart, the Tujue officers arrived in large numbers at the Tang camp to surrender. One of them brought with him a severed head. The Tang officers soon identified it as that of Ashina Nishufu Khan.

***

Ashide Wenfu, the other Tujue chieftain, had fled south as far as Xiazhou.[6] There he met up with Ashina Funian, a second cousin of Xieli Khan of Eastern Tujue. Together they would raise another Tujue army with Funian as the new khan.

***

In the fourth month of 680, the emperor, accompanied by the empress, went on a previously scheduled trip to the Zigui (Purple Cinnamon) Palace.[7] The main purpose of the trip was to get away from the hustle and bustle of Luoyang and be invigorated by the fresh air of the country. But the salubrious clime in the mountains did not seem to produce the expected benefit. At the end of a four-month sojourn, the emperor and the empress returned to Luoyang. By then, the emperor was still the nominal sovereign of the realm. But, in reality, he depended entirely on the empress to run the country.

***

The first month of 681 saw a major wave of Tujue attacks in Yuanzhou and Qingzhou.[8] In the third month, things got much worse. One of Pei Xingjian's generals, under attack by Ashide Wenfu north of the Great Wall (near Hohhot, Inner Mongolia), fled west to the Heng River,[9] where he was trounced by Ashina Funian Khan.

Pei Xingjian, faced with an enemy gaining momentum, adopted a different strategy. From his new headquarters in Daizhou,[10] he dispatched secret agents deep into enemy territory. Using jewelry and silver pieces as gifts, they befriended some of the middle-ranking Tujue officers with access to the leadership. Through them, the Tang agents drove a wedge between Ashina Funian and Ashide Wenfu, the two top chieftains.

In a matter of weeks, this strategy turned the situation around. The Tang forces were now in pursuit of the enemy. Ashina Funian was the first one to be cornered. He sued for peace and even went out of his way to entrap and capture Ashide Wenfu and deliver him to the Tang camp in person. Pei Xingjian then made him a promise that at the minimum his life would be spared. Funian, for his part, had no reason to doubt Pei's promise. Granting lenient treatment to surrendered Tujue officers had been a standard policy of the Tang since Taizong's time.

***

Four years after her ordination as a Daoist nun, Princess Taiping bid goodbye to monastic life. By an empress's decree, she was laicized in the summer of 681.

In the interim, Tang-Tubo relations had worsened.

After suffering a disastrous defeat by General Heichi Changzhi in Qinghai, the Tubo had turned their attention away from the Tang, at least for a while. They moved down south to dominate the Six Tribes in Yunnan and extended their influence as far north as Xinjiang. Against this backdrop, the Tubo had stopped requesting royal brides from the Tang court for quite some time and were unlikely to start doing it again any time soon.

The empress, who had just returned to Chang'an with the emperor, decided that the time had come for her daughter to return to lay life. Thus, on her orders, Princess Taiping moved out of the Taiping Convent and was betrothed soon thereafter to one Xue Shao. Tianhou had picked him from a dozen or so qualified candidates. His father was chamberlain of the Court of Imperial Entertainments,[11] and his mother was the princess of Chengyang,[12] a daughter of Taizong and a sister of the current emperor. His lineage—the Xues of Hedong—was one of the most prestigious in the north.[13]

On an early autumn day in the seventh month the wedding kicked off with a grand ceremony in the Taiji Basilica of the Palace City of Chang'an. The emperor and the empress, accompanied by hundreds of senior court officials, graced the event with their presence.

After dark, the mile-long wedding cavalcade carrying the newlyweds and their distinguished guests proceeded south through the central avenue of the Imperial City. Hundreds of guardsmen holding firebrands were lighting the way. From the center of the Imperial City, the cavalcade turned east and moved through the Jingfeng Gate[14] to the outside. It then turned south and moved three *li* to arrive at the Western Gate of Xuanyang Ward.[15] Along the way, many of the locust trees that had lined the city streets had caught fire and burned down.

In the southeast quadrant of the ward, the wedding carriage came to a stop at the gate of the Wannian County[16] compound. The bride got off to find out what was up and saw the coachman and the seneschal in the middle of a heated discussion on how to get the vehicle through the gate.

"Can't you just use axes to widen the gate?" shouted the bride with impatience.

"No, Taiping," said the emperor, who had just come over. "You can't do that. The gate was built by the Sui architect Yuwen Kai when he founded the city almost 100 years ago. It is not just another gate. It is an architectural marvel."

With reluctance, the bride and bridegroom switched to a smaller carriage to enter the compound.

Inside, the couple hosted an all-night food-and-wine party, where the guests sitting at more than 200 tables were regaled with a multi-course banquet prepared by the palace chefs.

The emperor, seated by the table closest to the front, nodded his head to Crown Prince Li Zhe and his brother Li Dan who came over to greet him. He then lifted his gaze beyond them as if in search of something, before asking the empress, "Where is Li Xián?"

"The ex-crown prince is now a commoner," she answered, undisturbed. "Commoners are barred from an event like this. It is only for the royals, nobles, and high officials."

"Oh?" The emperor shook his head in disappointment.

Before the year was out, on the empress's secret orders, Li Xián would be transferred out of Chang'an to Bazhou,[17] a remote prefecture in a semi-civilized area in west Sichuan.

***

Among the distinguished guests at the banquet was one Xue Kai,[18] elder brother of the bridegroom, sitting at one of the front tables. He was worried sick when he noticed the extravagant ceremony, the overbearing manner of the bride, and the permissiveness of her doting parents. "Do you consider my brother lucky?" he asked under his breath his grand uncle Xue Kegou[19] by his side.

"An imperial nephew marrying an imperial princess—this has been a standard practice in this dynasty," the uncle said. "I hope there is nothing to worry about. But for some reasons, I can't stop thinking about this proverb, 'To marry a princess is to get into trouble with the court.' "

"I share your concern," Xue Kai said. "My brother has to be extra careful to avoid trouble."

But trouble began brewing almost as soon as the banquet was over when the empress noticed that the spouses of Xue Kai and his little brother Xue Xu[20] did not come from illustrious families.

Tianhou thought of the recently completed *Record of Clans and Lineages*, where the first-class lineages included not only the royal Lis of Longxi but also the Wus of Wenshui.[21] She asked herself, "How can my daughter, the offspring of two first-class lineages, rub shoulders with those country bumpkins?" So she issued a decree to demand in unambiguous terms that Xue Kai and Xue Xu divorce[22] their wives and return them to their parents' homes.

The empress did not stop pushing her demand until someone pointed out that Xue Kai's wife was related to Xiao Yu,[23] a founding chief minister of the Tang and a Southern Dynasties first-class noble.

***

One morning in the ninth month of 681, on the second floor of the Gatetower of the Danfengmen, the southern main entrance to the Daming Palace in Chang'an, a grand ceremony was taking place to celebrate the Tang's victory over Tujue. As the prisoners of war were presented, Ashina Funian and Ashide Wenfu, both trussed up in rope, were pushed onto the dais to kneel in front of the emperor and the empress. The emperor motioned to his attendants to untie them and made a condemnation of the Tujue leaders before having them taken away.

General Pei Xingjian, commander-in-chief of the expeditionary army and the star of the ceremony, read a report on the captured equipment and animals, and key prisoners-of war. The emperor and the empress took turns to praise him in glowing terms.

After the ceremony came to a close, the members of the court leadership came up to the general one by one and gave him kudos. But unbeknown to the general, the public attention he received made some of the top officials uncomfortable. At head of this group was Pei Yan, a gaunt-faced, tall man in his sixties who was the de facto leader of officialdom.

Like Pei Xingjian, Pei Yan was a member of the Peis of Hedong, one of the noblest clans in the north. But his rise in officialdom was mainly a result of his own effort. An expert in the *Zuozhuan*[24] in his own right, he would probably have an easier time rising to chief ministership, if he had been a recipient of the prestigious *jinshi* degree instead of the *mingjing*.[25]

For Pei Yan, General Pei Xingjian's achievement was a cause for worry. With his recent military exploits and past administrative experience, he would probably be appointed the top leader of the court. Should that happen, political equilibrium would be thrown out of kilter.

In his memorial to the throne, Pei Yan asserted that, the Tujue were forced into submission, thanks mostly to the effort of Pei's lieutenant Cheng Wuting and to the help provided by the Uighurs; and that Pei Xingjian could not claim much credit for it at all. He further suggested that the Tujue chieftains and their associates be put to death. Only by executing the rebel leaders could would-be copycats be deterred, he argued.

In the end, Pei Xingjian received neither an official accolade nor a reward of gold; and those surrendered or captured Tujue officers—there were more than fifty of them—were put to death in public in the Western Market, despite Pei's strong objection. Notably among them were the top leaders Ashide Wenfu and Ashina Funian. By this point, the court leaders seemed to have forgotten that it was Ashina Funian who had captured Wenfu and delivered him to the Tang camp.

Pei Xingjian heaved a long sigh and said, "I am old now and can do without another reward. But if you kill those who surrendered, who will ever do it again?" He then submitted a letter to request permission for retirement in the country on grounds of old age, which was then rejected.

***

In 682, the Western Tujue started a rebellion in Central Asia. The first man the emperor thought of was Pei Xingjian. After a brief consultation with Chief Minister Pei Yan, the emperor appointed him commander-in-chief of another expeditionary army. Well over sixty, General Pei was in poor health. Still, he accepted the task out of loyalty to the throne. But just as he was about to set off with his army, he fell seriously ill and passed away.

At the court session the following morning, the senior court officials and top generals joined the emperor in honoring the memory of General Pei. General Cheng Wuting, Pei Xingjian's lieutenant on the recent expedition, spoke of his uncanny ability to see into the future, citing as an example his remarks on the Four Eminences (of the Early Tang). These were the four most celebrated belletrists of the day. Their literary accomplishments were regarded as an indication for future success. But Pei Xingjian was not impressed, saying, "A successful career in officialdom calls for a magnanimous mind and insightful judgment rather than literary talent. These fellows are excellent poets and prose writers all right. But they are rash and lack depth. I am not sure if they will attain high office. Of these, Yang Jiong is a bit less pushy than others, and can perhaps end up in a county magistrate's post. As for the rest, they are lucky to have a magistrate's post at all." Later on, Yang Jiong died when serving as magistrate of Yingchuan County;[26] Wang Bo, Prince Li Xián's reader-companion, drowned himself at sea;[27] Lu Zhaolin, who suffered from chronic paralysis, jumped to his death in the Ying River after quitting his job as county defender;[28] Luo Binwang had never held a post higher than vice magistrate.[29]

The emperor sighed and said to Cheng Wuting, "Xingjian was a great leader of troops. But he did not even receive a reward for his brilliant victory, because someone argued that most of the credit should go to you, Wuting."

"No, no, Your Majesty," responded Cheng without hesitation. "I won a few battles. But the overall strategy all came from General Pei Xingjian. Like a master go player, he often saw ten steps ahead of his rival. I just could not compare."

The emperor muttered to himself, a wistful look on his face, "General Pei, where are you when the country needs you the most?"

***

From late 681 to early 682, Guanzhong was hit by two consecutive seasons of poor harvests. It turned out that the fertile land in the Wei River valley was far from enough to support a growing population in the capital, now fast approaching one million. Rice prices had risen manifold to 300 cash per peck (*dou*) in a short time. Starving peasants with their wives and children swarmed the city streets, wards, and markets, begging for food and shelter. And many had fallen down dead.

The emperor and the empress could be shielded from the sight of misery and death so long as they used the network of "covered passageways" (*fudao*) for intra-city travel, which connected the Palace City, the Daming Palace, and the Hibiscus Garden[30] in the southeast. But occasionally, they chose to travel on the city streets incognito, which allowed them to witness firsthand the sufferings of the hungry multitude.

Returning from one such trip, the emperor was sickened by what he had seen and decided to leave for Luoyang. After appointing

Crown Prince Li Zhe as prince-regent,[31] he departed in haste with the empress, in a long cavalcade of carriages and oxcarts under the escort of thousands of cavalry. Along the way, they often saw corpses of the destitute scattered by the roadside and were harassed by petty thieves and robbers. Even dozens of royal guardsmen died of hunger.

Not long after the emperor and the empress had settled themselves in Luoyang, a severe rainstorm inundated much of the city. It was obvious that the gods were not happy with the situation on the ground and needed to be appeased. With that in mind, the emperor took part in sacrificial rites at the various altars devoted to the gods at the Eastern Capital and planned to go on pilgrimages to the Five Marchmounts—holy mountain sites of the north and the south—following the example of his recent trip to Mount Tai (also one of the five).

***

Like many high-ranking officials in the provinces, Area Commander of Qianzhou Xie You[32] went out of his way to make the empress happy. He set his sights on Prince Li Ming, now a resident in his prefecture. As one of the emperor's younger brothers, Li Ming had been banished after Li Xián's fall from grace. On Xie You's orders, his henchmen raided Li Ming's home on trumped-up charges and forced him to take his life.

Whereas the empress might regard the death of another troublesome Li as a good riddance, the emperor was grief-stricken. In a departure from his usual hands-off approach, he ordered the disenrollment of Xie You and his associates.

For his part, Xie You, reduced to a commoner, settled down in the country. But that was not too bad a deal, since he was able to live in comfort in the company of a dozen or so concubines and maids. Then one night, someone beheaded him in his sleep, to the great horror of his women, and his head went missing. The murder remained an unsolved mystery for years until one day when Li Ming's home, where one of his sons still lived, was raided for an unrelated crime. Among the confiscated articles was a chamber pot made of a human skull. An inscription on its surface linked it to Xie You. It thus became clear that the thugs hired by Li Ming's son had carried out the beheading.[33] Subsequently, the son went to the gallows.

***

While the Western Tujue remained untamed on the western frontier, new trouble arose in the north. Ashina Gudulu, a distant relative of Xieli Khan, the erstwhile overlord of Eastern Tujue, had survived Pei Xingjian's military campaign and fled into the mountains and soon started hostilities against the Tang. Commanding a Tujue force of 700 he stormed the town of Heisha.[34] Thereafter, he swelled the ranks of his army to 5,000 by recruiting the remnants of Funian's army while his men increased their livestock numbers by seizing hordes of horses and sheep from the neighboring Tiele.[35] And that gave him enough confidence to declare himself khan, with his brother Mochuo as his lieutenant.

It was about this time that the Tubo invaded the Heyuan Garrison[36] in the west.

These actions, though not coordinated and on small scales, threatened to whittle away the resources of the Tang empire.

***

As General Xue Rengui was leading a small troop of riders on a recon mission in Yunzhou[37] in the autumn of 682, his thoughts drifted to his checkered career in recent years.

After his defeat by the Tubo in the Dafei Plain (670) he had been disenrolled. The following year, due to an emergency situation in Koguryŏ, he had been restored to favor and appointed commander of a regional force to fight the rebels and their Silla supporters, only to be banished to Xiangzhou[38] in the far south for an offense. Several years had gone by, and the court seemed to have forgotten about him. The general, for his part, had given up hope for return to the capital and been prepared to spend the rest of his days in exile in a semi-civilized, sparsely populated area until one day in 681 when he received a summons. He rode posthaste to Luoyang. By then, Su Dingfang and Pei Xingjian were no more, and Liu Rengui was too old. Xue was appointed, at an audience with the emperor, chief administrator (*zhangshi*) of Guazhou, a key area sitting astride the Silk Road.[39]

Soon he was transferred again, this time to Daizhou[40] (in north Shanxi) to the east as its area commander. Meanwhile, the Tujue had made more inroads, having captured Lanzhou close by. Just as General Xue shifted his thoughts to its prefect Wang Demao,[41] who had lost his life defending the city, the clatter of horse hooves pulled him out of his musings. He raised his head and caught sight of an enemy general across a brook.

"Who is your commander-in-chief?" the Tujue officer asked from a distance.

"Xue Rengui."

"You can't fool me. I know for a fact he was banished to Xiangzhou, where he died."

"I am not trying to fool you," General Xue shot back as he pushed up his helmet.

The Tujue general, taken aback, dismounted and made an obeisance to show respect.

That very night, Xue Rengui launched a surprise attack and thrashed the main Tujue force before it could strike camp and withdraw north, killing more than 10,000 and capturing more than 20,000. That victory effectively stopped the thrust of their southern advance.

***

The Tang forces reversed the situation on the Tubo front as well. Lou Shide, the court envoy, launched eight attacks near the Baishui Brook, all victorious.[42]

At a ceremony to present awards in Luoyang's Palace City, the emperor saw for the first time the legendary Lou in person, a large, corpulent man in his early fifties. Amused, the emperor said to him, "You look different from what I expected."

"Your Majesty, I know what is on your mind. I do not look the part. Because of my round figure, I have to admit, I have a hard time mounting a horse, let alone riding it."

"How did you do it anyway?" the emperor asked.

"Well, as they say in the *Records of the Historian*,[43] it did not prevent me from 'devising winning strategies from the headquarters tent,' did it?"

"Of course not. What were you before the campaign?"

"I was an investigative censor."[44]

"What are your credentials?"

"I have a *jinshi* degree."

"Good for you! You are one of the very few officials who are experienced in dealing with both civil and military affairs. No wonder the empress has nothing but praise for you." The emperor cast a glance at an open scroll on the table and continued, "Now, on the recommendation of Tianhou, I hereby appoint you, Lou Shide, to deputy frontier commissioner of the Heyuan Garrison.[45] Don't try to decline it!"

"No, Your Majesty, I will not," answered Lou with a grin.

Notes

1 The Chanyu Grand Protectorate (Chanyu da duhu fu 單于大都護府): it lay in the northeast Ordos and the area to its north; seat: old town of Yunzhong 雲中 (northwest of present-day Horinger, Inner Mongolia). In 664, it was renamed from the Yunzhong Protectorate. Its nominal leader was the grand protector (*da duhu* 大都護). See *Jiu Tang shu* 4, 麟德元年.

2 The chief administrator (*zhangshi* 長史): a top administrator of a prefecture/commandery, protectorate, area command, garrison command, or a princely establishment.

3 The commander-in-chief (*da zongguan* 大總管) of the Dingxiang District Expeditionary Army (Dingxiang dao xingjun 定襄道行軍). The term *dao* 道 usually refers to one of the ten large administrative areas translated as "Circuit." Here it refers to an ad hoc district.

4 The Shuo Plain (Shuochuan 朔川): near Chanyu Protectorate (seat: near Horinger, Inner Mongolia).

5 The Black Mountains (Heishan 黑山): northwest of present-day Baotou, Inner Mongolia.

[6] Xiazhou 夏州: prefecture; it lay in Hanggin Qi and others, Inner Mongolia, and Yan'an and others, Shaanxi.

[7] The Zigui Palace 紫桂宮 was a touring palace located west of Mianchi, west Henan, completed in 679. See *Zizhi tongjian* 202.6390.

[8] Yuanzhou 原州: prefecture that lay in Guyuan and others, Ningxia, and Pingliang and others, Gansu. Qingzhou 慶州: prefecture that lay in Qingyang and Huanxian, Gansu, and adjacent areas in Shaanxi.

[9] The Heng River 横水: northwest of Hangjin Qi, Inner Mongolia.

[10] Daizhou 代州: prefecture that lay in Daixian, Fanshi, Wutai, and Yuanping, north Shanxi.

[11] Xue Shao's father was chamberlain of the Court of Imperial Entertainments (*guanglu qing* 光祿卿); the Court was one of the Nine Courts.

[12] The princess of Chengyang 成陽公主.

[13] There were three powerful lineages of Hedong 河東 in the north: the Xues, the Peis 裴, and Liŭs 柳.

[14] Jingfeng Gate 景風門.

[15] Xuanyang Ward 宣陽坊 was southeast of the Imperial City and west of the Eastern Market.

[16] Wannian County 萬年縣: one of the two urban counties of Chang'an. See *Tang liangjing chengfang kao* 3.57–58.

[17] Bazhou 巴州: prefecture that it lay in Bazhong, Pingchang, and others, northeast Sichuan.

[18] Xue Kai 薛顗.

[19] Xue Kegou 薛克構.

[20] Xue Xu 薛緒.

[21] The Lis of Longxi 隴西李氏 were the imperial lineage, and the Wus of Tianshui 文水武氏, the lineage of Wu Zetian.

[22] "To divorce" is the translation of *xiu* 休 or *chu* 出, "to cast out a woman." It was justifiable only when one of the seven offenses had been committed, including "being unfilial to her parents-in-law, infertility, extramarital affairs, jealousy," and others.

[23] Xiao Yu 蕭瑀.

[24] The *Zuozhuan* 左傳 (Zuo Commentary) is a chronological history of the Spring and Autumn period and a Confucian classic, completed in the fourth century BCE.

[25] The *mingjing* 明經 (Classicist) degree with its focus on the Confucian classics was much less prized than the *jinshi* 進士 (Advanced Scholar) degree with its focus on literature.

[26] Yang Jiong 楊炯 was magistrate of Yingchuan 盈川 County (in Quzhou, Zhejiang). He was known for his prose and five-syllable verses.

[27] Wang Bo 王勃 was a poet and the author of the piece on cockfight he wrote for Prince Li Xián. He was best known for his prose piece "Tengwangge xu" 滕王閣序 (Preface to the Prince of Teng's Pavilion).

[28] Lu Zhaolin 盧照鄰 was a poet, whose poetry was colored by a sense of melancholy. The Ying River 潁水 originated from Dengfeng, Henan, and ran southeast to empty into the Huai.

[29] Luo Binwang 駱賓王 was known for his mastery of parallel-style prose. He would perish in the Li Jingye 李敬業 rebellion. On the Four Eminences, see *Zizhi tongjian* 203.6408.

[30] The "covered passageways" (*fudao* 復道) were elevated passageways. The Hibiscus Garden (Furong yuan 芙蓉園) was a large scenic area open to the public in the southeast corner of Chang'an. It was home to the Serpentine River (Qujiang) Pond. See *Tang liangjing chengfang kao* 3.92.

[31] The prince-regent (*jianguo* 監國): designation of a prince appointed to exercise control over the central government when the emperor was away for an extended period of time.

[32] The area commander (*dudu* 都督): commander of an area command (*dudu fu*). *See* note in Part I, Chapter 13. Qianzhou 黔州: prefecture with its seat east of Pengshui, southeast Chongqing.

[33] *Tangren yishi huibian* 4.202.

[34] Heisha 黑沙 was north of Hohhot, Inner Mongolia.

[35] The Tiele 鐵勒 were a people of Turkic descent.

[36] Heyuan Garrison 河源軍: seat: southeast of Xining, Qinghai.

[37] Yunzhou 雲州: prefecture in Datong and others in north Shanxi.

[38] Xiangzhou 象州: prefecture in Guangxi. *See* note in Part I, Chapter 6.

[39] Guazhou 瓜州: prefecture that lay west of present-day Jiuquan, Gansu.

[40] Daizhou 代州: see above.

[41] Lanzhou 嵐州: prefecture in Lanxian and others in north Shanxi. Wang Demao 王德茂 was its leader.

[42] The Baishui Brook 白水澗 was in present-day Datong County (north of Xining), Qinghai.

[43] The *Shiji* 史記 (*Records of the Historian*) was a masterpiece by Sima Qian 司馬遷 (W. Han), sometimes called China's Herodotus.

[44] The investigative censor (*jiancha yushi* 監察御史): *see* note in Part I, Chapter 12.

[45] The deputy frontier commissioner (*fu jinglue shi* 副經略使): top aide to the commissioner. The Heyuan Garrison 河源軍 was headquartered southeast of Xining, Qinghai.

16. Fengtian Palace (683)

ONE MORNING IN the early winter of 683, the imperial cavalcade out of Luoyang was progressing southeast. Under the escort of twenty-four regiments of mounted guardsmen and garrison troops, the procession extended over ten *li*. The emperor and the empress rode in their own carriages, each drawn by six horses and each followed or preceded by its own team of auxiliary carriages.

In the entourage, apart from three chief ministers was Crown Prince Li Zhe, who had been summoned to Luoyang only recently from Chang'an, where one of his brothers had stayed behind to serve as prince-regent.

About two weeks later, the emperor and his entourage reached their destination, the Fengtian (Heaven-Worship)[1] Palace about 160 *li* southeast of Luoyang. It was on his recent visit to the Imperial Hot Spring in the area that the emperor had ordered the founding of the palace on the southern slopes of the Taishi Mountains, which form part of the Central Marchmount—Mount Song.

***

Within the palace precincts, the planners had enclosed two private homes where Tian Youyan and Pan Shizheng lived. The emperor and the empress remembered with fondness their previous visit to the two recluses and had given explicit orders to preserve and renovate their residences.

Tian's home was fronted by the old gate. On its lintel hung a new horizontal board with the inscription "Home of Tian Youyan" in the emperor's own hand.

At the entrance to the Dell of Happy Excursions close by, where Pan Shizheng's home was located, was erected a new gate, with its name the "Gate of Transcendents" (Xianyou men) inscribed on a huge rock by the side of the pathway. The name echoed in spirit that of the Gate of the Perfected (Xunzhen men) set in the northern outer wall of the palace.[2] Both "Xianyou" and "Xunzhen" were dedicated to the Daoist master.

While it was obvious that the construction of the palace served the purpose of honoring the Daoist deities and the Perfected Persons,[3] for the emperor, however, the main draw of this visit was the Imperial Hot Spring.

***

On the arms of two eunuchs, the emperor entered his bedchamber, well lit by oil lamps and candle-holder lamps, in the principal basilica of the mountainside palace. Exhausted by the long journey, he flung himself into bed and went to sleep.

The next morning, the emperor, feeling refreshed, held court in the reception area with the chief ministers. About half an hour passed when he suddenly scrunched up his face in agony, while pressing his palms against his temples.

"This headache is killing me," he moaned, shutting his eyes.

As soon as he tried to open his eyes again, he shrieked in a terrifying voice, "My eyes! My eyes!" while holding out his right hand in front with fingers stretched out.

The palace physician came rushing. He checked the pulse, tongue, and facial color of the patient, and said, "I will perform bloodletting on the top of Your Majesty's head now. It may ease the pain and help restore eyesight."

"Stop it!" a shrill female voice shouted. The empress emerged from behind the bamboo screen. "To do bloodletting on the head of the Son of Heaven? That is a capital crime. How dare you?"

"Spare me, Empress!" The physician was down on his knees, kowtowing.

"Let him do it," said the emperor in a weak voice.

"Why don't you try acupuncture first?" the empress asked the physician.

The physician heaved himself to his feet and said to the empress, "Your Majesty, there are hundreds of acupoints on the body. One can do bloodletting on all of them, but to do acupuncture on some can be lethal. So bloodletting on acupoints is very safe. For certain diseases, it is even more effective."

"Are you sure?"

"I swear to Buddha that is the case."

"Let him do it," the emperor urged again.

"All right," she murmured.

The physician moved close to the patient. He fixed his eyes on two acupoints—*baihui* (the highest point of the head) and *naohu* (about half an inch above the occiput)[4]—and pierced a thick needle into each to let out several drops of blood. He then used a white silk to wipe the wounds clean.

"Do you have any sensation of light at all, Your Majesty?" the physician asked.

The emperor blinked his eyes a couple of times and muttered in a feeble voice, "Ye . . . s, I can see a tiny sliver of light right now."

The empress held out two fingers in front of him, asking, "How many? Can you see them?"

The emperor stared at them hard and said with hesitance, "Three… four? Two, I suppose?"

"And the headache?"

"I think it is fading."

"Great! It is obvious Your Majesty is on the mend."

The physician wrote out a prescription and handed it to the eunuch on duty before leaving.

Amazed at the "miracle," the empress ordered to have 100 bolts of colored silk sent to the physician's home.

In two days' time, the headache came back with a vengeance, made worse by dizziness and vomiting. On the empress's orders, no one, except for his personal eunuch officers and the palace physician and his assistants, was allowed access to the emperor while he recuperated. As soon as his headache receded somewhat, the emperor, with the empress by his side, set off on his return journey to Luoyang.

***

In the twelfth month, the court adopted a new reign title, Hongdao (Increscent Dao), to mark the founding of the Fengtian Palace in hopes of bringing blessings down from the gods. In accord with ritual, the emperor was to ride a tall horse to the Zetian Gate[5] and ascend its gatetower to make the announcement. Because of his health condition, two eunuch officers instead brought him a docile pony and helped him into the saddle. Gasping for air, the emperor was too weak to even sit upright. In the end, the venue of the event had to be moved to the Zhenguan Basilica and the emperor was carried there in a palanquin. On the dais of its audience hall, he set himself down in the throne and declared to a roomful of court officials in a soft voice the new reign and a general amnesty. Then he asked, "My subjects, are you pleased . . . with the decision?"

Someone in the crowd answered, "We are! We all benefit from the amnesty and are immensely grateful."

"Ex . . . ex . . . excellent!" the emperor mumbled, as he was seized by a violent coughing fit. "I'm in serious trouble," he said to his attendants. "I do hope that Heaven and Earth would extend my life for one more month so that I can return to Chang'an. I will then go without regret. Is that too much to ask for?"

"Of course not. Your Majesty will get better soon," an attendant said as he wrapped him in a thick blanket and helped him to his feet.

***

That evening, just as preparation for the return trip to Chang'an was underway, the emperor breathed his last in bed in his bedchamber inside Luoyang's Zhenguan Basilica. His "Testamentary Edict" was issued at court the next morning. It ordered that, among other things, Crown Prince Li Zhe succeed to the throne in front of his coffin, and all important military and state affairs henceforth be handled by Tianhou, the Heavenly Empress.

Notes

1 The Fengtian Palace 奉天宮 was north of Dengfeng, Henan.

2 On the Dell of Happy Excursions (Xiaoyao gu 逍遙谷), the Gate of Transcendents (Xianyou men 仙游門), and the Gate of the Perfected (Xunzhen men 尋真門), see *Xin Tang shu* 121, 潘師正傳.

3 The Perfected or the Perfected Persons (*zhenren* 真人): those who have attained the Dao. Oftentimes, *zhenren* is used as part of an honorific title of a famous Daoist master.

4 The *baihui* 百會 is one of the most important acupoints. The *naohu* 腦戶 is for bloodletting only.

5 The Zetian Gate 則天門 was the south central entrance to Luoyang's Palace City. Later, it would be renamed "Yingtian Gate" 應天門. See *Tang liangjing chengfang kao* 5.132.

Part II.

Sole Sovereign

1. Li Zhe and Li Dan (684)

In the Middle East, Caliph Mu'awiyah II, son of Yazid I, died. Marwan I succeeded.

THE YEAR 684 marked a new beginning in Tang history. Under the close tutelage of his mother Tianhou, the emperor Li Zhe (temple name: Zhongzong) began his rule in the Sisheng (Heir-Sage) reign period. At twenty-nine *sui*, Li Zhe was a short, average-looking man with average intelligence, fun loving and a bit wayward. One of the first steps he wanted to take was to promote the son of his wet nurse to a Rank-5 position and his father-in-law Wei Xuanzhen, a low-ranking provincial official, to president of the Secretariat, a top leadership post at court.

At a morning court session in the second month, Chief Minister Pei Yan, one of the two regents appointed by Gaozong before his death, made a strong argument against the two promotions.

An infuriated emperor pounded the table, shouting, "You can't stop me even if I let my father-in-law rule over all under Heaven."

"Soothe your temper, Your Majesty," said Pei Yan, who was taken aback by the sudden burst of imperial wrath. "Please wait until I consult Tianhou."

"Do it!" the emperor growled.

Pei Yan took his leave in a hurry.

***

At an emergency audience granted to Pei Yan in her residential basilica in the afternoon, Tianhou learned what had just happened at court. She sighed and said, "To be frank, I planned to let him sit on the throne only as a *figurehead* and did not expect him to take his job seriously. Who does he think he is? He has neither control of the military, nor the Palace Guards, nor the chief ministers. Had I not placed him on the throne, he would have been a nobody."

The next morning, Li Zhe held court as usual in the main hall of the Qianyuan Basilica. As he stared down at the Hundred Officials on their knees making obeisance, the doors were flung open. With two dozen armed flying cavalrymen[1] leading the way, Tianhou entered, along with a small group of officials—Chief Minister Pei Yan, Vice President of the Secretariat Liu Yizhi,[2] Generals of the Yulin Army[3]

Cheng Wuting and Zhang Qianxu, and others. She walked down the central aisle, with the officials in tow, and mounted the dais. As she turned to face the audience, the vice president of the Secretariat announced her decree in a stern voice:

> *Pursuant to the* Tang Code, *it is hereby decreed that Li Zhe be deposed and demoted to prince of Luling.*[4]

With a puzzled look on his face, Li Zhe shouted, "Mother! Mother! What have I done to deserve this? I am innocent!"

"Innocent?" Tianhou said sharply. "Didn't you want to promote a clown to a senior position because he is the son of your lousy wet nurse? And to have a country bumpkin called Wei Xuanzhen rule over the realm because he is your father-in-law? Do you still claim innocence?"

The two generals seized hold of the emperor's arms and marched him out of the hall as he screamed in protest.

Li Chongrun at three *sui*, one of Li Zhe's sons, who had just been made "crown grandson," was now reduced to commoner status.

Soon afterwards, Li Zhe was banished to Junzhou[5] in the south together with his wife Consort Wei. Wei Xuanzhen, his father-in-law, was banished farther down south to Qinzhou,[6] where he would soon perish.

***

Prince Li Dan, Tianhou's youngest son, at twenty-three *sui*, was enthroned as emperor. In temperament Li Dan (temple name: Ruizong) took after his father, the late emperor Li Zhi (Gaozong)—modest, respectful, filial, and friendly. Like his disgraced brother Li Xián, he had established a reputation as a bookish scholar of sorts with an interest in lexicological works, in particular the *Script Explained and Graphs Explicated* by the Eastern Han lexicographer Xu Shen.[7] A lover of calligraphy, he was an accomplished master of both the cursive and clerical hands. Ascension to the throne did not excite him in the least. Nor did the strict rules set by Mother bother him that much at all. He would conduct his official "business" in a side basilica; and not be allowed to meddle in court affairs. Neither did he care, committed as he was to the Daoist idea of *wuwei* (non-being or non-action).

The bamboo screen in the principal basilica was taken down and put away for good. Tianhou had officially taken over the reins. She was now in everything but name the true emperor.

***

Tang zoning rules governing urban centers required that businesses be concentrated in the designated commercial areas separate from residential neighborhoods. In Luoyang, there were three of them, namely, the Northern, Southern, and Western Markets. Food and drink establishments like taverns were exempt from these rules.

It was in one of those neighborhood taverns in a residential ward east of Luoyang's Imperial City that a dozen or so flying cavalrymen were drinking and chatting about the recent bloodless coup they had taken part in. One inebriated cavalryman said, "We put our lives on the line for her. Where are our rewards? Where?"

A fellow cavalryman, equally tipsy, answered, "The commandant made us the promise. But he was overruled, so I heard."

The first cavalryman seized the second one by the neck and shouted, "By whom?"

"Who else?"

"If I knew she was so stingy, I'd have supported the son."

Others joined them, venting their fury in foul language.

As the carousal went on for a while, a third cavalryman stood up to use the toilet and left the room. By the time he came back about one hour later, he had brought with him three dozen armed guardsmen. They took all the cavalrymen present except the informant into custody.

Within the week, punishments were handed down. The one who had made the treasonous remark was to go to the gallows. The rest, guilty of complicity, were condemned to a slightly more dignified form of death—decapitation. The informant who had squealed on his comrades got a promotion from rank-and-file soldier to Rank-5 officer.

Throughout all this, Tianhou had not said a word. Her underlings had done the job for her in the name of protecting her reputation and authority.

This incident pushed forward a new trend that had already been underway, in which people informed against their bosses, comrades, neighbors, and relatives to show their allegiance to Tianhou in exchange for monetary rewards and promotions.

***

In late February, Tianhou visited the Shangyang Palace to enjoy cherry blossoms in full bloom along the Luo. She stopped at a pavilion on the riverbank to host a drinking party. At her request, officials, generals, and scholars in her entourage played a game of poem-recital, where they took turns to chant couplets by known poets. Tianhou recited the first one. Song Zhiwen, a great-looking poet in his late twenties, followed with one that began with the last character of the first couplet. One of his colleagues declaimed anther couplet following the same rule. The game went on like this until someone, a general, failed to respond with an appropriate couplet. For his punishment, he gulped down a goblet of wine. Tianhou then started another round of poem-recital.

When the party ended at dusk, Tianhou called General of the Left Jinwu Guard[8] Qiu Shenji aside, a top security officer known for loyalty to the sovereign and cruelty to prisoners.

Tianhou showed him a poem,[9] which read,

Below the Yellow Terrace melons were planted,
They then became ripened with seeds in abundance.
After one picking, the melons grew better,
After two pickings, the melons became less,
After three pickings, some still remained,
After four pickings, only vines were left.

"What do you think?" Tianhou ask.

"To be frank with Your Majesty, I do not know what to make of it."

"It complains against me! Can you guess who wrote it?"

"I cannot, Your Majesty."

"Li Xián, the ex-crown prince. There is no place for this kind of innuendo."

Tianhou paused briefly before saying in a sharp tone, "Shenji, I want you to silence him."

"By what means, Your Majesty?"

"By whatever means. I don't ever want to hear from him again."

About a month later, Qiu Shenji arrived in Bazhou (in Sichuan), and went with his henchmen straight to Li Xián's residence. Qiu's plan was to tie up the ex-prince and terrorize him until he promised to shut up for good. The moment they turned up on his doorstep, the prince went into a panic. In the scuffle that ensued, Qiu's men had him in a headlock and choked him a bit too hard and he stopped breathing.

Upon return to Luoyang, Qiu Shenji briefed Tianhou on what had happened. Thereupon, Tianhou sent him to jail before banishing him to Diezhou[10] in the west.

About two weeks later, Tianhou held a massive funeral for Li Xián in the palace of Luoyang, at which she joined in the ritual wailing and ordered the posthumous restoration of his prince's title.

In the meantime, Qiu Shenji was quietly recalled from banishment to resume his post as general of the Left Jinwu Guard at the Eastern Capital.

***

The court diviners chose the *jiazi* day of the second month (in early March) for a ritual ceremony, because it was fraught with significance. As the first of the Sexagenary Cycle, it marks an important beginning and an auspicious day of the zodiac.[11] On that day Tianhou mounted the dais of the Wucheng Basilica to the west of the Qianyuan Basilica[12] in the Palace City of Luoyang to receive exalted titles from her son the emperor Li Dan and the Hundred Officials.

Three days later, she held court while sitting on the yellow throne under an embroidered purple canopy on the front terrace of the Zichen Basilica.[13] At the end of the court session, another ceremony took place, in which Tianhou conferred upon Wu Chengsi, son of Wu Yuanshuang, the title of "successor emperor."[14] This newly created post implied that Chengsi was now a serious contender for the right to succeed the throne.

***

In the ninth month, the announcement of another amnesty marked the beginning of a new reign period—Guangzhai (Shining Residence). With that, Tianhou launched her Revolution.

The Eastern Capital Luoyang was renamed "Divine Capital." The Palace City was now known as the Palace of "Taichu" or "Grand Beginning," inspired by Laozi's *Class of the Way and Its Virtue* (*Daode jing*). The top executive agency, the Department of State Affairs, now became the Wenchang Terrace,[15] a name inspired by its eponymous constellation in Ursa Major in the Purple Tenuity Enclosure,[16] which encompasses the circumpolar area. The two co-leaders of the Department were renamed from "vice premiers" to "left and right chancellors."

The Six Boards under the Wenchang Terrace (Department of State Affairs)—the Boards of Personnel, Revenue, Rites, War, Justice, and Works—were now renamed as the Boards of Heaven, Earth, Spring, Summer, Autumn, and Winter,[17] based on precedents recorded in the *Rites of Zhou*.[18] The Chancellery was renamed the Simurgh Terrace; and the Secretariat, the Phoenix Pavilion. The Terrace of Censors

(Censorate) was split into the Left and Right Terraces of Government Discipline.[19] Other Departments (*sheng*), Courts (*si*), Inspectorates (*jian*), and Commands (*shuai*) underwent similar nomenclatural changes.

***

As the Revolution continued apace, officials and common subjects were encouraged to present innovative ideas to reform the existing political, military, economic, and ritual institutions. In response, her nephew "Successor Emperor" Wu Chengsi wrote in his memorial, "The Tang has its Ancestral Temple with seven chambers, dedicated to the ancestors of the Li royal house and deceased Tang emperors, in Chang'an. But now the Wu house is ruling over the country and the capital is Luoyang. In my humble view, another temple with seven chambers, dedicated to the illustrious ancestors of the Wu lineage, should be set up in Luoyang."

Tianhou, taken by surprise, asked him, "What do you hope to achieve by setting up this Wu temple?"

"To worship the Wu ancestors and eventually make it *the* Ancestral Temple of the country."

"And?"

"It will then help legitimize the Wu line of succession."

"But you are already the 'successor emperor.' I twisted many arms to get you that title."

"Your Majesty, I greatly appreciate the favor. But the post of 'successor emperor' is not based on a precedent, nor is it documented in the sources. As we all know, the crown prince is still the official successor to the throne. So long as the emperor Li Dan's eldest son Li Chengqi is the crown prince and so long as there is no ground for his removal, the 'successor emperor' is only a titular post, a fairly good one though."

"Chengsi, sooner or later, I will take measures to promote the Wu lineage. But I am not sure if now is the time. And your idea of the Wu seven chambers will be a much harder sell to the court."

Suddenly, Wu Chengsi dropped on his knees, his face flushing, as he continued in an agitated voice, "Your Majesty, I beseech you! Now *is* the time. If you don't seize the moment, it may never come back. After you pass on, the Wu lineage will be in danger."

"Get up, Chengsi!"

As soon as her nephew was back in his seat, she said, "Well, I can give it a try, if you insist."

The next morning, she brought up the issue at the court session. Although she expected disagreement from her senior advisers, the muscles of her face tensed when she heard Pei Yan voice his view.

"Your Majesty, as the ruler over the realm, should demonstrate a thorough dedication to the public, without a trace of self-interest. The proposal to build the Wu temple of seven chambers by Wu Chengsi, I must say, is self-serving. Not only that. The idea itself is disconcerting. One should never forget the lesson of Empress Lü[20] of the Han dynasty."

"Chief Minister, I have to disagree with you there," Tianhou responded, struggling to contain her anger. "Empress Lü gave power to her relatives while they were still alive. What we are trying to do is granting honors to the deceased Wu ancestors. What harm can it do?"

"Well, this proposal for an additional temple of seven chambers is a deviation from a cardinal principle since antiquity—there cannot be two suns in the same sky. If one does not put a stop to it at the outset, it will be a detriment to the country and shake it to the foundations."

Tianhou paused to search for an adequate answer. Failing to find one, she had the proposal tabled.

But Pei Yan's contentious argument triggered in her a defensive response. In the days that followed, the more she mulled over it, the more she became inclined towards her nephew's view. What at stake here was not just the new temple with seven chambers, which she actually could do without, but her authority to dominate the court.

In the end, overcoming strong resistance at court, Tianhou ordered to have two more ancestral temples set up. The first one consisting of five chambers went up in Luoyang. They were dedicated to the Wu ancestors, including her great-great-great-grandfather, great-great-grandfather, great-grandfather, grandfather, and father, who was given the posthumous titles of grand preceptor and King Ding of Wei.[21] The second temple, also dedicated to the Wus, was set up in Wenshui, their ancestral hometown.

***

For months in 684, the burial place for the late Emperor Li Zhi remained undecided. Most court officials believed that the emperor's remains should be interred in the Qianling Tomb Park north of Chang'an. But there were also eloquent voices against it. The young poet Chen Zi'ang, for instance, argued that Chang'an, always under threat from Tujue and Tubo, had been in decline for years. What was more, it had been suffering from a prolonged drought; the imperial cortège going west would only worsen the situation. Luoyang, on the other hand, with its natural beauty, wealth, economic advantages, and rich inheritance, deserved to be the last resting place for the late Heavenly Emperor.

Tianhou took notice and granted him an audience. The spirited argument Chen presented sure piqued her interest, but his short stature and plain-looking face did not inspire much confidence. Still, impressed with his literary talent, she hired him on the spot as a minor court official.[22] In the end, she chose not to act on his advice. Instead, she had the emperor's body transported back to Guanzhong, where it was laid to rest in Qianling in the eighth month. Thereupon, he was given the temple name Gaozong.

***

Ashina Gudulu's declaration as khan in 682 had marked the founding of a new Tujue state (known in history as the Later Tujue Khanate) in the vast territory of the now-defunct Eastern Tujue Khanate. Since then, the Tujue in the east had grown stronger. They conducted raids into settled communities not only on the frontier, but also in prefectures farther down south, including Bingzhou, Lanzhou, Yuzhou, and Shuozhou in present-day Shanxi; and Dingzhou and Guizhou in present-day Hebei.[23] In other words, the northern part of the Central Plain was now under threat.

"When the late emperor was alive, I was mainly in charge of civil affairs," Tianhou said to Pei Yan at a meeting of the Chief Ministers' Council. "But now the issue of northern frontier security is crying out for my attention. Chief Minister, in your opinion, which of our top generals can lead the fight against the Tujue raids?"

Pei Yan answered, "Recently, we lost two great frontier generals, Pei Xingjian and Xue Rengui (683). General Liu Rengui is still alive, but he is well over eighty and frail. So far, no one of their caliber has emerged. However, General Pei Xingjian did mentor a few good commanders, including Cheng Wuting, Zhang Qianxu, Wang Fangyi, Liu Jingtong,[24] Li Duozuo, and Heichi Changzhi, to name a few. Of these, in my opinion, Cheng Wuting and Heichi Changzhi are the most experienced. Cheng Wuting was Pei's lieutenant when they defeated Ashina Funian. Heichi Changzhi has repeatedly trounced the Tubo forces."

"Isn't Heichi posted in the west?"

"Yes, Your Majesty. He is our best general guarding the west."

"That leaves us with only one person, Cheng Wuting?"

"Unless Your Majesty wants to promote someone from the lower ranks."

"No, that won't be necessary. General Cheng will be fine. What kind of appointment then will be appropriate?"

"How about the pacifying commissioner of Chanyu District[25] with the task of defending the northern frontier?"

"Excellent."

Notes

[1] Flying cavalrymen (*feiqi* 飛騎): designation of soldiers with good horse riding and archery skills stationed at the Xuanwu Gate 玄武門 under the command of the Left and Right Barracks Guards (*tunwei* 屯衛; one of the Sixteen Guards).

[2] Vice President of the Secretariat (*zhongshu shilang* 中書侍郎) Liu Yizhi 劉禕之 (630–686).

[3] The Army of the Forest of Plumes (Yulin jun 羽林軍): an elite Praetorian Guard force.

[4] Prince of Luling 廬陵王.

[5] Junzhou 均州: prefecture in Shiyan and others, northwest Hubei. Later, Li Zhe would be transferred to Fangzhou 房州.

[6] Qinzhou 欽州: prefecture in present-day Qinzhou and others, Guangxi.

[7] The *Script Explained and Graphs Explicated* (*Shuowen jiezi* 說文解字) by Xu Shen 許慎 is one of the earliest dictionaries that survive.

[8] The Left Jinwu Guard (*zuo Jinwu wei* 左金吾衛): a prestigious unit of the imperial bodyguard and one of the Sixteen Guards.

[9] "Huangtai gua ci" 黄臺瓜辭.

[10] Diezhou 疊州: prefecture in Têwo (south of Lanzhou), Gansu.

[11] In astrology, the zodiac and celestial equator are divided into twelve stations or constellations, matched with twelve divinities. Six of them are considered auspicious, so are the days when they are on duty. The rest are considered "inauspicious."

[12] The Wucheng 武成 (later known as Xuanzheng 宣政) Basilica was the place where the sovereign held court regularly. It was located west of the Qianyuan Basilica 乾元殿 (also known as Hanyuan Basilica 含元殿). See *Tang liangjing chengfang kao* 5.134.

[13] The Zichen Basilica 紫宸殿 was the second of the axial structures, located north of the Qianyuan 乾元. See *Zizhi tongjian* 203.6419. Cf. its namesake in the Daming Palace, Chang'an. See *Tang liangjing chengfang kao* 1.22.

[14] The post "successor emperor" (*si huangdi* 嗣皇帝) was Tianhou's invention.

[15] The Department of State Affairs (*shangshu sheng* 尚書省) or the Wenchang Terrace (Wenchang tai 文昌臺) was the leading first-tier central government agency, and one of the Three Departments (*san sheng* 三省).

[16] In astrology, the areas north of the zodiac and the celestial equator are divided into the Three Enclosures (*sanyuan* 三垣). The Purple Tenuity Enclosure (*ziwei yuan* 紫微垣) in the circumpolar area is one of them.

[17] After Wu Zetian's reform, the Six Boards were renamed: The Board of Personnel was converted to the Office of Heaven; Revenue to Earth (*diguan* 地官); Rites to Spring (*chunguan* 春官); War to Summer (*xiaguan* 夏官); Justice to Autumn (*qiuguan* 秋官); and Works to Winter (*dongguan* 冬官).

[18] The *Rites of Zhou* (*Zhouli* 周禮) is a Confucian classic on ritual, probably completed in the Warring States period.

[19] The Chancellery (*menxia sheng* 門下省): the Simurgh Terrace (*luantai* 鸞臺). The Secretariat (*zhongshu sheng* 中書省): the Phoenix Pavilion (*fengge* 鳳閣). The Terrace of Censors (*yushi tai* 御史臺): the Left and Right Terraces of Government Discipline (*zuo you suzheng tai* 左右肅政臺).

[20] Empress Lü of the Western Han, after the emperor Liu Bang's death, adopted a policy of packing the court leadership with members of her own lineage, which was reversed after her death.

[21] King Ding of Wei 魏定王.

[22] His post was "proofreader" (*zhengzi* 正字).

[23] Bingzhou 并州 (seat: near Taiyuan, Shanxi); Lanzhou 嵐州 (seat: Lanxian, Shanxi); Yuzhou 蔚州 (seat: Lingqiu, Shanxi); Shuozhou 朔州 (seat: Shuozhou, Shanxi); Dingzhou 定州 (seat: Lunu, Hebei); Guizhou嬀州 (seat: southwest of Zhuolu, Hebei).

[24] Liu Jingtong 劉敬同.

[25] The pacifying commissioner of Changyu District (Chanyu dao anfu dashi 單于道安撫大使).

2. Rebellion (684)

BY THE TIME Wu Chengsi was appointed successor emperor, Wu Sansi was vice commanding officer of the Right Guard. As these two nephews of Tianhou helped strengthen the power base of the Wu lineage, they also went out of their way to ferret out members of the Li royal house who might pose a threat to their aunt and the Wus.

They set their sights on Princes Li Yuanjia (general-in-chief) and Li Lingkui (grand preceptor of the crown prince).[1] Both were younger brothers of Emperor Taizong and high-ranking officials occupying positions of vital importance. And both enjoyed great prestige among the senior officials and officers.

After the two nephews had dug up some dirt on the Li princes based on hearsay, they urged their aunt to take action against them. With a roll of her eyes, she said, "To deal with those two princes, I may need a broad base of support."

She then took up the matter with the court leadership. Chief Minister Pei Yan was the first one to raise an opposing voice, which was echoed by a number of court leaders. And she was forced to put the plan aside. Although not too surprised, she was nonetheless annoyed.

Meanwhile, a massive campaign had been underway all over the country to degrade the influence of the Li house, with the princes as the main targets. Those judged to have failed to switch allegiance from Emperor Gaozong to Tianhou were subject to demotion and banishment. Each time a prince was punished, dozens or even hundreds of people under or around him would go down with him.

***

One night in the ninth month, four disgraced officials were having a secret meeting behind closed doors on the second floor of a teahouse on the north bank of the Yangzi in Yangzhou.[2] As the purge carried out by Wu Chengsi and Wu Sansi was spreading east, this cabal of conspirators decided to advance their date of action to avoid capture.

The next day, Supervising Censor[3] Xue Zhongzhang, on the instruction of the cabal, barged into the Yangzhou Government Office. Acting on the authority of the Censorate, he had Chief Administrator Chen Jingzhi taken into custody.

Hot on his heels was the lead conspirator Li Jingye, a man in his late forties with a towering stature like his famous grandpa Li Ji. Armed with a forged edict, he appointed himself assistant prefect to take over the prefectural government.[4] In that capacity, he had the top official Chen Jingzhi decapitated, and opened the Prefectural Storehouse and Treasury to the masses. He then recruited thousands of prison inmates and artisans working for the prefectural government as rebel soldiers, arming them with weapons seized from the prefectural armory.

Within ten days, Li and his associates had taken control of the military personnel throughout the prefecture, numbering more than 100,000. When his minions found a lookalike of the late Crown Prince Li Xián, they declared the prince to be alive and had him endorse the rebel cause. Thereupon, Li Jingye set up the Yangzhou Protectorate. He himself acted as its leader with the title of "grand protector."

As Li Jingye's rebel army sacked towns and cities and captured territory in Yangzhou, it began to pose a serious threat to two neighboring prefectures—Chuzhou to the north and Runzhou[5] to the south.

***

At an emergency meeting of the Chief Ministers' Council, Tianhou was addressing the first serious rebellion on her watch. It was particularly alarming because it had disrupted the flow of revenue from the south and done great harm to farming in Yangzhou and surrounding areas in the lower Yangzi valley.

An attendant arrived with a scroll marked "top secret" and "urgent." She unfurled it to reveal the title of the essay "A Call to Arms against Wu." She handed it back to the attendant and said, "Read it. We have nothing to hide."

The attendant began:

> *Wu the usurper, who dominates the court, is churlish by nature and lowly by birth. When first admitted into the palace, she was one of many who stood around in the Audience Hall and attended on Emperor Taizong when he changed clothes. Concealing her intimate ties with Taizong, she ingratiated herself with his son Gaozong and became his favorite in the Rear Palace. She ascended the throne of empress dressed in resplendent attire, having lured the sovereign into incest. As a fratricide and sororicide, a regicide and matricide,[6] she is condemned by humans and gods alike. Neither will she be tolerated by Heaven and Earth. With a malicious heart, she covets the throne. She confined Gaozong's favorite son in a side basilica and placed her thuggish relatives in positions of power. . . . And yet, we know for certain that, in today's world, which house in the end will prevail and rule over all under Heaven. . . .*

Tianhou sighed and asked, "Who wrote this?"

"Luo Binwang," the attendant said.

"One of the Four Eminences," said she, forcing a smile. "How can a man of such talent fail to get noticed by the court? The chief ministers are to blame for this neglect!" She paused to wait for a response from the top leaders.

"I recognize the name," Pei Yan said. "After he committed an offense, he was banished to the south. I never heard about him again. My apologies, Your Majesty."

"That is all right. Now let's return to the rebels. I've got someone in mind as leader of the expedition against them: General-in-Chief

Li Xiaoyi. I'll grant him the title of commander-in-chief of Yangzhou District. What do you think?"

"An excellent choice, Your Majesty!" Pei Yan said. And others concurred.

"Well, I have to admit, dealing with military affairs is not my cup of tea. What I need urgently now is your assessment of the situation and your strategies for dealing with it."

Pei Yan, old but still spritely, straightened his wiry frame and said in a serious tone, "Your Majesty, there seems a better way than war. The emperor Li Dan came of age a while ago and was expected to exercise his power as sovereign. But so far, he has not, because Your Majesty is reigning on his behalf. That was the pretext the scoundrels used to rebel in the first place. In my humble opinion, if true power is restored to the emperor today, the rebellion will lose any claim to legitimacy, and fall apart by itself."

Tianhou scowled without uttering a word. The pallid color of her face suggested extreme displeasure, which was not lost on the court officials present.

A few days later, taking his cue from Tianhou's facial expression, Supervising Censor Cui Cha submitted a memorial. It said, "Pei Yan is already the leading powerholder at court. Still, he wants to force Your Majesty off the throne. In so doing, he must have an ulterior motive."

Cui Cha is right, Tianhou thought. *What Pei Yan is trying to do is replace me with a weakling like Li Dan so that he can amass more power. No wonder he has shown no interest in fighting Li Jingye and his rebel followers.*

She ordered to have fifty bolts of silk sent to Cui's home as a reward.

Feeling emboldened, more officials came forward to censure the lead chief minister. One of them, Secretariat Drafter[7] Li Jingshen, went so far as to accuse him of collusion with the rebels. His evidence: The rebel leader Xue Zhongzhang—the investigative censor who had imprisoned the de facto governor Chen Jingzhi—was Pei Yan's nephew.

Someone then filed a request for Pei Yan's immediate arrest. It jogged Tianhou's memory. The first time she had seen him was in 680 when he was transferred in from a provincial post in Shandong. Gaozong had soon promoted him to leading chief minister. Although Tianhou had endorsed him, something about him had always bothered her. She had known all along that he was no pushover and was fine with it. What sometimes drove her up a wall was his bull-headedness. She could never forget how he had badmouthed General Pei Xingjian, opposed the prosecution of Li Yuanjia and Li Dingkui, and fought against the setup of the Wu Temple tooth and nail. Now he was asking Li Dan to rule over the realm! *That's the last straw*, she thought. *It gives me no choice but to take him down, at least a peg or two*. She gave assent to the request for his arrest.

Stripped of his powers, the chief minister was taken into custody.

But the charge against Pei did not sit well with many leading officials and officers. Cheng Wuting, the most powerful general in charge of safeguarding the northern border, sent in a secret memorial in which he vouched for the character of Pei Yan.

De facto Chief Minister Liu Jingxian and Vice President of the Secretariat Hu Yuanfan both came to Pei Yan's defense at court. They argued that, as a meritorious court elder, Pei Yan had served Her Majesty with utter devotion and selflessness, a fact known to all under Heaven. He could not possibly be a rebel.

Tianhou said, "I've seen convincing evidence that proves his intention to rebel. You just don't know it yet."

"Your Majesty, if Mr. Pei is a rebel, so am I," responded Liu Jingxian curtly.

"So am I," Hu Yuanfan echoed.

A flush swept across her face as Tianhou cast a stern look at the two court leaders and her thoughts went back to her decision to oust Chu Suiliang. The two youngest chief ministers at that time, Hann Yuan and Lai Ji, had turned out to be the most stubborn opponents to her order. Now Liu Jingxian and Hu Yuanfan were treading in their footsteps. And she did not like it a bit.

"I know for a fact neither of you are a rebel," she said. "But I am certain Pei is. There are a lot of rumors floating around. One claims that Pei once planned to kidnap me when I was about to visit Longmen and to have the imperial power restored to Li Dan. He gave up the attempt only when rain prevented me from making the trip. Another claims that Pei Yan was one of the original conspirators against me and was in secret liaison with Li Jingye through Luo Binwang. You know what? I find neither credible. But he has opposed me almost at every turn, *and* he wants me to step down, for heaven's sake!"

The two court leaders fell silent. Tianhou could sense their displeasure.

***

At night, a question kept popping up in her mind, "Does all this make Pei Yan a rebel?" With that in mind, the next morning she paid a visit to Pei Yan in person to hear him explain himself. Despite her harsh rhetoric, she was still willing to show leniency if he owned up to his guilt with sincerity.

When she eventually saw him face-to-face, she was dumbfounded at his refusal to fess up to his crime at all.

She left the prison in disappointment. When she called in his prosecutor for questioning later, she was told, "We asked him to show contrition to save his skin, but he would not do it, saying, 'When a chief minister is thrown into jail, do you really expect him to survive?' "

She scrunched her eyebrows together and uttered through clenched teeth, "All right, Chief Minister, I'll oblige you."

Tianhou forthwith appointed Censor-in-Chief of the Left Qian Weidao de facto chief minister to head the prosecution. And Qian delivered the expected outcome within days, convicting Pei of rebellion with death by decapitation as his punishment.

Tianhou waited two more days. When no report of confession showed up on her table, she gave her approval to the punishment.

On the day of his execution, as Pei Yan was transported in a prison cart to the Luoyang Posthouse, he felt the leaden weight of a wooden cangue on his neck. He shut his eyes to hear the Sage's voice one more time, "There are cases where gentlemen of high purpose have to accept death in order to have benevolence accomplished."[8] Throughout the whole ordeal, he had been sustained by Confucian teachings like this, staying calm and strong, without shedding a single tear.

The cart came to a halt. After he was pushed off, he raised his head and saw two old men dressed in rags with tears pouring down their cheeks. The moment he recognized them as his brothers, Pei felt a lump in his throat and burst out crying.

"It's all because of me!" he blurted out. "You are being banished to the far south! When I had power, it never did you any good. Now I've fallen into disgrace, and you have to suffer!"

As he struggled to hold his head straight, two guardsmen dragged him onto a wooden platform and a sword fell on his neck.

Meanwhile an officer leading a group of guardsmen raided the Pei's residence. He found no fresh evidence against him, but a sparsely furnished home that did not even have an extra bushel of grain.

***

Apart from the two brothers, all other male members of the Pei Yan household were banished, and all female members were forced to labor in the Lateral Palace as bondwomen, as was the standard practice. Only one nephew of seventeen *sui* named Pei Zhouxian had escaped punishment. The young man made a request to see Tianhou and was, to his surprise, granted an audience.

"Your uncle plotted rebellion. What do you have to say to that?" Tianhou asked.

"I am not here to complain but to propose something for Your Majesty's benefit."

"Oh?" Tianhou was curious.

"Your Majesty, as a woman married into the Li house, has taken over the court after the late emperor passed on. Your Majesty has suppressed the Lis and promoted the Wus. My uncle, for all the loyal service he rendered to the country, was maligned and killed, and his descendants banished. All this may do harm to Your Majesty's lineage in the long run. But, if Your Majesty restores the rule of your son, Your Majesty will enjoy a peaceful life in retirement and the Wu family line will continue forever. Otherwise, when a change of regime happens, things will become hopeless."

"Nonsense, utter nonsense!" Tianhou growled and motioned to have the brat taken out.

As he was being dragged away by two guardsmen, the teenager turned his head and shouted, "Follow my advice before it is too late!"

After receiving a flogging of 100 blows ordered by Tianhou in the Audience Hall, Pei Zhouxian was sent in exile to the far south. As for why Tianhou spared his life nobody knows. What was clear was that Tianhou was in no mood to slow down the purge any time soon. Even the Daoist Master Pan Shizheng, then living in Luoyang as Tianhou's guest, was not spared. After he was found guilty of close association with Pei Yan, on Tianhou's orders, he was sent back to his old home on Mount Song.

***

In the flagship moored to the bank of the Xia'e Brook in Gaoyou,[9] Li Jingye was meeting with the top rebel leaders—Li Jingqiu (his brother), Wang Naxiang (a subordinate officer of his grandfather Li Ji), and Luo Binwang—to discuss how to ward off the next wave of assault by Li Xiaoyi's men. Already outnumbered five to one by the enemy, the rebel army would be at a fatal disadvantage, if the Tang army was joined by General Heichi Changzhi's massive reinforcements now moving posthaste towards Gaoyou. In the last engagement, the rebels had simply lucked it out. Their superior naval battle skills allowed them to take on and wipe out the entire attack force of 5,000 men before they could establish a foothold ashore.

The meeting adjourned after the rebel leaders had planned out their escape routes by sea to Silla, in the event of a disastrous defeat.

Li Jingye set himself down by the main mast of the ship. He was to sit up all night as the commanding officer on duty. It was pitch-dark all around except for a few flickering torch lights at the prow and stern. The other leaders had left to catch a short sleep in their own ships before dawn. The enemy could resume their attack any moment.

As a fishy breeze from the river was blowing into his face, Li Jingye thought back to his first river battle at a time when he had under his command more than 100,000 men. A few weeks later, he lost more than four-fifth of them. The previous week was the toughest. They had to fend off attacks by hordes of enemy every day. Feeling thoroughly exhausted like everyone else, he drifted to sleep.

A short while later, he awoke to bright flares that lit up the sky, accompanied by noisy war cries. A volley of arrows rained down on the ship and ripped through "Great Tang" banner at the bow and the topsail. He shouted orders to his adjutants, picked up his long sword and bow, slung a quiver of arrows across his shoulder, and rushed ashore. He watched in despair as his fleet of ships was being consumed by hundreds of fires.

At the designated meeting place, Li Jingye joined the other members of the leadership: his brother Li Jingqiu, Luo Binwang, and Wang Naxiang. Under the escort of about thirty cavalry provided by General Wang, they fled south to Jiangdu (Yangzhou). After a short break, they started heading east towards Hailing.[10] Their plan was simple: after the main road took them from Hailing to the seaport, they would commandeer a ship to go on a sea voyage north.

About fifty *li* shy of their destination, the party stopped for a much-needed respite in a small village. The Li brothers and Luo left their baggage behind and went on a recon mission as they rode into the semidarkness of the early morning, accompanied by a dozen or so riders. At a crossroads, the three rebel leaders dismounted to check directions. Some escort riders eased off their horses and skulked after them, swords drawn. When they finally sneaked up behind their leaders, they attacked and hacked them down.

The next day, General Wang Naxiang surrendered to a commanding officer of the Tang army, bringing with him the severed heads of the three rebel leaders in a blood-stained wicker chest.

With this act of treachery, the Li Jingye War, the costliest internal conflict under Tianhou, was over, after the loss of more than one hundred thousand lives.

Legend had it that the head of the top leader betrayed and killed by Wang Naxing was not really that of Li Jingye but his double. Li Jingye himself went into hiding in the Dagu Mountains,[11] where he lived as a monk until he was in his nineties. But few put much stock in the story.

***

On Tianhou's orders, Liu Jingxian and Hu Yuanfan, the two younger court leaders who had defended Pei Yan, were imprisoned and then banished to the far south. Convinced of their innocence, she nonetheless decided to punish them. At this stage of her career, she could ill afford to tolerate people who showed the slightest sign of disloyalty.

Pacifying Commissioner of Chanyu District Cheng Wuting, the greatest general after Pei Xingjian's death, had gone out on a limb for Pei Yan. In so doing, he had crossed the line. An envoy bearing Tianhou's secret decree, escorted by a dozen armed riders, paid a surprise visit to him in his campaign tent on the northern frontier. Before he fully understood what his crime was, he was trussed up and gagged and executed in situ. His surviving family members were later slaughtered to a man.

On hearing the news of Cheng's death, the Tujue north of the border held several parties to celebrate. Before long, they realized that, by dying a wrongful death at the hands of Tianhou, General Cheng had been transformed into their patron god of war. A shrine in honor of the fallen general was set up. The Tujue would often pray at the shrine for his protection before going into battle.

***

At a victory ceremony held on the front terrace of the Qianyuan Basilica in Luoyang, Tianhou, sitting on an embroidered yellow throne under a purple canopy was conferring Certificates of Commendation upon a group of meritorious officers, headed by Commander-in-Chief Li Xiaoyi. They were honored for their distinguished service in the recent Li Jingye (Xu Jingye)[12] War.

Tianhou singled out the low-ranking clerk Liu Zhirou for special praise. Under his advice, the government troops had adopted the fire attack tactic, resulting in the death of 7,000 rebels in combat and many more by drowning.

A grand reception followed inside the main hall of the basilica. After several rounds of boisterous toasting to Her Majesty's eternal health, the distinguished guests—high court officials and top commanders—went quiet, as the female sovereign in resplendent attire began to address them in a commanding voice:

I served the late emperor for more than twenty years. His Majesty was constantly in poor health. At his request, I assisted him in running the country. My great concern then was the well-being of all under Heaven. In the meantime, the entire realm was at peace, and you—my senior officials and officers—had become rich and powerful. After His Majesty departed from this world, I have continued to carry out his behest, caring for the people to the point of forgetting the self.

Still, some rose against me—Pei Yan, Li Jingye, and Cheng Wuting, to name a few. And yet, among the leading officials, was there anyone who was more tenacious and unyielding than Pei Yan? Among members of the nobility, who could gather a larger following of desperados than Li Jingye? Among the top military commanders, who was more able to command a large force to win battles than Cheng Wuting? These powerful men with tremendous prestige all wanted to topple me. I fought back and eliminated them all. Let it be known, if you, my officials and my officers, stay loyal to me, you will continue to enjoy wealth and power. Otherwise, the aforementioned three men are your examples.

A suffocating silence descended upon the spacious hall for a few moments until cheers broke out as people in the crowd shouted, "Long live Tianhou!" again and again.

Notes

[1] Grand preceptor of the crown prince (*taizi taishi* 太子太師): one of the three preceptors of the crown prince (*taizi sanshi* 三師) and a highly prestigious appointment.

[2] Yangzhou 揚州 was a prefecture in south Jiangsu.

[3] The investigative censor (*jiancha yushi* 監察御史): *see* note in Part I, Chapter 12.

[4] The assistant prefect (*sima* 司馬) was the lowest ranking member of a prefectural leadership, next to prefect (*cishi*), vice prefect (*biejia*), and *zhangshi* (chief administrator).

[5] Chuzhou 楚州: prefecture in Xuyi, Yancheng, and others, north Jiangsu. Runzhou 潤州: prefecture in Danyang, Zhenjiang, and others, south Jiangsu.

[6] "A fratricide and sororicide, a regicide and matricide": in reference to the killings of her nephews Wu Weiliang and Wu Huaiyun, and of her sister's daughter the state mistress of Wei. She banished her brothers Wu Yuanqing and Wu Yuanshuang to hardship places in Sichuan and Anhui, which quickened their death. There are no records of her getting involved in killing the sovereign (Gaozong) and her own mother (Lady Yang). Thus the charges of her being a "regicide and matricide" are groundless.

[7] The Secretariat drafter (*zhongshu sheren* 中書舍人) was a post of upper middle rank responsible for handling government documents.

[8] *Lunyu* 15.9.

[9] The Xia'e Brook 下阿溪 was in Gaoyou 高郵 (present-day Gaoyou, Jiangsu).

[10] Hailing 海陵: county east of Yangzhou in present-day Taizhou, Jiangsu.

[11] The Dagu Hills 大孤山 were in the middle of Lake Poyang in Hukou 湖口, Jiangxi.

[12] The rebel leader Li Jingye by then had been deprived of the royal surname Li and become Xu Jingye again.

3. Xue Huaiyi (685–687)

In the Middle East, after Caliph Marwan I died, Abd al-Malik succeeded in 685. Under his reign (until 705), peace and prosperity prevailed in the Arab Empire.
In the West, Pepin II of Herstal, father of Charles Martel and mayor of the palace of Austrasia, became the de facto ruler of the Frankish Kingdom (687).

ON A SUMMER day in 685, the head eunuch announced the arrival of the abbot of the White Horse Monastery.[1] Situated in the eastern suburbs, the Buddhist cloister had been built in 68 CE to celebrate the arrival of two Indian monks with the first batch of sutra scrolls from India carried on the back of a white horse. Hence the name. Now it was the most important Buddhist institution at Luoyang.

"I'll be ready in a moment," Tianhou said to the eunuch. She sat at a dressing table as a palace maid was painting her lips.

"How about it, Your Majesty?" asked the maid, stepping back.

Tianhou checked her own face meticulously in a bronze mirror. At sixty-two *sui*, she looked like someone thirty years her junior, with reddish smooth skin and a well-shaped body. Beneath her light crown a tuft of luxurious silver hair added to her seductive charm. She motioned to dismiss the maid and moved towards the door.

As Tianhou entered the waiting hall, the abbot got to his feet.

"I am *very* delighted to see you," she said.

"I, a poor monk, am at Your Majesty's service." He bowed in obeisance.

"Sit down, the Reverend Xue." She took her seat beside him.

The abbot was in his late thirties. His muscular physique and beautiful facial features made him irresistible to many women.

As usual, the abbot stayed for a private dinner with Tianhou, a simple, relaxing meal served with local rice wine. After that, she stepped into her boudoir to freshen up.

She reemerged a few moments later, wearing a revealing red dress that lit up the hall.

"What do you think?" she asked.

"I like the vibrant color, Your Majesty."

"The dress?"

"The lips too."

She stretched out her hand, a smile on her face. He took it as she guided him towards the adjoining room.

***

Strictly speaking, Li Zhe's successor Li Dan (Ruizong), despite his emperor's title, was not even a figurehead. He was never allowed to hold court and his every move was under the close watch of Tianhou's men. The emperor, for his part, knew his place and did everything possible to avoid suspicion.

There was no doubt that Tianhou was the sole ruler of the realm. And yet, she was not content with her role as a de facto Tang emperor and the guardian of the Li house. She had introduced changes to the patriarchal institutions that had dominated the court for thousands of years. She had set up the Wu Ancestral Temple to rival the Li Temple of the Tang. She had appointed someone of the Wu lineage as successor-emperor. And she had eliminated or exiled a large number of the Li princes.

One institution that irked her the most was the Rear Palace, home to the emperor's 200-plus ranked consorts and concubines. To say nothing of the unranked palace ladies and maids, numbering in the thousands. All of them were His Majesty's potential bedmates. At least in theory, this institution of male domination was set up to ensure the continuation of the royal line. Under a female sovereign, all this became moot. But she did not mind having her own male playmates. Even though she had long passed her prime, she could still feel sexual urges and a strong desire for intimacy and companionship with men.

This was where Abbot Xue Huaiyi came in. He was of humble peasant stock with a corny name: Feng Xiaobao (Feng the Little Treasure). He had neither a *jinshi* (Presented Scholar) nor a *mingjing* (Classicist) degree. Nor did he know much about the classics or the great works of literature. But he had taught himself how to read and write. When he was selling medicinal herbs in the Southern Market of Luoyang, his great looks had attracted the attention of a pretty young maid. After she had given up her body to him, they had had frequent sexual encounters. When some subtle changes had begun to show in the maid's voice and gait, her master, Princess Qianjin,[2] the eighteenth daughter of Emperor Gaozu, had taken notice. Although she could have had the maid clubbed to death for fornication, she had not. She had let her go instead, after keeping her lover in custody.

In a time and age where Tianhou was actively going after the princes and princesses of the Li house, Princess Qianjin lived with the fear that she could become a victim any time, and believed that one sure way to protect herself was by exploiting one of Tianhou's weaknesses: her love for good-looking men of much younger age.

The princess then had the herb seller, disguised as a monk, smuggled into the palace, so that Tianhou and he could have their first meeting. Tianhou took an instant liking to him. To show her appreciation for the gift, Tianhou granted the Wu surname to the princess, after adopting her as a daughter.

On Tianhou's orders, Feng Xiaobao had his head shaved bald to become a professional monk and abbot of the White Horse Monastery. He then received a much more respectable given name, Huaiyi, and an aristocratic surname, Xue, from Xue Shao, the husband of Princess Taiping and Tianhou's son-in-law. At Tianhou's insistence, the monk also became Xue Shao's adoptive uncle. This way, Xue Huaiyi had become an honorary member of the nobility.

By conventional standards, Xue Huaiyi was not well educated at all. However, there was no denying that he was a highly ingenuous man. When Tianhou put him in charge of renovating palace structures, there was no objection among the court officials. But the presence of this hunk of a man in the palace grounds did raise some eyebrows.

A strait-laced remonstrator submitted a memorial which said, "In Emperor Taizong's reign, a musician was tasked with teaching palace ladies how to play the pipa. He was castrated to do his job. I would like to propose that Xue Huaiyi be subjected to the same procedure to avoid accidents in the Rear Palace."

It went unheeded. Xue Huaiyi continued to come to the palace to work and have rendezvous with Tianhou.

History is full of examples of powerful women keeping virile men as sex partners. As early as the Qin dynasty, Consort Zhao, the First Emperor's mother, bedded the false eunuch Lao Ai[3] for his sexual prowess. Empress Lü of Han, Liu Bang's wife, carried on an open affair with her butler Shen Yiji.[4] Empress Dowager Feng of the Northern Wei, bereaved of her husband in her twenties, had no less than three handsome high-ranking officials as lovers, including Li Chong,[5] the architect of Northern Wei Luoyang. So what Tianhou did was just tread in the footsteps of these women.

***

As Tianhou continued to shower favors upon Xue Huaiyi, she requested the cruel enforcement officer Suo Yuanli to be his protector and adopt him as his son. Now, with Suo having his back and with Tianhou as his lover, the herb-seller-turned-monk was virtually beyond the law. Even the most powerful of the Wus—Chengsi and Sansi—were in awe of him.

When he traveled, Xue always rode a tall bay horse, escorted by a dozen or so attendants and servants—mostly hooligans he had recruited from the marketplace and tonsured as professional monks. With Xue's connivance, his men often captured pedestrians on the street at random and bloodied their heads with whips for fun. They especially enjoyed roughing up their religious rivals—Daoist adepts, tearing up their robes and shaving off their hair.

For one honest censor named Feng Sixu, Xue Huaiyi and company had gone too far. He requested his impeachment on several occasions. While no action was taken against the accused, Feng Sixu did not have to worry about his own safety. It was so because of a time-honored tradition that regarded the post of censor as sacrosanct. Its holder was given the rare privilege to impeach any high-ranking officials and even criticize the throne with immunity. This had always been the case until one late afternoon when Feng was riding home through Luoyang's neighborhoods. A rabble of hooligans swarmed around him, pushed him off his horse, tackled him to the ground, and bludgeoned him. He narrowly escaped death, only after two passers-by saw him lying unconscious in an alleyway and rushed him to a doctor's for treatment.

***

At the advanced age of seventy-nine *sui*, Left Chancellor Su Liangsi insisted on coming to work on a regular basis. One morning, as he was shuffling with the help of two aides towards the Southern Office area, all senior officials who met him along the way hastened to bow in courtesy, out of respect for his rank, age, and seniority.

In the Audience Hall, Su came face to face with the bald-headed Xue Huaiyi, and bowed his head in obeisance. The abbot did not deign to look in his direction.

"Who is this arrogant baldhead?" Su Liangsi shouted.

"Old Bastard! Is that the way to address your daddy?" Xue Huaiyi was as impertinent as ever.

"How . . . how dare you?" Chancellor Su gasped in anger, his hands shaking.

"Did I do anything wrong?"

"Court etiquette requires lower-ranking officials to bow to the court leaders."

"I for one do not buy into that shit," shouted Xue Huaiyi, grimacing.

"Attendants!" rasped the chancellor hoarsely. "Teach him a lesson."

About half a dozen men jumped on the monk and seized hold of his arms and shoulders. A musclebound man slapped him no less than nine times before letting him go.

***

In the late afternoon, the Reverend Xue had a scheduled meeting with Tianhou. The first thing she noticed were the bluish stripes on his face. The moment she asked about them, he broke into sobs as he told her how Chancellor Su's men had roughed him up.

Tianhou heaved a deep sigh and said, "Why did you want to hang out in the Southern Office in the first place? This is where the formal chief ministers gather. You don't belong there. Don't you understand?"

The monk nodded his head and stopped sobbing.

"There is something else I want to ask you," Tianhou continued. "Why did Censor Feng Sixu get beaten?"

"I . . . I do not . . ."

"Don't tell me it was not done by your minions," Tianhou cut him off sharply. "Don't you know that the body of the censor is inviolable? Whatever you do, don't touch the censors! Otherwise, even I won't be able to protect you."

The monk fell quiet.

***

Outside the south main entrance to the Imperial City, an enclosed kiosk popped up one morning in the summer of 686. Inside, one saw a heavy bronze chest installed at the center. It served as a receptacle for suggestions from the populace. In the top of this heavy metal box, there were four slots facing the four cardinal directions. The eastern one bore the label "Panegyric" (for pieces singing praises to Tianhou); the western one, "Injustice" (for complaints and grievances against officials); the northern one, "Occult" (for reports on disastrous astrological signs and military intelligence); and the southern one, "Remonstrances" (for criticisms of court policies and policy suggestions).

At first blush, the Bronze Chest seemed intended as a way to gather four different types of information from the masses. But its main purpose was to serve as the medium through which secret, oftentimes anonymous, accusations reached Tianhou's table unhindered. It had thus become de facto her "accusation letter box." It would also function as a tool for helping Tianhou hunt down undesirable elements in society, especially pro-Li royalists.

If an informer was willing to come forward, Tianhou would provide him gratis with the use of relay horses and delicious meals befitting officials of Rank 5,[6] including rice, wheat foods, wine, mutton, melons, fermented soybeans, edible salt, green onion, ginger, and sunflower seeds. Once in Luoyang, he would be housed in a government guesthouse and even given an audience with Tianhou. It did not matter if he was a low-born peasant or woodcutter. If Tianhou liked what she heard, she would appoint him to an official post without regard for rules and regulations. If an accusation turned out to be false, she would not fault the accuser.

But this policy was not sustainable. There were simply too many freeloaders who cost the court dearly. And cost was not the only concern. Doubtless, there were those who had vital information to share with her. But there were many more who were false accusers.

***

To keep the war on her opponents going, Tianhou relied on the so-called Legalist[7] law officers. They would do her bidding no matter what, going after members of the Li house and their followers. People in the street and high-powered court officials alike stood in fear of them.

Among these, three stood out as the most effective. The first one was the aforementioned Suo Yuanli, a man in his fifties with a hooked nose and deep-set eyes. At first glance, he could be taken for a Sogdian merchant from Central Asia. After his first meeting with Tianhou, he was granted the prestige title[8] of guerilla general,[9] which was exclusively reserved for entry-level prosecutors, and was charged with the task of interrogating suspects.

Suo and his associates invented a slew of imaginative methods for extracting confessions with such telling names as "Blood Vessel Fixer," "Suffocater," "Growler," "Instant Confessor," "Out-of-Wits," "Same as Rebellion," "Rebellion as Fact," "Worries of a Dying Pig," "Plea for Death," and "Plea for Ruining the Family." Using these methods, he had little trouble forcing an accused to fess up and implicate dozens of others. Because of his ingenuity and great success as interrogator, he was granted many audiences with Tianhou, who showered him with material rewards and honors.

One of the cases that made Suo famous concerned Yu Baojia, the inventor of the Bronze Chest. Through a twist of fate, Yu fell victim to his own invention. He was denounced by an anonymous letter as a weapon-maker for the rebel Li Jingye.

Suo Yuanli interrogated him, but Yu refused to own up to his crime under torture. Suo then had his new gadget brought out—an iron head cage equipped with sharp bamboo spikes pointing inwards. As he was about to jam the device on his head, Yu caved and gave a self-incriminating confession. That allowed Suo to have him condemned and beheaded.

The remaining two members of the triad were Vice President of the Board of Justice Zhou Xing and Vice Censor-in-Chief Lai Junchen. They rose to prominence later than Suo but obtained higher ranks. They were not merely the ruler's henchmen who hunted down her enemies and roughed them up but members of the law enforcement elite.

Zhou Xing was known for his brutal interrogation methods. It had earned him the epithet "Oxhead." Numerous people had lodged complaints against him. He responded in defiance, "When you ask defendants if they have been wronged, all will say yes. But there is no need to worry. They will shut up after their execution." He then wrote down these words on a piece of paper and had it posted on his office door.

Lai Junchen, the third one of the triad, was known for his cruel streak even as a boy and became an active informer as a young adult. Once caught in a theft, he was punished with a flogging of 100 blows on orders from the local prefect Prince Li Ji.[10] Later, when Li Ji was in trouble with Tianhou, Lai trumped up a charge of rebellion against him, sending him to the gallows. As his reward, Lai was allowed to have an audience with Tianhou and got hired on the spot.

With the Bronze Chest set up to encourage snitching, and with the Legalist law officers actively going after Tianhou's enemies and detractors, imagined and real, a Reign of Terror had descended on Luoyang and the provinces.

***

Since the Li Jingye War, General-in-Chief Heichi Changzhi had been the top commander of the northern defense forces against the Tujue. No one in the military could rival him in the art of war and the number of enemies slain and captured. Tianhou had granted him a most distinguished enfeoffment title, the state duke of Yan.

This giant of a man with handsome features had already been a formidable military leader when he was in the service of the Paekche court. Under the Tang, he had been mentored by Liu Rengui and Pei Xingjian, and risen to the top of the military after the death of his mentors. A master of surprise attacks, he was very effective at raiding enemy camps at night. He treated his officers and rank and file like family, always sharing war spoils with them, while showing no interest in amassing personal wealth at all. No wonder those fighting under his command were often willing to risk their lives for him.

In the battle of the Ordos in 686,[11] General Heichi, leading a troop of 200 cavalry, had an encounter with 3,000 Tujue riders. Just as the Tujue men dismounted to put on armor, he struck and scattered them.

One night not long afterwards, Heichi received intelligence that a massive Tujue attack was imminent. He ordered to have many campfires lit inside and outside his camp. That trick must have sown doubt in the heads of the Tujue commanders, and as a result, the planned attack did not take place after all.

When the Tujue mounted a major invasion in the seventh month of 687, it was Heichi Changzhi, with General Li Duozuo as his lieutenant, who trounced them at Huanghuadui, Shuozhou.[12]

In the tenth month, one of Heichi's subordinate generals, Cuan

Baobi,[13] led a cavalry of 13,000 men to give chase to a recently defeated enemy army. In his headlong rush across the vast Tujue territory, Cuan did not wait for Heichi's reinforcements and must have been driven by a desire to claim sole credit for the victory. As his advance troops were closing in on the enemy, he sent out envoys to ask for battle. Although in so doing he gave away the element of surprise, something tabooed in Sunzi's *Art of War*, he could not care less, because he enjoyed momentum, high morale, and strength in numbers.

It was then that the Tujue khan Gudulu saw his chance and made a surprise countercharge and routed the Tang army.

The defeat was so thorough that General Cuan was the only one to make it back to the headquarters camp.

An irate Tianhou had him executed for his monumental failure, and censured General Heichi Changzhi as his superior. She vowed to seek revenge, but her action for now was only limited to changing the name of Gudulu to Buzulu (Eventually Without Pay).[14]

Notes

1 The White Horse Monastery (Baima si 白馬寺) east of Tang Luoyang was the first officially built monastery in China on record.

2 Princess Qianjin 千金公主.

3 The story of Consort Zhao 趙姬 (280–228 BCE) and Lao Ai 嫪毐 (–238 BCE) is recorded in Sima Qian's *Shiji*. Its authenticity is doubted by some modern scholars. But that is open to debate. See *Shiji* 6.

4 Shen Yiji 審食其.

5 Li Chong 李沖 (450–498) became rich thanks to Empress Dowager Feng's largesse. The other two famous lovers were Li Yi 李弈 (–470) and Wang Rui 王叡 (434–481).

6 *See* "ranks" in Glossary.

[7] Legalism can be traced to the Warring States period. It is a philosophy that stresses the paramount importance of law and punishment and absolute loyalty to the sovereign.

[8] *See* "prestige title" in Glossary.

[9] *Youji jiangjun* 遊擊將軍.

[10] Li Ji 李績 (d. 689): grandson of Taizong.

[11] The Ordos primarily refers to the area within the great loop of the Yellow River in present-day south Inner Mongolia, Shaanxi, Ningxia, and others.

[12] Huanghuadui 黄花堆 (Huangguadui 黄瓜堆) in Shuozhou 朔州 was northwest of Yingxian, Shanxi.

[13] Cuan Baobi 爨寶壁.

[14] Buzulu 不卒祿.

4. Mingtang (688–689)

AN AGE-OLD TRADITION required that the capital should be equipped with a host of national ritual centers, most of which were located in the suburbs. In the city proper, two ritual centers were of paramount significance: the Ancestral Temple (*zongmiao*) and the Altars of the Soil and Grain (*sheji*). The former was dedicated to the royal ancestors, the guardians of the dynasty. The latter symbolized all the lands within the empire and their bounty. Since ancient times, it had been the standard practice to set up only one set of these urban ritual centers in the capital.

After she had made Luoyang her permanent home, Tianhou threw this tradition out the window, because it stood in her way. She ignored it when she established two more ancestral temples: one for the Tang ancestors in Luoyang (on the same level with the Ancestral Temple in Chang'an); and the other called the Temple of Ancestral Worship[1] for the Wu ancestors in Chang'an. Thus, on her watch, there were three national Ancestral Temples active at the same time, if the one at Wenshui was not counted.[2]

The more controversial ritual structure Tianhou set up inside the city of Luoyang was the Mingtang (Hall of Brilliance or Bright Hall), which had existed in far antiquity and the Han dynasty. The *Rites of Zhou* records its specifications but says practically nothing about its ritual functions. The *Annals of Lü Buwei* and the *Elder Dai Record of Rites*[3] address various aspects of the Mingtang and differ on the number of chambers it should have. During the Sui dynasty and the first two reigns of the Tang, Confucian scholars had debated about its layout, size, and location. They had never reached a consensus.

Tianhou, for her part, regarded it as a ritual center of the highest order, and was determined to have it built. Since she was not interested in the endless academic bickering among the Confucian curmudgeons, she turned to the much younger Northern Gate academicians. After a careful study of the ancient ritual sources, they came up with a Mingtang plan and a suggestion for its location: three to seven *li* south of the Divine Capital.

To that Tianhou responded, squinting her eyes, "That means that each time I conduct a ritual, I have to make a long trip: traveling south across the Palace City and through dozens of residential wards to reach the southern suburbs. A large area of the city proper has to be cordoned off for the passage of my procession. What a hassle for my subjects and me!"

A scholar replied, "Your Majesty, the trouble is if the ritual structure is located in the wrong place, it will not work."

"Really? I disagree. The location you and your colleagues proposed is at best based on guesswork."

In the end she chose a site herself: the prime spot of the Palace City. The only problem was that it was already occupied by the principal palatial structure, the Qianyuan Basilica, the tallest and the most expansive building in the country, which served as the venue for a host of important ritual activities, including the great state ceremonies for the New Year's Day and the Winter Solstice, and the periodic assemblies of court and capital officials to pay homage to the emperor.

But, once she made up her mind, nothing could stop her.

She named Abbot Xue Huaiyi as project manager, not for his expertise in architecture but for his loyalty to the sovereign. Under his leadership, a team of architects and laborers numbering in the tens of thousands tore down the old basilica, leveled the ground, and began to erect the new structure in early 688.

***

Meanwhile, an auspicious event unfolded nearby. A Luoyang resident discovered by chance in the legendary Luo River a granite slab bearing an enigmatic diagram and eight characters in purple, meaning, "When the Holy Mother is reigning over the masses, the imperial cause will be eternal." He immediately presented it along with a memorial to the court. Tianhou was delighted with the implication that the female ruler was in favor with Heaven. She gave the discoverer a hefty reward and renamed the artifact the *Treasured Chart* (*Baotu*). It harkens back to the famous *River Chart* (*Hetu*)[4] documented in the ancient sources. Later she gave it an even more prestigious name, the *Holy Chart from Heaven* (*Tianshou shengtu*).[5] It was in response to the discovery of the

Holy Chart that Tianhou took on the title of Holy Mother and Divine Sovereign (Shengmu Shenhuang).[6]

To celebrate the divine revelation from the Luo, Tianhou planned to make a ceremonial trip to the river. According to her published schedule, on the day of her visit, she would preside over a grand ceremony to pay homage to the river; travel to the Southern Suburban Alter to make a sacrifice to the Lord on High;[7] and upon return to the palace, give a grand reception to the court officials at the Mingtang. A Tianhou's decree was issued to the effect that, ten days prior to the scheduled event, area commanders (*dudu*), prefects, royals, and consort relatives should arrive in the Divine Capital to take part in the ceremony and the Mingtang reception.

***

When the Li Jingye War broke out a few years back, hopes were raised among loyalists that power would be restored to the Li house. However, at that point, none of the surviving Li princes was willing to risk an open break with the court by siding with Li Jingye. And his rebel army crumbled.

With the Mingtang project underway in 688, things seemed to have changed. As soon as Tianhou's decree reached the princes, a rumor began to circulate among them that the *Holy Chart* on the granite slab was a fraud and the Mingtang reception was a trap to ensnare the royals. It struck fear into the hearts of the princes. Li Yuanjia (prefect of Jiangzhou)[8] and Li Lingkui (prefect of Xingzhou),[9] both Emperor Taizong's brothers, were likely the first to fall. Both had been slated for elimination. It had not happened thanks to strong opposition from the court leadership. Now that was no longer possible.

Taizong's less prominent brothers—Li Yuangui (prefect of Qingzhou), Li Zhen (prefect of Yuzhou), and Li Shen (prefect of Beizhou)[10]—were gravely concerned. If Yuanjia and Lingkui fell, it was almost certain that the lesser princes would too.

Li Yuanjia's son Prince Li Zhuan, prefect of Tongzhou,[11] who was on sojourn in Luoyang, was the first royal to take action. He forged a letter by the emperor Li Dan to plea for help and forwarded it to Li Chong, Li Zhen's eldest son and prefect of Bozhou.[12]

Now in his forties, Li Chong was one of the bravest of the princes. The letter riled him up so much that he could not have a moment's rest the whole night through. The emperor's voice kept ringing in his ears, "I am now in virtual custody. I am imploring you, the princes, to come to my rescue with an army." The next morning, he forged an imperial letter himself. He made several copies of it and had them sent out to the royals. In this letter he warned through the emperor's voice that "Tianhou is now planning to eliminate all the Lis," in the hope of stirring them up to rebellion.

In the eighth month, when the day set for coordinated action arrived, Prince Li Chong was the only one who took up arms, leading 5,000 men from Bozhou (near Liaocheng, Shandong) to fall on the county seat of Wushui to the southwest.[13] While laying siege to the town, the rebels dumped stacks of straw outside the southern gate, and set them ablaze. Flames soon engulfed the gatetower until, without warning, the wind changed directions and started blowing south, killing dozens of rebel attackers and scattering the rest. Li Chong then beat a hasty retreat, with several dozens of his servants, back to Bozhou, where outside a city gate, he fell to an arrow.

***

By the time Commander-in-Chief Qiu Shenji with a large government force arrived in Bozhou, where Li Chong had called home, the rebellion had been squelched. Bozhou officers and officials, dressed in white, came out to welcome the general. Qiu's men rounded them up along with their families before killing them all. They then went on to ravage the city, wrecking more than one thousand homes.

***

Not long after the start of the Li Chong Rebellion, his father Prince Li Zhen based in Yuzhou (in Henan) sent out his envoys to the royals, with a request to rise up against Tianhou's tyranny. He felt encouraged when he received some positive responses. One of them was from Grand Princess Changle, sister of Taizong, wife of Zhao Gui, prefect of Shouzhou.[14] She said, "In the past, when General Yuchi Jiong[15] realized that Yang Jian of Sui had designs on the Northern Zhou throne, he started a rebellion. Although only a nephew to the Zhou emperor, he nonetheless raised an army to save the dynasty. Even though he didn't succeed, he set an example for all of us. Today, the Li house is in mortal danger. The princes—the sons of Gaozu and brothers of Taizong—must join the cause without hesitation. As Tianhou is stepping up the purge of the royals, we are probably all doomed. But, if we have to go down, let us go down fighting!"

A few days later, Li Zhen declared his own rebellion, in the hope of drumming up support for the cause and taking the pressure off his son. But, in the end, the actions promised by the other princes did not take place. It was obvious that they had gotten cold feet in the last moment. After Li Zhen learned of his son Li Chong's defeat, he decided to go all the way. At Shangcai,[16] a key county on the Central Plain, he cobbled together a ragtag army of 5,000 men, while forcing 500 officials to put their life on the line for him. At his request, the rebels all wore talismans for protection, while Buddhist monks and Daoist adepts were on site to recite sutras and scriptures aloud to shield them from harm.

The arrival of the expeditionary army led by Qu Chongyu[17] in the eastern suburbs caught Li Zhen unprepared. When his son Li Gui's effort to check the advance of Qu's troops failed, Shangcai soon came under siege. By the third week, morale among the rebels had all but vanished.

General Qu, escorted by a dozen riders, rode to the edge of the moat outside a town gate. One of his men shouted out a message to the defenders on the wall: "Prince Li Zhen, do you want to surrender now or get captured and killed in a humiliating way?"

That night, Qu's men stormed the gates and poured into the town. Their vanguard troops broke into the magistrate's compound and found the corpses of Prince Li Zhen and his lieutenant and Li Gui, as well as their wives. They had taken their lives rather than surrender.

General Qu had the severed heads of the rebel leaders transported posthaste to Luoyang, where they were put on display hanging from the tall watchtower outside the End Gate (Duanmen), the southern main entrance to the Imperial City.

A campaign soon followed to root out the followers and sympathizers of the rebels. On Tianhou's orders, Investigative Censor Su Xiang was tasked with reviewing the cases of those princes exposed as accomplices. After he failed to produce a report days later, Tianhou summoned him to the palace for questioning. When she heard from the censor that the evidence against the princes was not convincing, she shook her head in disappointment and said, "Well, perhaps this job is not suitable for a gentleman like you. I am taking you off the case." Then she sent him to a post in faraway Hexi (in mostly Gansu) in the northwest.

As Su Xiang's replacement, Vice President of the Board of Justice Zhou Xing wasted no time in sending his men after the royals. They arrested Princes Li Yuanjia, Li Lingkui, and Li Zhuan (Yuanjia's son), and Princess Changle, and raided their homes. Convictions and sentences soon followed. With Tianhou's approval, all died by their own hands in a Luoyang jail. Their next of kin, friends, and associates, and officials and clerks working under them were all executed.

In the months that followed until late 689, Tianhou's henchmen continued their campaign against Li Zhen's intimates. It was as thoroughgoing as it was merciless. Notable among those implicated were the Xues of Hedong. Their most distinguished member Xue Shao was none other than Tianhou's son-in-law and the husband of Princess Taiping. He and his brothers were arrested for their close association with the rebel leader and subsequently put to the sword.

Prince Li Yuangui (prefect of Qingzhou), sixty-seven *sui*, was condemned as Li Zhen's co-conspirator and banished with his son Li Xu[18] to Qianzhou (in Chongqing). Old and frail, he had a hard time coping with the bumpy ride in an open prison-cart and perished en route.

Prince Li Shen (prefect of Beizhou), around sixty, was the only brother of Taizong's who had opposed the rebellion at the outset. He was banished anyway and died before reaching the destination in the far south. Two years later, five of his sons would die by the sword.[19]

When Li Shen's filial daughter Li Chuyuan[20] heard of her father's death, she became inconsolable and lost her voice for weeks because of wailing. Thereafter she stopped primping herself for a good twenty years.

On Tianhou's orders, the surname of those royals tainted by the rebellion was changed to Hui (Viper).[21]

***

In the wake of the rebellion, Left Vice Chancellor Di Renjie was appointed prefect of Yuzhou, Li Zhen's home base, with the mission to pacify the local populace. In his first week on the job, he found the situation on the ground troubling. Previously, some officials from the Court of Judicial Review,[22] under the guidance of the Legalist policy, had done much to clean up this rebels' den, condemning two thousand local men to death—the so-called followers of Li Zhen and their close relatives—and punishing five thousand men with the forfeiture of their family assets.

The more Di Renjie examined the cases, the more it became clear that the prosecutors had gone too far. He paid a visit to the prefectural prison and found that those on death row were farmers, traders, Buddhist monks, and Daoist adepts, just like ordinary subjects one might encounter in a street or marketplace. They were crowded together like cattle, wearing heavy shackles and cangues day and night.

Di balled his clammy hand into a fist and slammed it against the wall as he barked out an order to have these restraining devices removed immediately. At night, he wrote a secret memorial to Tianhou, asking for leniency, and submitted it through a court courier the following morning.

It said, "Keeping silent on crucial facts one is aware of runs counter to the spirit of compassion, the essence of Buddhism, in which Your Majesty believes. Having read the files of the condemned criminals and met them in prison in person, I have come to the conclusion that, in the last analysis, these people under sentence, guilty as they are, are not evil by nature. Many of them were simply misled or forced by threat of death to join the rebels. . . ."

A few weeks later, Di received a decree from Tianhou. It commuted the death sentence of those poor folks to banishment to the northern border area in Fengzhou.[23]

***

After the prisoners were let out of jail, they were on their way. When they stopped by a village in Ningzhou,[24] they learned from the villagers what Prefect Di had done for the locals before he was transferred to Luoyang and it was his effort that had saved the condemned prisoners from the gallows.

With the locals leading the way, the prisoners paid an homage to a rare artifact: the "Stela of Good Government" dedicated to Prefect Di. In front of the tall stone monument, the prisoners fell on their knees, making sacrifices while crying their hearts out. They went on ritual fasting for three days to express their gratitude before moving on.

Upon arrival in their place of banishment, they set up another stela in honor of their savior. Thus, Di Renjie became the only court official in the entire realm to have two stelae dedicated to him while still alive.

***

On January 21, 689, a grand ceremony was in progress south of the End Gate of Luoyang. A makeshift stepped altar was set up for the occasion in the square outside the gate, the southern main entrance to the Imperial City.

Tianhou arrived, accompanied by the emperor Li Dan, Crown Prince Li Chengqi (Li Dan's eldest son), and senior officials and officers, as well as tribal chieftains of Tujue, Tubo, Uighur, and others. In front of the altar, rare birds and exotic beasts were on display and, in an unprecedented show of wealth, a rich variety of treasures were arrayed: strings of pearls, gold and silver hairpins, necklaces and bracelets, and other *objets d'art* inlaid with gemstones—rubies, diamonds, carnelian beads, lapis lazuli stones.

After Tianhou and her followers made sacrifices at the altar, they went down to the bank of the Luo, the river running from west to east through the city proper of Luoyang. The discovery of the granite slab, the *Holy Chart*, was then reenacted. After it revealed itself in the river, the ritual officials hauled it ashore and "transmitted" it to Tianhou sitting under a canopy.[25]

Several months later, Tianhou heard a rumor that the sacred artifact had been forged by her nephew Wu Chengsi. If proven, it would make him liable for the crime of *lèse majesté*. But Tianhou chose to look the other way, thinking, *If it advances the cause of justice, even if it is forged, what does it matter?*

***

On the old site of the Qianyuan Basilica, the building of the Mingtang (Hall of Brilliance) continued under the direction of the project manager Xue Huaiyi, and was brought to completion in early 689.

On the day of its inauguration, Tianhou appeared in person to host the grand ceremony. She could not help being impressed by the spectacular view of the new structure. With an imposing height of 300 *chi* (feet), this three-story building measured 300 *chi* at each of the four sides. It had a circular roof ornamented with pearls; resting on nine coiling dragons, it was symbolic of Heaven. On the rooftop was mounted an iron phoenix ten *chi* in height decorated with gold.

Stepping inside the spacious hall, Tianhou was dumbfounded by the wooden column ten fathoms (*wei*) in circumference that rose from floor to roof interior at the center, and delighted to notice that beams, purlins, and rafters were all in *nanmu*. Going in and out, she felt dazzled by the contrast between the dark green of the interior wall and the bright red and white of the exterior wall. As she toured the ground level, she was intrigued by the miniature iron canal circling around the central building and learned from Xue that it symbolized the Biyong[26] (Jade Disc Moat), another ancient ritual structure, where ritual music was performed and moral teaching enunciated.

Tianhou felt so inspired by the visit that she gave the Mingtang another name—the Divine Palace of Myriad Images.[27]

Despite its mind-boggling façade and enormous dimensions, some scholars found the building gaudy and grandiose with a touch of vulgarity. It nonetheless stood as a testimonial to the bold vision of its initiator and the architectural ingenuity of its builder, Xue Huaiyi.

On the heels of the Mingtang project, Xue Huaiyi was given

another most important task: to build a Buddha statue of great height and have it set up on the central axis north of the Mingtang. Workmen under Xue's management first sculpted the statue in clay, and then wrapped it with layers of painted ramie cloth, before giving its surface several coatings of lacquer. When completed, it was the tallest statue in the realm. A little toe had room for several adult men. To house the statue, a tall structure called the "Hall of Heaven" was erected. It stood like a supersized pavilion with carved columns, upturned roofs, finely finished edgings, and latticed windows.

When the Hall of Heaven was completed, Tianhou was so pleased that she appointed its builder Xue Huaiyi general-in-chief of the Left Guard[28] while granting him another enfeoffment title: the state duke of Liang.[29]

***

On the first day of the standard month (January 27, 689), for the first time, the annual Grand Sacrifice took place at the Divine Palace aka the Mingtang. Donning the imperial ritual regalia, Tianhou herself served as the initial sacrificer. With a *dagui* (large jade tablet) tucked in her waistband, she held a *zhengui* (anchor jade tablet)[30] in both hands. Following her at a distance were the emperor Li Dan as the second sacrificer and Crown Prince Li Chengqi as the last sacrificer. They knelt down and made sacrifices by turns to the spirit tablets of the Lord on High, Gaozu (Li Yuan), Taizong (Li Shimin), Gaozong (Li Zhi), and the First King of Wei (Wu Shiyue, Tianhou's father). They then made offerings to the Five Directional Heavenly Emperors.[31] Thereafter, Tianhou proceeded south to the Zetian Gate, the main southern entrance to the palace, and mounted the upper level of the gatetower to announce a general amnesty and the change of the reign title to Yongchang (Eternal Prosperity).

Two days later, she graced the Mingtang with another visit. Seated in her throne on the dais of the main hall, she received felicitations from the court officials and officers. It was followed by a celebration lasting two days, which ended in an elaborate banquet Tianhou hosted to regale her officials and officers.

Notes

1 The Temple of Ancestral Worship (*chongxian miao* 崇先廟).

2 Later she would move the Altars of the Soil and Grain from Chang'an to the western part of the Imperial City in Luoyang. *See* Part II, Chapter 6; *Tang liangjing chengfang kao* 5.139, 太社.

3 The *Annals of Lü Buwei* (*Lüshi chunqiu* 呂氏春秋) was compiled under the auspices of the Qin chancellor Lü Buwei during the late Warring States period. The *Elder Dai Record of Rites* (*Da Dai Liji* 大戴禮記) is a collection of pieces on ritual by Spring and Autumn and Warring States scholars edited by Dai De 戴德 (W. Han).

4 The *Baotu* 寶圖 (*Treasured Chart*). The *Hetu* 河圖 (*River Chart*) allegedly emerged from the Yellow River in predynastic times.

5 The *Holy Chart from Heaven* (*Tianshou shengtu* 天授聖圖).

6 The Holy Mother and Divine Sovereign (Shengmu Shenhuang 聖母神皇).

7 The Lord on High (Haotian Shangdi 昊天上帝): the god of Heaven and the highest deity in the national pantheon.

8 Jiangzhou 絳州: prefecture in south Shanxi.

9 Xingzhou 邢州: prefecture in south Hebei.

10 Qingzhou 青州: prefecture in Shandong. Yuzhou 豫州: prefecture in Henan. Beizhou 貝州: prefecture in south Hebei and Shandong.

11 Tongzhou 通州: prefecture in northeast Sichuan.

[12] Bozhou 博州: prefecture in west central Shandong with its seat near Liaocheng.

[13] Wushui 武水 was southwest of Liaocheng, Shandong.

[14] Zhao Gui 趙瓌 (–688). Shouzhou 壽州: prefecture in south Anhui.

[15] Yuchi Jiong 尉遲迥 (516–580) started a rebellion against the usurper Yang Jian 楊堅 to save the Northern Zhou.

[16] Shangcai 上蔡 was in southeast Henan.

[17] Qu Chongyu 麴崇裕 was a member of the ex-royal family of Gaochang and Tianhou's favorite.

[18] Li Xu 李緒.

[19] *Jiu Tang shu* 76, 李慎傳. Cf. *Zizhi tongjian* 204.6458.

[20] Li Chuyuan 李楚媛.

[21] Hui 虺.

[22] The Court of Judicial Review (*dali si* 大理寺) was one of the Nine Courts.

[23] Fengzhou 豐州: prefecture in Baotou and others, Inner Mongolia.

[24] Ningzhou 寧州: prefecture in Ningxian and Zhengning, northeast Gansu.

[25] *Zizhi tongjian* 204.6454.

[26] Biyong 辟雍.

[27] *Wanxiang shengong* 萬象神宮.

[28] The Left Guard (*zuowei* 左衛) was one of the Sixteen Guards.

[29] *See* "duke" in Glossary.

[30] *Dagui* 大圭: a long jade tablet with a pointed top. *Zhengui* 鎮圭: a jade tablet slightly longer than a foot.

[31] The Five Directional Heavenly Emperors (*wufang tiandi* 五方天帝): they represent the five directions—east, west, south, north, and center. Normally, they were worshipped in their own ritual centers in the suburbs of the capital.

5. Legalist Law Officers (689–690)

AFTER HEICHI CHANGZHI'S transfer to the northern frontier, the western frontier was badly in need of a top general to fend off Tubo raids. That task eventually fell on the shoulders of Right Chancellor and Chief Minister Wei Daijia, now appointed commander-in-chief of the Anxi District Expeditionary Army. At that time, Wei was also president of the Board of Personnel, the most important one of the Six Boards. Coming from a first-rate aristocratic family, Wei had risen to power and fame as a general. He felt uncomfortable as chief minister and had requested on several occasions a transfer back to the military without success. He welcomed this new appointment as a nice break.

In the seventh month of 689, while marching along the northern edge of the Tarim Basin, his army had an unexpected encounter with the enemy near the Yinshijia River[1] and was trounced. It was then hit by an unseasonable snowstorm when it turned icy cold in a few hours. Much of the baggage train that carried clothing and provisions was lost. Countless Tang soldiers died of cold and hunger. General Wei was forced to pull his army out of the Western Regions into neighboring Shazhou[2] to the east.

A few days later, when Tianhou read a report on the military disaster and the loss of the Western Regions to Tubo, she felt a sudden rush of blood to her head and meted out punishments for the commanders: Wei Daijia would be disenrolled and banished to Xiuzhou[3] in the far south; and his lieutenant would face the gallows.

Tianhou could have mobilized her troops for another expedition against Tubo. But after much pondering she resisted the urge. First, she realized that the central government's coffers were running low and a military operation on a massive scale in a faraway place was too costly. Second, good generals familiar with the area were few and far between. Third, she needed to focus more on the Tujue in the north; the threat they posed was far more direct and dangerous. Fourth, which was the most important, she was planning on a thorough overhaul of the government, which would bring about earth-shaking changes to the regime; and she needed all the resources she could get. So she accepted the status quo in the Western Regions as a new normal.

***

One summer afternoon, as General Heichi Changzhi was fast asleep on a thick straw mattress in his campaign tent on the northern border, he felt a jerk of his shoulder, opened his eyes, and found himself surrounded by a group of armed men in black, weapons in hands. As he was thinking how to pull his sword from under the pillow, a middle-aged official came over. From the red robe he wore and the gold-colored pouch he carried at his waist, Heichi realized he was dealing with a high-ranking official sent by the court. After the man showed him an official document bearing the seal of the Board of Justice, Heichi let himself be taken into custody without a struggle.

He was in the dark about the reason for his arrest until he found himself face-to-face with his interrogator Vice President of the Board Zhou Xing in a Luoyang prison. His jaws dropped when he heard Zhou announce his crime—colluding with a certain General Zhao Huaijie[4] in plotting rebellion. The proud officer of Paekche descent refused to confess, even when subject to all sorts of torture at the hands of Zhou's henchmen. He clung to hope that Tianhou would come to his rescue—only recently had she lauded him as the bulwark of defense against the Tujue. When the tenth month of 689 came and he still heard nothing from her, he broke in despair and hanged himself in his prison cell.

When Tianhou first learned of the case, she was suspicious, but did not intervene because she would rather err on the side of caution. She could not afford, she believed, to allow the most powerful general accused of disloyalty to remain at large. With Heichi gone, Tianhou started looking for his replacement and did not go very far before she set her sights on the "right man," the Reverend Xue.

The choice might be surprising to many top officials and officers. However, with the successful Mingtang project under his belt, the Reverend Xue was ready for some military adventure. With Tianhou having his back, he was appointed commander-in-chief of the Xinping District Expeditionary Army[5] and charged with leading the fight against the Tujue. He then marched a massive army north as far as the Purple River.[6] Having encountered no enemy, he had a panegyric on his exploits inscribed on a cliff face and returned. Upon his return to Luoyang, Tianhou rewarded him with another accolade.

***

Meanwhile, the effort to exterminate the royals of the Li house in the wake of the Li Chong-Li Zhen rebellion continued without letup. In the fourth month of 689, a wave of raids was carried out against less prominent princes in places as far apart as Lianzhou and Chenzhou.[7] Twelve of them were executed, their families banished, all because of their perceived threat to Tianhou's rule. Obviously, the recent general amnesty did not apply to them. In the ninth month, six more went to the gallows, and six others were sent in exile to the far south.

The relentless ongoing campaign to weed out the Tang royals and loyalists disloyal to Tianhou was sustained by a culture of informers, where lowborn commoners were able to rise to prominence. Hou Sizhi, for example, had been a flat-cake seller before he was hired by a guerrilla general as his manservant. That gave him access to his first legal cases. In 690, when a clerk was punished with flogging for offending his boss Prefect Pei Zhen, Hou encouraged the clerk to inform against him. Although Hou was as unlearned as the next person, he was smart enough to suggest that the clerk tie Prefect Pei Zhen to a disgraced royal. So the clerk, relying on the flimsiest of evidence, filed an accusation against Pei Zhen for plotting rebellion with Prince Li Yuanming (Gaozu's son). After General Qiu Shenji took over the case, he had both condemned and executed.

Tianhou took notice of Hou Sizhi's "talent," promoted him from nobody to guerrilla general, and granted him an audience.

"I heard you want to be an attendant censor?"[8] she asked.

"Yes, Your Majesty," Hou answered.

"But that is a court-appointed position with many very important responsibilities. You are a total illiterate. How can you read cases?"

"It is true I do not read, Your Majesty, but neither does the unicorn. Still, it butts its horn against the evil and disloyal. I want to be Your Majesty's unicorn."

Tianhou chuckled. While she could not bring herself to like this vicious-looking man, she made the appointment he requested anyway. At this critical juncture, she needed people like Hou who would fight for her under any circumstances.

A few weeks later, Hou's great performance at work came to her attention again. She rewarded him with a nice house confiscated from a rebel leader.

"I am very sorry, Your Majesty, but I cannot take it," Hou Sizhi responded. "I do not want to live in this house, because it used to belong to a rebel leader. I despise rebels."

Tianhou was impressed with his intense hatred of evil and granted his wish.

***

Among Hou Sizhi's colleagues, Wang Hongyi stood out as having a particularly checkered past. When still a little-known young village boy, he was already a troublemaker. One summer, when his request to taste a melon from his neighbor's garden was rejected, he reported to the county authorities on the sighting of a white rabbit near the neighbor's house. The county immediately sent dozens of men to search for it. While they were at it, they trampled the melon crop. No complaint could be filed against them since they were from the government, looking for an auspicious animal for Tianhou. Later, when Wang became a law officer, people called him behind his back the "White Rabbit Censor," because of this incident.

On another occasion, while passing through a village in Zhaozhou,[9] Wang saw some villagers busy preparing a vegetarian feast for Buddhist monks. He asked to have a bite, and they said no. He then informed against them for harboring rebels. Acting on his tip-off government troops raided the village and rounded up the villagers. In the end, more than two hundred of them lost their lives.

Like Hou Sizhi, Wang Hongyi too was given a guerrilla general's title and appointed attendant censor. In such capacity he once travelled to Shengzhou to investigate Area Commander Wang Anren.[10] No sooner did he arrive than the general showed up in his office, wearing a cangue and fetters, obviously as a way to profess his loyalty to the throne. But Censor Wang felt so offended that he, in a burst of anger, chopped off General Wang's head. Momentarily, when the general's son arrived on summons, the censor beheaded him as well. He then put the two severed heads in a wicker case, and took it to Luoyang. Since

General Wang Anren was condemned as a disloyal officer, no one even bothered to ask about how he and his son had died.

On yet another occasion, Wang Hongyi went to Fenzhou[11] on errand. As he was having lunch with Assistant Prefect Mao,[12] all of a sudden, the censor was seized by a murderous rage, rose to his feet, drew out his sword, and lopped off the head of the poor prefect. A few days later, Wang entered Luoyang on horseback, holding a pike on which was stuck Mao's head.

In theory, guerrilla generals like Hou Sizhi and Wang Hongyi were supposed to follow laws in the *Tang Code* and rules in the state statues. In reality, they often ignored them and could get away with murders, a fact that added to their notoriety as "cruel officials."

As Tianhou continued to recruit people like Hou and Wang, a clique of Legalist law officers took form under the leadership of Lai Junchen and Zhou Xing. They targeted the royals, high-ranking officials and officers, and rank and file, bringing treason charges against them. The dominant presence of these cruel officials at court and in the prefectures had completely altered the nature of law-enforcement and the legal discourse.

When they arrested a person, they would send him or her straight to the state prison inside the Lijing Gate.[13] Almost nobody who had entered the gate had come out alive. Thus, Wang Hongyi, the "White Rabbit Censor," dubbed it the Gate of Despair,[14] a name that stuck in the minds of Luoyang residents.

***

Late one night in the fall of 690, a dozen or so young officers and men were taken into custody, trussed up with ropes, and transported through the infamous gate into the state prison. They all belonged to the prestigious Left Jinwu Guard, one of the Sixteen Guards, with its headquarters in Qinghua Ward[15] east of the Imperial City. These men had been drinking wine in a tavern in the ward. After they had paid for the drinks, ready to leave, three dozen policemen, armed with swords and spears, broke in, and apprehended the drinkers on the charge of libel against the court.

At their interrogation two days later, they learned the true reason for their arrest: reciting a popular ditty while playing a drinkers' wager game. The ditty went: "When mother and son get separated, the stand falls down with it." Here the "mother and son" referred to "an oil-lamp with its tray." The ditty simply meant, "The oil lamp and the tray are overturned." On the surface, it was silly, nonsensical, and entirely innocuous. To Tianhou, however, it was an innuendo about her tense relations with her son Li Zhe, whom she had banished to the south after deposing him. At court, everybody understood this was a taboo subject. Even a slightest hint of it could lead to trouble.

Some high-level officers of the Guard went to the prison to negotiate their release, but in vain. Under the management of Lai Junchen, there was a stringent policy: "It is better to kill many innocents than let a single culprit escape." Those unlucky men of the Jinwu Guard were soon put on trial, found guilty, and beheaded in the Southern Market.

***

The year 690 was an *annus horribilis* for the royal Li house. In the fourth month, two remaining prominent princes, Li Sujie, and Li

Shangjin, both Emperor Gaozong's sons *not* born to Tianhou, were taken in, thanks to the tireless effort of Zhou Xing (taking his cue from Wu Sansi) to frame them. They were transported from their places of banishment to Luoyang to face charges of plotting rebellion. En route, Li Sujie caught the sound of some folk wailing over a loved one who had just died of a disease. Sujie sighed and said, "To die of a disease—how I wish I could do that! To say nothing of being mourned by others after death!" He had held on to the hope that Tianhou, who had once spared his life after killing his mother, would probably do it again. That hope faded in Longmen in the southern suburbs of Luoyang when he was visited by two burly men in black. Unceremoniously, they grabbed the scruff of his neck and strangled him. The semi-starved Sujie hardly put up a fight. Meanwhile, his half-brother Li Shangjin committed suicide on orders from the court. The next of kin and associates of the two princes were also eliminated.

In the eight month, twelve more titled royals were killed. Then came the death by flogging of the two sons of the late Crown Prince Li Xián. It did not matter at all that they were Tianhou's flesh and blood. By then, a total of thirty-four royals had been dead. The plan to exterminate the undesirable ones was nearly complete.

In view of all this, the survival of Princes Li Zhe's and Li Dan's sons was nothing short of a miracle. Maybe because they were too young, or maybe because Tianhou still recognized their royal status, and decided to let their branches of the Li clan live. But their fate was by no means certain, since she could change her mind in a flash.

Among her surviving offspring, Princess Taiping was the only one Tianhou truly cared for. Now in her mid-twenties, she was blossoming into a beautiful, mature woman, with a full forehead suggestive of extraordinary intelligence. Tianhou liked her because she resembled herself in looks and character, and because she possessed a rare gift—strategic thinking. Ever since the death of her husband Xue Shao, who had perished in the aftermath of the Li Chong-Li Zhen rebellion, Tianhou had been on the hunt for his replacement. She set her sights on Wu Youji, the grandson of her uncle Wu Shirang. Wu Youji was the cautious type, honest and boring, with hardly any political ambitions, in other words, the most suitable husband material for Taiping. The only problem was: he was still married and there was no reason for him to divorce his wife.

Then, not long afterwards, she was found dead one mid-afternoon, with blood oozing from her orifices. It was rumored that one of her housemaids, working secretly for the law officers, had laced her morning tea with "crane's crest red," a kind of arsenic known for its great potency.

Two months later, the marriage between Tianhou's favorite daughter and the widower Wu Youji, who had overcome the sorrow of losing his wife to food-poisoning, was consummated.

Notes

1 The Yinshijia 寅識迦 River is identified as the modern Aksu River.

2 Shazhou 沙洲: prefecture that lay in Dunhuang and others, west Gansu.

3 Xiuzhou 繡州: prefecture that lay in Guiping (southeast of Liuzhou), Guangxi.

4 Zhao Huaijie 趙懷節 (–689): general of the Right Soaring Hawk Guard (*you yingyang wei jiangjun* 右鷹揚衛將軍). The Guard, previously known as the "Right Militant Guard" (*you wuwei* 右武衛), was one of the Sixteen Guards.

5 The Xinping District Expeditionary Army (Xinping dao xingjun 新平道行軍). Xinping was a town northwest of Yingxian, north Shanxi.

[6] The Purple River (Zihe 紫河) was south of Horinger, central Inner Mongolia.

[7] Lianzhou 連州: prefecture that lay in present-day Lianzhou, Yangshan, and others, northeast Guangdong. Chenzhou 辰州: prefecture that lay in Yuanling and others, central Hunan.

[8] The attendant censor (*shi yushi* 侍御史): censorial official under the Censorate with general surveillance and impeachment powers.

[9] Zhaozhou 趙州: prefecture that lay in Zhaoxian and others, Hebei.

[10] Wang Anren 王安仁. Shengzhou 勝州: frontier prefecture that lay in Shenmu, Shaanxi, and neighboring areas in Inner Mongolia.

[11] Fenzhou 汾州: prefecture that lay in south Shanxi.

[12] Mr. Mao 毛.

[13] The Lijing Gate 麗景門: the southern gate on the west side of the Imperial City in Luoyang.

[14] The Gate of Despair (Liejingmen 例竟門).

[15] Qinghua Ward 清化坊.

6. Wu Zhou Dynasty (689–690)

ON THE FIRST day of the eleventh month of 689, Tianhou adopted a new reign title—Zaichu ("Beginning of the Era"). This was one of the many steps she took to forge her own identity. Next, she abandoned the existing Xia calendrical system[1] in favor of the Zhou system, placing the standard month (*zhengyue*) in the eleventh month of the lunar calendar and renaming the twelfth month as the *la* (sacrifice) month.[2]

To celebrate this symbolic change, Tianhou mounted the Divine Palace (Mingtang) to announce a general amnesty and a slew of additional measures to accentuate the regime's continuity from antiquity by giving prominence to the celebrated sovereigns of the past and ranking their descendants according to their relevance to the Wus and their historical importance. The royal offspring of the Zhou and

Han, also known as the Two Dynasties, were the highest. Next came those of Shun, Yu, and King Tang of Shang, collectively called the Three Reverends.[3] Below them were those of the Northern Zhou and Sui.

She ordered her nephew Qin Zongke to invent twelve alternative characters. One of them *zhao* 曌 was to become her given name. Consisting of the sun and moon above and the sky below, it shows her ambition and vision.

She took steps to bolster the civil service examination system, a system that had evolved since the Sui dynasty with roots in the Western Han. For her, it was a most effective way of recruiting talented young people, especially those of non-aristocratic background, into governments at various levels.

Of the three academic degrees the aspirants could hope to earn through examination—the Cultivated Talent (*xiucai*), the Classicist (*mingjing*), and the Advanced Scholar (*jinshi*)[4]—Tianhou especially favored the last one with its focus on literary accomplishment. The *jinshi* before her rise to power had already been the most prestigious of the three. During her reign, it had almost become the *sine qua non* for promotion to chief minister, particularly for those without a powerful family background.

In addition, Tianhou introduced a new degree, *gongshi*.[5] Recipients of *gongshi* were local examination passers eligible to attend the central examination for the prestigious *jinshi* (Presented Scholar) degree.

Tianhou had a personal interest in recruiting qualified young people from society and took it upon herself to administer oral examinations to *gongshi* candidates in the Luocheng Basilica[6] of Luoyang's Palace City in early 690. From then on, this "Basilica Examination"[7] tradition was to continue down to the Qing dynasty.

***

One morning in the ninth month of 690, more than 900 self-proclaimed loyal subjects from Guanzhong were hanging around the southern main entrance to the Palace City. A Phoenix Pavilion (Secretariat) official came out to receive them. Their leader Attendant Censor Fu Youyi delivered a petition with two revolutionary demands:

> *(1) the dynastic title be changed from Tang to Zhou, and*
> *(2) the emperor's surname be changed from Li to Wu.*

Although Tianhou granted neither, she nonetheless promoted Fu to supervising secretary,[8] a high-ranking post in the Simurgh Terrace (Chancellery).[9] In the days that followed, the court was flooded with petition letters. All told, there were more than 60,000 of them. The petitioners ranged from senior court officials, royals, common subjects far and near, and chieftains of barbarian tribes to Buddhist monks and Daoist adepts. They all voiced their support for Fu Youyi's requests. Even the emperor Li Dan submitted his own petition, offering to give up his surname Li for Wu.

It was about this time that some senior officials reported two unusual scenes. First, a phoenix was seen taking flight from the Mingtang to the Shangyang Palace, where it perched on a phoenix tree (flame tree) in front of the Left Terrace (Censorate) for hours before taking off to the southeast.

Soon thereafter, a large flock of vermilion birds were seen descending on the roofs of the Audience Hall and in its courtyard where they strutted and cooed for hours.

Faced with these auspicious omens that heralded the arrival of a *Pax Sinica*, and overwhelmed by the flood of letters, Tianhou found it futile to resist the powerful message they conveyed. Or so it seemed. With apparent reluctance, she finally agreed to comply with the intent of the people and Heaven.

She mounted the Zetianmen gatetower and announced one more general amnesty, the change of the dynastic title from Tang to Zhou (or Wu Zhou), and a change of the reign title to Tianshou (Heaven Given). Finally, she took up the imperial mantle by adopting the honorific title of Holy Emperor.[10]

The emperor Li Dan was demoted to imperial heir,[11] with Wu as his new surname, while his crown prince Chengqi was redesignated imperial grandson.[12]

The Wu Ancestral Temple of seven chambers was officially inaugurated in the Divine Capital. To the original five Wu ancestors were now added two Zhou figures—King Wen as the original ancestor, and Ji Wu, the youngest son of King Ping (Ji Yijiu).[13] It was believed that Ji Wu's given name *wu* (marshal) later became the surname of a new lineage, and Tianhou (Wu Zhao/Wu Zetian) was its fortieth-generation descendant.

A salient feature that distinguished the Wu Temple from all others was the fact that each chamber contained not one, but two spirit tablets dedicated to a male ancestor *and* his mother. Therefore, seven male and seven *female* ancestors were worshipped together. In introducing this practice, Tianhou broke a centuries-old tradition and elevated the status of women in a male-dominated world. Thus, at least in the ritual arena, a deceased mother commanded the same level of reverence as her male spouse.

***

Because of his help in founding the Zhou dynasty, Fu Youyi received promotion to chief minister and was gifted with the imperial surname Wu.

This fast-track rise in officialdom was unheard of in Tang history. Within a year, his official robes changed colors from black, green, and red to purple, which coincided with the four seasons, as he climbed from a bottom rung of the official ladder to the top. People referred to him jocularly as a "four seasons official."

As chief minister Fu proposed new measures to enhance Wu Zhou's dynastic identity. One of them was replacing "prefecture" (*zhou*)—the name of a Tang local government below a Circuit (*dao*)—with a defunct name, "commandery" (*jun*), and replacing the title of its leader "prefect" (*cishi*) with "governor" (*shou*). After it went into effect with Tianhou's approval, six grandsons of her brothers were created commandery prince. Before long, however, a court official pointed out a fatal flaw. The character *zhou* (prefecture) and the new dynastic title Zhou were homophones. Thus, "to abolish prefectures (*zhou*)" could also mean "to abolish Zhou." And that was not auspicious at all.

"I'll be damned!" Tianhou snarled. Thereupon she ordered to roll back the change. Within days, commanderies reverted to prefectures.

This error, however, did not affect Fu Youyi's favorable standing with Tianhou. He was still a leading Legalist law officer of the day, bent on eradicating elements hostile to Tianhou.

About one year later, Fu got caught up in a bizarre event that would bring about a reversal of fate. One night he had a dream in which he roamed about in the palace alone and ventured into the Zhanlu

Basilica,[14] a royal building where the sovereign received the top court leaders. Intrigued, he shared this strange experience with a close relative in confidence. The relative then leaked the secret to a senior court official, who reported it to the authorities. When Tianhou learned about the dream, she was alarmed. This seemingly innocent dream showed that Fu was covetous of the throne! On her orders, he was then stripped of his official titles, thrown into jail, and committed suicide.[15]

***

Different from previous dynasties, the founding of the Tang had been predicated not only on sanction from Heaven but also the Daoist gods. The alleged founder of the religion, Lord Lao (aka Li Dan), was considered the initial ancestor of the Li royal house; and Daoism, the state religion, was ranked above both Buddhism and Confucianism. But Tianhou disagreed with the ranking. Although she held Daoism in high esteem, she was first and foremost a Buddhist. When she sought divine blessings on her regime, she would go to the Buddha first. And, for quite some time, she had been wanting to re-rank the "Three Religions."[16] An incident of Buddho-Daoist rivalry provided a perfect opportunity.

When the iconic Buddhist cloister in Chang'an, the Daxingshan si (Great Rising Goodness Monastery),[17] was destroyed in a fire, the Daoist adept Li Rong[18] composed a satirical poem, which read:

To call it "good" is actually no good;
To name it "rise" is to see it fall.
With the Buddha statue reduced to ashes,
Only a bunch of monks remain.

Tianhou did not take too kindly to this type of disparagement. She condemned the poem and used it as grounds for demoting Daoism and elevating Buddhism. She withdrew all support for the construction of new Daoist abbeys but increased court sponsorship for Buddhist projects.

In the tenth month she issued an edict on the founding of two Buddhist monasteries, both named Dayun (Great Cloud), respectively in Luoyang and Chang'an. Each would house a copy of the *Great Cloud Sutra*, a Buddhist work of special significance to Tianhou.[19]

The central theme of the sutra is about a woman prophesied to be the sovereign of Jambudvīpa,[20] the island-continent in the south. There had been a translation of the sutra by the Indian monk Tanwuchen[21] (385–433). On Tianhou's orders, Master Xue Huaiyi and Master Faming[22] leading a team of monks completed a "new translation." But what the translators did was copy the old version almost word for word. The team's main contribution was a subcommentary that identified the Heavenly Empress (Tianhou) as the reincarnation of Maitreya. A divine figure residing as a bodhisattva in the Tushita heaven,[23] Maitreya is destined to come down to earth to expound the dharma ("law") at a time when the teachings of Sakyamuni (the historic Buddha) will have perished. Dubbed the future Buddha, Maitreya was then the most worshipped god in Buddhism.

Tianhou was very impressed with the team's achievement. She conferred the title of "county duke"[24] (*xiangong*) upon nine of the monks who had taken part in the project. Each also received a purple cassock and a silver turtle ornament as proof of his rank.

In view of the significant role the *Great Cloud Sutra* had played in founding the new dynasty, providing a religious legitimacy to its existence, a few months later, Tianhou issued an edict to rank Buddhism as the highest religion in the nation, a notch higher even than Daoism, which had helped the Lis justify their replacement of the previous Sui dynasty.

***

In the *standard* (eleventh) month of 690,[25] Tianhou attended a grand ceremony at the Divine Palace (Mingtang) to officially receive the honorific title of "Holy Emperor" and proclaim Red as the proper color of the new Zhou dynasty and its flag. A flurry of ritual-related activities followed. First, the authorities relocated the Altars of the Soil and Grain[26]—one of the two state ritual centers inside Chang'an—to Luoyang. Then, they moved the spirit tablets of the Wu Temple into *the* Ancestral Temple in Luoyang. Then again, upon demoting the old Ancestral Temple in Chang'an, they renamed it as the Xiangde Temple.[27] Of the seven spirit tablets therein, only the last three (those of Gaozu, Taizong, and Gaozong) continued to receive offerings on a seasonable basis. The chambers for the four earlier ancestors were shuttered.

Not long afterwards, a grand sacrificial ceremony took place in the Mingtang, where offerings were made to the Lord on High and a host of other gods. Accompanying these gods were the Seven Ancestors of the Wu Temple and the Three Ancestors of the Li Temple. This event conveyed an unmistakable message: in the ritual arena, the Wus were gaining the upper hand over their rivals the Lis.

***

As Tianhou was seriously considering setting up an heir to her Zhou dynasty, with Wu Chengsi as the most likely candidate, a scandal broke out that shook her hard.

It concerned one of Wu Chengsi's women called Jasper (Biyu).[28] Originally Court Rectifier[29] Qiao Zhizhi's bondwoman, Jasper possessed many qualities that made her attractive to educated men. Apart from being young and beautiful, she was a great dancer and singer, a good pipa player, and a gifted literary companion. For her sake, Qiao Zhizhi had turned down all marriage proposals by matchmakers.

After a chance encounter, Wu Chengsi took a shine to her and made a request to her master to borrow her for a few days. She would teach his courtesans how to apply makeup. Qiao Zhizhi had no reason to turn down the request. So she left, but never returned. Wu Chengsi ended up taking her in as his concubine. Dying to see her again, Qiao Zhizhi penned an emotion-laden essay called the "Sorrow of Green Pearl"[30] on a silk sash. It ended with this sentimental poem in the voice of Green Pearl, a third-century courtesan:

The Shi House liked the new songs in its Golden Vale Garden,[31]
Ten bushels of shining pearls went to buy graceful elegance.
On that day you took pity and promised yourself to me,
At that moment my singing and dancing captured your heart.
The boudoirs of your household were never locked up,
For you loved to let others watch my singing and dancing.
Driven by bold emotions and unbound by reason,

A man haughty with power rudely stepped in.
To be apart from you, to leave, this I could never bear,
Vainly struggling to hide behind my sleeve, I mar my makeup.
With the pang of eternal separation in the loft-building,
This great beauty of her time will meet her end for you.[32]

Here Qiao Zhizhi alluded to the story of Shi Chong, a Western Jin man of fabulous wealth. Among the many beautiful courtesans he kept, Green Pearl was his favorite. The poem speaks in the voice of the courtesan, who eventually killed herself for him.

Upon reading the poem, Jasper was conscience-stricken and haunted by a subliminal message to tread in Green Pearl's footsteps. After three days without food and sleep, she wrapped the sash around her waist and plunged herself into a well and drowned. After Wu Chengsi had the corpse pulled from the well, he took off the waist sash, unfurled it, and read the piece, which was still legible. Livid with rage, he rushed to his pal Lai Junchen for help. Although the author of the piece Qiao Zhizhi was not a high-powered official, he was of formidable family background: his maternal grandfather was Li Yuan, the founder of the Tang dynasty. But Lai Junchen could not care less. He condemned Qiao on trumped-up charges and had him beheaded in public in the Southern Market of Luoyang.[33]

Tianhou was scandalized. Scrunching her face into a frown, she asked herself, "If this is what Chengsi would do for a low-class woman, how can I consider him as a serious contender for crown prince?" The whole thing filled her with disgust and anger.

Notes

[1] The Xia Calendar places its standard month (*zhengyue* 正月) in the first month of the lunar calendar. Under this system, the Chinese calendar was roughly one month *behind* the Julian Calendar.

[2] The Zhou Calendar places its standard month in the eleventh month of the lunar calendar. Under this system, the Chinese calendar was roughly one month *ahead* the Julian Calendar.

[3] The Three Reverends (*sanke* 三恪).

[4] Cultivated Talent (*xiucai* 秀才), Classicist (*mingjing* 明經), and Advanced Scholar (*jinshi* 進士).

[5] *Gongshi* 貢士.

[6] The Luocheng Basilica 洛城殿 was south of the Yinyu Basilica 飲羽殿 in the southwest corner of the Palace City of Luoyang.

[7] *Dianshi* 殿試.

[8] The supervising secretary (*jishi zhong* 給事中).

[9] The Simurgh Terrace (*luantai* 鸞臺) was previously known as *menxia sheng* 門下省 (Chancellery).

[10] The Holy Emperor (*shengshen huangdi* 聖神皇帝).

[11] The imperial heir (*huangsi* 皇嗣).

[12] The imperial grandson (*huangsun* 皇孫).

[13] Ji Wu 姬武; Ji Yijiu 姬宜臼.

[14] The Zhanlu Basilica湛露殿: its precise location is unknown.

[15] Fu Youyi's epitaph suggests that his downfall was due to Lai Junchen's effort to frame him, which is different from the accounts in the sources.

[16] The "Three Religions" (Buddhism, Daoism, and Confucianism) can also be rendered as the "Three Teachings." Essentially, Confucianism is not a religion.

[17] The Daxingshan Monastery 大興善寺 was in Jingshan Ward 靖善坊 east of the central axial street and south of the Imperial City in Daxingcheng (later known as Chang'an). West of the axial street was the Xuandu Abbey 玄都觀 as its Daoist counterpart in Chongye Ward 崇業坊. Occupying the entirety of a ward, the monastery was built before the city. The monastery and the city were both named after the title of Yang Jian (duke of Daxing). See *Tang liangjing chengfang kao* 2.38.

[18] Li Rong 李榮.

[19] The *Great Cloud Sutra* (*Mahāmegha-sūtra*; *Dayun jing* 大雲經).

[20] Jambudvīpa (Yanfuti 閻浮提).

[21] Tanwuchen 曇無讖 (Dharmakṣema).

[22] Faming 法明 was based in Luoyang.

[23] In Buddhism, the Tushita heaven is one of the Buddhist heavens.

[24] *See* "duke" in Glossary.

[25] The Wu Zhou adopted the Zhou calendar, and the eleventh month of the lunar calendar now became the standard month (first month). See *Zizhi tongjian* 204.6462.

[26] The Altars of the Soil and Grain (*sheji* 社稷).

[27] The Xiangde Temple 享德廟.

[28] Biyu 碧玉.

[29] The court rectifier (*buque* 補闕): middle-ranking remonstrance official.

[30] "Lüzhu yuan" 綠珠怨.

[31] The Shi House refers to the house of Shi Chong 石崇.

[32] *Tangren yishi huibian* 9.440. Translation is from Sanders 2006, 266, with modifications.

[33] On Qiao Zhizhi's death, see *Xin Tang shu* 4.90.

7. Enter the Vat, Please! (691)

TRADITIONALLY, IN METING out punishments to officials, there were "Confucian" elements to consider, for example, the Eight Deliberations,[1] which took into account such extenuating factors as blood and other ties to the throne, virtue, capability, past meritorious service, and official rank, among others. But when the Legalist law officers tried their cases, they often disregarded these elements. Their rivals, the Confucian law officers—those who made allowances for mitigating circumstances—were so rare that you could count them on the fingers of one hand. The best known of them was Xu Yougong.

While still a middle-ranking official in the provinces, Xu Yougong had established a reputation for being lenient and humane. At a time when physical torture was the standard way of extracting confessions, Judge Xu was probably the only one in the realm who refused to apply that standard. He had tried thousands of cases, but had never ordered a single flogging, nor had he handed down a single death sentence.

Having served as a judge in the Court of Judicial Review, he was promoted to a bureau director in the Board of Justice,[2] where he saved hundreds of condemned men and their relatives from the axe.

In the wake of the Li Chong-Li Zhen rebellion, the campaign to root out their confederates and sympathizers went on for months. In the end, Tianhou issued the Yongchang Rescript in a reconciliatory spirit. Considering the fact that the ringleaders of the rebellion had been eradicated, it ordained that unexposed accomplices should all be pardoned.

It was against this backdrop that Xu got involved in the case of County Defender Yan Yuqing[3] accused of being a confederate of Li Chong. Using torture, Lai Junchen extracted from him a self-incriminating confession and recommended the death sentence. After a review of the case at Tianhou's request, Xu reduced the sentence to "lifetime banishment." That did not go down well with the Legalist law officers at all.

At a court session, when someone brought up the issue, Tianhou turned to Xu and asked, "Why did you revise Lai Junchen's judgment?"

"Your Majesty, according to the Yongchang Rescript, Yan Yuqing is merely an accomplice who escaped punishment, but not a ringleader."

"He collected debt and purchased bows and arrows for Li Chong. Didn't that make him a ringleader?"

"Your Majesty, while he did collect debt, he had nothing to do with the bow and arrow purchase."

"He exchanged letters with Li Chong. Didn't that make him at least a co-conspirator?"

"The so-called 'letters' are never found and are based entirely on his confession. My view is that one should not pin the crime of rebellion on him. The evidence is simply not there. If the court insists on sending him to the gallows, I, your humble servant, will have no choice but to quit."

Taken aback at Xu's blunt way of speaking, Tianhou rolled her eyes and shouted, "None of your impudence."

Xu Yougong dropped on his knees. For a moment, the hall became so quiet that one could hear the drop of a needle as the two hundred-odd officials present held their breath and listened. They knew that by contradicting the sovereign, Xu was risking his own neck.

"Sit down, Yougong!" Tianhou ordered. "Write up your opinion. I need to read it no later than day after tomorrow. Can you do it?"

"Yes, Your Majesty." Xu Yougong was now back in his seat.

Tianhou had Xu's long report in her hands the following day and spent much of the night studying it. Here Xu backed up his view with similar cases during Gaozong's and Tianhou's reigns and quotes from the *Tang Code*. Finding no holes in Xu's argument, Tianhou gave it her approval.

Yan Yuqing lived, and his family escaped the fate of bondage in the Lateral Palace.

But Xu Yougong soon got himself in serious trouble. It had to do with the case of the Li brothers—Prefect of Daozhou Li Xingbao and his brother Magistrate of Yuci Li Changsha.[1] It was one of several similar cases involving the Lis. When these two were charged with conspiring to restore the Li house to power, they were condemned to death together with their entire clan in 690. As a bureau director in the Board of Justice Xu Yougong reviewed the case and suspected a frameup; he argued strenuously against the recommended sentence. Tianhou, who would rather err on the side of excess, was not pleased.

Sensing Tianhou's anger, Xu's immediate boss Zhou Xing, vice president of the same Board, filed a secret report against him.

"According to a Han precedent," it said, "those who curry favor with the inferior and deceive the superior should be punished by waist chop.[5] The *Record of Rites* says, 'Those who engage in sophistry are punishable by death.' Xu Yougong attempted to set free condemned rebels by making convoluted and deceitful arguments and is thus guilty on both accounts. I demand that he be prosecuted for his unpardonable crime."

Thus Xu Yougong himself became the object of an investigation and ended up in jail. Now he had to suffer the indignity of wearing a cangue and fetters while keeping company with murderers, rapists, and other hardcore lawbreakers. On his second day in custody, his interrogator allowed him to steal a look at the report. Although the author's name was blotted out, he was able to figure out, based on style and content, that Zhou was the author. He was not too surprised. As a most hated Confucian law officer at court, he had been maligned by his Legalist colleagues before on numerous occasions.

After the interrogator's judgment in favor of the report was in, Tianhou gave it a careful reading. Common sense convinced her to rule against it. Besides, she needed people like Xu to counterbalance the influence of his rival camp. Nonetheless, so as not to disappoint the Legalist officers too much, she dismissed Xu from office after releasing him.

A few weeks later, Xu Yougong turned up on summons in Tianhou's study. A eunuch envoy read out her edict, ". . . it is hereby decreed that Xu Yougong be rehabilitated and promoted as an attendant censor of the Censorate."

Xu prostrated himself at her feet, tears streaming down his face, and said, "I am afraid, I cannot do it, Your Majesty. I am awfully sorry. But I cannot."

"Why?" She sounded angry and confused. This position would afford him more protection from baseless charges and give him the power to review legal cases involving high-powered officials.

"I heard that a deer can run around freely in the mountain woods, but its fate ultimately rests in the hands of hunters or chefs. If Your Majesty appoints me as a law-enforcement officer, like that deer, my fate will no longer be in my own hands. I will not bend the law of Your Majesty, nor dare I. But if I follow the law to the letter, I will incur the wrath of many and risk dying soon with my boots on."

"Yougong, stop worrying! Just do what you need to do, and I will have your back. By the way, do you know what kind of punishment they proposed for you in the Li brothers' case? Death by waist chop. I shielded you from harm, because we need people like you at court to keep those Legalist law officers in check."

Xu Yougong knelt up and made a deep bow of gratitude.

***

Tianhou was viewing a celadon ware placed on a red sandalwood table on a fine afternoon. She was amazed at the jade green color and the spider web of tiny cracks under the translucent glaze. Its bulbous belly recalled an extravagant vase. But its wide flared mouth gave it away as a spittoon. Still, as a rare palace ware of the Liang dynasty, it had transcended its functionality to become a treasured connoisseur's item.

"What do you know about the donor, Wan'er?" asked Tianhou as she kept her gaze on the celadon.

"Your Majesty," answered Shangguan Wan'er, now a palace attendant at twenty-eight *sui*, "she is a palace lady and has been in the service of the Tang sovereigns since Taizong's time."

"She doesn't ask for any compensation?"

"No. She just hopes to see Your Majesty in person."

With a flick of her hand, Tianhou said, "All right, request granted."

Momentarily, Yidu Neiren,[6] a good-looking woman in her early fifties with bright eyes and a high forehead, was brought in. The meeting went so well that when it was getting dark Tianhou asked her to stay for the evening meal. Over wine and food, Tianhou and the palace lady continued their conversation. To Tianhou this occasion was relaxing, unlike a meal with a top official, where protocol created a sense of distance.

Tianhou enjoyed the visitor's company because she never bowed and scraped, although she remained deferential. Tianhou was particularly impressed that she knew as much about the history of the Han and the poetry of the Tang as antique prices in the Southern Market.

The next morning, Neiren came again, not as a visitor, but as a confidante, an unofficial adviser. Tianhou needed someone like her, who was not in the pocket of the court leaders or the Legalist law officers but was in close contact with the populace. After the evening meal, they talked behind closed doors far into the night.

Sensing Tianhou's anxiety about the state of her rule, Neiren offered a candid analysis. As the first female emperor in history, she argued, Her Majesty should feel secure on the throne. The embers of rebellion were snuffed out, and hostile forces were all but destroyed. The time had come to shift attention to the center and deal with the Legalist law officers. True, they had played an indispensable role in helping Her Majesty consolidate power. But they often went out of their way to ravage loyal subjects residing in Luoyang and elsewhere. Under the guise of weeding out Her Majesty's opponents, they carried out many atrocities. They took bribes and committed murder and rape with immunity. In truth, they had already done much harm to the court's reputation.

Neiren's advice confirmed what Tianhou had suspected for months: the power of the Legalist law officers must be curtailed before it got out of hand. After further discussions of the issue with a few trusted court leaders, Tianhou made up her mind to conduct a purge.

The first one who had to go was Qiu Shenji. It was true that he was one of Tianhou's most ardent early followers, but his hands were tainted with the blood of Prince Li Xián, the officials of Bozhou at the time of the Li Chong Rebellion, and many others.

Soon Qiu was run in. When he heard his charge—plotting against the throne, he was flabbergasted. He insisted on seeing Tianhou to clear his name. But she chose not to respond to his request. "His accusation is probably unfounded," she thought. "But I would rather believe it." So General Qiu, while still hoping for an audience, was executed by decapitation.

The news of Qiu's death got people in the street talking excitedly about the riddance of a much-hated cruel official.

In the meantime, a secret report had reached Tianhou's table. It pointed a finger at Qiu's colleague Zhou Xing, a heavy hitter. His machinations had caused the deaths of more than a thousand victims. He was also one of the lynchpins that supported the Reign of Terror and a leader of the powerful Board of Autumn. To start an investigation on him, Tianhou realized, she had to proceed with great caution, because she did not want him to find out about it too early and make trouble. So she gave Lai Junchen a secret order to take him in for questioning in the first month of 691.

Lai Junchen waited until he had occasion to have a private moment with his colleague at lunch.

"Sometimes one encounters a tough prisoner who refuses to confess," Lai said casually as he sipped his wine. "What is the best way to make him talk?"

"Easy," Zhou Xing said with confidence. "Get a large vat first. Put some charcoal beneath it, light the charcoal to heat up the vat, and then ask the prisoner to enter the vat. He will own up to everything."

"Great idea!" exclaimed Lai Junchen, who paused to speak to his underlings. About twenty minutes later, they brought into the room a huge pottery vat, moved it onto a low metal stand, and shoved a brazier with burning charcoal beneath it.

"Will that do?" Lai Junchen asked.

"Perfect!" Zhou Xing shouted.

Turning to his colleague with a smile, Lai said, "Mr. Zhou Xing, would you like to try it?"

"What?" Zhou Xing asked in puzzlement.

"Enter the vat, please!" Lai shouted.

"Why?" a horrified Zhou Xing asked.

"I have read a secret report collected from the Bronze Chest, and it is about *you*."

All of a sudden, Zhou Xing dropped on his knees and knocked his head against the floor again and again, while asking for mercy in a shaking voice. But it was no use. He was immediately taken into custody.

It did not take long before Lai Junchen found him guilty and handed down the death sentence.

Tianhou intervened. Taking into consideration his past merit, she reduced it to banishment to the far south.

While he was en route, his past caught up with him. One of his enemies tracked him down and killed him.

***

The Caucasian-looking Suo Yuanli was run in as well, charged with taking bribes. A close subordinate of Zhou Xing, he was every bit as murderous as Zhou.

"I demand to be granted an audience with Her Majesty." Suo was adamant at the start of his interrogation.

"Her Majesty has no time for a petty criminal like you," the interrogator answered.

"You'd better be careful with what you say. When I get out, I'll—"

"Stop dreaming. You have to own up to your crime now if you want a 'good death' by waist chop. Otherwise, you will be flayed to one thousand pieces, alive."

"Does Master Xue know about this?" asked Suo, getting the jitters.

"Yes. But Master Xue Huaiyi doesn't want to have anything to do with you."

"That's not true. He is my adopted son. He must help."

"Baloney! Are you going to talk or not?"

"I refuse. Not before I see Her Majesty or Master Xue."

"All right, we'll see." The interrogator waved his hand. A prison guard brought in a nondescript bundle and placed it on the floor. He lifted away the hempen cover to reveal a small iron cage equipped with bamboo spikes pointing inwards.

Suo Yuanli was quiet for a few moments, his face ashen. Faced with his own ingenious contraption, he had no choice but to start talking. In the end, with Tianhou's special approval, he was sent to the gallows.

***

Like Zhou Xing and Suo Yuanli, Lai Junchen was a leading Legalist law officer. Known as the scourge of the literati, he was universally feared. Tianhou trusted him to go after the other Legalist law officers not only because of his self-professed blind loyalty, but also his efficiency in getting results thanks to his profound understanding of the art of interrogation.

Based on his experience, he had formulated an elaborate theory on interrogation. Working hand in hand with his colleague Wan Guojun, he distilled this theory into a book called the *Classic on Framing*.[7] It shows that his evil wisdom knows no bounds. First, in a Legalist vein, he stresses the absolute importance of ingratiating yourself with your boss:

> *No superior is unintelligent; no inferior is very virtuous. All merit is due to the superior, and all faults are due to the inferior. Always be on alert and never let your guard down. Never show off your intelligence, nor your bravery. Be prepared to cut ties with your next of kin. Never refrain from doing something because it is evil. So long as you follow this advice, after you have won the favor of your superior, it will never depart from you.*

What is more important, Lai shows how to entrap and incriminate the innocent:

> *Whereas death is bearable, pain is not. So we choose the most unbearable type of torture on people. The literati cannot bear to be insulted and common folks are afraid of implicating their kin. Thus we act accordingly and punish them where it hurts most. If a man refuses to admit to his crime, increase the charge against him. If the evidence is not readily available, create it to make his case believable. Torture has its limitations, but slander does not. They should be used in combination for maximum effect. One should not worry if a charge lacks merit; one should only worry if it fails to convince the sovereign.*

All these years, the *Classic* had been the Scripture of investigators. Like many court leaders who read the book, Tianhou was concerned about the author's total lack of moral restraint. But she retained his service for carrying out the purge, in the belief that she could "fight poison with poison."

For his part, Lai Junchen continued to exercise unstrained power. He took into custody General-in-Chief Zhang Qianxu and his Supply Commissioner Fan Yunxian on trumped-up charges in the eighth month of 691. When General Zhang launched out into a monolog about what he had done for the country, Lai Junchen ordered his guardsmen to put an end to the prattle, and they struck him down with swords. When Fan babbled on and on about his long service to the court, Lai Junchen, in a fit of rage, ordered to have his tongue hacked off.

***

"How is the living shrine doing in Runan (south Henan)?" Tianhou asked Di Renjie, not without a touch of sarcasm. It was the ninth month of 691 and Di Renjie had just been promoted to de facto chief minister together with Pei Xingben.

"Your Majesty, my apologies," Di Renjie said. "I was transferred to Luoyang before I had time to have the stela torn down."

"No, no, don't get me wrong. When the masses are singing praises to one of my officials, it does me proud."

"I, your humble servant, thank Your Majesty."

"But I must tell you, your promotion has made a few folks green with envy."

"Oh?" Di Renjie did not sound surprised.

"Some accuse you of harboring grand ambitions."

"Do they?" Di Renjie was undisturbed.

"What's the matter with you? Aren't you curious about who badmouthed you?"

"I am awfully sorry. But if Your Majesty points out my errors, I will do my best to correct them. If Your Majesty does not believe I have done anything wrong, I do not have to worry at all. Either way, I will continue to serve Your Majesty with diligence and loyalty. As for who my accuser is—that is not of my concern."

"Really?"

"Really, Your Majesty."

"You don't mind losing the opportunity to protest your innocence or perhaps take revenge?"

"Well, if I am guilty, no matter how much I protest my innocence, I will be exposed as a liar. If I am truly innocent, in the end, I will be vindicated, without having to resort to revenge."

"You are really weird, Renjie. You are different from them all." Tianhou sighed and continued, "Things would be very different if people at court were like you."

Di Renjie frowned.

"For the better," she added.

***

Tianhou was reclining in a divan reading a scroll when Right Chancellor Cen Changqian and President of the Board of Revenue Ge Fuyuan, both de facto chief ministers, were brought in.

"Who is this Wang Qingzhi?" asked Tianhou, putting the scroll down on the low mahogany table by her side.

"Your Majesty, he is a commoner from Luoyang," Cen Changqian said.

"He has gathered a whole bunch of signatures on the memorial." Tianhou picked up the scroll and handed it to Ge Fuyuan.

"What do you think?" she asked both.

"Your Majesty, it is absolutely scandalous," Cen Changqian said. "Wu Chengsi is not Your Majesty's descendant. How can he be appointed crown prince? Furthermore, Imperial Heir Li Dan is still residing in the Eastern Palace. He has done nothing wrong and does not deserve to be deposed."

"Are you with Cen Changqian on this?" Tianhou asked Ge Fuyuan.

"I completely agree with him, Your Majesty," answered Ge, handing the scroll to Cen. "In fact, in my humble opinion, what this Luoyang commoner Wang Qingzhi proposes is bordering on the preposterous."

"But hundreds of petitioners are waiting at the southern main gate to the Palace City. We need to give them an answer," said Tianhou, her brows furrowing.

"Your Majesty, I can order them to go home," Cen said.

"Can you? All right, do it later. Now, what I want is this: despite your reservations, ponder over the proposal to see it has any merit at all. Don't jump to conclusions."

"Your Majesty, we have given it careful consideration already," Cen Changqian said. "What we have arrived at is not a rushed decision."

"What if I, by an imperial edict, order you to reconsider?" asked Tianhou, sounding annoyed.

"In that case, I may have to refuse Your Majesty's order with great regret," Cen Changqian said.

"I may have to do the same, Your Majesty," Ge Fuyuan said.

After the meeting ended on an unpleasant note, Tianhou wondered if she had made the right decision by promoting Cen and Ge to de facto chief ministers in the first place. She expected her top advisers to say no to her sometimes. But ganging up on her like that? Again?

Tianhou had never felt so pressured by a pair of upstarts since Hann Yuan and Lai Ji had publicly opposed her promotion to empress.

Wu Chengsi soon picked up on his aunt's displeasure. He went to Lai Junchen with a request for help.

After laboring with his minions for a couple of weeks, Lai announced the discovery of a clique of conspirators, headed by those arrogant chief ministers—Cen Changqian and Ge Fuyuan! They, together with several dozen others, were soon taken into custody, tortured, and forced to confess to a plot against the throne. With a nod of Tianhou, the ring leaders and their accomplices were decapitated in public.

***

At a meeting with Tianhou, Di Renjie asked in a cautious voice, "Will Your Majesty make Wu Chengsi crown prince based on Wang Qingzhi's proposal?"

"Not necessarily, Renjie."

"Isn't that true that Cen Changqian and Ge Fuyuan were removed because of their opposition to Chengsi?"

"Not really. What aroused my ire was their tone and attitude. Who were they to challenge my authority and defy my edict? As for who should be my heir? I haven't made up my mind yet."

***

Wang Qingzhi the petitioner had become a hero. As the clamor for a new crown prince was getting louder every day, he, with the backing of Wu Chengsi, obtained permission to see Tianhou in the Renshou Basilica.[8]

"Give me a reason why I should depose him?" Tianhou said. "The imperial heir is my son."

"Your Majesty," Wang Qingzhi answered. "The ghosts will never accept offerings from the wrong people. Nor will people make offerings to ancestral spirits other than their own. Today, who reigns over all under Heaven? Your Majesty. Why then should a Li be Your Majesty's successor? After you assumed the imperial mantle, Your Majesty replaced the Li ancestors with the Wus in the Ancestral Temple. People in the street were overjoyed. Now they are all hoping that the Wus will rule over the realm for ever and ever and rooting for Wu Chengsi as heir. He is capable, intelligent, and mature, and is the most eligible candidate. Since he is already successor emperor (*si huangdi*), to rename him as crown prince is simply to bring his status in line with reality."

"Well, it seems you are on to something, Qingzhi. I'll bring this matter up with my advisers." Tianhou waved her hand, and two eunuch officers came up to take the visitor away.

All of a sudden, Wang Qingzhi prostrated himself at Tianhou's feet, weeping and wailing, and saying, "Appoint Chengsi as crown prince, Your Majesty!"

The eunuchs dragged him to his feet. As they were pushing him towards the door, Tianhou said, "Wait." She walked over and handed him a sheet of paper with her imperial seal.

"Show this pass to the gate guards and they will let you in," Tianhou said. "However, don't brother to come unless you have something really important to report."

In the following weeks, Wang Qingzhi paid a visit to her once every three or four days. In the end, Tianhou had enough and told him to stop coming.

Concerning the point Wang had raised, Tianhou turned to the senior leadership for advice. Vice President of the Secretariat Li Zhaode gave a carefully worded answer, saying, "Wang's proposal certainly deserves close consideration. In my humble view, after the late Heavenly Emperor Gaozong entrusted the throne to Your Majesty, you have ruled over all under Heaven and should pass down the throne to your posterity, not to a nephew and his lineage. Suppose the nephew did come to power, would he worship his aunt in the Ancestral Temple? I think not. Because, if he would, that would have been unheard of since antiquity. Thus, if Chengsi were to succeed to the throne, the imperial line would come to an end."

With knitted brows, Tianhou turned to Di Renjie and asked, "And your comments?"

"Li Zhaode seems to have a point, "Di Renjie said. "After Your Majesty passes on, you should be worshipped as the founding emperor of the Zhou dynasty in the Ancestral Temple. But that would change if Wu Chengsi ascends the throne, because he is obligated to honor his father Wu Yuanshuang as his ancestor, not you."

Tianhou brooded darkly for a while, then said, "Zhaode and Renjie, let us leave the matter aside, at least for now."

***

Li Zhaode was standing at the entrance to the residential basilica, holding a gold-plated scepter in his hand. This recently appointed chief minister in his forties was competent and efficient. If he came across as a bit overconfident, one could put it down to Tianhou's backing.

Holding his special pass in his hand, the petitioner Wang Qingzhi said in an urgent tone, "Vice President, I need to see Tianhou right now."

Li Zhaode snatched the pass from him and moved his eyes to Tianhou's red seal and a brief statement above it: "Upon presentation of this document, the bearer is permitted to enter the residential basilica for an audience with Tianhou."

Without showing any expression, Li ripped the pass up, piece by piece.

"How dare you?" a wrathful Wang Qingzhi shouted.

Two guardsmen came up and pushed Wang south to the Guangzheng Gate.[9] Li Zhaode followed. At the gate, waving the scepter over his head, he gathered the officers and men on duty and announced an imperial rescript: "The wicked man called Wang Qingzhi insists on deposing the imperial heir and setting up Wu Chengsi in his place. I hereby order his elimination."

With a stunned look on his face, Wang Qingzhi was lost for words. A barrage of sticks rained down on his raised forearms, head, and shoulders until he collapsed onto the ground.

***

On the first of the first month, 692, Tianhou granted an audience to nominees for office recommended by relief commissioners[10]—high-ranking court officials sent to various prefectures to coordinate relief work. Only recently had the court, taking its cue from Tianhou, begun to recruit candidates in large numbers through this channel, contrary to convention. The most talented were hired as Secretariat drafters and supervising secretaries in the Chancellery; the rest were appointed to lower posts as supernumerary attendants, attendant censors, court rectifiers, court reminders, editors, and others.[11]

A limerick mocking this practice rose to popularity. It ran:

Court rectifiers were delivered by the cart load;
Court reminders were weighed by the catty.
Attendant censors were pitchforked into their job;
Editors all came out of the same mold.

One candidate added his humorous quip, "The relief commissioners have their brains filled with flour paste; / The emperor has her eyes half shut."

A censor was not amused. He could not find the author of the limerick but tracked down the sarcastic candidate and had him arrested. He wanted to impeach him for libel against court policy and made a request to punish him with flogging.

When Tianhou read the report, she chuckled and said, "If they do their jobs well, they don't have to worry about what others say about them, do they? Set him free!" The candidate was spared, and the censor was put to shame.

***

So far it was clear that Tianhou's recruitment policy had not worked as well as expected. But there was no mistaking that she was fully in charge here. That was why she was bold enough to break with tradition, where birth, experience, and academic talent all came into play. And she shifted the focus to talent. By so doing, she loosened the stranglehold the old aristocratic families had held on recruitment, and created a much more merit-based system. As for those unfit for their jobs, they were either removed, sentenced to time in prison, or, in rare cases, executed. Now that she held firmly in her hands the power of punishment and reward, dominating all under Heaven and making her own policy decisions, some of the best and brightest of the day began to fall over one another to offer their services to what they regarded as a perceptive and decisive sovereign.

Notes

[1] The Eight Deliberations (*bayi* 八議).

[2] The Board of Justice, known as *xingbu* 刑部 under the Tang, was called *qiuguan* 秋官 (Office of Autumn) under the Wu Zhou.

[3] Yan Yuqing 顏餘慶.

[4] Li Xingbao 李行褒 of Daozhou 道州 (prefecture that lay in Xintian, Jianghua, and others, Hunan). Li Changsha 李長沙 of Yuci 榆次 (county southeast of Taiyuan, Shanxi).

[5] Waist chop (*yaozhan* 腰斬): a type of execution that kills the condemned by severing his torso.

[6] Yidu Neiren: concerning this woman, the Tang man of letters Li Shangyin 李商隱 keeps a record. See *Quan Tang wen* 780, 宜都內人.

7 The *Classic on Framing* (*Luozhi jing* 羅織經).

8 The Renshou Basilica 仁壽殿 was to the northwest of the Hanyuan Basilica in Luoyang's Palace City.

9 The Guangzheng Gate 光政門 (Changle Gate 長樂門): the western gate in the south wall of the Palace City.

10 Relief commissioners (*cunfu shi* 存撫使).

11 Secretariat drafters (*fengge sheren* 鳳閣舍人). Supervising secretaries (*jishi zhong* 給事中): fairly important upper middle ranking positions with the task of monitoring the flow of documents between officials and the throne and their implementation. Supernumerary attendants (*yuanwai lang* 員外郎) were those hired outside the authorized official quota with smaller stipends; they often served as vice bureau directors. Court rectifiers (*buque* 補闕) and court reminders (*shiyi* 拾遺) were remonstrance officials.

8. The Chief Ministers' Clique (692)

IN HER STUDY in the Zhenguan Basilica, Tianhou was reading for the third time a secret memorial submitted by Lai Junchen. She was so focused that she did not have time to take a sip of the red date tea in a celadon bowl on the mahogany small table. It had gone cold.

She was alarmed by the accusation. If true, it would expose her most trusted senior official, de facto Chief Minister Di Renjie, as a fraud and the ringleader of the most menacing anti-emperor clique at court since the start of the Revolution. It named two more de facto chief ministers—Ren Zhigu and Pei Xingben—and four others: Chamberlain of the Court of Imperial Sacrifices[1] Cui Xuanli, former Left Vice Chancellor Lu Xian,[2] Vice Censor-in-Chief Wei Yuanzhong, and Prefect of Luzhou Li Sizhen.[3]

So far Di Renjie, together with Xu Yougong and Li Zhaode, had served as a counterweight against the Legalist law officers headed by

Lai Junchen. Their removal from office would surely tip the balance of power in favor of the latter. Tianhou did not want that to happen. But the case was too serious to be ignored.

As a matter of procedure, it now came under review by a panel of judges, including Li Qiao, a supervising secretary; Zhang Deyu, vice chamberlain of the Court for Judicial Review;[4] and Liu Xian,[5] an attendant censor. They soon found that the whole thing was baseless. Li Qiao, a strait-laced Confucian, felt duty-bound to act. "Seeing what is right but refusing to do it is a sign that you have no courage," he cited Confucius. In his strongly worded memorial to the throne, he protested the innocence of the accused.

As soon as she finished reading the memorial, she tossed it onto the small table and uttered, "Stupid pedant!" Thereupon, she issued an edict to have Li Qiao transferred out of the capital to a lower provincial post. In demoting Li, she acted on impulse because she was pissed off with his moralizing tone. *Who is he to lecture the emperor on how to run her court based on Confucian teachings?* But there were deeper reasons as well. First, she did not want to alarm the Legalist law officers too early. Second, she wanted to "get to the bottom of things." Third, she was interested in knowing how far Lai and company would go.

The two judges still on the panel, anxious to avoid the fate of their colleague, completed their final assessment report that echoed Lai Junchen's judgment.

***

With the go-ahead from Tianhou, Lai Junchen went to the state prison to try the imprisoned conspirators in situ. In the "interrogation room," a whole array of instruments was on display: bamboo sticks of different thicknesses, bamboo nail-crushers, whips with metal tips, foot presses, torture racks, an iron head cage, and others. A long bench stood beside a tall brazier. Two iron rods were partially buried in the burning charcoal.

"I am sure you are familiar with this edict of leniency," said Lai Junchen to Di Renjie, in cangue and shackles, who had just been hauled into the room by two guardsmen.

"Yes, Your Honor?" answered Di, with a puzzled look on his face. This medium-sized man of middle age looked tiny in an ill-fitting gray prison uniform.

"Whoever confesses in the first session will be spared death." He handed the prisoner a paper document.

"If that is the case...." His eyes ran across the vertical lines of characters from right to left and settled on the red imperial seal at the bottom, as he said, "I confess."

"Really?" Lai Junchen was taken by surprise. "You want to fess up to everything?"

"Yes, everything."

"Why?"

"I have no choice," said Di, giving the document back to Lai. "The founding of the Wu Zhou dynasty ushered in the Revolution, and it is still with us today. Everything under the sun must change. I was an official of the previous regime. That fact alone makes me guilty. To save my skin, I confess to every charge, including plotting rebellion against the throne."

"Board President, you know what? I am really shocked. You, Her Majesty's favorite, of all people, are the first to confess!"

"That won't help. In fact, the other day, the moment I passed through the Lijing Gate, I was reminded of its nickname, the Gate of Despair. As of now, few prisoners have come out of the Gate alive and none in one piece. I figure, I'd better come clean now and hope for leniency. At least I will live. 'So long as the green hills are there, one should not worry about a shortage of firewood.' "

"Yes, where there is life there is hope," a gleeful Lai Junchen said. "Well, I can certainly help. I'll get the document ready, you'll sign it, and I'll submit it to Her Majesty."

"Will you, please?" a grateful Di said.

"Yes, I will." Lai motioned to have the prisoner taken out of the room.

***

As the news of Di Renjie's cowardly confession began to spread among the officials, Wang Deshou, Lai Junchen's assistant, came up with a plan to take advantage of the situation.

"Board President, I have brought the four treasures for you," Wang said to Di Renjie while visiting him in his prison cell. He placed a small hamper on the floor.

Di Renjie opened the lid and swept his gaze over what was inside: a scroll of paper, an ink stick, two writing brushes, and an ink slab.

"Thank you so much, Brother Wang," Di said.

"Not at all," Wang Deshou said. "Just let me know if there is anything else."

"I think I am fine. Lai's visit gave me hope that I will only get banishment to the far south with my family. But I do not know if that is for real."

"Of course, it is. But it will take a while. Hang in there."

"I will try to keep myself in one piece."

"You don't have to worry too much. I will take good care of you."

"I am so grateful." Di gave him a kindly look.

Wang Deshou glanced at the floor a few seconds and said in a low voice, "I wonder if you can help *me* with something."

"Yes? What is it?"

"You know we are under tremendous pressure to expose conspirators."

"So?"

"I am sure you know de facto Chief Minister Yang Zhirou."

"Of course, we were colleagues."

"Well, he has defied Her Majesty and we need to bring him down, but so far with no luck."

"Yes?"

"It would be great if you would bring a charge against him."

"How?"

"For example, you can name him as a member of the clique, your clique."

"What? Do you want me to frame an innocent man?"

"Hey, that doesn't sound nice."

"Lord on High! Why this thing is happening to me?" Di Renjie gruffed. Suddenly, he banged his forehead three times against the wood pillar near him as fresh blood streamed down his face.

"Hey, I take it back! I take it back! All right?" a frightened Wang Deshou said as he backed away, taking his hamper with him.

***

A few weeks later, Wang Deshou visited Di Renjie again, bringing with him a bundle which contained two egg pancakes, some preserved lard, a small jar of plum paste, and some clothing. He then asked the prisoner what else he needed.

"Just thank my wife for everything, please."

"Sure, I will do that." Wang turned to leave.

"Wait," Di Renjie said suddenly. "Can you do me a favor? And take this padded jacket to my wife?"

"With pleasure."

Di rolled the jacket into a bundle and used a hemp rope to tie it tight. "It is getting too warm here," he added. "Don't forget to tell her to take out at least a layer of batting."

"I will take care of that," Wang Deshou said and left the room with the bundle.

***

"Your Majesty," Lai Junchen said to Tianhou in her study, "after a thorough examination of the Di Renjie Anti-Emperor Clique case, the interrogators and reviewers have reached a consensus opinion: guilty. All the major conspirators, except for one, have confessed to the crime of plotting rebellion against the throne. Di Renjie even wrote a confession letter."

Yidu Neiren took a piece of paper from Lai and handed it to Tianhou.

"Do I hear that one of them refuses to confess?" Tianhou asked, while browsing through Di Renjie's letter.

"Yes. It is Wei Yuanzhong, Your Majesty."

The name jogged her memory of the man. She saw Wei Yuanzhong for the first time when he made his appearance in front of Emperor Gaozong to give a secret report in the late 670s. The emperor was impressed with the eloquence and calmness of this low-ranking official. But Wei, on taking his leave, failed to make a deep obeisance as required by ritual. The emperor commented, "What an egghead! That breach of ritual—I put it down to his ignorance. Still, I think he is chief minister material. I'm certain of that."

"Your Majesty," Lai's voice brought her back to the present. "Hou Sizhi has used almost everything we have on him."

"You mean every instrument of torture?" Tianhou asked.

"Your Majesty is very, very perceptive. Despite all that, he has remained defiant. He even said, 'Why don't you just lop off my head?' "

Tianhou tut-tutted her tongue while shaking her head.

"If Your Majesty gives us more time, say a month, I will find a way to make him talk."

"That won't be necessary," said Tianhou with a dismissive flick of her right hand. Keeping her eyes on the letter, she continued, "I am flabbergasted that that Renjie went to such a great length to scheme against me. I thought I treated him well enough. Unbelievable. But the signature is real." Lifting her gaze, she said to Lai, "What kind of punishment do you propose for the clique?"

"Execution and extirpation of the Three Clans."

"For all of them?"

"Except for Di Renjie. He confessed at his first trial. We propose to banish him to the far south for life."

"Let me think it over."

After sending Lai Junchen out of the room, Yidu Neiren closed the door, returned to sit next to Tianhou, and asked, "May I, Your Majesty?" She was anxious to voice her view.

"Fire away!"

"Your Majesty, the report is almost watertight, complete with eyewitness accounts and material evidence. Since the death of Qiu Shenji, Zhou Xing, and Suo Yuanli, Lai Junchen has become the most important Legalist law officer. He has done a great job, removing potential threats against Your Majesty. One should not take his report lightly."

"Do you think I should approve the suggested punishments?"

"Not really. No doubt Lai has done a lot for Your Majesty. However, I would, if I may, also like to remind Your Majesty of his *Classic on Framing*. In this short book, he professes his belief in the power of evidence, so much so that he is willing to create it out of thin air."

"Are you intimating that this report of his is based on manufactured evidence?"

"Not necessarily, Your Majesty. But one should keep that possibility in mind when dealing with the case. Especially when so many senior officials including chief ministers are involved."

"Indeed, the case is too complex. And we can't afford to rush it, can we? I'll put it on hold for now. The next round of executions won't take place until after the autumn harvest anyway. Meanwhile, I should probably appoint another panel consisting of non-Legalist judges like Xu Yougong. What do you think?"

"That is a great idea, Your Majesty," her confidante said.

***

Five days later, at Tianhou's request, a boy of eight or nine *sui* was brought into her study. Tianhou was intrigued by what this son of former de facto Chief Minister Yue Sihui[6] wanted to talk about.

"Where do you work?" Tianhou asked.

"Your Majesty, I work at the Court of State Grain Reserves."[7]

"How did you end up there?"

"After my father's execution, the family was broken up. Grownup men went to the far south. Women and children became bondservants working in the Lateral Palace or government agencies."

"You are a bondservant too at such a young age?" asked Tianhou, shaking her head.

"Yes, Your Majesty. But I have learned to cope."

"Anything important you want to share with me?"

"Yes. It is this. I am lodging a complaint against . . ." The boy dithered. He lifted the white tea bowl from the mahogany low table, took a sip of the hot tea, and nearly scalded his lips.

"Don't be afraid! Go ahead."

"I am lodging a complaint against the Legalist gang."

"You mean my law-enforcement officers."

"Yes. Your Majesty's laws on the books are just and fair. No one should complain about them. Least of all me, your humble servant. But the Legalist law officers have twisted them beyond recognition. If an innocent, honest court official falls into their hands, they will charge him with treason, torture him, and made him confess to his crime. On the bones of my ancestors, what I said is the absolute truth."

"I eliminated quite a few Legalist law officers already."

"But Lai Junchen is still there. He is the true ringleader of the Legalist gang. Now he seems to have more power than ever."

"Knowing that, you still want to complain against him?"

"Well, I don't have that much to lose, apart from the head on my shoulders."

"Do you have specific cases you want to complain about?"

"Di Renjie and Wei Yuanzhong are cases in point."

"You believe the anti-emperor gang is wrongly charged?"

"I suspect so, Your Majesty."

"I appreciate you sharing this with me. But what I have under me is an incredibly complex empire. I need a huge cadre of officials to keep it running from day to day, including law-enforcers like Lai." She waved her hand. A eunuch officer came up to take the young man away.

Turning to Neiren, Tianhou said, "Treat him to a good meal, and have him taken back to the Court of State Grain Reserves."

As Neiren was heading for the door, Tianhou added, "Give the boy fifty catties of silver, and restore his status as a subject."

"Yes, Your Majesty," Yidu Neiren said.

***

After the morning levee two days later, Tianhou made her way back to her study. Yidu Neiren came in, closed the door shut, turned around, and whispered in a low voice, "Your Majesty, we have got a break in the Di Renjie case." She drew a piece of silk from her bosom and handed it to Tianhou, saying, "I got it from his son."

This was an appeal letter that began with,

> *Your guilty subject Di Renjie basked in the radiance of Your Majesty's glory and rose to the pinnacle of officialdom. For that he is eternally grateful. He has devoted himself whole-heartedly to the service of the throne to the point of forgetting the self. So long as he breathes, he will remain the loyal servant of Your Majesty. On pain of death, he solemnly swears that the charge against him as head of an anti-emperor clique is preposterous and completely unfounded. . . .*

Tianhou looked up from the silk letter and asked quizzically, "How did Di Guangyuan[8] obtain this letter from his father? Renjie was in jail inside the Gate of Despair!"

"Di Renjie tore off the top cover of his quilt and wrote this letter on it. He then hid it inside a padded jacket. It was Wang Deshou who took it out of the prison."

"Bring him in immediately," Tianhou ordered.

"Wang Deshou?"

"No, Di Renjie the prisoner."

By early afternoon, when Tianhou was about to take her usual nap, she heard the sound of footfall outside, and made for the door in a hurry, followed by two female attendants. She saw a gray-haired man groveling over the threshold. Tianhou extended a hand to help him to his feet.

With Tianhou's permission, Di Renjie took his seat, with tears streaming down both cheeks. After Tianhou dismissed the female attendants, Di Renjie said in a shaky voice, "Your Majesty, I have been wronged!"

"Tell me how. Don't worry, I'll have your back!" shouted Tianhou, standing up, as if Di was hard of hearing.

"The whole thing is a setup by Lai Junchen."

"Why did he do it?"

"I, your subject, do not really know. Maybe he is power-hungry. It seems obvious that, after bringing down all the de facto chief ministers, he will replace them with his men."

"Let us assume this is what he is after, but why did you own up to the crime in the first place?"

"Well, Your Majesty, when I read the *Classic on Framing*, it gave me gooseflesh all over. When I learned that the author of that book Lai Junchen was in charge of my case, I knew I had to confess. If I did not, I could have lost my tongue, or, worse, been tortured to death. Or Lai Junchen with his brutal interrogation methods could have forced me to confess to any crime."

"However, why did you offer to write that confession letter? It gives the impression that you committed the crime and are contrite about it."

"What letter, Your Majesty?" Di Renjie asked with a perplexed look on his face.

Tianhou raised her hand. Yidu came over, picked up a piece of yellow paper from a pile of documents on the table, and handed it to him.

The moment he cast his eye on the letter, Di Renjie exclaimed, “Your Majesty, it is a fake! A complete fabrication! May I remind Your Majesty that when I sign my name, I always add an extra dot to the character *jie* 傑 . The forger made the mistake of ‘correcting’ it.”

“Did he?” asked Tianhou, her face darkening.

“Yes, I swear on the bones of my ancestors, Your Majesty,” Di Renjie said as he dropped on his knees and began to kowtow.

“All right, all right, Board President. Sit down.”

He heaved himself to his feet. With a trembling hand grasping the back of the chair, he plopped himself down.

***

By the time Tianhou gave Di Renjie permission to leave, the sun outside was setting. She sat down in her lounge chair to read today’s memorials that Yidu Neiren had selected for her. Several of them pleaded for leniency for the “conspirators,” and none supported Lai’s proposal.

After a lengthy discussion with Yidu Neiren and Shangguan Wan’er at dinner, Tianhou issued her edict on the case, “The ancients used killings to prevent further killings; I want to use grace to stop these executions. I would grant each of them a second chance at life and an official post, in the hope that they will make amends.”

Unwilling to see his hard work go to waste, Lai Junchen filed an appeal that targeted the treasonous crime of one of them, President of the Board of Works Pei Xingben, requesting his decapitation.

Xu Yougong, as the case's review officer, filed a rebuttal, saying, "Our enlightened sovereign offers a gift of life. What Lai Junchen proposes runs counter to it in spirit and can only do harm to the Sage Ruler's Way of grace and trust. While a subject should always loathe evil, he should also, when serving the sovereign, be in tune with her virtuous decisions."

On reading that, Tianhou reaffirmed her initial rule. Subsequently, all members of the clique were punished with banishment from the capital. Of the original seven "conspirators," only Pei Xingben and Li Sizhen were sent to true hardship places in the far south.

***

As a minor member of the clique, Chamberlain of the Court for State Sacrifices Cui Xuanli was demoted to the post of magistrate of Yiling,[9] a county on the north bank of the Yangzi. For his maternal nephew Censor Huo Xianke, this was the time to take a principled stand. He remonstrated with Tianhou, demanding the execution of Di Renjie and his gang including Cui Xuanli.[10]

"What?" a surprised Tianhou said. "For heaven's sake, Cui Xuanli is his uncle!"

"It seems that Her Majesty does not want to kill him," Huo responded. "That leaves me no choice but to end my life to show my selfless loyalty to the throne." He thereupon banged his forehead against the marble steps of the audience hall in the principal basilica until it was bespattered with blood.

A few days later, Tianhou spotted Huo in the audience hall, his head bandaged in a green silk band. She rolled her eyes in disgust and ordered his banishment from the court.

Notes

[1] The chamberlain of the Court of Imperial Sacrifices (*sili qing* 司禮卿).

[2] Left Vice Chancellor (*wenchang ge zuocheng* 文昌閣左丞) Lu Xian 盧獻.

[3] Luzhou潞州: prefecture that lay in Wuxiang and others, Shanxi, and Shexian and others, Hebei. Li Sizhen 李嗣真 (–696) was formerly vice censor-in-chief.

[4] The vice chamberlain of the Court for Judicial Review (*dali si shaoqing* 大理寺少卿).

[5] Liu Xian 劉憲.

[6] Yue Sihui 樂思晦.

[7] The Court of State Grain Reserves (*sinong si* 司農寺).

[8] Di Guangyuan 狄光遠 was Di Renjie's son.

[9] Yiling 夷陵 was in present-day Yiling, Hubei.

[10] *Zizhi tongjian* (205.6481) mentions Cui Xuanli only; but *Xin Tang shu* (115.4210) records "Di Renjie and others."

9. Tuan'er (692–693)

TIANHOU HAD RELIED on the Legalist law officers to go after her enemies since the Chuigong Reign (685–) under the Reign of Terror. Hundreds of the Tang royals and nobles had perished. Hundreds of senior court officials, culpable by association, were put to the sword, and their families destroyed. Condemned prefects and commandants[1] (*langjiang*) and those ranking below them were countless.

Once in a long while, an outspoken official stepped forward to stand up to the Legalist law officers. De facto Chief Minister Li Zhaode was one of them. But, as had been proven time and again, being chief minister afforded one no protection. He had remained immune from attacks by the Legalist law officers because of the support he received from Tianhou.

After he had helped her suppress Wang Qingzhi's petition campaign, Li Zhaode wanted to bring down the powerful forces that had been operating behind the scenes. And the only way to succeed was to win over Tianhou.

He saw his chance at a private audience with her one late afternoon.

"How could Wang Qingzhi have the guts to make demands with such tenacity?" Tianhou asked.

"Your Majesty," Li Zhaode answered, "in my opinion, the Luoyang commoner could not have done so without his backers."

"You mean Wu Chengsi?"

"And the other Wus as well. They used people like Wang Qingzhi to show that Chengsi's appointment to crown prince was popular with the masses."

"But he is my nephew."

"Yes, but that is all the more reason to be careful."

"You are not serious, are you?"

"I am very serious. Please allow me to ask Your Majesty: are aunt-nephew ties closer than father-son ties?"

"Of course not."

"Still, it is not uncommon for sons to commit patricide to seize the throne. A recent case was Emperor Yang of Sui.[2] To say nothing of nephews. I understand Your Majesty uses the Wus in the struggle against opposition at court. But entrusting too much power to the Wus will expose the throne to danger. Take Chengsi for example. He is the prince of Wei, one of the two chancellors, *and* the one and only successor-emperor. Still, he is not satisfied and wants more. Recently, he made a bid for the seat of crown prince and almost succeeded. If he became crown prince, it would be hard to rein him in. He might even be tempted to tread in the footsteps of Taizong."[3]

Tianhou listened without saying a word, a grave look on her face.

***

In the autumn of 692, a grand ceremony was going on at the Zhenguan Basilica in Luoyang's Palace City to celebrate the renaming of Bingzhou[4] as the "Northern Capital." On the same occasion, with pomp and circumstance, a host of key appointments were made, and high-sounding titles granted. Chancellor Wu Chengsi received the highest prestige title *tejin* (Specially Advanced).[5] President of the Chancellery Wu Youning—grandson of Wu Zetian's uncle Wu Shirang[6]—was named president of the Board of Works. President of the Board of War Yang Zhirou[7] was named president of the Board of Revenue. Simultaneously, these top officials were relieved of their duties as chief ministers, official or de facto, a fact that was not lost on them.

Those who were thus kicked upstairs soon flooded the court with complaints against the "peremptory way" in which Li Zhaode had handled their appointments.

Tianhou summoned Wu Chengsi, the leader of the group, to her study. With her permission, her nephew launched into a long talk about the grievances he and his colleagues suffered at the hands of the upstart.

With a flick of her hand, she cut him short, rose from her seat, and told him in a stern voice, "I can't sleep well at night unless Zhaode is in charge. To be frank with you, he is doing my bidding. You and your colleagues will do well to stop bitching! Do you understand?"

With sweat breaking out on his forehead, Wu Chengsi said cravenly, "Yes, of course, Your Majesty."

***

It was an open secret that Tianhou was interested in omens, especially ones that confirmed divine sanction. People would go to unbelievable lengths to look for them. In early 692, one subject from Shandong presented a rock with red veins as a propitious omen. Li Zhaode got down on one knee to examine it and then said with disdain, "To me, this is just an ordinary stone. What makes it special?"

"See those red veins, Chief Minister?" The man in his early forties ran his callused hand over the surface. "They represent a loyal red heart."

Li Zhaode gave a snort of contempt and said, "If this stone is loyal, does it mean other stones are disloyal?"

Amid a hearty laugh from those around him, Li Zhaode rejected the propitious rock out of hand.

A few days later, a man of Xiangzhou called Hu Qing[8] presented a divine turtle, whose underbelly bore the red characters *tianzi wanwan nian*[9] ("ten thousand years to the Son of Heaven"). Li Zhaode pulled out a dagger to scrape the characters, and red paint began to come off. "It is a fraud!" he shouted. Two guardsmen came over and arrested the forger. Tianhou then intervened to set him free, under the belief that "the man had done no harm." Had she not done so, this peasant of Xiangzhou would be languishing in jail for years.

***

Tianhou had ordered the banning of cats in the Palace City of Chang'an soon after Consort Xiao had issued the "cat threat." When she made the palace of Luoyang her home, she had adopted the same policy for fear that Xiao would morph into a cat-demon to haunt her place. But, over time, her love of feline animals had gotten the better of her. As soon as she received a Persian kitten as a gift from a foreign emissary, she fell in love with its snow-white long fur and grumpy face and decided to keep it close to her bedchamber.

Then she received a pair of parrots as tributary gifts from Chenla[10] (in Southeast Asia). The first time they were brought into the palace, the cat gave out a purring growl. The birds, one red and one green, fluttered their wings, but showed no signs of panic. The kitten was too small to pose a threat after all. In the following months, birds and cat were able to keep one another's company in peace, much to the pleasant surprise of Tianhou. In fact, she would often show them to court officials as an example how different types of animals could live together in perfect harmony.

Li Zhaode could not believe his eyes when he saw the scene. He cited a passage from the Confucian classic the *Venerated Documents* (*Shangshu*), "Obsession with playthings will inevitably sap the spirit," as he remonstrated with her against the keeping of the pets. But Tianhou showed no interest in mending her ways.

In the end, the unthinkable happened. The parrots one morning vanished. Only a handful of red and green feathers remained scattered on the floor. Obviously, the Persian, in a moment of hunger, had taken his companions for lunch. Tianhou felt embarrassed, took the blame on herself for the mishap, and banished the cat from the palace for good.

***

In 692, with the Legalist law officers restrained and their nemesis Li Zhaode riding high, an era of tolerance seemed to have arrived. There was a sudden increase in the number of memorials to Tianhou by middling and low-ranking officials.

For example, Court Rectifier Xue Qianguang[11] advised on how to improve the efficiency of civil and martial examinations designed to recruit officials and officers.

Chief Archivist Xu Jian[12] spoke of Taizong's Three Verifications,[13] which used to be enforced before each execution. He put it down to the utmost importance Taizong attached to human life and urged the court to revive them. That, he asserted, could only enhance the authority of the throne.

Court Rectifier Zhu Jingze,[14] having given praise to the successful banning of dissident opinion with the use of severe punishment, called attention to the need to lighten punishment and promote leniency now that the dynastic change had already taken place and the masses had been pacified. To prove his point, he cited the cases of Chancellor Li Si of Qin and Gaozu of Han (Liu Bang).[15] The former adopted a policy of severe punishment in eliminating the local lords, which brought about his own destruction. The latter founded a dynasty that lasted twelve generations, thanks to his ability to adopt lenient policies and make changes in response to the needs of the times.

Attendant Censor Zhou Ju, emboldened by his colleagues, presented a most critical memorial, in which he pointed an accusatory finger at the Legalist interrogators. He singled out two procedures they had invented to break the interrogated. The first one called *yuchi*[16] or "jail maintenance" began with filling the ears of the prisoner with mud before forcing him to wear by turns an iron head cage, a heavy cangue, and an iron headband on his forehead tightened with wedges. It ended with crushing his rib case, piercing his nails with bamboo skewers, hanging him by the hair, and fumigating his ears.

The second one called *suqiu*[17] or "overnight imprisonment" involved the deprivation of food, an all-night interrogation, and constant shaking of the body to keep the prisoner awake.

When subject to these tortures, he argued, prisoners often broke on the first day and fessed up to whatever crime they were charged with. With this threat hanging over their heads, the court officials passed their days as if on pins and needles and lived under the constant fear that Her Majesty, their best friend in the morning, would turn into their worst foe at night.

Zhou Ju ended his passionate memorial with a stern historical lesson: "The Zhou thrived after adopting the rule of benevolence; and the Qin perished after imposing severe punishment. It is my hope that Your Majesty lightens punishment and practices benevolence. For that all under Heaven will feel grateful."[18]

Over the years, Tianhou had learned not to be offended by critical memorials like these anymore. To be sure, she did not relish reading them, but nonetheless took them seriously, especially those by Zhu

Jingze (to whom she even gifted 300 bolts of silk as a reward) and Zhou Ju. She mulled over their proposals for weeks before, under the advice of Yidu Neiren and Shangguan Wan'er, she decided to act on some of them. Over time, punishment in general was greatly reduced in severity and the number of men and women in custody fell by a large margin. It gave hope to men in the street that, at length, a new age of benevolence was dawning.

***

Also in the year 692, there was a resurgence of Wu Zhou power in the Western Regions, a strategic area sitting astride the Silk Road connecting China with the Roman Orient.[19]

Back in 670, when a Tang army had marched into the area to protect the Four Garrisons, it had suffered a disastrous defeat in the hands of Tubo, the new overlord of the Western Regions. Vice Commander-in-Chief Wang Xiaojie was taken captive. But, once there, he was surprised to receive a royal treatment during his long captivity. It was so because, he was told, he bore a resemblance to the *zanpu*'s father. By the time he left Tubo, he had gained a good knowledge of its strengths and weaknesses.

Twenty-two years on, Wang Xiaojie, along with his lieutenant Ashina Zhongjie, returned with a large Wu Zhou expeditionary army. After they scored a decisive victory against the Tubo, they seized from their hands a massive area of Central Asia extending from Xinjiang to Western Turkestan, and reestablished the Four Garrisons of Anxi at Qiuci, Yutian, Shulê, and Suiye.[20]

***

Since his deposition in 690, Prince Li Dan and his five sons had existed under the constant threat of banishment to the far south or extermination, as the campaign to eliminate the Li royals had continued. One reason for their survival had been Tianhou's decision not to appoint a Wu as crown prince. They were safe so long as Li Chengqi, Li Dan's eldest son, held on to his title of "imperial grandson," and Li Dan his title of "imperial heir." But there were no lack of Legalist law officers and Wu Chengsi supporters at court who would gladly see them disappear. By necessity, Prince Li Dan and his sons lived their lives with great caution, "as if they were standing on the edge of a steep cliff or walking on thin ice," as they say in the *Classic of Odes*.[21] So did Li Dan's two wives—Consort Liu and Consort Dou[22]—both of whom were exemplary, aristocratic women.

A mishap then struck the prince's household when one of his maids had a spat in the Northern Market with a palace bondwoman. In the heat of the argument, the maid called the bondwoman "bitch," "slave."

That night, Li Dan gave the maid a good dressing-down and a serious warning. That would have been the end of the story except that the bondwoman called Tuan'er was no ordinary bondservant. She had spent her childhood as the daughter of a senior official until she was forced into bondage in the Lateral Palace after his father's fall from grace and banishment from the capital. After someone close to the throne noticed that she was quick on the uptake, they had her transferred to the palace. Now one of Tianhou's favorite girl servants, she decided to turn the incident into a boon for herself. Instead of complaining about the maid, she cooked up a story about her masters, Consort Liu and Consort Dou, accusing them of practicing witchcraft against Tianhou, a capital crime. With Tuan'er as their guide, Tianhou's men went to a suburban house the two consorts had frequented and unearthed a couple of wooden effigies, linking them to black magic.

The two consorts were still in the dark when they came a few days later to the Jiayu Basilica[23] in the palace to pay homage to Tianhou. After the ceremonial visit was over, they, along with the maid, exited the basilica door, walked across the courtyard, and disappeared through the main gate, never to be seen again. It was rumored that some of Tianhou's hatchet men knocked them down with thick sticks and dumped their bodies into one of the abandoned wells, of which there were many in the palace grounds.

The loss of his two wives hit Prince Li Dan hard. Still, he had to keep his sorrow to himself and look calm or put on a smile whenever he was in the presence of Tianhou for fear of getting on her nerves. He said nothing when a few months later a court order condemned his late wives for doing witchcraft.

***

Tuan'er, for her part, felt encouraged by her success and decided to try her hand at "conjecturing," a game only the best-informed people near the throne had the guts to play. That was, to figure out Tianhou's real intention on a major issue and make an anticipatory move. Through listening in on Tianhou's conversations with her advisers, Tuan'er concluded that the succession struggle was far from over and Tianhou would place a Wu on the crown prince's seat sooner or later.

The only reason that she had not done so was that she still recognized Prince Li Dan as heir. But the fact that she called him "imperial heir" instead of "crown prince" showed her reluctance to support him all the way. *If I can help to drag him through the mud,* Tuan'er figured, *it will enhance Wu Chengsi's chances. If he ascends the throne, I will be rewarded with restoration to free-subject status at the minimum. That will in turn open a vista of opportunities, including promotion to official posts and even marriage.*

Tuan'er made her move in late 692, charging Li Dan with practicing black magic. But she was not in a position to know what Tianhou's real thoughts on succession were. After Wang Qingzhi's campaign to make Wu Chengsi heir failed and after Wu himself was caught in the Jasper scandal, Tianhou had given up on grooming him as successor. When she read Tuan'er's report against Li Dan, it immediately raised a red flag. She was alarmed that even her servant had begun to meddle in succession politics. On her orders, an investigation was launched and it soon exposed Tuan'er as a liar and a fraud. The bondwoman finally fell victim to her own machinations. In early 693, she was dispatched with a barrage of thick sticks. Her body ended up at the bottom of one of those abandoned wells.

By ordering Tuan'er's death, Tianhou showed that she was still unwilling to abandon Prince Li Dan as heir. Neither could the condemnation of his two wives, Consorts Liu and Dou, seriously affect his status. However, these events put Tianhou on guard as she continued to worry about efforts to restore Tang rule.

One late afternoon, she received a secret report on an unauthorized visit two high-ranking officials had made to Prince Li Dan. She lost no time in having the visitors—President of the Directorate for Royal Manufactories Pei Feigong and Inner Regular Attendant[24] Fan Yunxian (whose tongue had been cut out recently)—arrested. Both were summarily executed by waist chop in the Southern Market. From then on, visits to the prince by court officials were permanently banned.

***

The case of Tuan'er did not happen in isolation. It was part of an ominous trend in which bondservants, maids, and domestics were encouraged by the Legalist law officers to accuse their masters.

Consort Dou's mother (Prince Li Dan's mother-in-law) Lady Pang fell victim to this trend as well. She was living comfortably in Runzhou where her husband Dou Xiaochen[25] was the prefect when her daughter vanished in the palace. A household bondwoman then started practicing black magic to blackmail his wife. A frightened Lady Pang gave in to her threat and joined her in her occult activities in the dead of night.

When someone tipped off the authorities, Supervising Censor Xue Jichang, a nephew of General Xue Rengui, travelled to Runzhou to investigate. In a week's time, he wrapped up the case and returned.

At a court session, he was asked to present his findings. When he had the floor, he broke into a sob that lasted several minutes before he blurted out, "Your humble servant finds it unbearable to even talk about what Lady Pang has done."

"Speak you must," Tianhou demanded.

With seeming reluctance, Xue Jichang went on to give a scathing report. Lady Pang, he concluded, had joined the late Consort Dou in practicing witchcraft.

"Against whom?" asked Tianhou.

"Your Majesty, I believe."

Subsequently, Lady Pang was sentenced to decapitation and Mr. Xue was rewarded with promotion to supervising secretary (*jishi zhong*).

The fair-minded Attendant Censor Xu Yougong, at the request of Lady Pang's sons, did a thorough review of the case and found that Censor Xue Jichang's conclusion rested, to a large extent, on unsubstantiated evidence (such as forced confessions by bondservants). He requested a stay of the execution while conducting his own investigation.

Censor Xue Jichang fought back by filing charges against Xu Yougong himself for covering up Lady Pang's crime, and got his law officer friends to make Xu Yougong guilty and condemn him to death by hanging. Everyone in the legal profession knew that this was a most undignified way of dying, even worse than decapitation. But when Xue Jichang sent his men to break the bad news, Xu Yougong looked as if nothing out of the ordinary had happened. He simply asked, "Am I the only one to die? How about the others? They will never die?"

By "the others," Xu Yougong probably referred to those corrupt Legalist law officers. At any rate, he showed neither regret nor remorse, which was actually his best hope for leniency. After his mid-day meal, he lay down in a cot and placed a wicker fan on his face to catch a sleep that lasted hours. He behaved in a way quite unlike someone on death row.

In the evening Tianhou summoned him into her basilica.

"You don't seem to be disturbed at all," she said.

"Not really, Your Majesty. What is the use to worry about death if it will happen no matter what?"

"But don't you regret your previous decision?"

"No, I do not, Your Majesty."

"Don't you know that, in the course of your career, you have erred on the side of leniency too often and acquitted too many people by mistake?"

"I plead guilty as charged, Your Majesty. However, when I, your humble servant, am wrong, it is because I acquit someone by mistake, and that is a small error. And when I am right, I save life, and that adds to the great virtue of Your Majesty the Sage Ruler."

Tianhou remained quiet for a while, then said, "I see your point. Let me think it over carefully before making a final judgment." She gestured to have him taken away.

She was reminded of Xu Jian's recent piece on the Three Verifications before every execution under Taizong and said to herself, "The Legalists take this as a perfect opportunity to remove Yougong, don't they?"

She read the three reports one more time and handed down her decision. Lady Pang would be banished with her three sons to the far south. Her husband Dou Xiaochen would be demoted to assistant prefect of Luozhou.[26] As for Xu Yougong, he would be punished with disenrollment. That meant that Judge Xu would still be around and could be recalled any day. A hell of a lot better than death by hanging.

***

To Lai Junchen, Tuan'er's failure to bring down Prince Li Dan was due to inexperience and lack of support at court. The recent execution of two high-ranking officials, Pei Feigong and Fan Yunxian, for visiting the prince sent a clear signal that he was still vulnerable. Lai Junchen formulated his own plan to topple the prince, in the belief he could, in his capacity as the top Legalist law officer, pull it off.

First, he hauled dozens of Li Dan's men to prison, put them through hellish torture, and forced them to confess their crimes. A workman called An Jincang snapped when faced with Lai as his interrogator, and blurted out in hysteria, "The prince has no ambition for the throne! If you don't believe me, I can show you the color of my heart to prove his loyalty!"

Lai shouted back, "If you don't do it, you are a coward!"

The workman pulled out a sword and slit open his lower belly where the heart supposedly lay and collapsed. As his guts were spilling out, he writhed in great pain on the blood-soaked floor.

Tianhou, upon learning what had happened, had An Jincang transported in her own palanquin into the palace. The palace physicians shoved his guts back into his abdomen before using a thread made of mulberry tree bark to suture up his wound and applying a fair amount of medicinal powder.

A couple of weeks later, as soon as Tianhou learned that the patient was on the mend, she paid him a visit. Although not known for giving in to tender feelings, Tianhou was moved to tears by the sight of An Jincang, a stoutly built, middle-aged man, wan and pale, knitting his brows in excruciating pain. She let out a long sigh and said, "My poor son Li Dan! He just can't defend himself. Otherwise, it would not have had to come to this."

Before leaving, she issued a rescript to stop Lai Junchen from harassing the Lis.

***

In early 693, Tianhou received an informer's report on a plot against the throne in the far south, organized by some vagabonds. Since the conspiracy was already nipped in the bud, there was no need to send an expeditionary army. Instead, Tianhou appointed the low-level officer Wan Guojun as investigative censor to head the investigation. Wan had gained some notoriety as the coauthor with Lai Junchen of the *Classic on Framing*, and a master of cruel investigative techniques in his own right.

Upon arrival in Guangzhou in Lingnan Circuit,[27] he had more than 300 vagabonds rounded up at daybreak. He then read out a forged Tianhou's rescript that granted them the honorable way of ending their own lives by suicide. The crowd broke into a mass hysteria with shouts of "Injustice!" Brandishing whips and spears, Wan's men drove them to the bend of a river, and slaughtered them to a man, making the river water turn red with blood.

Based on fabricated evidence, Wan Guojun, upon return, wrote a report that not only justified his action but also warned Tianhou against vagabond threats elsewhere. Tianhou was impressed. She conferred upon Wan a much higher prestige title: counselor for closing court,[28] and appointed five more low-ranking officials as ad hoc censors to prosecute rebels in five other Circuits. Looking up to Wan Guojun as their model, they engaged in a killing competition, with death tolls ranging from 100-plus to 700.

Before long, Wan Guojun's scheme was exposed. Wan himself was thrown into prison in Luoyang and died in custody. Fantastic rumors about him began to surface. According to one, once when he was traveling in the south of the city, he was intercepted by demons at the Tianjin Bridge. He jumped off his horse to fall on his knees and kowtow repeatedly, begging for mercy. He was then lifted back onto the horse, beaten savagely, and died lying prone on the saddle in great pain.

The ad hoc censors were all banished to faraway places.

Notes

1 The commandant (*langjiang* 朗將): often commanding officer of a garrison in the *fubing* system.

2 Emperor Yang of Sui 隋煬帝 (r. 604–618): he was suspected of having a hand in his father's (Emperor Wen Yang Jian) death.

3 Taizong had risen to power after the Xuanwu Gate incident of 626.

4 Bingzhou 并州 was the name of Bing Prefecture and its seat near Taiyuan, Shanxi.

5 *Tejin* 特進 (Specially Advanced): a prestigious supplementary title (*jiaguan* 加官).

6 Wu Shirang 武士讓.

7 Yang Zhirou was Tianhou's favorite because she considered him as a member of her mother's clan.

8 Xiangzhou 襄州: prefecture that lay in Xiangfan, Yicheng, and others, Hubei. Hu Qing 胡慶.

9 *Tianzi wanwan nian* 天子萬萬年.

10 Chenla (Zhenla) 真臘: country in Indochina with its core area in Cambodia.

11 Xue Qianguang 薛謙光 was court rectifier (*buque* 補闕).

12 Xu Jian 徐堅 was chief archivist (*zhubu* 主簿) in Wannian 萬年 County, Chang'an. *Zhubu* sometimes rendered "assistant magistrate" was the third top leader of a county.

13 The Three Verifications (*sanfu zou* 三覆奏) refer to the policy to verify a death sentence three times before it was carried out. See *Zizhi tongjian* 193.6087–88.

14 Zhu Jingze 朱敬則 was right court rectifier (*you buque* 右補闕).

15 Chancellor Li Si 李斯 of Qin. Gaozu of Han (Liu Bang 劉邦).

16 *Yuchi* 獄持.

[17] *Suqiu* 宿囚.

[18] *Jiu Tang shu* 191, 索元禮傳.

[19] The Silk Road is a network of roads connecting China, Central Asia, West Asia, the Middle East, and the Mediterranean area. It has existed since the early Western Han. But the name was first used in the late nineteenth century.

[20] Suiye 碎葉 (Tokmak, Kyrgyzstan) now replaced Yanqi as one of the Four Garrisons.

[21] *The Classic of Odes* (*Shijing* 詩經) is a Confucian classic and the most ancient collection of poems.

[22] Consort Liu 劉妃; Consort Dou 竇妃.

[23] The Jiayu Basilica 嘉豫殿 was perhaps in the northwest corner of the Palace City, just east of the Jiayu Gate, which was the northern gate on the west side of the palace.

[24] The Directorate of Royal Manufactories (*shaofu jian* 少府監): a third-tier government agency on a par with a Court. The inner regular attendant (*nei changshi* 內常侍).

[25] Dou Xiaochen 竇孝諶.

[26] The assistant prefect (*sima* 司馬). Luozhou 羅州: prefecture in Huazhoushi, Guangdong.

[27] Lingnan Circuit 嶺南道: the southernmost administrative region encompassing Guangdong, Guangxi, north Vietnam, and others.

[28] The counselor for closing court (*changsan dafu* 朝散大夫).

10. Li Zhaode (694)

FOLLOWING THE DEATH of Wan Guojun and the banishment of his associates, Tianhou's patience with the Legalist law officers was wearing thin. She decided that the time had come for another purge. The first one whose luck had run out was Attendant Censor Hou Sizhi. Acting on an anonymous tip, the authorities raided his home and uncovered a large quantity of silk brocades. He was immediately hauled to jail since the hoarding of silk brocades had been banned repeatedly by the court. Sensing Tianhou's change of attitude towards the Legalist law officers, the prosecutor Li Zhaode sentenced him to death. With his plea for mercy falling on deaf ears, Hou Sizhi, a most-feared and -hated guerrilla general and one of Tianhou's favorites, was clubbed to death in 693.

Then, a fellow guerrilla general Wang Hongyi fell from grace in late 694. He was banished to the far south for his abusive treatment of laborers. When he was halfway to his place of banishment, he received a special pardon from Tianhou. So he turned around and went on his return journey. As he was travelling along the Han River, he encountered a court envoy, who asked him to present his travel documents. Hou showed him an edict from Tianhou. That, upon close examination, was a fake. That meant that Wang had "deceived the sovereign" on purpose, a capital crime. Therewith he was clubbed to death on the envoy's orders.

About the same time Lai Junchen himself stumbled. After he was exposed for taking bribes from merchants, he was tried and found guilty and sentenced to death. Tianhou then reduced it to demotion to adjutant in Tongzhou.[1] That was tantamount to banishment. Before long, however, he was transferred to Hegong[2] County to serve as its defender. This suggested that Tianhou still intended to keep him close by.

Originally known as "Henan," Hegong was one of the two royal counties of Luoyang. Hegong and Luoyang Counties together covered the entire walled area of the Divine Capital.

***

With Lai Junchen's fall, Li Zhaode had emerged as the most powerful official at court. Different from other de facto chief ministers, Li Zhaode had won the complete trust of Tianhou and was the only one allowed to carry a gold-plated scepter that invested in him the power to make life-and-death decisions on most people without prior approval by Tianhou.

When a massive northern expeditionary army was launched against Tujue, Li Zhaode was appointed its deputy commander-in-chief so that he could gain some valuable experience in the military while keeping an eye on Commander-in-Chief Xue Huaiyi and Assistant Commander-in-Chief Su Weidao.[3] Under their command were eighteen generals, each with his own sizeable contingent of foot and horse.

Prior to this, General Wang Xiaojie had already scored two consecutive victories in the Outer Western Regions, respectively against Tubo and remnants of Western Tujue.

In the third month of 694, the expeditionary army marched north to confront the Later Tujue khan Mochuo, successor to Gudulu,[4] who had recently raided Lingzhou.[5]

A few days into the march, the army command received news of Mochuo's withdrawal, and called a stop to the operation.

***

While Li Zhaode was on campaign in the north, Tianhou was busy keeping the company of the Three Visitors, all endowed with magical power. The first one was Old Nun of Henei[6] with the title of "Pure and Light Tathāgata,"[7] now residing in the Linzhi Convent.[8] It was believed that she had the ability to see into the future.

The second one was a Mount Song-based Daoist called Wei

Shifang. By his own account, he had been born during the Chiwu[9] Reign (238–251) of the Three Kingdoms period.

The third one was a Central Asian known as Old Hu (Old Caucasian).[10] Reportedly, he was 500 years old, even older than Wei Shifang. He and Master Xue had been acquaintances for 200 years. But he still looked like someone in his forties.

Tianhou might find these claims incredible. But convinced that the Three Visitors were on the verge of immortality, she was eager to learn their techniques.

On Tianhou's orders, they took up residence inside the palace and were treated like distinguished guests of state. The Daoist Wei Shifang, the most learned of the three, was even appointed by a special edict as de facto chief minister.

Although the Three Visitors espoused three different religious beliefs—traditional Buddhism, Daoism, and Tantric Buddhism—they all claimed to share one commonality that contributed to their longevity: abstention from evil indulgences such as sex and consumption of meat and wine. Inspired by their preachings, Tianhou had issued several edicts to ban slaughter of animals.

When Tianhou asked the Three Visitors to divulge their secrets on longevity, the clairvoyant Old Nun was the first one to reveal hers: eating one flaxseed and one kernel of rice a day.

Old Hu, who was on intimate terms with Old Nun, gave Tianhou a secret Tantric formula.

The Daoist Wei Shifang showed Tianhou an esoteric recipe handed down from generations.

Tianhou was fascinated with these novel approaches but found it hard to benefit from them.

Old Nun's diet called for extreme deprivation, which was as good as starving, and was more than Tianhou's aging body could endure.

Old Hu's formula was a nonstarter, precisely because it was prepared with a Tantric method. Tianhou still remembered what had happened to Emperor Taizong. The Tantric drugs he had taken to prolong life had probably achieved the opposite effect.

Wei Shifang's nostrum held out the greatest promise. But it contains ingredients not available in the north. On her orders, Wei then went on an herb-gathering mission in the Lingnan area in the far south.

***

After his return to Luoyang, Li Zhaode resumed his duties at court, but with a changed work schedule. Before the expedition, he had been routinely summoned to discuss important court and government issues with Tianhou. Since he came back, for months he had not been summoned once. Li Zhaode chalked it up to the presence of the Three Visitors, who had kept Tianhou occupied.

It was about this time that some unflattering reports on Li Zhaode reached Tianhou's table. For example, one filed by a low-ranking official said,

> *Prior to the Tianshou Reign (690–691), Your Majesty made decisions on government affairs herself. Starting in the Changshou Reign (692–694), however, much decision-making power fell into the hands of Li Zhaode. Since he was appointed de facto chief minister and given access to state secrets, he has often shown a penchant for arbitrary action and vaunting himself. He*

fails to follow the fundamental principle governing sovereign-subject relations: "Attribute everything good to the sovereign, and acknowledge every error as your own." It seems to me that his bravado is bigger than can be contained by his shell and he puts on airs that boggle the mind. As the proverb says, "Ant holes can destroy a tall dam; a pinpoint can deflate the air." If he goes on behaving like this, his fall is almost guaranteed.

Then a Guard commandant wrote a scathing treatise called *Shilun* (On Stone).[11] After it was passed around among the court officials, a Secretariat drafter submitted it to Tianhou. Apart from railing against Li Zhaode's high-handed way of decision-making, it asserted that, over the years, Li had formed a clique of supporters at court, who always sided with him. The treatise ended with a warning to Tianhou: Li had amassed so much power that he had become a menace to the throne.

By and by, with attacks like these, Tianhou's perception of Li Zhaode began to change. Faced with repeated requests by the Legalist law officers for an investigation, Tianhou gave her nod. Until recently, Tianhou had used Li as a counterweight against the Legalist law officers. By now, the most notorious of them had fallen, and she was much less dependent on Li's service than before. Still, when the Legalist law officers recommended the forfeit of life as his punishment, Tianhou intervened. In view of the service he had rendered in the past, she reduced his punishment to demotion to county defender before banishing him to the far south.

Li Zhaode's ouster impacted the five remaining chief ministers as well, especially Doulu Qinwang (president of the Secretariat), Su Weidao, and Wei Juyuan. All were demoted to prefects in the provinces.

Notes

[1] The adjutant (*canjun* 參軍): low-level adviser on military matters, especially in a prefecture or a princely establishment. Tongzhou 同州: prefecture that lay in Dali, Shaanxi, and areas to its north.

[2] Hegong 合宮 (also known as Henan 河南): county with its office in Kuanzheng Ward 寬政坊 in the southwest area of Luoyang. See *Tang liangjing chengfang kao* 5.167; *Xin Tang shu* 38, 河南府河南郡.

[3] The deputy commander-in-chief (*zhangshi* 長史); the assistant commander-in-chief (*sima* 司馬). Note: in a princely establishment or prefecture, the *zhangshi* was one of its top leaders and is rendered as "chief administrator"; and *sima*, which was below *zhangshi*, as "deputy chief administrator" or "assistant prefect."

[4] *Zizhi tongjian* 205.6493.

[5] Lingzhou 靈州: prefecture that lay north of Zhongwei and Zhongning, Ningxia.

[6] The Old Nun of Henei 河内老尼. Henei: county in Qinyang, Henan.

[7] The Pure and Light Tathāgata (Jingguang Rulai 淨光如來). Tathāgata is one of the ten major titles of Sakyamuni.

[8] The Linzhi Convent 麟趾尼寺 was in Xingyi Ward 興藝坊 in the northeast corner of Luoyang.

[9] Chiwu 赤烏 was a Wu reign title.

[10] The Old Hu 老胡 (Old Caucasian).

[11] *Shilun* 石論.

11. Xue Huaiyi (694–695)

XUE HUAIYI HAD no reason to doubt that his lucky star was still in the ascendant. After Censor Feng Sixu had made a vain attempt at impeachment, no censor had bothered to bring charges against him. Since his unpleasant encounter with the old curmudgeon Su Liangyu at the Southern Office, he had never met a single official who dared to stand up to him. The old bastard had died anyway. On the recent northern expedition, Li Zhaode, then-current favorite of Tianhou, had tried to challenge his strategy. On the spur of the moment, Xue had him thrashed outside his campaign tent. That was enough to silence him.

A few years back, when the Hall of Heaven project was halfway through, it was hit by a powerful gale and reduced to rubble in a matter of minutes. Instead of blaming Xue Huaiyi, Tianhou gave him permission to rebuild. For several years, he commanded an army of ten thousand laborers to work on the project every day. At his request, the best master craftsmen were hired and pest-resistant *nanmu* trees were transported by river and land from the far south for use as timbers. To keep the project going, the state treasury was almost exhausted. But Tianhou refused to ask questions.

Pampered by Tianhou, Master Xue spent money like dirt, money that did not belong to him. His alms-giving gatherings (*pañca-vārṣika-pariṣad*) were often held on a lavish scale. On one occasion, he attracted a large throng of young men and women packed shoulder to shoulder. On his orders, ten cartloads of cash (bronze coins) were scattered into the crowd, setting off a stampede, that trampled many of the small and weak to death.

Over time, however, Tianhou's passion for him had waned. Age did not seem to be the issue. True, she was approaching seventy, but still exuded much charm and energy indicative of good health. Recently, she had grown new teeth and black hair, a clear sign of physical rejuvenation. But still she had summoned Xue much less often.

For the life of him, Xue Huaiyi could not figure out why until he caught sight of her personal physician Shen Nanqiu, a well-preserved man in his fifties. He clung to her like a leech and the way he spoke to her suggested that they were on intimate terms with each other: "Huagu, don't forget to take your herbal tea before breakfast!" or "Huagu, put on more clothes when you go out, it is getting cold!" or "Huagu, it's time for your decoction!" The shameless tone of the physician stoked the fire of rage in the monk.

Eventually, Xue Huaiyi managed to put a cap on his emotions. He began to stay away from the palace as much as possible, in the hope that distance would make him more desirable. As abbot of the suburban White Horse Monastery, he had ordained as many as a thousand musclemen as monks. That made Attendant Censor Zhou Ju suspicious. Fearless and inexperienced, the censor obtained, after several efforts, Tianhou's permission to prosecute Xue for possible illegal ordinations.

At the Censorate, where they had agreed to meet, Zhou Ju saw Xue Huaiyi sitting bare-chested on a chair at the bottom of a flight of steps. As soon as Zhou's men approached him, Xue rose to his feet, jumped onto a horse, and galloped away.

Zhou Ju reported this to Tianhou.

"The man is sick," she responded. "It is not worth your while to go after him like this. Why don't you focus on his followers first?"

So Zhou Ju with his men raided the White Horse Monastery. He rounded up all the ordained musclemen and had them banished to faraway prefectures.

Soon, because of merit, Zhou was promoted to vice bureau director in the Board of Personnel. Just as his career in officialdom was about to take off, he got entangled in a frameup, punished at the hands of Xue Huaiyi's buddies in law enforcement, and in the end disenrolled.

***

On December 6, 694, Xue Huaiyi held an alms-giving gathering at the Mingtang. He planned to pull off something extraordinary to impress Tianhou. In preparation for this, he had had a hollow five *zhang* (50 ft) deep dug into the floor of the building. Inside the hollow, his men had created a makeshift structure, called "the basilica," decorated with silk ribbons of different colors. On the day of the event, Buddha statues were pushed out one by one from the basilica as a vast crowd watched on.

The next day (December 7), he had a gigantic Buddha painting set up south of the Tianjin Bridge. It was executed with the blood of a freshly slaughtered ox. Xue Huaiyi claimed that his own blood was used on the painting as well, blood that he had let out from a self-inflicted stab wound in his leg. It was in front of the painting that he held a vegetarian feast, where he used a wooden ladle to dole out millet and veggie dishes to hundreds of clergy lining up in a queue.

For two days, Xue Huaiyi had hoped against hope that Tianhou would send a eunuch officer, or better still, make a personal appearance at one of the events. By the late afternoon of the second day when the last ceremony was drawing to a close, and there was no sign of Tianhou or her envoy coming to join him, Xue was struck with dismay and disappointment, and then anger, upon realization that he had lost favor with Tianhou, who had fallen for that evil doctor Shen Nanqiu.

***

That night, a full moon shone faintly through dark clouds. The reddish lunar aureole was hardly visible. In the wee hours, a spark started a small fire at the foot of the giant statue inside the Hall of Heaven. It simmered for about half an hour until its flames licked up the feet, legs, body, and head of the giant Buddha, and the roof of the Hall, breaking the darkness of the landscape and erupting into a conflagration that lit up the sky.

Before eunuchs and palace maids rushed to the scene bearing lanterns, flaming torches, firebrands, and buckets of water, the Hall and the statue had been reduced to piles of rubble and ashes.

The Mingtang nearby had caught fire as well; it had sustained so much damage that restoration and repair was no longer feasible.

Meanwhile, strong wind sweeping from the north tore down the Buddha painting south of the Tianjin Bridge and shredded it into hundreds of pieces.

An investigation followed. When every piece of evidence pointed to Xue Huaiyi as the culprit, Tianhou called a stop to it. In fact, she was so ashamed of what had happened that she only allowed a made-up story to be released: the fire had been started by accident by laborers working on the ramie-cloth statue in the Hall of Heaven.

This act of Heaven was interpreted as a warning from the Lord on High that the mortals on earth had been going down the wrong path. To appease the divine wrath, it was suggested that all festivities and celebratory gatherings be suspended. Tianhou agreed and wanted to go one step further and issue a self-blaming edict.

Chancellor Yao Shu demurred. "In the past," he said, "when a hall on a terrace in Chengzhou[1] was on fire (593 BCE), a divination predicted greater prosperity for later generations; the destruction of the Bailiang Terrace (104 BCE) under Emperor Wu of Han made way for the rise of the Jianzhang Palace.[2] Traditionally, only the destruction of the Ancestral Temple calls for self-blaming pronouncements. But neither the Mingtang nor the Hall of Heaven is an ancestral temple.

The Mingtang is the place for proclaiming public policies, and the Hall of Heaven, the structure for housing the Buddha statue. In neither case is a self-deprecating action necessary."

The convoluted argument gave her pause.

But the Mingtang and the Hall of Heaven would be rebuilt. On Tianhou's orders, Xue Huaiyi was again appointed the project's commissioner.

To lend might to the new Mingtang, Tianhou ordered the reproduction of the Nine Tripods of Xia[3]—symbolic of the Nine Provinces and the authority of the Son of Heaven—and the creation of the statues of the Twelve Zodiac Animals,[4] and had them installed in appropriate locations in its courtyard.

***

After the destruction of the Hall of Heaven and the partial destruction of the Mingtang, Tianhou for a while was busy with the reconstruction of the two buildings, and did not have time to be with the Three Visitors at all.

In late 694, Old Nun paid a visit to offer her condolences.

On seeing the nun for the first time in months, Tianhou was reminded of her claim to clairvoyance, and asked, "Aren't you the one who can see far into the future?"

"Yes, Your Majesty. As your humble servant, I am always ready to offer my service."

"Where have you been recently?"

"I have been here in Luoyang, Your Majesty."

Suddenly, Tianhou stood up and asked sharply, "Where were you when the Hall of Heaven went up in smoke? And the Mingtang was damaged beyond repair?"

The Old Nun fumbled for words. Tianhou continued, "Why didn't you warn me about the fire?"

"Your Majesty, I was . . ."

"You are a fraud, aren't you? Get out!" Tianhou glowered as Old Nun backed away, shamefaced.

Therewith Tianhou issued an edict that banished Old Nun from Luoyang to Henei where she had been based. Her disciples in the capital and her friend Old Hu vanished without a trace.

Gradually, unsavory reports by informers began to reach Tianhou about Old Nun and Old Hu and dozens of their female followers. According to one of them, after dark, these self-professed vegetarians, teetotalers, and ascetics gorged themselves on beef and mutton and drank wine like water. They then held night orgies together.

Tianhou felt betrayed. "How could they break their religious vows of abstinence?" she asked. "How could they fool me like that?" On her orders, Old Nun and her disciples in Henei went back to the Linzhi Convent in Luoyang. Not long thereafter, they were taken into custody before being condemned to bondage in the Lateral Palace.

On his way back from the south, the Daoist Wei Shifang stopped in Yanshi,[5] a small town east of Luoyang. It was there that he heard what had happened to the other two visitors and he got scared. When he realized that his days were numbered, he hanged himself at his inn.

***

One afternoon in late spring Tianhou was reposing on a sandalwood lounge chair in the forecourt of the residential basilica, with Yidu Neiren sitting by her side. They were having a casual chat.

"As Your Majesty knows," Yidu said, "since antiquity, it has been a given that men are superior and women are inferior."

"Of course, beyond a shadow of a doubt."

"In ancient times, the first female sovereign was Nüwa.[6] She is lumped together with Fuxi and Shennong[7] as the Three Sovereigns. However, she never really ruled as a Son of Heaven, but only as an assistant to Fuxi, helping him run the Nine Provinces."

"That was such a long time ago. Maybe a thousand years before the Xia dynasty?"

"Yes, Your Majesty. Nüwa nonetheless was the first of a long line of powerful women, empress dowagers, and grand empress dowagers, who stepped out of their boudoirs to play a decisive role in governing the world. But they never became true rulers. They ruled either on behalf of a weakling or a minor."

"So what?"

"Your Majesty is different. You are the *only* woman in history who has actually received the Mandate of Heaven. You have given up the golden bracelets and diamond necklaces to don the imperial regalia. Auspicious omens arrive at the court often. And not a single senior court official dares to make a noise against you. You are the true female Son of Heaven ruling over the realm in name *and* in reality."

Tianhou half closed her eyes, a slight smile on her face.

"In view of all this, I, your humble servant," Yidu continued, "would like to propose something for your consideration."

Tianhou nodded her head slightly and Yidu continued, "From this day forward, Your Majesty should dismiss all those gigolos and firmly establish your control, independent of outside influence, over all under Heaven. That will greatly enhance the yang of your rule, making the males emasculated and the females dominant for myriad generations."

After Yidu left, Tianhou spent a long time pondering her advice. *Yes, I need to enhance the yang of my rule and make the females dominant. But, do I have to send away all the gigolos? Not really. I can twist them around my little finger and manage without getting rid of them. Whenever I want to have fun, they are at my beck and call. What's wrong with that? Of course, I do have to watch them. Those who challenge my rule will have to go. I can tolerate them for acting weird, but not for threatening my power*. She thought of Xue Huaiyi and heaved a sigh.

After the fire that burned down the Hall of Heaven and damaged the Mingtang, Xue Huaiyi had often experienced intense mood swings. One moment, he loathed himself as a kept man so much that he wanted to put an end to his miserable existence; the next he felt on top of the world—even Tianhou had to yield to his whims. When in such an exhilarated state of mind, he would make threatening, disrespectful utterances.

Tianhou heard reports of them from her snoops and felt threatened. For added security, she surrounded herself with a hundred specially trained stout palace maids.

***

The sun was setting one late afternoon in early 695. Xue Huaiyi finished his work on the new Mingtang, as he had done every day for weeks recently. He got on his horse and started riding towards home. While passing through the forecourt of the Yaoguang Basilica,[8] he was accosted by a group of musclemen in black. They pulled him off his horse, tackled him to the ground, and dragged him under an old tree as he kicked and screamed in violent protest.

Without warning, Tianhou's nephew Wu Youning came into view on horseback. Xue went quiet as his face darkened. Wu dismounted, read out an edict, and waved a hand. And a volley of sticks rained down upon Tianhou's disgraced lover until his body went limp. The men in black then transported his lifeless body in a cart to the White Horse Monastery. There it was turned into ashes before being buried in the foundation of a pagoda. Xue's disciples and attendants were thereupon banished to faraway hardship places. Memories of this rags-to-riches legend, great architect, and head of the most powerful monastery in the country would be purged from public consciousness.

Notes

1 Chengzhou 成周: at that time there were two urban centers in the Luoyang area. The eastern one located east of present-day Luoyang was called Chengzhou, which was the capital.

2 The Bailiang Terrace 柏梁臺: Western Han structure in the Weiyang Palace 未央宮. The beams of its building were made of cypress (*bai*), hence the name. In 104 BCE, after it was destroyed by lightening, a lavish suburban palace called Jianzhang 建章 was built.

3 The Nine Tripods: according to legend, Yu, at the founding of the Xia dynasty, created the Nine Tripods symbolizing the Nine Provinces.

4 The Twelve Zodiac Animals are twelve animal signs that are matched with the years in the twelve-year cycle of the lunar calendar and the twelve Earthly Branches.

5 Yanshi 偃師.

6 Nüwa 女媧.

7 According to legend, Fuxi 伏羲 was the inventor of the Chinese script. Shennong 神農 (Divine Farmer) was the inventor of farming and medicine.

8 The Yaoguang Basilica 瑤光殿 was in Luoyang's Palace City. Its precise location is unknown. See *Zizhi tongjian* 205.6502. Cf. *Xin Tang shu* 76.3483; *Jiu Tang shu* 183.4743.

12. Heavenly Pivot (695–696)

IN THE SUMMER of 695, the Heavenly Pivot (Tianshu), a commemorative column, was erected south of the End Gate (Duanmen) outside the Imperial City on Tianmen (Heavenly Gate) Avenue—the main north-south road—that ran all the way to the Dingding Gate, the southern main entrance to the city. To the south of the End Gate was the famous Tianjin (Heavenly Ford) Bridge across the Luo River.

Tianhou's nephew Wu Sansi and a few foreign chieftains had come up with the idea. Some foreign chieftains and notables had raised a large sum of cash for purchasing the copper and iron needed for the project.

This imposing artifact consisted of a bronze column 105 *chi* (feet) tall and 12 *chi* thick rising from a cluster of miniature iron hills resting on the backs of auspicious bronze animals—dragons, lions, and unicorns. Over the top spread a canopy 30 *chi* across covered with cloud patterns. Crouching on the canopy were four dragons, each holding a fire ball in its mouth.

The copper nameplate at the base of the column bore its full name: the "Great Zhou's Heavenly Pivot of the Myriad States in Praise of Virtue"[1] in Tianhou's own hand. Beneath that was a long inscription composed by Wu Sansi. It gives praise to Tianhou's Revolution while expressing disdain for her Tang predecessor. It was followed by a long list of donors, including the Hundred Officials and the barbarian chieftains.

The column may have drawn its inspiration from a foreign source. The Indian king Aśoka had erected his commemorative pillars as early as the third century BCE. The project leader Abraham was a Jew who hailed from Persia now under the Umayyad Caliphate, a land famous for its ancient commemorative pillars with animal capitals.

In astrology, the Heavenly Pivot (Tianshu) was also the name of the first star of the Big Dipper (Ursa Major), symbolic of the center of power. The naming of a commemorative column as Tianshu near the Heavenly Ford (Tianjin) and on Heavenly Gate (Tianmen) Avenue accentuated the celestial nature of Tianhou (Heavenly Empress) and her city, Luoyang, now known as the "Divine Capital."

More than sixty years before in 630, Taizong had been crowned the title of "Heavenly Khan" (*tian kehan*). In a way, the event was comparable to the inauguration of the Heavenly Pivot. Both involved foreign chieftains in adulation of a Chinese sovereign and both were associated with Heaven.

However, there was a major difference. While Taizong's title of Heavenly Khan was suggested by foreign chieftains, Tianhou's Heavenly Pivot was proposed by Wu Sansi, her nephew, and built with money donated by foreign chieftains and notables.

To celebrate the erection of the Pivot, Tianhou paid homage to the Southern Suburban Altar south of Luoyang on October 22, 695. After making sacrificial offerings to Heaven and Earth, she assumed the title of "Heaven-Appointed Great August Emperor of the Gold Wheel,"[2] and announced a general amnesty and the change of the reign title to Tiance Wansui (Ten Thousand Years on Heaven's Appointment).

The propitious occasion was enhanced by the good news that Mochuo Khan of Later Tujue had made a plea for submission. Tianhou welcomed the gesture; she appointed him general-in-chief of the Left Guard and granted him the title of state duke of submission. But Tianhou knew that, calculating and unpredictable, Mochuo probably did not have a complete change of heart. In fact, by offering to submit he did not lose an iota of his military and political autonomy.

***

On January 10, 696, Tianhou, accompanied by a procession stretching for dozens of *li*, set off for Mount Song, where she would conduct the *fengshan*[3] sacrifices. The traditional venue for *fengshan* was Mount Tai. Tianhou selected a different site on purpose even if it meant defying tradition. For her, Mount Song was the "Divine Marchmount"[4] and the closest one of the Five Marchmounts to the Divine Capital.

On January 20, Tianhou was carried in a palanquin to the top of the Great Chamber,[5] the main peak of Mount Song, where she conducted the *feng* rite to Heaven. On the same occasion, she announced another general amnesty, the change of the reign title to "Wansui Dengfeng" (Ten Thousand Years on Ascent for Feng Ritual), and the nationwide exemption of grain tax for a year. These announcements kicked off a Grand Drinking Festival for all under Heaven lasting nine days.

On January 23, she reached the top of the Lesser Chamber,[6] another peak of Mount Song, where she conducted the *shan* rite to Earth.

Two days later, on January 25, she mounted the Altar of Pilgrimage to receive felicitations from the Hundred Officials and the chieftains.

Upon return to the Luoyang Palace on the 29th, she paid a ritual visit to the Ancestral Temple the following day to wrap up the *fengshan* event.

On the heels of this flurry of ritual activity, the Wu temple in Chang'an, which had been known as the Temple of Ancestral Worship[7] and the Temple for the Worship of Worthies,[8] was quietly redesignated as *the* Ancestral Temple. The Li temple of the Tang was shoved to the sidelines.

***

With the recovery of the Western Regions, Wang Xiaojie was celebrated as the new ever-victorious general since Heichi Changzhi. Now appointed commander-in-chief of the Expeditionary Army of Shuofang District, he was leading another campaign against Tubo. Lou Shide, a man in his mid-sixties, was assigned as vice commander-in-chief of the same army. But the two top commanding officers could not be more different. Wang was slim and of medium height, a great horse-rider and a sharp archer. Lou was portly and tall, a poor horse-rider and a lousy bowman. Nicknamed "Dumpy," Lou Shide was clumsy in public, but approachable and good-tempered, and would split his sides with laughter when he heard a good joke. Behind his back, people loved to tell stories about him.

It was said that once when Lou was on his way to the court, his colleague Li Zhaode, then at the height of his power, caught up with him from behind. Impatient with Lou's slow movement, Li shouted, "Hurry up, you stupid country bumpkin!"

Lou answered with a smile, "You are absolutely right, Chief Minister. If Shide is not a country bumpkin, who is?" The expression "country bumpkin" suggested association not only with "rural background," but also "uncouth manners" and "a lack of refinement." As a *jinshi* degree holder since twenty *sui*, Lou Shide clearly did not fit the mold. Still, he readily accepted the epithet for the sake of geniality.

When his younger brother was appointed prefect of Daizhou, a strategic prefecture in the north, Lou Shide was gravely concerned. He admonished his brother thus, "I am a chief minister and you the governor of a key prefecture. Both of us are in a position of high power. It is only natural that people may look upon us with envy and hatred. What are you going to do to avoid that?"

The brother dropped on his knees and answered, "Elder Brother, I promise: even if somebody spits on my face, I will not fight back. I will wipe off the spittle instead."

With a troubled look on his face, Lou Shide said, "That is exactly what worries me. When someone spits on your face, it is because he is angry with you. If you wipe it off, you will make him angrier. You should instead smile and let the spit go dry by itself!"

This kind of humility, rare among top officials, made Lou a great colleague to work with. Thanks in part to his smooth cooperation with General Wang, the expeditionary army won a series of easy victories at the beginning of the campaign.

But their luck soon ran out. As the Tang troops were marching into Taozhou in the third month of 696,[9] a Tubo army ambushed them in the Suluohan Mountains[10] and thoroughly trounced them. Both commanding officers fled in rout.

Wang Xiaojie was the first to be punished. He was disenrolled and banished to a distant place.

Lou Shide was in his office revising a document when he learned his own fate. He would be deprived of his noble title and demoted to supernumerary assistant prefect of Yuanzhou.[11] That would knock him down from the pinnacle of power to the bottom rung of the hierarchy. Although Yuanzhou was not in the middle of nowhere, it was quite far from the Western Capital. His initial response was one of disappointment. He asked the eunuch who came to deliver the message, “Am I losing both my post and title?” Before he got an answer from the eunuch, he came around and said, “Fine. I’ll just start over.” It was obvious that he did so because he realized that he still got a respected government job, and that was not too shabby at all.

The crushing defeat in the hands of the Tubo was an ominous sign. The northern frontier was by no means secure and tough challenges might lie ahead.

Notes

1 *Da Zhou wanguo songde tianshu* 大周萬國頌德天樞.

2 *Tiance jinlun dasheng huangdi* 天冊金輪大聖皇帝.

3 *Fengshan* 封禪.

4 *Shenyue* 神嶽.

5 Taishi 太室.

[6] Shaoshi 少室.

[7] Chongxian 崇先.

[8] Chongzun 崇尊.

[9] See *Zizhi tongjian* (205.6504). *Jiu Tang shu* gives 695 (97, 婁師德傳, 證聖元年). Taozhou 洮州: prefecture that lay in Lintan and others, Gansu.

[10] The Suluohan Mountains 素羅汗山 were east of Lintan, Gansu.

[11] Yuanzhou 原州: prefecture that lay in Guyuan and others, Ningxia, and Pingliang and others, Gansu.

13. Threat on the Frontier (696)

THE GREATEST THREAT to the security of the northern frontier in 696 was neither the Tujue nor the Tubo, but a rather obscure people, the Qidan (Khitan).[1] The Qidan had emerged in history in the late fourth century, after they had spun off from the Xianbei during the Disturbances of the Five Barbarians.[2] By the early seventh century they had formed a tribal confederation. After submitting to the Tujue, they switched allegiance to the Tang under Taizong. Their lands, encompassing southern Manchuria, northern Hebei, and neighboring areas in Inner Mongolia, were then placed under a Tang area command.[3]

Under Tianhou, Area Commander of Yingzhou[4] Zhao Wenhui was assigned to govern the Qidan. But Zhao turned out to be a poor choice for the job. He was arrogant and unpleasant as a person and showed little compassion for his non-Han subjects. When the area was ravaged by a famine and the starving Qidan came to him for help, he refused to provide relief grain. Even worse, he treated their leaders Li Jinzhong and Sun Wanrong as if they were his slaves.

When summer came, the deep-rooted hatred against Zhao Wenhui and his cronies exploded. Under Li and Sun, the Qidan staged an open revolt against the court, sacking the city of Yingzhou and killing Area Commander Zhao Wenhui himself.

In the Qidan War that followed, twenty-eight generals, each with a large contingent of troops, marched into Yingzhou the prefecture to confront the rebels. Prince of Liang Wu Sansi was appointed pacification commissioner of Yuguan[5] District to take charge of the entire operation, with Yao Shu as his lieutenant.

Tianhou, for her part, placed a curse on the rebel leaders by having their names changed: Li Jinzhong ("Li the Thoroughly Loyal") now became Li Jinmie ("Li the Thoroughly Destroyed");[6] and Sun Wanrong ("Sun with Ten Thousand Honors"), Sun Wanzhan ("Sun with Ten Thousand Decapitations").[7]

***

In its first major engagement against the Qidan, the Wu Zhou army suffered a humiliating defeat with hundreds of officers and men captured. The captives, while being kept in a dungeon, learned from their Xí[8] prison guards that the Qidan soldiers were starving and that, everything considered, they were no match for Tianhou's army.

When a Qidan general came to feed them with a standard meal consisting of bran porridge, he said, almost with an apology, "This is the best we can do. We don't even have enough grain to feed ourselves." He then released them.

As soon as the captives returned to the Wu Zhou camp in Youzhou,[9] they briefed the commanding officers about what they had seen and heard. Based on this and other intelligence, they launched a general attack. Along the way, they passed by many animals, all emaciated. In the Huangzhang Vale,[10] they were greeted by a band of white-flag-waving Qidan soldiers. Most of them were in their forties and fifties, too old for regular military duty, and many were weak and sickly. All this affirmed the resolve of the leadership to go after the enemy main force.

General Cao Renshi,[11] commanding officer of the vanguard, could not wait to clinch a major victory. Leading a forward troop of cavalry, he pushed deep into enemy territory, leaving the baggage train far behind. With no logistical support and reinforcement, the cavalry rushed into an ambush and were almost wiped out, with the commander himself taken prisoner.

The foot soldiers trailing behind were caught in a surprise attack in a valley. Both General-in-Chief Zhang Xuanyu and his lieutenant Vice Chamberlain of the Court of the National Granaries Ma Renjie[12] fell into enemy hands after their horses were tripped by ropes.

To make things worse, the Qidan now had General Zhang's seal. They used it to forge an order: "The government forces have defeated the rebels. If you don't come to Yingzhou in a timely manner, the generals will be beheaded. The soldiers will not get their merit awards." They then forced Zhang Xuanyu to affix his signature under threat of death.

Two area commanders, upon receiving the order, marched their troops posthaste north. With little time for sleep and food for days, both men and horses were exhausted by the time they fell into a trap sprung by the enemy and were annihilated.

***

The devastating defeat the Wu Zhou army suffered in the hands of the despised Qidan left Tianhou distraught. She dismissed Wu Sansi and Yao Shu from their posts after censuring them, and appointed Prince of Jian'an Wu Youyi as commander-in-chief of the Expeditionary Army of Qingbian District[13] to lead the operation. To swell the ranks of the anti-Qidan forces, she authorized the recruitment of prisoners and bondmen for military service in the war-torn area. But this policy hardly improved the situation.

A war of attrition followed that dragged on for months.

The Tujue, forgetting their recent pledge of allegiance and commitment not to conduct raids, made an opportunist assault on Liangzhou,[14] capturing Area Commander Xu Qinming.[15]

***

It was about this time that a large Tubo mission arrived with harsh demands. Tianhou immediately suspected a conspiracy where the Qidan, Tujue, and Tubo were ganging up on her. In reality, there was no strategic coordination between them. Tubo, in particular, was very much on its own.

At Tianhou's request, Guo Yuanzhen, adjutant of the Armaments Section of the Right Militant Guard,[16] went to meet with the Tubo emissary at the border to find out about their real intentions.

At forty-one *sui*, Guo was no ordinary functionary. He had obtained the prestigious *jinshi* degree at the young age of nineteen *sui*. Everyone then had believed he would be considered for fast-track promotion.

Chief Minister Zhang Jiazhen for one had been struck by his graceful carriage and intelligence.

"Hey, young man, how about becoming my son-in-law?" Zhang suggested.

"I am greatly flattered, Chief Minister. But I don't want to rush into a marriage. I know you have five daughters. How can I be sure that they are not plain-looking?"

"Yuanzhen, I can assure you all my daughters are great beauties. Customs don't allow you to see them right now. But I can still give you an opportunity to make a choice. How about that?"

That left Guo Yuanzhen no choice but to accept the offer.

A few days later, when Guo found himself in a large room in the Zhang residence, he saw five silk ropes in different colors sticking out from behind tall purple curtains. After a brief hesitation, Guo picked up the red one, and pulled. Out came the chief minister's third daughter. Since Guo was not able to find a single blemish with her looks, he accepted her as his wife, and they got married soon afterwards.

After his first appointment as defender of Tongquan[17] County, what happened next disappointed everybody. He did not seem to care about career advancement, and often engaged in illegal activities including coin counterfeiting and human trafficking. No wonder people in the county hated him and he got stuck in this low-level position for a good twenty years.

Eventually, Tianhou had enough of this corrupt official. As she seriously considered ways to make an example of him, she summoned him into the palace for questioning. Minutes into their first conversation, however, Tianhou was convinced that she was in the presence of a genius. At her request, Guo presented some of his written works. She was impressed with his style of writing and took an instant liking to one of his poems entitled the "Treasured Sword."[18] Thereupon, she transferred him to a post at court after pardoning his past transgressions on condition he would make amends in the future.

Guo Yuanzhen was chosen to deal with Tubo because of his talent, his intimate knowledge of Tubo, and his flair for analysis. Even though there were many more experienced officers of much higher ranks who could also do the job at hand.

At the meeting with the Tubo, Guo was taken aback when he saw for the first time the great Lun Qinling himself, head of the Tubo mission and *the* power-holder at the Tubo court.

At the top of the list of demands Lun handed him was *heqin* or "marriage alliance,"[19] an age-old institution that dated back to the early Western Han dynasty. By marrying off a "royal princess" to a powerful barbarian chieftain, the emperor would become the father-in-law of the chieftain, and deter him from making attacks. It was hoped that this kind of marriage ties would guarantee peace on the border between the two peoples for generations to come.

The request brought back memories for Guo of the 677 *heqin* mission from Tubo when the *zanpu* insisted on having Princess Taiping as his bride. Tianhou had used a subterfuge to prevent that from happening. *But the alliance this time,* Guo Yuanzhen thought, *does not involve her own daughter, so it is more acceptable. She can select any royal princess or even a nonroyal young lady as bride after granting her royal status.*

The next on the list was the abolition of the Four Garrisons in Central Asia and the withdrawal of Zhou garrison troops and civil officials from the area.

The third demand was permission to take over lands previously controlled by the Ten Tribes of Western Tujue in the Suiye (Chu) River[20] Valley and areas to its west, now under Wu Zhou's nominal control.

Guo Yuanzhen was aware of how strong the Tubo military had grown under Lu Qinling, but the aggressive tone of his demands still shocked him.

He took a breath to collect himself, and responded, "People living in the Four Garrisons and the Ten Tribes areas are quite different from the Tubo. Still, you ask us to withdraw our troops and hand over their lands to you. That shows you are interested in territorial expansion, something you promised not to do."

"I disagree," Lun Qinling said. "If we covet more territory, we would have invaded Ganzhou[21] and Liangzhou much closer to us. Why should we care about lands ten thousand *li* away?"

In the end, Lun Qinling was not swayed by Guo. He continued with his journey east and arrived in Luoyang with his original demands.

That left Tianhou in a bind. With the Tujue encroaching upon prefectures on the northern border and the Qidan carving out their turf in the northeast, she could ill afford to have another hostile power on the western frontier. But, among her top commanders of troops, the Wus were essentially useless. Lou Shide and Di Renjie were the only ones she could count on, but both were in exile. Lou was in Yuanzhou[22] in the northwest, and Di was in the south. Both were in low-level posts. It was too late to recall them. The trouble was that she had never felt comfortable dealing with China's neighbors in the first place. Neither could her female advisers—Shangguan Wan'er, Yidu Neiren, and others—offer much help. It was then, when Tianhou was almost at the end of her rope, that she received Guo Yuanzhen's secret report:

Lun Qinling's requests—withdrawal of troops and territorial cessions—are of grave concern. We should not treat them lightly. But if we flatly turn them down, it will no doubt trigger a deep crisis on the border: our Ganzhou and Liangzhou may soon be under attack. This may happen before we begin to benefit from having the Four Garrisons in our possession. So we have to keep these issues in mind while making decisions.
In my humble opinion, for now, it is essential to keep the Tubo's hope for peace alive. To that aim, I would like to propose that we say the following in our reply,

"The Four Garrisons and Ten Tribes areas were originally of little value to the Central Kingdom.[23] Our rationale for stationing troops there was to safeguard the Western Regions and to discourage hostile forces from moving into areas further to the east. As for the lands you request, we will consider giving up half of the Ten Tribes area on condition that you return the former Tuyuhun area and the Qinghai area in the east, which you recently captured. We hope that this suggestion is acceptable to you, considering you have expressed no interest in an eastern invasion."

The offer will no doubt be turned down by Lun Qinling, but it will probably keep him from pressing his demands further and thus help to prevent the Tubo from severing ties with the Zhou, which is dangerous.

As for marriage alliance, it will bring peace. The Tubo people have long been tired of heavy corvée and garrison duties, and most of them are in favor of peace. However, Lun Qinling, being the military dictator he is, does not really want a marriage alliance. In my opinion, if the court sends a marriage emissary to Tubo, Lun Qinling will do his utmost to sabotage his mission. But his act will expose his true intention and deepen his people's distrust of him, which may even bring about his downfall.

Tianhou was sold. She took the report to her chief ministers for discussion the following morning. As expected, they failed to offer anything better. She then authorized a carefully worded response to Lun Qinling essentially based on Guo Yuanzhen's proposal. In the end, Lun Qinling left with an agreement to conclude a marriage alliance, but without any territorial gains. An international crisis was thus averted. As for the marriage alliance itself, it did not come to fruition precisely because of Lun Qinling's lack of sincerity.

***

A significant number of Tujue nomads had been settled in six northern prefectures: Ling, Xia, Feng, Sheng, Shuo, and Dai.[24] In 696 Mochuo made a demand for the return of all the Tujue households and the lands of the Chanyu Grand Protectorate,[25] in addition to requesting material aids. By now, under Mochuo, Later Tujue had grown into a force to be reckoned with. When they threw their weight around, they caused a lot of jitters south of the border.

While the Wu Zhou was still at war with the Qidan in the northeast and struggling to resist erosions by the Tubo in the west, hostilities with the Tujue would spell disaster.

After a heated debate at court, Tianhou, sensing the prevailing sentiment against taking on the Tujue, authorized the return of the Tujue households and a shipment of 40,000 *hu* (bushels) of grain seeds, 50,000 bolts of colored silk, 3,000 farm tools, and 40,000 catties (*jin*) of iron. These gifts, it was believed, were to contribute to the material basis for the rise of Later Tujue as a dominant power in the north.

About two months later, as Tianhou was still waiting with bated breath for a response from the north, a Tujue delegation arrived. To her relief, Mochuo's letter his emissary presented was rather friendly. First and foremost, he expressed his wish to be Tianhou's adopted son; second, he sought the hand of a royal prince for his daughter in a marriage alliance" (*heqin*); third, he asked permission to launch a campaign against the Qidan. At the bottom of the list was a "modest" request for the return the Hexi[26] households who had surrendered to the Wu Zhou.

At Tianhou's request, the court officials debated about how best to respond to Mochuo's letter. The most prominent issue here was by far marriage alliance (*heqin*). Since the Han dynasty it had always meant marrying off a Han princess to a barbarian chieftain. What Mochuo looked for—a prince for his daughter—was just the opposite. But strictly speaking, it was not that different. As was expected, it split the court into the pro- and anti-*heqin* camps. Members of the pro-*heqin* camp included Yang Zaisi, Guo Yuanzhen, Yan Zhiwei, and others. Belonging to the anti-*heqin* camp were Li Qiao, Zhang Jianzhi, Tian Guidao, and others.

At a court session, Yan Zhiwei and Tian Guidao sparred over the issue. Yan Zhiwei asserted, "Marriage alliance can be very effective. After Wang Zhaojun's marriage to a Xiongnu *chanyu*, the northwestern frontier remained peaceful for a good sixty years."

Tian Guidao countered, "But Mochuo has never been a reliable partner. As certain as spring will follow winter, he will go back on his words. A marriage alliance with him will be an exercise in futility."

"How do you know without even trying?"

"I have dealt with him before and know how fickle he is."

"I too have dealt with him. I think he is someone we can do business with."

So the bickering went on until Tianhou ordered them to stop.

The *heqin* topic was brought up again at a later court session. The focus was then shifted to the northern border strategy. The majority of the key officials present concluded that, in view of the internal and external challenges it faced, the court should use *heqin* to avoid conflict with Tujue.

Tianhou, in the end, sided with the pro-*heqin* camp and decided to send a friendly mission to Tujue, headed by General-in-Chief Yan Zhiwei and Acting Chamberlain for Tributaries[27] Tian Guidao. They would confer two high-sounding titles (those of general-in-chief and khan) upon Mochuo and discuss *heqin* and other issues with him in person.

***

In the tenth month, the Qidan leader Li Jinzhong died. Just as Sun Wanrong was stepping into his shoes, his people suffered a surprise attack by Mochuo's Tujue forces in Songmo[28] and both Sun's wife and Li Jinzhong's widow fell into their hands. Tianhou took note and granted Mochuo two more prestigious titles.[29]

Despite their heavy losses, the Qidan eventually rallied under the new chief, and were soon on the offensive, not against the Tujue, but the settled communities in Wu Zhou territory. They sacked Jizhou[30]—slaughtering several thousands of its official and civilian residents including the prefect—and swooped down on Yingzhou.[31] For a while, the entire Hebei area was within their grasp.

Notes

[1] The Qidan 契丹 (Khitan) were a non-Han ethnic group active in the Tongliao area in the Xiliao River valley and neighboring areas in Inner Mongolia, with roots going back to the Northern Wei.

[2] The Disturbances of the Five Barbarians (304–439) refer to a time when five non-Han ethnic groups invaded and ruled North China: Xiongnu (Hun), Jie, Qiang, Di, and Xianbei.

[3] On the area command (*dudu fu* 都督府), *see* note in Part I, Chapter 13.

[4] Yingzhou 營州: prefecture that lay in west Liaoning.

[5] Yuguan 榆關.

[6] Li Jinzhong 李盡忠; Li Jinmie 盡滅.

[7] Sun Wanrong 孫萬榮; Sun Wanzhan 萬斬.

[8] Xí 霫: non-Han ethnic group of Xiongnu origin, active north of the Xar Moron River, Inner Mongolia. They should not be confused with Xi 奚.

[9] Youzhou 幽州: prefecture that lay in north Hebei and Liaoning.

[10] The Huangzhang Vale 黃麞/獐谷 was in the southeast of Lulong, Hebei.

[11] Cao Renshi 曹仁師.

[12] Zhang Xuanyu 張玄遇. Vice Chamberlain of the Court of the National Granaries (*sinong shaoqing* 司農少卿) Ma Renjie 麻仁節.

[13] Qingbian District 清邊道.

[14] Liangzhou 涼州: strategic prefecture that lay in Wuwei, Jinchang, and others, Gansu, and Alxa Youqi and others, Inner Mongolia.

[15] Xu Qinming 許欽明.

[16] The adjutant (*canjun* 參軍): a low-ranking staff officer (*see* note in Part II, Chapter 10). The Armaments Section (*zhoucao* 冑曹) was in charge of weaponry. The Right Militant Guard (*you wuwei* 右武衛) was one of the Sixteen Guards.

[17] Tongquan 通泉 was a county in the southeast of Shehong, Sichuan.

[18] The "Treasured Sword" ("Baojian pian" 寶劍篇).

[19] *Heqin* 和親.

[20] The Suiye River 碎葉水 (Chu River 楚河) was close to Tokmak, Kyrgyzstan.

[21] Ganzhou 甘州: prefecture that lay east of Jiayuguan, Gansu.

[22] Yuanzhou 原州: prefecture and its seat and chief city (Guyuan, Ningxia).

[23] Here I use "Central Kingdom" in place of "Middle Kingdom" to avoid confusion with the Middle Kingdom period of ancient Egypt.

[24] Ling 靈, Xia 夏, Feng 豐, Sheng 勝, Shuo 朔, Dai 代: six northern prefectures (*zhou* 州) extending from north Ningxia through the Ordos to north Shanxi.

[25] The Chanyu Grand Protectorate (*chuanyu da duhu fu* 單于大都護府): it lay in the northeast Ordos, Inner Mongolia, and areas to its north. *See* note in Part I, Chapter 15.

[26] Hexi 河西 : the Hexi Corridor in Gansu.

[27] The acting chamberlain for Tributaries (*she sibin qing* 攝司賓卿): previously known as *honglu qing* 鴻臚卿.

[28] Songmo 松漠: north of Chifeng, Inner Mongolia.

[29] Mochuo received one khan title and one "great chanyu" title.

[30] Jizhou 冀州: prefecture that lay in present-day Jizhou and others, southeast Hebei, and Dezhou, Shandong.

[31] Yingzhou 瀛州: prefecture that lay in Gaoyang, Hejian, and others, Hebei.

14. Xu Yougong (696)

IN 692, WHEN the anti-emperor case was drawing to a close, Tianhou was unhappy with the fake confession letter allegedly by Di

Renjie. But a secret discussion with her confidante convinced her to leave the chief suspect Lai Junchen alone, if only for the purpose of maintaining a balance of power between different factions at court. Besides, there would be occasions again where attack dogs like Lai could come in handy.

Di Renjie, as a member of the clique, had to leave for his place of banishment in the south. While en route, he stopped in Kaifeng for a brief stay at an inn.

Huo Xianke then was the magistrate. After his attempt to profess his loyalty to Tianhou backfired, he had been transferred to this post.

As soon as he got news of Di Renjie's arrival, he paid him visit, escorted by a few underlings.

"What brings you here?" the magistrate asked.

"I injured my right foot while in custody. I am here to see a famed chiropodist. As soon as I am done, I'll leave."[1]

The magistrate would have none of it. He served Di with an ultimatum: "Get out of my county by sunset, or else."

Di Renjie in the end had to cancel his room and leave without the treatment. He felt saddened, not so much by the ill-treatment at the hands of a petty man like Huo as by his own new pariah status in officialdom.

After he settled down in Pengze[2] County to serve as its magistrate, he gradually restored his self-confidence. Situated south of the Yangzi and removed from the Central Plain, Pengze had been made famous by one of the poetic greats of the Six Dynasties, Tao Yuanming. To be its magistrate, even though by way of demotion, was not too shabby a deal after all, considering what could have happened if Lai Junchen and company had gotten their way.

***

One rainy afternoon in the tenth month of 696 when Di Renjie was presiding over the hearing of criminal and civil cases in the main hall of the magistrate office, a eunuch officer arrived on horseback with an urgent edict. It ordered him to go north therewith and report for duty in Weizhou.[3]

Located in the southernmost part of Hebei, Weizhou was one of the most populous prefectures in the country. With the Qidan poised to push south, it could become the new frontier soon. To its south lay open country that led straight to Kaifeng, the eastern outpost of Luoyang. In peace times, the area's flatlands yielded an abundance of grain. In times of trouble, an invading army could roll across with ease, unobstructed by natural barriers.

While Di Renjie appreciated his promotion from county magistrate to prefect of a major prefecture (*zhou*), he also realized that, with it came a serious responsibility: to stop the Qidan's southern advance. To avoid being caught off guard by an unexpected maneuver of the enemy, his predecessor had forced a large number of suburban residents into the walled area of the prefectural seat also known as Weizhou and shored up its defenses. However, this had the unintended consequence of depressing local farming and trade.

"I am afraid the cure is worse than the disease," said Di Renjie to his men. "The Qidan bandits are still far away. We don't need to worry about them until they show up. By then, I promise I will lead the fight in person against them." He issued an order that allowed outside residents to return to their homes in the suburbs and beyond and encouraged everyone to carry on with their productive and trading activities as usual, especially farming.

The masses welcomed the decision. They had to make a living to survive, even when the barbarians were at the gate.

***

In the meantime, Di Renjie's colleague Xu Yougong also had a similar twist of fate. After his disenrollment, he had been living the life of a commoner but his reputation had continued to spread among the populace. Chief Archivist of Lucheng County[4] Pan Haoli wrote a passionate piece about him. To his own surprise, the piece took off in official circles. In imitation of the Han rhapsody style, it took the form of a dialog between a host and a fictitious guest.

It begins with the guest asking a question, "Nowadays, who can Mr. Xu be compared to?"

The host answers, "In the wide world, there are numerous personalities. Some hide their whereabouts and others conceal their sharpness. Although I am not in a position to judge them all, I am certain that Mr. Xu is unique among them. In fact, you can only find someone like him among the ancients."

The guest asks, "How does he compare with Zhang Shizhi?"

The host answers, "Pah! What Zhang Shizhi accomplished in the Western Han was easy. And what Xu Yougong did was very, very difficult. Who is superior and who is inferior is self-evident. Zhang Shizhi was active in Emperor Wen's reign when peace reigned over the realm. Of course, there were still undesirable activities. For instance, the theft of the jade ring from Gaozu's temple, Emperor Wen's horse shying on the Wei Bridge,[5] and others. But all Zhang needed to do was go by the book. Wasn't that easy? Xu Yougong, however, lived in an age of revolution and change. Some courtiers of the previous court harbored evil intentions, sowing doubts and suspicions in the mind of the sovereign. Law officers such as Zhou Xing and Lai Junchen were no different from the Four Evildoers[6] in the age of Yao and Shun. They hid their evil tongue and framed up men of virtue. Never deviating from the Way, Xu Yougong did his utmost to get to the bottom of cases, often risking his own imprisonment, and, on several occasions, getting caught up in the web of law."

"Indeed," the guest says. "If he is appointed chamberlain of the Court of Judicial Review,[7] he will be able to give full play to his talent."

The host says, "You only see him as a fair-minded person, and that is why you recommend him for the position in law enforcement. My observation tells me that he is good at everything. Any task you assign him to do he will do very well, not just as head of the Court of Judicial Review!'

Pan Haoli ends his piece with, "As someone who follows the Way, practices benevolence, and adheres to honesty and integrity, Xu Yougong is a man who will give up life and wealth for probity."

After reading the rhapsody, Tianhou sighed and commented, "It is time that Xu Yougong came out of retirement." She thereupon appointed him palace attendant censor of the Left Censorate.[8]

***

For reasons not entirely clear, Shangguan Wan'er, for the first time since her appointment as document-drafter, fell out of favor.

Rumor had it that it was her secret love affair with a court official. Having intimate relations with men was tabooed and may have also aroused in Tianhou a strong sense of jealousy. After she had the poor fellow banished to the northeastern frontier, a grief-stricken Shangguan turned to poems to express her emotions. One of them read:

When first leaves fall on Lake Dongting,[9]
I long for you ten thousand li *away.*
In heavy dew my scented quilt feels cold,
At moonset, brocade screen deserted.
I would play a Southland melody,
And yet, I crave to seal my letter to Jibei.[10]
The letter has no other message but
This misery in living long apart.[11]

At any rate, an incensed Tianhou inflicted on Wan'er a most insulting punishment called "blacking."[12] After the center of her forehead was branded by a hot iron, the wound was permanently colored with a kind of black powder so that she would bear the scar of shame for the rest of her life. The scar, however, did not really disfigure her, but, in a morbid way, added to her charm.

With the passage of time, Tianhou's ire subsided, and her trust in Shangguan Wan'er returned. Now an "inside drafter,"[13] she was given access to all the top secrets of the state and was even allowed to take part in the decision-making process. In fact, she had become Tianhou's behind-the-scenes chief minister in everything but name.

Notes

[1] *Tangren yishi huibian* 8.371.

[2] Pengze 彭澤: southeast of Hukou, Jiangxi.

[3] Weizhou 魏州: prefecture in south Hebei with its seat near Daming.

[4] A chief archivist (*zhubu* 主簿). Lucheng 鹿城 County: near Xinjishi, Hebei.

[5] The Wei Bridge 渭橋: from Qin to Tang there were three bridges on the Wei River near Xi'an (Tang Chang'an) known as the Wei Bridges: Eastern, Western, Central.

[6] The Four Evildoers (*sixiong* 四兇): legendary evil figures under Yao and Shun.

[7] *Sixing qing* 司刑卿.

[8] The palace attendant censor (*dianzhong shiyu shi* 殿中侍御史).

[9] Lake Dongting 洞庭 is on the border between Hunan and Hubei.

[10] Jibei 薊北 was in present-day Beijing.

[11] Translation from Chang and Saussy 2000, 50, with modifications.

[12] *Qing* 黥.

[13] The post "inside drafter" (*nei sheren* 內舍人) was more prestigious than *sheren*.

Part III.

Sunset Years

1. The Two Zhangs (697)

THE DEATH OF Monk Xue Huaiyi had left a void in Tianhou's heart. She surrounded herself with good-looking male servants and gigolos like Shen Nanqiu,[1] but still longed for intimate companionship with a macho man who matched Xue Huaiyi in looks and intelligence.

It was then that Zhang Changzong the "Sixth Brother" in his mid-twenties burst into her life like a breath of fresh air, thanks to Princess Taiping's good offices. His lack of machismo was more than made up for by his delicate, handsome looks, which made him stand out from all the men in Tianhou's service. It was said that his whole body was so perfect that one could not find a single blemish from head to toe.

On Changzong's recommendation, his elder half-brother Zhang Yizhi the "Fifth Brother" entered the service of Tianhou as well. A couple of years older, Yizhi was not as stunningly handsome as Changzong. Nevertheless, he was a fine-looking young man. He held a special attraction for Tianhou, not just because of his good looks, but because of his intelligence and ingenuity. His skill at making longevity drugs, for instance, served to enhance his charm.

The job of the Two Zhangs (or the Zhang brothers) consisted of playing the zither, reciting poems, gambling, and drinking wine as Tianhou's intimate companions. Soon Tianhou began to favor them over all other men around her, and to please them, she even granted noble titles to their mothers, Lady Wei and Lady Zang. When Tianhou learned that Lady Zang (Yizhi's birthmother) was widowed, she set her up with a handsome officer of a much younger age who had divorced his wife for being unkind to one of his housemaids.[2]

Thanks to the Two Zhangs' easy access to Tianhou, the court leaders toadied up to them. Even the Wu princes, particularly Wu Chengsi and Wu Sansi, often visited them at home to offer their services and, on several occasions, were seen holding horse reins and whips for them.

***

In the spring of 697, General-in-Chief Yan Zhiwei, grandson of the famous architect Yan Lide, set off on his mission to Tujue. Along the way, he crossed paths with a Tujue emissary going in the opposite direction. Eager to make peace with Tujue, Yan gifted him with a red robe and a belt with silver ornaments. In his memorial to the court, he suggested that the emissary be given a royal treatment and entertained in a grand tent, which was usually reserved for a head of state.

Yan's lieutenant Acting Chamberlain for Tributaries Tian Guidao did not like what Yan had done and sent a secret memorial to voice his concerns: Yan Zhiwei should not have given away gifts to the Tujue emissary intended for a chieftain, nor should the court be expected to use the grand tent to welcome him.

Tianhou agreed with Tian, but still treated the emissary swell.

***

As soon as the Wu Zhou mission arrived in the Tujue headquarters camp (in Outer Mongolia), the two emissaries were summoned for an audience. Yan Zhiwei, upon entering Mochuo's grand yurt, threw himself face downward on the carpeted floor to kiss the tip of the chieftain's boot. By contrast, Tian Guidao stood with his feet planted apart and his hands by his sides in a way that seemed to show his dignity.

"Who the hell are you?" a displeased Mochuo asked Tian. "Why don't you bow in obeisance?"

"You mean kneeling down like Yan Zhiwei? Never. I won't kiss the boot of my own sovereign, let alone the leader of a neighboring state."

"I can kill you for being impertinent!" Mochuo growled as he brandished his sword over his head.

An adviser rushed over to whisper something into his ear. That apparently dissuaded Mochuo from carrying out his threat.

Several days after the unpleasant audience, Yan Zhiwei set off on his return journey. But his lieutenant Tian Guidao was held in captivity. Mochuo did not let him leave until three months later.

***

With Di Renjie's and Xu Yougong's return to favor, the morale of the Confucian camp at court was raised. It received another boost when Li Zhaode was reappointed as investigative censor[3] after a brief banishment.

In her effort to keep a proper balance between the Confucians and the Legalists, Tianhou rehabilitated Lai Junchen as well.

About the same time, she promoted Ji Xu, a young law officer with a rising reputation, who was not enamored of severe punishment.

Ji Xu had gotten his first lucky break through the help of Wu Chengsi, whom Ji came to know because of a family mishap. His father, then a prefect, had been sentenced to death for embezzlement. Ji Xu, as erudite (*boshi*) of the Court for State Sacrifices, did not have an influential friend to turn to. In desperation, decided to do something risky. One afternoon, when he spotted the carriage carrying Tianhou's nephew south of the Tianjin Bridge, he summoned up enough courage to drop on his knees in front of it.

"Great Prince, I am so sorry to have committed a crime against you," he said to Wu in a beseeching voice.

Wu got off, pulled him to his feet, and asked, "What is it?"

"Without your permission, I have asked my two younger sisters to be your concubines."

"Well, that is a problem," said Wu with a straight face. "Why? Do they have trouble getting married?"

"No, no! I can assure you they are very presentable."

The next day, the two sisters arrived in an ox-cart. Wu Chengsi was pleased with their looks, and took them in.

But in a matter of days, he noticed a serious problem: neither would speak except for single utterances. When he could not take it any longer, he forced them to make a choice: either they would tell him the truth, or they would be sent back to their mother's home.

With great hesitation, they told him the story about their father.

Wu Chengsi resented being used by strangers but did not want to part with his new concubines. So he did what was expected of him, using his pull to help the old man get off the death row and then out of jail.

As for Ji Xu himself, through his sisters, he became a relative of Wu Chengsi, sort of. But to climb to the top of the bureaucratic ladder, he was pretty much on his own. In 697 his first opportunity came when he got involved in the case of Liu Sili.

***

Years before when Liu Sili was still a young man, he got to know an occultist named Zhang Jingcang, who predicted that Liu would become prefect of Jizhou[4] and receive the title of grand preceptor, the highest of the Three Dukes. Decades later, he was appointed to a prefectural post. The first part of the prediction had come true!

But, to make the second part happen, he would have to render significant meritorious service as a top leader at court. With that purpose in mind, he began to do face readings himself, in hopes of recruiting as many supporters as he could. He made generous predictions of career advancement for quite a few court officials. For example, to someone from Luozhou named Qi Lianyao[5] he said, "With that 'dragon aura' of yours, you look like a grand emperor. At the minimum you will acquire very noble status." More often, he would say to a middle-ranking official, "You will rise to a Rank-3 position in the not-so-distant future."

Ji Xu, then defender of Mingtang[6] County in Chang'an, was the first one to notice the shenanigans. Not sure how to file a charge against it, he contacted his colleague in Luoyang, Lai Junchen. It was Lai who reported it to the court and attracted much attention.

At Tianhou's request, Wu Yizong took charge of the investigation. Now in his mid-fifties, Wu was a short man with a plain-looking face and hunched back and spoke with a soft, low-pitched voice. Despite his gentle demeanor, he had earned the reputation as a cruel Legalist law officer after he had tried a certain Yang Qizhuang,[7] a *heqin* commissioner who had failed his mission. Wu had him tied to a wood drum stand, his hands and feet nailed to the frame. On Wu's orders, his men hit the condemned man with a hail of arrows that turned his body into a hedgehog. Wu then came up close and struck open his chest with one sword stroke and ripped out his heart. After he tossed it onto the ground, it kept beating for dozens of times.

As a relative of Tianhou, Wu Yizong had been promoted to positions of power and prestige: commandery prince of Henei and general-in-chief. To ensure the full cooperation of Liu Sili, Wu went soft on him first. After promising him immunity from death, Wu set him free.

For his part, Liu became hopeful that he would receive a light punishment for his crime, and the second part of the prediction would still be fulfilled. He got in touch with as many his colleagues and associates as he could, whom he later nailed as his "confederates." In the end Liu Sili himself and members of more than thirty families he had ensnared were executed. More than a thousand people associated with the case were banished.

The Liu Sili incident cast Lai Junchen into the limelight. He wanted to take full credit for exposing the culprit. With the help of his gang of thugs, he charged Ji Xu as one of the confederates as well. Ji Xu fought tooth and nail to defend himself.

When the dispute came to Tianhou's attention, she summoned both into her study for questioning one afternoon. Lai was brought in first to make his case. Although Tianhou found the "evidence" he presented unconvincing, she was nonetheless amazed that after his demotion many months before, he still possessed the kind of relentless vigor that had made him famous when hunting down members of the Li house. Since she had already made up her mind to reuse him, she appointed him on the spot as vice chamberlain of the Court of the Royal Equipages.[8]

After a eunuch escorted Lai out, Tianhou leaned back, took a few sips of the green tea on her table, and clapped her hands. In came Ji Xu, a well-built middle-aged man of six feet. The moment he made his first utterance in his melodious booming voice, Tianhou was mesmerized. As soon as his twenty-minute presentation came to an end, Tianhou dismissed the charge against him and promoted him to vice censor-in-chief.[9]

***

A man in his early twenties walked up to the entrance to the Audience Hall one sunny afternoon. Wearing a white headband with the character *yuan* (injustice) on it, he mounted a flight of steps to enter the building. An armed guard with a halberd stopped him. The young man told the guard the purpose of his visit: to file a petition to clear the name of his father Pan Jian,[10] a low-ranking functionary wrongly executed for plotting rebellion. But the guard refused to let him in.

The young man then entered the kiosk nearby instead. Casting a glance at the famous Remonstrator's Drum, he picked up the drumstick, and started drumming. Within one hour, a small crowd had gathered, but no grievances officer had come out as expected. In desperation, he pulled out a knife and plunged it into his lower belly in protest, fell to the ground in pain, and started bleeding his life away.

After Vice President of the Board of Justice Liu Ruxuan[11] witnessed the incident, he shed a few tears in his office. He was soon denounced by a servant. Lai Junchen took him in and charged him as an accomplice to the criminal and sentenced him to death by hanging. Only thanks to Tianhou's timely intervention was his sentence reduced to banishment.

Lai Junchen had a particular reason for going after Liu Ruxuan with such ferocity. He himself had been behind the framing of the young man's father Pan Jian in the first place. Besides, the accolade Lai Junchen had received from the court for exposing the Liu Sili Clique filled him with confidence that he was again in favor with Tianhou. Now he took aim at his old nemesis Li Zhaode.

Though only an investigative censor, Li Zhaode was as sharp and combative as ever. But he was no longer vested with the power of a chief minister. Nor did he enjoy Tianhou's unconditional backing as before. That left him vulnerable.

On Lai Junchen's orders, his minions spent days digging into Li Zhaode's past before they discovered a skeleton in the closet that in the end landed Li in jail. It turned out that Li Zhaode had once received money and valuables from the Qidan chieftain Sun Wanrong. Not long afterwards, Sun had been raised to the third rank, allegedly on Li's recommendation.

In the meantime, the minions uncovered a rescript Li Zhaode had issued in the name of Tianhou, which they believed they could use to their advantage. It said,

> *He who has committed a crime involving government matters punishable by forced labor, a crime involving private matters punishable by banishment, or a crime deserving a more serious type of punishment must confess the said crime to the authorities within one hundred days of the announcement of an amnesty. Otherwise, he would be prosecuted according to the law.*

After Sun Wanrong started the anti-government rebellion as leader of the Qidan, many amnesties had been announced. Li Zhaode had not responded to any of them, nor had he fessed up to his crime at all. Clearly, he had missed the deadline repeatedly.

Backed by Tianhou, Lai Junchun went out of his way to destroy his enemy and condemned him to death on the evidence of corruption.

While Li Zhaode was on death row and Xu Yougong in poor health, Lai Junchen was having the fun of his life. Whenever he set his sights on a pretty young woman, it did not matter whether she was the wife or concubine of a miserable commoner or a high-ranking official, he would frame her husband and get him executed, before obtaining an edict to take possession of the woman.

As his reward for exposing Liu Sili, Lai Junchen was allowed to claim ownership of ten bondwomen. One morning, he visited the Court of the National Granaries[12] to claim his prize. As he sized up those available, he kept shaking his head in disappointment until he saw this beautiful young woman. Lai instantly took a fancy to her exotic looks and expressed his interest, only to be told that she already had her owner, the Western Tujue Khan Ashina Huseluo, who had led his people to submit to the Wu Zhou in 690.

Lai's minions then started a campaign to frame the khan for plotting rebellion. In response, dozens of Tujue chieftains presented themselves at the court. Following an honored Tujue tradition, they cut their noses, ears, and chins to protest their leader's innocence. The moment she heard about this, a horrified Tianhou issued an urgent order to put the case on hold.

Meanwhile, Lai Junchen, driven by an urge to go after somebody, fashioned an innovative method for picking his targets. He ordered his minions to set up a row of bricks on the bank of the Yi River in Longmen south of Luoyang. On these bricks were inscribed the names of court officials. The minions would then hit the bricks with stones from a distance. Whenever a brick fell, they would go after the person whose name was on it. By this way alone, Lai Junchen ruined dozens of lives. With nobody willing to stand up to him, Lai Junchen could convict almost anyone who was brought to trial.

Perhaps because of age, Tianhou had adopted a hands-off approach to Lai's atrocities. Moreover, the two young lovers she had recently taken on—Zhang Changzong and Zhang Yizhi—had kept her very busy.

Lai Junchen, for his part, never felt so invincible in his life and wanted to do more. He drew up a secret plan to eliminate the most powerful figures around the throne, including the princes of the Wu lineage, Princess Taiping, the Imperial Heir and ex-emperor Li Dan (Ruizong), and the ex-emperor Li Zhe (Zhongzong), as well as the top government and military leaders. For obvious reasons, he only allowed a handful of his most trusted followers to have access to the plan.

One evening, Lai Junchen and his pretty wife, whom he had recently seized from another man, were holding a banquet to entertain her folks in his mansion. A certain Wei Suizhong[13] arrived at the gate, asking to get in. The gatekeeper knew that this disheveled man with stinking breath was not an invited guest, and told him to go away, because Mr. Lai was not home.

Although not a high-ranking official, Wei Suizhong had close ties with Lai because of his profound learning. That evening, however, Wei was roaring drunk, and Lai was in no mood to receive him. But Wei refused to believe what he was told, pushed the gatekeeper aside, and barged in.

As he broke into the dining hall, he saw Lai and his wife with their guests sitting at a large round table. He fixed his gaze on Lai's young wife, and blurted out, "You whore!"

His ears burning red, Lai Junchen, with a flip of his hand, ordered half a dozen of his men to close in on Wei. They gave him a good thrashing and tossed him out of the gate.

***

For weeks after that unforgettable evening, Wei Suizhong had been laid up in bed nursing his wounds. He tried hard to forget everything about Lai Junchen, but when he closed his eyes the terrible scene at Lai's home would sometimes replay in his head. With each passing day, his hatred for Lai and his desire for revenge grew stronger. As soon as he could get up and hobble around, he began to look for ways to get even. It was then that he got wind of the secret plan. With the help of one of his housemaids, Wei paid a secret visit to Princess Taiping and told her what he knew.

Before Wei was done, Taiping's face had turned ashen with fright and anger. She was convinced that, having been driven into a corner, she had to put up a fight if she wanted to survive at all. She plunged into action and alerted Lai's intended targets to his sinister scheme. In a matter of days, the Wus, the Lis, and the court leaders coalesced around her to expose the infamous plan and make sure that Tianhou was informed of its evil intentions.

Suddenly, Lai found himself under attack by powerful enemies all around him. Before he could launch a counterattack on any of them, he was arrested. Following a speedy trial, he was found guilty, and sentenced to death.

***

Tianhou glanced at the scroll lying on her table, a memorial from the Board of Justice recommending Lai's execution. It had reached her three days before. So far, she had refused to put down the character *zhun* ("approved") in red on the document. She thought of her first audience with the young Lai when he had just uncovered the rebellious plot of a Li prince, and of his meritorious deeds in purging the other Lis. She sighed and made up her mind to save Lai's neck.

***

At dawn on a cool summer day, Tianhou was getting ready for her visit to the Western Park. She would pass through the Jiayu Gate[14] in the west wall of Luoyang to enter the royal parkland. The gate was the only physical link between the Palace City and the park, both heavily guarded by palace guard troops and off limits to the public. Since there was no need for extra security measures, such as roping off the roads and stopping the flow of traffic, she would travel in a "light" carriage, followed by a small escort.

She beamed with apparent delight when she saw from the window of her palanquin the coachman on duty standing beside the two black stallions at the gate to her residential basilica.

"How are things outside the palace, Ji Xu?" she asked, after she had stepped down.

Vice Censor-in-Chief Ji answered with his head lowered, "Your Majesty, everything is fine inside and outside the palace in Luoyang. Except for one thing. I wonder if Your Majesty is interested in hearing it."

"What's that? Tell me."

"People in the street are wondering why it takes so long for the memorial to get approved. Some even doubt if it will be approved at all."

"I have given it a lot of thought, Ji Xu. Lai Junchen is a meritorious officer. We have to take that into account when meting out his punishment."

"Your Majesty, no matter what great service he rendered in the past, Lai Junchen is now exposed as the arch-villain who committed some of the most heinous crimes. He framed the innocent, took an enormous amount of bribe, and caused a countless number of wrongful deaths."

The carriage rolled forward as Tianhou pondered her options. After a short ride, Tianhou and her entourage reached the picturesque Jicui (Jadeite) Palace[15] in the depth of the park.

With the help of her coachman, Tianhou got off the carriage and, accompanied by him, started strolling towards the Jicui Pond nearby.

"What else do you have on him?" she continued.

"He has ravaged dozens and dozens of women, after causing the death of their masters and husbands on trumped-up charges. Most important, Your Majesty, he recently hatched a plan to destroy the prominent members of the Li *and* Wu houses and the entire court leadership."

"He is out of control."

"He is out of his mind, Your Majesty."

"I agree, Ji Xu. What do you think should happen?"

"He deserves no mercy."

With her eyes half closed, she paused for a moment, then said, "I'm afraid so."

"Your Majesty approves the memorial?"

She uttered a faint "um-hum."

***

On the early morning of the third of the sixth month (June 26, 698), death-row prisoners were transported to the wooden platform in the Southern Market. Li Zhaode was the first to go. There was an eerie silence among the large crowd that had gathered in the light drizzle to watch as the ex-chief minister ended his life's journey by hanging.

As more executions were carried out, the audience began to get worked up. The sight of the last prisoner Lai Junchen being pushed onto the platform, trussed up and blindfolded, sent the spectators into a frenzy. As he was still kicking and writhing on the gallows, dozens of people jumped onto the platform, and fell over one another to tear the body into shreds.

By and by, Tianhou became more aware of the intense hatred people felt for Lai Junchen. With the memories of his past merit fading, she issued an edict to extirpate his clan and confiscate his family assets.

With Lai Junchen's death, the Western Tujue Khan Ashina Huseluo was set free as the case against him unraveled. Soon he was reunited with his lovely bondwoman.

Notes

1 In the sources, there is no record on how Shen Nanqiu died. He probably died of natural causes. There are claims that he died of poisoning, which is unfounded.

2 Her worn looks did not inspire the officer. Her strong urges for sex drove him to the brink of insanity. In the end, he had to turn to drinking to drown his frustration in wine. See *Tangren yishi huibian* 8.404–5.

3 *Jiancha yushi* 監察御史: *see* note in Part 1, Chapter 12.

4 Jizhou 箕州: prefecture that lay in Zuoquan and Heshun, east central Shanxi.

5 Luozhou 洛州: prefecture that lay in Luoyang and neighboring areas. Qi Lianyao 綦連耀.

6 Mingtang 明堂.

7 Yang Qizhuang 楊齊莊.

8 *Sipu shaoqing* 司僕少卿. See *Xin Tang shu* 208 (cf. *Jiu Tang shu* 136). Note: *sipu* was previously known as *taipu* 太僕.

9 *Yushi zhongcheng* 御史中丞. *See* note in Part 1, Chapter 4.

10 Fan Jian 樊戩.

11 Liu Ruxuan 劉如璿.

12 *Sinong si* 司農寺.

13 Wei Suizhong 衛遂忠.

[14] The Jiayu Gate 嘉豫門 was the northern gate on the west side of the Palace City.
[15] The Jicui Palace 積翠宮 was the largest palace inside the Western Park. At its center was the Jicui Pond. See *Tang liangjing chengfang kao* 5.144.

2. Lou Shide (697–698)

The Arab general Hassan ibn al-Nu'man seized Carthage from the Byzantines. Byzantine rule in North Africa came to an end (698).

IN THE THIRD month of 697, Tianhou launched another campaign against the Qidan. General Wang Xiaojie, recently recalled from banishment, led an advance detachment to meet an enemy force head-on in Hebei and trounced them. Wang then went on a perilous chase in the mountains until he fell into a trap in the East Xia Stony Vale.[1] As he turned back in retreat, he tumbled off a cliff into the abyss below. The remainder of the expeditionary army broke in a rout.

Prince Wu Youyi commanding a large army happened to be close by. But he was too shocked by Wang Xiaojie's death to act. By the time he summoned up enough courage to engage the enemy, Youzhou had fallen into the hands of the Qidan without offering much resistance.

In the fourth and fifth months, Tianhou massed a force of 200,000 men in two columns. One of them, the Shenbing District Expeditionary Army, was the main force, under the command of Commander-in-Chief Wu Yizong. The other was the auxiliary army, under the command of Lou Shide, recently rehabilitated, and the Paekche general Shazha Zhongyi.

***

Having vanquished Wang Xiaojie's forces, Sun Wanrong set up a settlement called New Town (Xincheng) nearby,[2] well protected by natural barriers, to store the newly acquired *materiel.* He then filled the town with captured Han people—mostly women, the weak, and the old—and appointed his brother-in-law as its leader.

On Sun's orders, five Qidan emissaries went on two separate missions to the southern headquarters camp of Tujue in Heisha.[3] The first mission arrived early and delivered Sun's letter to Mochuo. It said,

> *I have just destroyed a Tang army of one million men. The Tang people are scared out of their wits. I would like to propose that the Qidan and Tujue join forces to take advantage of the victory and capture Tang territory to the south.*

To Mochuo, "one million" was no doubt a bogus figure, and "Tang" showed Sun's refusal to recognize the Wu Zhou's legitimacy. He would not nitpick over these issues. The problem was that he had just made a promise to Tianhou to take on the Qidan and was not sure that switching sides at this juncture was the best choice. After spending hours interrogating the three Qidan emissaries in person, he was finally convinced that the proposed Tujue-Qidan alliance would benefit him much more than the alliance with the Wu Zhou.

***

By the time the second mission arrived a few days later, Mochuo had officially accepted Sun Wanrong's proposition and rewarded each of the three emissaries on the first mission with a Tujue red robe—a precious gift reserved only for the most distinguished non-royal guest.

At the audience Mochuo granted to the second mission, he asked curtly, "Why so late? Don't you know I hate laggards?"

"We got lost, Your Highness," the leader of the mission said.

"How come they didn't and got here days earlier? I just don't find that convincing." The Tujue khan looked up into the inner dome of the grand yurt, then down at the two emissaries, and said, "I don't want to waste my time on losers like you." Raising his head again, he shouted in a matter-of-fact manner, "Guards! Take them away and kill them!"

"Not so fast, Your Highness!" the leading emissary screamed in desperation. "I am sure we have something you want. Please hear me out before you kill me."

Mochuo waved a hand to stay the execution.

At a secret meeting behind closed yurt flaps, the two emissaries revealed the real situation in Qidan.

"Despite their recent victories," the leading emissary said, "the Qidan are on their last leg. What is the evidence? They are surrounded by the Wu Zhou army and outnumbered by at least ten to one. There is a great shortage of everything, especially food and weaponry. Their only allies are the Xi.[4] But the Xi are by no means loyal and may revolt any time. After Li Jinzhong's death, the new leader Sun Wanrong is not popular at all. He has managed to stay in power only through violence."

"How can I trust you?"

"If Your Highness launches an attack on Qidan, we will lead the way. If anything I said turns out to be incorrect, Your Highness can do whatever you want with me."

Mochuo had an emergency meeting with his advisers. After a short debate, he decided on what he considered the best course of action for his people. On his orders, his men retrieved the red robes from the three emissaries of the first mission and hacked them to death. They then gifted one robe to each of the two emissaries of the second mission.

Guided by the two turncoats, Mochuo led a contingent of his troops in a surprise attack on New Town and stormed it in two days.

***

With their relations with the Qidan already strenuous, the Xi people took the fall of New Town as a sign of the latter's weakness and went over to the Wu Zhou camp. A joint attack by the Xi and Wu Zhou against the Qidan soon followed that thoroughly routed them.

With a high prize on his head and thousands of pursuers hot on his tail, Sun Wanrong beat a frantic retreat west and did not take a break until he reached the Lu River.[5] By then, his escort of several thousand men was reduced to a single bondservant. Flopping down on the grassy bank, he heaved a sigh and said, "I want to submit to the Tang, but I can't because of the crime I committed. Neither can I go to Silla because it is too far. Nor can I go to Tujue because it is my enemy. Where can I go?"

Suddenly, the bondservant brought a broadsword down on his neck and hacked off his head. The bondservant then made his way to

Luoyang with it and claimed a prize. The head was then hoisted on a pike for display outside the main gate of the Hotel of the Four Quarters,[6] a favorite haunt for foreign visitors.

***

In the winter of 697, Di Renjie was once again appointed de facto chief minister, and readmitted into Tianhou's inner circle under Lou Shide's leadership. In the months that followed, Di Renjie, through force of character, emerged as the dominant figure, elbowing Lou Shide aside. Each time they appeared together, the brilliant Di outshone the slow-spoken Lou. Over time, Di Renjie grew to look down upon his colleague, and even made disparaging remarks about him.

Tianhou, concerned about a growing rivalry among her top leaders, called Di Renjie into her study in the residential basilica and said, "I hope you and your colleagues can work together in harmony. It is especially important today when we are under the constant threat of the Tujue on the northern border."

"Your Majesty, there is no reason to worry. I collaborate with the chief ministers very well."

"How about Lou Shide?"

"I have not worked with him lately, but neither did I get into trouble with him."

"I'm glad to hear that. But what's your opinion of him, anyway? Is he talented?"

"Your Majesty," Di Renjie answered, "I think Mr. Lou is a conscientious administrator and a cautious general. But I won't call him talented."

"Is he a discoverer of talent?"

"I have known him for a long time, but never been under the impression that he is good at discovering talented people."

"How were you promoted to the top job?"

"I suppose, Your Majesty, I was promoted because I wrote my reports and memorials in an honest and straightforward manner, not because I had connections."

Tianhou paused to collect her thoughts, then said, "Previously, I didn't know much about you at all. I began to take notice of you only after someone recommended you in the strongest of terms. Do you know who?"

Knitting his greyish eyebrows into a frown, Di Renjie shook his head and said, "It is really stupid of me, but I do not know."

"Lou Shide." Turning to Yidu Neiren, Tianhou said, "Show him the documents."

Yidu Neiren fetched an oblong basket filled with paper scrolls on a long table to Tianhou's left and set it down on the table in front of her.

Di Renjie picked out one scroll. The moment he opened it he recognized the elegant handwriting as that of his colleague. He went on to unfurl and read them all—memorial after memorial praising him in glowing terms.

Di Renjie sighed and said, his face red and his eyes teary, "That . . . that a surprise. I didn't know what a big-hearted gentleman Shide is until today!"

***

When Sun Wanrong was besieging Youzhou, he issued a declaration of war, in which he claimed to have staged the uprising in the name of Prince of Luling Li Zhe. Everyone knew that the Qidan leader had no intention of restoring the prince's rule. But the fact that he used the prince's name as a pretext to challenge Tianhou's power proved that he had not accepted the Wu regime as legit. Mochuo's communications sometimes reflected the same attitude. One way to lay it to rest was to name an official heir immediately. That would go a long way in lending legitimacy to her rule and discouraging future contenders for the throne. So the argument by many remonstrators went.

Ever since the Jasper scandal, Tianhou had not seriously considered the succession issue. Now in 698, with the crushing of the Qidan rebels, it was once again on the agenda.

Wu Chengsi, for his part, was still hoping for the day when he would be named crown prince, but his time was running out. As he struggled through his sixth decade, his health was failing him. It was his paternal cousin, the much younger Wu Sansi (also Tianhou's nephew) who would have a real shot at getting her nomination.

With Chengsi's backing, some court leaders had recommended Sansi as heir apparent on several occasions recently.

"Since antiquity," they contended, "a Son of Heaven has never chosen his heir from a different clan."

To Tianhou, it was obvious that they were forcing the issue. And she did not like it a bit. But as she continued to age, she had no choice but to address it one way or another.

To her surprise, it was Di Renjie who raised the most forceful voice of opposition. He said in his memorial,

After the Great Emperor Gaozong received the throne from Taizong, he entrusted two of his sons to Your Majesty's care before he passed on. Both are possible successors to the throne, and both are alive and well. And yet, some people have made much noise about naming an heir from outside the Li clan. Is it not against the will of Heaven? Furthermore, how can the bond between aunt and nephew be compared with that between mother and son? If you set up one of your two sons as heir, after ten thousand years, you will still be worshiped in the Ancestral Temple. If you set up a nephew as heir, things will be very different. When he becomes the Son of Heaven, will he worship his aunt in the Ancestral Temple? I am afraid not.

Tianhou rolled her eyes in anger and said to Di at court, "This is my family business. Don't get involved."

"Well, Your Majesty," Di Renjie responded in a raised voice. "I, your humble servant, have to respectfully disagree. The sovereign regards the entire realm as her family, and rightly so. Within the Four Seas, every individual is her subject, and every matter of import is her family business. The sovereign is the chief, and her court officials are her right-hand men. In essence, they belong to the same entity. In that sense, selection of an heir should concern every subject of the empire, especially people like me who occupy the highest positions of power. In my view, there is no reason for me *not* to get involved."

Tianhou's face darkened as she fell into a brown study.

In the next few days, she received more memorials from the pro-Li party that urged her to set up one of her sons as heir.

As she was still between two minds, she saw Di Renjie again in her study and said, "In my dream the other night, I saw a huge parrot struggling to take off. But its wings were broken. No matter how hard it flapped them, it just couldn't free itself. What does this all mean?"

"The parrot, or *yingwu*, stands for 'Wu.' The broken wings are the two sons of Your Majesty. The parrot will be able to fly the moment you set up one of the two sons as crown prince."[7]

"I see," Tianhou said. She was not necessarily swayed, but, from then on, she would no longer consider Wu Sansi as a serious candidate for crown prince.

Notes

1 Dongxia Shigu 東硤石谷: northeast of Qian'an, Hebei,

2 New Town (Xincheng 新城): the sources record numerous towns by that name. According to *Zizhi tongjian*'s (206.6521), the Xincheng in question lay 400 *li* northwest of Liucheng 柳城 (present-day Liaoyang, Liaoning).

3 Heisha 黑沙: in Wuchuan, Inner Mongolia.

4 Xi 奚 (Kumoxi 庫莫奚): ethnic group of Donghu origin active in west Liaogning and north Hebei, and parts of Inner Mongolia. They should not be confused with "Xí" 霫.

5 The Lu River 潞水: the present-day Bei Canal 北運河 in the southeast of Beijing.

6 The Hotel of the Four Quarters (Sifang guan 四方館) was located south of the Yingtian Gate 應天門 and west of the central axis in the Imperial City, Luoyang. See *Tang liangjing chengfang kao* 5.139.

7 On Di's comment on *yingwu* 鸚鵡, see *Zizhi tongjian* 206.6526. For a variant account, see *Xin Tang shu* 115, 狄仁傑傳.

3. Crane-Riders (698)

TO MANAGE TIANHOU'S gigolos and male favorites, a special agency was created, known as *konghe jian*[1] or the Directorate of Crane-Riders. The crane was an auspicious bird and a symbol of longevity. Crane-riders were oftentimes a reference to legendary immortals in the past who had allegedly ridden cranes in their ascent to Heaven. Members of the Directorate were known by the more mundane term *gongfeng*[2] (palace attendants).

***

One late afternoon, Zhang Changzong and Zhang Yizhi, the most prominent palace attendants of the Directorate, were having a chat with their colleague Ji Xu. The Two Zhangs, with Tianhou at their back, did not seem to have a care in the world, but what Ji Xu would say would alarm them.

"Do you know how the world sees you nowadays?" Ji Xu asked.

The Two Zhangs shook their heads.

"People believe you enjoy so much power and privilege not because of your virtue, but because of your status as Tianhou's favorites. To be brutally frank with you, my friends, that's why they hate you. Well, nobody knows what the future may bring. We may wish Her Majesty to live forever, but we can't deny the fact that she is getting on in years. You may need to protect yourself soon if you want to survive her passing."

"What will you suggest?" asked Zhang Yizhi the elder brother.

"All under Heaven nowadays still remember the kindness of the Tang and still think fondly of the prince of Luling (Li Zhe). I know for a fact that Tianhou has been looking for a successor. As far as I can tell, she is not considering the Wu princes. If you can persuade her to set up Li Zhe as heir, it will please the people. And this is the best way to avoid disaster and keep your wealth and power when the inevitable happens."

The Two Zhangs nodded in agreement.

***

Two days later in the evening, the Two Zhangs brought up the subject of setting up an heir to the throne in the after-meal conversation with Tianhou.

"You guys never poked your nose into my family business before," said she in astonishment. "This is quite out of character. Where the hell did you get the idea?"

The Zhangs hummed and hawed.

Tianhou kept pressing them for an answer until they gave away the mastermind behind the idea. She decided to call him in for questioning.

***

The audience Tianhou had with Ji Xu was short. After she sat him down in a seat across the table, she gave him the go-ahead to speak, and words poured out from his mouth in an unending stream. She could not argue with the point he was trying to make, but his contentious tone got on her nerves. So much so that she had to cut him off halfway and sent him away with a flea in his ear.

As she was still undecided about naming her heir, a few days later, she received a memorial from Di Renjie that harped on the same theme. In the week that followed, more memorials by court leaders came in, all written in a similar vein.

All this time, she had been suffering from a lingering cough and a persistent chest pain. That made her painfully aware of her own physical decline and the impossibility of putting off the matter any longer. Only then did she make the crucial move.

About three weeks later, an envoy arrived in Fangzhou[3] in the third month of 698 to announce an edict, whereby Prince of Luling Li Zhe, accompanied by his consort and sons, was to travel to the Divine Capital for the treatment of his ailment and for convalescence. Six more months later, upon a request by the Imperial Heir Li Dan, Li Zhe was officially appointed crown prince with much fanfare.

***

Tianhou in the end chose her nephew Wu Yanxiu (Chengsi's son) as the future son-in-law of Mochuo, despite strong opposition from court officials like Secretariat Drafter[4] Zhang Jianzhi.

Yan Zhiwei was to head a *heqin* mission of sorts to fetch the Tujue bride. Among the officials to join him for the trip was Pei Huaigu with a secret mission of his own: to watch Yan's every move on behalf of Tianhou. Although only an investigative censor, Pei had already enjoyed a formidable reputation as savior of the wrongly accused. He had gained Tianhou's respect by the way he handled the *cause célèbre* of Monk Jingman of Hengzhou.[5]

Back then, someone jealous of Jingman's accomplishments had a painting inserted in one of his books. The central figure therein is Jingman himself drawing his bow to aim at a woman sitting at a window in a loft-building. Tianhou was livid with rage when she saw the painting. She took it as an innuendo attack on herself and wanted the monk dead. It was Pei Huaigu who found the monk innocent and acquitted him in defiance of Tianhou's orders.

In the middle of summer (in the sixth month of 698), Yan Zhiwei, Pei Huaigu, Prince Wu Yanxiu, and others started off from Luoyang, bearing with them a generous collection of gifts—a large amount of bronze cash, gold and silver vessels, and silk—as bride price. After they traversed miles and miles of grassland on the Mongolian Plateau, they arrived at the Tujue headquarters camp in Heisha. By then autumn had already begun in earnest.

At the official reception, Mochuo stared down with fierce dark eyes at the members of the mission, as a Tujue officer with a sword at waist introduced them. Without warning, he rose from his felt futon, shouting in anger, "I told you I wanted to marry off my daughter to a son of the Son of Heaven. That hasn't changed. Who needs a Wu boy? Guards! Take him away!"

Two Tujue soldiers armed with scimitars came up to Wu Yanxiu and pushed him out of the large yurt.

Mochuo lifted his eyes towards the delegates and said with a smile, "Relax. I am not going to harm you. We, the Tujue, have been indebted to the Lis for generations. We will repay them for their kindness. But I heard some disturbing news about them: except for two sons of

Gaozong, the Lis have been killed off. If that's true, I will use my power to help restore their rule." Turning to Yan Zhiwei, he continued, "Would you like to help me do that and serve as a leader of the new Tang regime?"

With sweat beading on his forehead, Yan Zhiwei was now on his knees, shaking.

"Let me see." Mochuo paused briefly to ponder something, then continued in a raised voice, "I, the Tujue khan, am naming you the khan of the south."

"Long live Your Highness!" Yan Zhiwei said feebly.

"Your Highness, we are on a mission on behalf of the imperial court," someone said in a loud voice. "We are not in a position to receive official appointments."

"Who are you?"

"Instigative Censor Pei Huaigu."

"Aha! I will name you Zhiwei's lieutenant!"

"With all the respect due to Your Highness, I have to decline. Tianhou is expecting us to return home soon."

"You are not willing to cooperate?" Mochuo asked, his tone harsh.

"No, Your Highness, I cannot."

"All right." With a clap of his hands, two armed guards walked up to Pei, grabbed his arms, and took him into custody.

In the months that followed, Mochuo made many attempts to suborn Pei Huaigu. None of them succeeded. In a fit of anger, Mochuo ordered his death.

But before the execution was carried out, Pei fled on a stolen horse. Two days into the journey, he lost his way. He sank to his knees and prayed to Heaven that he would end his life in his homeland. After he fell asleep, a bald-headed old man appeared in his dreams and pointed to a path of escape. Waking up, he realized Monk Jingman had come to his rescue. Following the path, he made his way to the border and crossed over into Wu Zhou territory.

***

A few days later, at a gate to Jinyang, one of the bustling metropolises of the north, some local garrison soldiers stopped an emaciated tramp. His tangled long hair and beard and tattered official robe aroused suspicion. They took him in as a spy, planning to chop off his head and use it to claim a reward. It was then that their commandant recognized the captive as Censor Pei. A few years back, it was Pei who had saved him from the gallows. He took it upon himself to save his savior and send him back on the road.

As soon as he arrived in Luoyang, Pei Huaigu was summoned to the palace for a secret meeting with Tianhou. He gave her a detailed account of what he had witnessed in Mochuo's yurt.

Notes

1 *Konghe jian* 控鶴監.

2 *Gongfeng* 供奉.

3 Fangzhou 房州: prefecture that lay in Fangxian, Zhushan, and others, Hubei.

4 *Fengge sheren* 鳳閣舍人. *See* note in Part 2, Chapter 2.

5 Hengzhou 恆州: prefecture that lay in Shijiazhuang, Fuping, and others, Hebei.

4. Di Renjie (698–699)

MOCHUO'S DECLARATION OF war arrived in the middle of the night. It caught Tianhou unawares. Notable among the complaints it listed were:

> *(1) Cooked seeds received from the Wu Zhou that yielded no crop at all;*
> *(2) Gold and silver vessels of inferior quality sent by the Wu Zhou as gifts;*
> *(3) A boy of the Wu clan sent to marry the khan's daughter; but the khan had requested a son of the Son of Heaven, not someone of a minor lineage.*

"Do you think that we gave them cooked seeds on purpose?" Tianhou asked Yidu Neiren, handing her the document on a scroll.

"I do not think so, Your Majesty. We did everything possible to avoid offending Mochuo. It served no purpose to send him seeds that wouldn't germinate unless we wanted to make him angry. I can have the Left Censorate check into it. But I can assure Your Majesty that the Board of Earth (Revenue) did not send cooked seeds. They never dared."

"Did we give the Tujue gold and silver vessels of poor quality?"

"Your Majesty, as we all know, the Tujue worship gold and silver. People in the Directorate for Royal Manufactories could not possibly risk their heads to send shoddy vessels as gifts to a Tujue khan."

"How about his refusal to accept Yanxiu as son-in-law?"

"Your Majesty, there is no need to let that bother you. Mochuo was not serious in the first place. Otherwise, he would not have suborned Yan Zhiwei and tried to suborn Pei Huaigu."

Tianhou muttered through clenched teeth, “He is forcing me to fight him.”

“Your Majesty may have to take him on.”

“No matter how much it costs?”

“I think so, Your Majesty,” Yidu said, putting the scroll down on the table.

***

By then, a massive Tujue army had intruded into Wu Zhou territory. After they had sacked Dingzhou, they started laying siege to Zhaozhou’s prefectural seat, a sizeable northern city.[1]

Yan Zhiwei, with a dozen or so Tujue riders, rode to the edge of the moat. They dismounted, linked hands, and started singing the Turkic “Song of Ten Thousand Years” while dancing to the tune.

A Wu Zhou general shouted from the wall, “Board President! Don’t you feel ashamed? Singing that barbarian song and dancing like them?”

Yan Zhiwei answered, “No, I don’t. The khan treats me swell and will treat you swell too. Just open the gates, will you, General?”

“Go to hell!” was the sharp answer.

Two days later, the Tujue took the city. It happened at dawn when the south gate was unlatched from the inside, and the Tujue soldiers pushed it open and poured in.

When they broke into Prefect Gao Rui’s mansion, they found him and his wife lying lifeless on the floor. Both had taken the *mafei* decoction,[2] a powerful sedative nostrum, to fake death. As soon as someone hit them with a splash of cold water, they regained their consciousness.

Mochuo came in to interrogate the prefect in person. Holding a belt with a golden lion head buckle in one hand and a purple robe in another, he said, "Look here. These represent great power. Just submit to me and they will be yours. Will you do that?"

Gao Rui kept his mouth shut. Mochuo stayed on for twenty minutes, did not get what he wanted, and left the room. Gao then turned to his wife lying beside him, and murmured, "Time to repay the country for all it has given me," and fell silent. The next morning, he and his wife were put to the sword.

By the time the Wu Zhou soldiers retook the city two days later, the invaders had left city. The soldiers surrounded Chief Administrator Tang Bore's mansion and took him into custody. Someone had fingered him as the one who had unlatched a city gate to let in the enemy. On Tianhou's orders, he was hanged in public, and his clan extirpated.

***

Tianhou raised in haste two large armies to confront the Tujue: first, the main army of 300,000 men led by Wu Chonggui, Shazha Zhongyi, and Zhang Renyuan; and second, the reinforcement army of 150,000 men led by Yan Jingrong.[3] Crown Prince Li Zhe was made field marshal to assume overall command of both, and Di Renjie was appointed vice field marshal to serve as his lieutenant. When the news began to spread, military-age volunteers flocked to army recruiters to offer their services.

Before long, Di Renjie took over the prince's responsibilities. On the day of his departure for the front, when he was attending a farewell ceremony outside the Shangdong Gate,[4] the northern gate in the eastern wall of Luoyang, he was surprised to see the unexpected arrival of a large imperial carriage in dark lacquer, accompanied by a long escort. With the assistance of two attendants, Tianhou stepped down from the carriage. Di hurried over to make an obeisance and thank her profusely for paying the visit.

With her face lit up, Tianhou, accompanied by her retinue of maids, eunuchs, attendants, and bodyguards, joined the audience.

At the close of the ceremony, Tianhou walked Di all the way to the main road and watched on as he clambered on to his bay horse and rode into the morning sun under the escort of a small troop of riders.

***

Following the sack of Dingzhou and Zhaozhou (both in Hebei), the Tujue pillaged the markets and homes there before retreating north. When the Wu Zhou army under Di Renjie began to close in on their rearguard, on Mochuo's orders, the Tujue slaughtered more than 10,000 men and women they had captured from the Wu Zhou cities. As they continued to flee north, the Tujue marauded through the Hebei territories, wreaking carnage upon the settled communities.

Weeks later, Mochuo led the bulk of his army across the Great Desert back into his headquarters camp in Okuten, a settlement named after a sacred mountain nearby in Central Outer Mongolia.[5] From there, he dominated the vast swathe of land north of the Great Wall. With an armed force of 400,000 men under his command and with northern and western barbarian tribes vying against one another to pledge allegiance to him, he was at the summit of his power and held the Central Kingdom in contempt.

***

Before the Tujue withdrew to the grassland, Yan Zhiwei went to see Mochuo on summons in his yurt and received a new mission: to return to Luoyang to live incognito and bide his time until Mochuo's come-back. As much as Yan feared being left behind, he had no choice but to accept fate with resignation, having hitched his bandwagon to the Tujue. He shed his Tujue outfit—high fur hat, kaftan, jackboots, belt with a lionhead buckle—and put on the brown garb of a Han commoner. After he had made a long, grueling journey south, he reached the Eastern Capital and settled down in a ward near the Southern Market. He grew a long beard and assumed a new identity as a small trader. But soon his cover was blown when he was having a drink in a tavern in his ward. Upon his arrest, he was denounced as an enemy collaborator. Despite his loud protest of innocence, he was condemned to death in public. Little did Yan know, Pei Huaigu had returned months before and briefed the court on his deal with Mochuo.

Early one morning before sunrise, Yan Zhiwei was transported from his prison cell to the south of the Tianjin Bridge. There with his cangue and shackles off, he was hogtied to a pole and shot by a barrage of arrows. Two slaughterers came up to finish him off, slicing his body and hacking his bones to pieces before dumping them in the wild. His Three Clans, including those who did not even know him, were extirpated.

***

Because of the Tujue invasion, the Hebei area had suffered a significant loss of registered residents. Many had worked for the Tujue under coercion and now gone into hiding for fear of punishment. Those who remained in their towns and villages were a restless lot. Having just endured the ravages of a brutal invasion, they continued to suffer at the hands of heartless officials. The almost impossible task of restoring order fell on the shoulders of Di Renjie, now pacifying commissioner of Hebei. With deep concerns over the situation on the ground, he submitted a memorial in the tenth month of 698:

> *. . . In the Shandong area,*[6] *one of the prime reasons for the locals' displacement was the excessive levy of corvée for military purposes. It drove many into bankruptcy. Moreover, the local officials, in the name of following court orders, appropriated their property; and on the pretext of military emergency, hauled many residents to jail to face interrogation and torture.*
>
> *During the invasion, many cities and towns had fallen into enemy hands, although they may have held out until they were forced to surrender. After the enemy withdrew, the court's army retook them. However, for the purpose of getting ample rewards, our officers and men often falsely claimed to have sacked the cities and towns. Thus, I fear, many of the rewards granted were without merit; and much of the punishment inflicted on those who had surrendered the cities and towns to the enemy was unjustified. Once a city or town had been occupied by the enemy, it had become a "wicked" place. So much so that, as soon as it was recaptured, the residents became fair game; their money and*

property were pillaged, and their wives and daughters molested and raped. The soldiers all knew that these acts were atrocities, but they did them anyway. Nor did their officers make an effort to stop them. That is why, after the enemy had left, the cities and towns suffered even greater devastation.

To drum up support from the populace for our troops and weaken the enemy forces, there was in place a policy that prohibited the soldiers from abusing the locals. Now it has been abandoned, causing much grief among innocent civilians. That really aches my heart.

People are flexible like water. If you dam it, it will become a spring; if you dredge it, it will become a river. Whether in a dam or a spring, it will flow at will and take no constant form. Those who are condemned as guilty will stay away from their homes, sleep in the wild, and take shelter in mountains and swamps to avoid capture. Some of them will even become reckless and cause trouble. Take the example of Shandong again: many people formed bandit groups precisely for this reason. But if you pardon them, they will come out of hiding and make livings as law-abiding subjects.

In my humble opinion, what should worry us most are not occasional skirmishes on the frontier but unrest at the center. In view of this, I sincerely hope that a special amnesty be extended to the various prefectures in Hebei under my jurisdiction. . . .

Tianhou closed her eyes for a few moments, picked up a writing brush on the table, and wrote next to the title of the long memorial a large *zhun* ("approved") in red. She then ordered Shanguan Wan'er to take it to the Secretariat for implementation.

***

With Tianhou's firm backing, Di Renjie started restoring peace and order in the region. People who had been abducted by the Tujue could now return to their villages or neighborhoods without harassment; relief grain was distributed among the poor and needy; and posthouses were repaired to facilitate the withdrawal of troops. On many occasions Di had ordered the generals and court envoys to be frugal and not to make excessive demands on the populace. To set an example, he ate coarse food every day (consisting mainly of millet and cabbages and turnips). He also let it be known to the officials and clerks working for him that harassment of the people was strictly forbidden on pain of death.

Before very long, Hebei bounced back as farming and trading activities returned to normal.

***

With his Hebei experience under the belt, Di Renjie had gained much respect from Tianhou. He could sense it when he was back in Luoyang by the way she addressed him now by his honorary epithet "State Elder."[7] But as he aged, he became increasing irascible and sometimes behaved like a grumpy old man.

Still, Tianhou almost always fell in with his wishes because she had gotten into the habit of believing that he always meant well for the country and the throne.

Even the Two Zhangs, her favorites, held him in awe.

One afternoon Di Renjie, accompanied by a bondservant, visited the Xuanzheng Basilica on business and saw Tianhou and Zhang

Changzong in a green coat sitting at a round table, ready for a game of backgammon. At Tianhou's request, Di took a seat opposite Zhang to play him at a game instead.

Tianhou asked with a smile on her face, "What do you want to wager, State Elder?"

"I play to win," said Di Renjie, with confidence. "I will wager the official purple robe I am wearing against Mr. Zhang's green feather coat."

"What?" Tianhou exclaimed. "It is made of kingfisher feather and is worth one thousand pieces of gold. Nanhai gave it to me as a tributary gift before I gave it to Changzong."

"I know, Your Majesty. But my robe is the formal attire a senior official wears when paying homage to the sovereign. The green feather coat is a gift given to a court favorite. In that sense, the robe is far more valuable than the coat."

"All right, all right" said Tianhou. "We'll use the coat and robe as wagers."

Zhang Changzong was put in a bad mood by Di Renjie's provocative tone and did not play well. Three games later, he had no choice but to yield his precious coat to Di Renjie.

Di Renjie rose to his feet and bid farewell to Tianhou. Holding the feather coat in one hand, he exited the basilica and strolled along the pathway as far as the Guangfan Gate.[8] Turning his head, he called out to his bondservant and tossed the coat to him.

"Don't fuss. Just take it," Di Renjie ordered.

"Yes, My Lord?"

"This is my gift to you."

***

Finally, the mighty kingdom of the Tubo was showing signs of weakening. Guo Yuanzhen's strategy of sowing seeds of discord between Lun Qinling and his sovereign seemed to have played a part. But what mattered more was perhaps the internal dynamics of Tubo politics. The zanpu (King) Chidu Songzan had succeeded to the throne as early as 676 when he was still a small child. The power-holder Lun Qinling of the Ga'er (Gar) clan had treated him as a figurehead ever since. With the support of his brother Lun Zanpo, Lun Qinling kept the Tubo court firmly under his thumb.

The zanpu, out of necessity, always kept up an affable façade when he was in the presence of one of the Lun brothers, but deep down he resented the way they ruled Tubo with an iron hand and yearned for the day when he would finally be released from their tutelage.

In 699, at thirty *sui*, he got his chance. With the senior official Lun Yan[9] at his back, the zanpu embarked on a secret plan to seize back power. While on a royal game hunt north of the capital Lhasa one summer morning, on his orders his large guard force turned their swords on Lun Qinling's followers of more than two thousand and butchered them to a man. The zanpu therewith issued a decree to summon Lun Qinling and his brother to the capital. Upon receiving Lun Qinling's defiant answer, the zanpu, commanding an expeditionary army in person, came after him and soon trounced his army.

Lun Qinling, the proud leader of Tubo for decades, was now labeled a traitor, and fell on his own sword.

His brother Lun Zanpo, along with the remainder of his brother's following, fled east and submitted to the authority of their old foe, the

Wu Zhou. When he entered the western suburbs of Chang'an, it was Guo Yuanzhen, no less, who welcomed him on behalf of Tianhou. All his doubts about his treatment in the hands of his erstwhile enemy were gone when he received the grand titles of *tejin* (Specially Advanced) and Guidê prince.[10] Not long thereafter, his nephew Lun Gongren,[11] Lun Qinling's son, joined the Wu Zhou as well, bringing with him 7,000 Tuyuhun households (tents), and received as his reward the title of commandery duke of Jiuquan.[12]

A few months later, Lun Zanpo was invited to the palace in Luoyang to see Tianhou and received from her the appointment of general-in-chief of the Right Guard and a generous reward of gold and silver and silk. After the audience was over, he, accompanied by his men, set off west to his new base in the Hongyuan Vale[13] in Liangzhou.

The defection of Lun Zanpo and his men was a great loss to the Tubo. Thereafter, there would not be another talented military leader in Tubo until the late eighth century.[14]

Notes

1 Dingzhou 定州 and Zhaozhou 趙州: two prefectures in west central Hebei.

2 *Mafei san* 麻沸散.

3 Yan Jingrong 閻敬容.

4 The Shangdong Gate 上東門.

5 The Great Desert: the Gobi Desert. Mt. Okuten (Yudujin 於都斤; Wudejian 烏德鞬) is probably part of the Khangai Range.

6 Shandong ("east of the mountains") in Tang times means "the area east of the Taihang Mountains," which lay in present-day Hebei, Shandong, and part of Henan.

7 *Guolao* 國老.

8 The Guangfan Gate 光範門 was south of the Xuanzheng Basilica and west of the Qianyuan Gate in Luoyang's Palace City. See *Henan zhi*, 唐城闕古蹟, 120.

9 Lun Yan 論巖.

10 Guidê prince 歸德王.

11 Lun Gongren 論弓仁.

12 Jiuquan 酒泉: commandery in present-day Jiuquan and others, Gansu. Note: at that time, Jiuquan Commandery was called Suzhou 肅州 (Su Prefecture).

13 The Hongyuan Vale 洪源谷 was in the southwest of present-day Wuwei, Gansu.

14 The second half of the eighth century saw the rise of Enlan Dazhalugong 恩蘭•達扎路恭 (Nganlam Takdra Lukhong), who once took Chang'an (762).

5. Ji Xu (699–700)

SINCE LI ZHE'S appointment as crown prince, Tianhou's angst had been mounting. She was concerned that the Wus and the Lis would not be able to get along after she was gone. One day in the summer of 699, she brought Li Zhe, Li Dan, Princess Taiping, Wu Youji, and other Wu princes together in the Mingtang. There they made sacrifices to Heaven and Earth and took turns to swear an oath to treat one another with kindness forever.

On her orders, an artisan from the Board of Rites crafted an Iron Certificate,[1] an iron sheet that bore the inscription of the oath in red, to be deposited with the Institute of Historiography.[2]

Traditionally, the Iron Certificate was one of the most sacred official documents. Its holder could use it to save himself from one death sentence. The sovereign issued it only to the most meritorious officials and generals. In this case, it served to accentuate the solemnity of the Wu-Li alliance.

***

As Tianhou continued to age, from time to time, she came down with an ailment that left her in bed for weeks. On one such dreadful occasion, she spent hours looking back on her past. She wondered what was happening to her. *Of course, there is aging, relentless, inevitable*, she thought. *No amount of longevity drugs can slow it down a bit. But there must be something else. Those lives lost due to my action? Empress Wang and Consort Xiao, dozens of the Li princes and princesses, and senior officials such as Zhangsun Wuji, Chu Suiliang, Pei Yan, and countless others. According to karmic laws, they can produce a negative effect on this and next life.*

While in search of divine forgiveness and blessings, she went on pilgrimages to Mount Song. On one such trip in 699, she first stopped in Goushi[3] to pay a visit to the Temple to the Immortal Crown Prince. It was dedicated to Crown Prince Jin who had lived under King Ling of Zhou in the sixth century BCE.[4] Tradition had it that, after his passing at a young age, he was seen riding a crane in his ascent to Heaven.

Inspired by the visit, Tianhou composed a long eulogy. She brushed the 2,000-plus characters on paper, which were then inscribed on a limestone stela, 6.54 m (more than 21 feet) high. On the obverse one finds the names of the most important senior officials in her entourage: Wu Sansi, Wang Jishan, Su Weidao, Wei Yuanzhong, Di Renjie, Lou Shide, Yang Zaisi, and Ji Xu.[5] Three of them, Wang Jishan, Di Renjie, and Lou Shide, were advanced in age like Tianhou herself. Two (Wang and Lou) would die before the year-end.

Before the imperial progress reached the final destination—Mount Song, Tianhou was taken ill, and could no longer endure the rigor of climbing the mountain in a palanquin.

At her request, Supervising Secretary Yan Zhaoyin[6] completed the final leg of the journey on her behalf. On the peak of the Shaoshi Mountains,[7] Yan conducted the ritual. Following an ablution, he lay face down on the bronze vessel containing the sacrifice and prayed to the gods to let him suffer Tianhou's ailment.

By the time Yan came down from the mountain and saw Tianhou again, she had already felt much better. As a token of thanks, she had 100 bolts of silk sent to Yan's home.

***

On her return journey, Tianhou received news of troubles in the west. She appointed Lou Shide as grand commissioner of the Longyou Armies, with the special task of pacifying those Tubo who had submitted to the Wu Zhou.

As Lou Shide was about to set off for his new assignment in 699 at the age of seventy *sui*, he passed away in his home.

An attendant read out his obituary:

> *. . . [Chief Minister Lou Shide] will be remembered for his distinguished career and his dedicated service in the Helong*[8] *area (through which the Silk Road passed), where he was on and off for a good forty years! Thanks to his industry, magnanimity, and benevolence, he was very popular with the locals. In an age where entrapment and frameups were common, he managed to survive without compromising his integrity. That in itself was an extraordinary accomplishment. . . .*

With a gloomy look on her face, Tianhou closed her eyes to reflect on the man—his awkward manners, hearty laugh, and thoughtful advice. She let out a deep sigh.

***

From the fourth to the seventh months of 700,[9] Tianhou sojourned in the newly constructed Sanyang Palace.[10]

It was Wu Sansi who had first proposed the building of this sprawling complex in the shadows of Mount Song and to the east of Luoyang for Tianhou. The name Sanyang meaning "three yangs" had been adopted after much debate and deliberation at court. They referred to her nephew Wu Sansi and her sons Li Zhe and Li Dan: the three most important individuals in her life now.

The idea had come about after the creation of the Iron Certificate had failed to ease her worries that, following her death, there would be a fierce Wu-Li struggle in which the three yangs would destroy one another. Naming the palace after these three men expressed her wish that permanent harmony would prevail among them.

The highlight of her stay was a special trip to Mount Song, again completed by someone else for her. The proxy was Hu Chao, a Buddhist monk from Hongzhou who had created a longevity drug for her.

Having scaled to the top of the main peak, the monk knelt down on a cliff, made a prayer for Tianhou, stood up, moved back a few steps, and dashed towards the edge while hurling with every ounce of his strength a gold tablet[11] into the abyss below as he voiced the hope that it would be received by the transcendents dwelling in Heaven. The inscription on the tablet read:

The sovereign of the Great Zhou, Wu Zhao, is a passionate follower of the Perfected Dao, transcendents, and divine beings. Now on her behalf, I am paying this visit to the entrance to the Central Marchmount, Mount Song. With the casting of this gold tablet, I am beseeching the Three Officials[12] *and Nine Agencies*[13] *to delete Wu Zhao's name from the list of sinners.*

The year of gengzi, the month of gengzi, and the day of jiayin.[14]

respectfully submitted by the humble envoy Hu Chao,[15]
bowing twice in obeisance.

Later, commentators observed that in seeking divine protection, Tianhou deployed an eclectic approach. It would have been frowned upon under usual circumstances. But it happened at her insistence: a Buddhist monk performed a ritual to appease the Daoist gods in order to alleviate her karmic burden.

***

One year after its founding, the Directorate of Crane Riders had attracted much unwanted attention. Everyone knew that Tianhou was behind its creation and growth, but that had never stopped detractors from coming forward. Counselor of Remonstrance Yun Banqian, a talented poet favored by Tianhou, did not like the term adopted for its members: *gongfeng*[16] (palace attendants). He memorialized to abolish it for lack of an ancient precedent.

Over the years Tianhou had mellowed to the point where she could listen to critical advice with equanimity. Still, she felt very uncomfortable with Yun's "attack," and demoted him for defying the court.

President of the Secretariat Wang Jishan complained against Tianhou's favorite courtiers affiliated with Directorate. Tianhou gritted her teeth but refrained from taking action against the chief minister. Tianhou had promoted him to the post for his candor in the first place. How could she bring him to book for offering his candid opinion?

It was only after Wang had submitted the fifth memorial dwelling on the same issue that Tianhou felt compelled to write him a reply, "Jishan, because of your advanced age, you don't have to accompany me when I am on a tour or at a banquet. What you need to do is take care of business in the Secretariat."

Wang Jishan sighed and said, "How can the president of the Secretariat not see the Son of Heaven every day?" He submitted his request for resignation in three letters. Tianhou rejected them all. Not long afterwards, Tianhou even promoted him to chancellor just before he passed on at the age of 82 *sui*.

After the Directorate of Crane Riders (*konghe jian*) had taken enough heat, it was given a more respectable name, "Palace Office" (*fengchen fu*)[17] in 700. Zhang Yizhi had continued to serve as its director, and the membership had even expanded to include sycophantic literati skilled at writing panegyrics and a few unsophisticated young men who had nothing to offer except youth and looks.

***

Tianhou was throwing a drinking party in the forecourt of the residential basilica. The Two Zhangs, the Wus, and the Palace Office pretty boys were in attendance. They teased and flirted, drank and gambled with abandon. Wu Sansi then declared that Zhang Changzong was Crown Prince Jin reincarnate, a son of King Ling of Zhou who had allegedly gone to heaven. An amused Tianhou, with Zhang Yizhi holding a large feather fan by her side, suggested that Zhang Changzong should put on a show for the party. Zhang Changzong thereupon disappeared into the building, only to come out a few moments later in a changed appearance. He was wearing a shiny feather coat to look like an immortal and riding a wooden crane. He strutted like a bird seeking a place to perch and, every now and then, stopped to play the flute. With Wu Sansi taking the lead, the Palace Office literati fell over themselves to write panegyric poems for the memorable occasion. When an attendant read them out to Tianhou, she could not stop laughing. At the end of the party, Tianzhou gifted a peck of pearls to each of the Two Zhangs.

***

The Two Zhangs' status as court favorites was a boon to their relatives as well. Zhang Changyi, one of their elder brothers, did not have any academic credentials, but was nonetheless promoted to head Luoyang County, the most important one in the nation. Thanks to his connections, there was no lack of people asking him for favors. A job candidate named Xue once gave him fifty ounces of gold together with a written request for an official appointment. Zhang Changyi passed the request on to his buddy Zhang Xi, vice president of the Board of Personnel.

When the vice president met Zhang Changyi again a few days later, he said, "I'm awfully sorry, but I've misplaced the written request. Do you remember who gave it to you?"

"Well, I only remember his surname, Xue," Zhang Changyi answered. "But it shouldn't matter. Why don't you just appoint everyone surnamed Xue?"

"Good idea! Thanks for reminding me," said the vice president, who went on to appoint *sixty* Xues to official posts.

This prompted Court Rectifier Zhu Jingze to file a memorial, in which he said, "I understand that Your Majesty needs the companionship of Zhang Yizhi and Zhang Changzong. But that should not give their relatives license to sell offices. What is more, the Palace Office under their control has recently experienced too much growth. That is hardly justifiable. Even vulgar people like Hou Xiang,[18] chief administrator of the Left Palace Gate Guard, sought appointment as palace attendant (*gongfeng*). That, if approved, will be in serious violation of ritual and etiquette. As a court remonstrator, I have no choice but to voice my concern."

Tianhou knew that the Zhangs had serious problems. But she also knew that the Zhangs—no matter how much mischief they might cause—acted, together with their literati associates, as a balance against the chief ministers, and they were never in a position to challenge the throne. She rewarded Zhu with 100 bolts of silk for candor but refrained from taking action against the Zhangs.

It was about this time that someone proposed a large-scale literary project: the compilation of a poem anthology entitled *Sanjiao zhuying*[19] (Essential Pearls of the Three Teachings) in the *leishu*[20] (encyclopedia) category. It was to be undertaken by the Palace Office. When completed, the massive collection would have 1,300 *juan* (scrolls or chapters).[21] After consulting a few court leaders, Tianhou was convinced of its advantages, and gave the go-ahead. First, it would provide the palace attendants with an opportunity to work on something that could be passed on to future generations. Second, it would lend legitimacy to the presence of the Two Zhangs in the palace. Third, it would give voice to her idea of religion as she attempted to promote Confucianism, Buddhism, and Daoism in tandem.

It was given out that Zhang Changzong was the book's editor-in-chief and Zhang Yizhi was actively involved in its compilation. However, according to one source, the Two Zhangs were semi-literate. They depended on the service of sycophantic literati such as Song Zhiwen and Yan Zhaoyin around them to write poems. So the Zhangs' contributions to the project were probably very limited.[22]

***

Apart from the gigolos such as the Two Zhangs and the literary hacks, the Palace Office (*fengchen fu*) was also home to some able administrators. One of them, Ji Xu, was also in favor with Tianhou. He enjoyed her patronage not just because of his virile looks, but also his competence and ambition. But that patronage would end soon.

After the sack of Zhaozhou, Ji Xu got involved in a quarrel with Wu Yizong over who deserved the most credit for helping take back the city. Out of curiosity Tianhou ordered them to make their cases in front of her. Ji Xu with his imposing height, booming voice, and eloquence stood in sharp contrast with the stubby Wu Yizong who stammered in a tongue-tied voice that was hardly audible. While she was convinced that Ji Xu won the debate hands down, she was also alarmed that a non-Wu had so easily insulted a Wu in her presence. *It is hard to imagine what he is going to do to the Wus after I am gone.*

The next day, Ji Xu came into her study on summons to report on the Palace Office. He held forth with elan, as usual, citing allusions to literature and history that vaunted his knowledge of classical scholarship. Suddenly, Tianhou slammed her hand on the table in front of her, her face creasing into a frown, and shouted, "Enough of your pedantic nonsense! Why don't you shut up for a change?"

A terrified Ji Xu sank to his knees.

"Let me tell you something," Tianhou continued. "When I was in attendance on Taizong, there was a tameless horse called the Lion nobody could break. I suggested using one of three instruments: an iron whip, an iron stick, and a dagger. Taizong praised me. Do you want me to try one of those on you?"

Ji Xu kowtowed and begged for mercy.

With a roll of her eyes, Tianhou ordered him to his feet and said, "Count yourself lucky today. I am not yet in a mood to stain my dagger with your blood." She waved her hand and let him go.

***

Wu Yizong and other Wu princes had always resented Ji Xu's peremptory ways and the favors he received from Tianhou, nor did they like his close ties with the crown prince. Soon they found an opportunity to bring him down. When one of Ji's brothers was caught masquerading as an official, they started a petition campaign to hound Ji Xu out of office, based on the principle of culpability by association. That was reason enough for Tianhou to demote Ji Xu to county defender at the bottom rung of the official ladder.

***

A few days later Tianhou granted Ji Xu an audience in her study before he took up office in the provinces.

With a glint of tears in his eyes, he said, "After I leave for a place far away from Luoyang, perhaps I will never see Your Majesty again." He broke into a sob, and continued, "I would like to give Your Majesty my parting advice, if I may."

"Yes?"

"Please allow me to ask Your Majesty: When soil and water are mixed together to make mud, is there a struggle between them?"

"No."

"Is there a struggle between Buddhism and Daoism?"

"Yes, there is."

"And between the royals and the Wus?"

"Obviously, there is a constant struggle."

"Today, the Lis are happy with Li Zhe as crown prince, but the Wus—the consort relatives—are not. Trouble is, they are still powerful princes. This is setting the Lis and the Wus up for a fight one of these days. I fear neither the royals nor the consort relatives will find peace."

"I agree. But at my request, my sons and daughter and the Wus took an oath together and they promised to live in permanent harmony. The whole thing is recorded in the Iron Certificate."

"The promise may not be enough, Your Majesty."

"I know. But it is impossible to take away the Wus' princely titles, if this is what you want to propose."

"Nothing can escape Your Majesty's sharp eye. Indeed, that is exactly what is on my mind. Let me hope that they, the Lis and the Wus, will never come to blows."

"Me too," Tianhou said with resignation. With her eyes closed, she wished in her heart that Ji Xu's dark premonition would never come true.

***

After the destruction of the giant Buddha statue, Tianhou had entertained the thought of its re-creation, but had yet to set the project in motion due to the lack of an adequate source of funding.

Then, in the autumn of 700, she read a proposal that promised to find a solution. It suggested building the second giant Buddha statue with a poll tax on the Buddhist clergy. She sent the proposal to the court leadership for comment and soon received a response in the form of a memorial that filled her with joy and excitement. *Last time I saw State Elder*, she thought, *he looked really old. With thinning white hair, he wobbled on a cane. Wonder if he is doing better now.*

She opened the scroll and started reading:

> *Your Majesty, nowadays, monastic buildings surpass palatial structures in grandeur. Those who build them are neither ghosts nor gods, but humans. The building materials do not come from Heaven, but from Earth. That being the case, how can these building projects avoid harming the masses? Here, I must say, in most cases, the Buddhists are to blame. In today's world, traveling monks are everywhere. Thanks to their work,*

sutra printshops are set up in the alleyways of the wards, and temples are built in the marketplaces. They want to convert people with a greater urgency than government levies. Their religious ceremonies are more demanding than imperial edicts. But do they do any good? Take, for example, Emperors Wu and Jianwen of Liang.[23] *As the most pious rulers in history, they gave alms to the Buddhist monasteries without restraint. But when turmoil arose in the Three Huai*[24] *area and the smoke of war enveloped the Five Mountain Ranges,*[25] *none of the countless Buddhist pagodas they had helped build could save the country from disaster. When their own lives were in danger, none of the monks and nuns in cassocks who packed the streets could save them from the axe.*

As for the suggested poll tax on monks and nuns, my calculation shows that what it amounts to is negligible and will cover less than one percent of the total cost. Why? Because of its large size, the statue, which cannot be exposed to the elements, needs to be housed in a colossal building. In addition, corridors and porticos will have to be built. All these greatly add to the cost.

In the past, when the Tathāgata[26] *Buddha founded the religion, he aimed at mercy and compassion and never wanted to run people into the ground in order to create useless ornaments. Besides, the people have already suffered a great deal in recent years. Water-logging and drought have often hit the farming communities, and our frontier is never at peace. If, in the process of building the giant Buddha statue, we use up the resources of the treasury and exhaust the labor force, with what can we help and rescue the people when disaster hits somewhere in the realm?*

Heaving a long sigh, Tianhou asked Yidu Neiren, "State Elder has passed seventy, has he not?"

"Yes, Your Majesty."

"Yet, all he cares about is the fate of the country. All he expects of me is to do good. How can I bear to go against his wishes?"

"No, Your Majesty cannot," answered her confidante. Thus, on Tianhou's orders, the giant Buddha statue project was shelved for good.

Notes

[1] *Tiequan* 鐵券.

[2] The Institute of Historiography (*shiguan* 史館): agency responsible for keeping historical records and compiling official histories. It had two branches, one in the Daming Palace, and the other in Luoyang. See *Tang huiyao* 63.

[3] Goushi 緱氏: county and town southwest of present-day Yanshi, Henan.

[4] The Temple of the Immortal Crown Prince (*shengxian taizi miao* 升仙太子廟). Allegedly, the temple was set up following King Ling of Zhou's 周靈王 son Crown Prince Jin's 太子晉 after-death appearance on Mount Goushi.

[5] The stone tablet is still standing in situ today. For Wu Zetian's eulogy, see *Quan Tang wen* 88. After the tablet was set up in 699, more text was added later.

[6] Yan Zhaoyin 閻朝隱.

[7] The Shaoshi Mountains 少室山.

[8] Helong (Hexi 河西 and Longyou 隴右): roughly present-day west Gansu.

[9] In the tenth month of 700, the Xia Calendar was restored, and the first month of the lunar calendar was once again the standard month (*zhengyue*). See *Zizhi tongjian* 207.6553.

[10] The Sanyang Palace 三陽宮 was west of Dengfeng, Henan. See *Zizhi tongjian* 206.6545.

[11] The gold tablet is the only known artifact of Wu Zetian extant today. It is now in the collection of the Henan Museum 河南博物院.

[12] The Three Officials (*sanguan* 三官) refer to three Daoist deities—the Officials of Heaven, Earth, and Water.

[13] The Nine Agencies (*jiufu* 九府) are Daoist offices. Each of the Three Officials (see above) has three palaces and nine agencies. In all there are twenty-seven agencies. The Nine Agencies here may refer to those that belong to any one of the Three Officials.

[14] *Gengzi* 庚子, *jiayin* 甲寅: names of years, months, or days in the Sexagenary Cycle.

[15] Hu Chao 胡超 of Hongzhou 洪州 (prefecture based in Nanchang, Jiangxi) is identified by some as a Daoist adept or a eunuch. Both are incorrect. In *Taiping guangji* (288, 胡超僧), he is recorded as a *seng* 僧 (Buddhist monk), who renounced the mundane world to study the Way of enlightenment.

[16] *Gongfeng* 供奉.

[17] The Directorate of Crane Riders (*konghe jian* 控鶴監); the Palace Office *(fengchen fu* 奉宸府).

[18] Hou Xiang 侯祥 argued that he deserved to be appointed as palace attendant because he was more virile than Xue Huaiyi.

[19] *Sanjiao zhuyin* 三教珠英.

[20] A *leishu* 類書 is a thematic collection of written pieces. The first *leishu* dates back to the Cao-Wei period.

[21] The project was launched in 700 (*Zizhi tongjian* 206.6546) and completed in the Chang'an rein (701–704) (*Jiu Tang shu* 101, 張說傳; 199, 沈佺期傳).

[22] *Jiu Tang shu* 78.2706.

[23] Emperor Wu of Liang 梁武帝 (r. 502–549); Emperor Jianwen of Liang 梁簡文帝 (r. 549–551). The former died while under siege in Taicheng 臺城 (the royal castle near Nanjing, Jiangsu) and the latter, his son, was killed by the rebel Hou Jing 侯景 (503–552).

[24] Three Huai (Sanhuai 三淮): the lower Huai valley. It was the area under Hou Jing's control before he rebelled in 548.

[25] The Five Mountain Ranges (Wuling 五嶺): the mountain ranges that separate Jiangxi and Hunan from Guangdong and Guangxi.

[26] Tathāgata: lit., "one who has thus come." It is a title Sakyamuni used to refer to himself. *See* note in Part 2, Chapter 10.

6. The Cabal (701)

In Japan, the influential Taihō Code (Taihō-ritsuryō 大寶律令) was completed under the influence of the Tang institutions.

AFTER TIANHOU READ a long letter delivered to the Bronze Chest in the early autumn of 701, she was surprised that the writer Su Anheng was not even a court clerk. But he showed a great level of familiarity with court affairs. In his letter, he attempted to address a highly sensitive issue—succession. Very few people at court were willing to touch it for fear of rubbing her the wrong way. In fact, Tianhou did not like Su Anheng's argument a bit, but was nonetheless intrigued by his erudition. She granted him an audience in the palace.

"You proclaim your loyalty to the throne," Tianhou said to Su, a man in his early forties. "But you also argue in favor of my abdication?"

"Yes, Your Majesty. That is precisely my point. Since Your Majesty took over the reins from the late emperor, almost twenty years have passed. The move then showed deference to Heaven above and in accord with the wishes of the people below. But now things are different."

"How?"

"Your Majesty, you are already in your mid-seventies. Your filial son, the current crown prince, on the other hand, is in the prime of his life. Lord Shun lifted the hem of his garment and left the throne to Lord Yu;[1] the Duke of Zhou at the height of his authority returned power to King Cheng.[2] Lord Shun and Lord Yu were at best distant relatives; the Duke of Zhou and King Cheng of Zhou were just uncle and nephew. The emotional bond between second- or third-degree relatives or between uncle and nephew cannot begin to compare with that between mother and son. If your son is allowed to succeed to the throne and run the country, it will be in accord with tradition, and will not be much different from your own rule."

Tianhou looked at him in amazement. If it were ten years before, she would have ordered his beheading for *lèse majesté*.

"Despite your advanced age, Your Majesty," Sun continued, "you reign over the realm as emperor, enjoying great prestige and popularity. But to be an emperor is a tiring business. With its heavy workload, it drains your body and spirit. Only by yielding the throne to the crown prince can you lighten the load and find pleasure and health."

"I see your point. But I won't quit the throne."

"Yes, Your Majesty, I understand." Su Anheng knitted his brows.

"Now, what's the other thing I want to discuss? Oh yes, the conferral of princely titles."

"Yes, Your Majesty. Since antiquity, there has never been a single case in which members of two different clans were created princes simultaneously."

"How about Gaozu of Han Liu Bang?"

"Your Majesty is right; I apologize. But that is an exception. Anyhow, Liu Bang soon realized his mistake and started eliminating the nonroyal princes. Today, however, the country has a host of them: Prince of Liang Wu Sansi, Prince of Ding Wu Youji, Prince of Henei Wu Yizong, and Prince of Jianchang Wu Youning.[3] They were enfeoffed not because of merit, but because of their ties to Your Majesty. As consort relatives, they can be much more threatening than the nonroyal princes of the past. In my opinion, this in the long run will be detrimental to the Wu clan and the country."

With his voice shaking and tears brimming his eyes, Su Anheng suddenly dropped on his knees, held up his hands together in front, and said, "I beseech Your Majesty! Demote the Wus to dukes and marquises, and assign them to insignificant posts, for the sake of the country."

"What else?" Tianhou asked, furrowing her brows.

"I also heard," Su Anheng answered, sitting up, "that Your Majesty has more than twenty grandsons; none has been enfeoffed yet."

"That's true."

"In my humble opinion, this situation cannot go on for long. I entreat Your Majesty to enfeoff them as princes and appoint mentors to edify them about filial piety and loyalty. I hope, before long, they will start playing an active role in guarding the throne."

"Well, I'm glad you brought it up today. Yes, I'll give it some thought," Tianhou said. With a wave of her hand, a eunuch on duty came up to take the visitor away.

***

Tianhou held several discussions with the court leaders and her confidantes Yidu Neiren and Shangguan Wan'er on the issues Su Anheng had raised. Lack of consensus of opinion gave her pause as to what action to take. Meanwhile, her male favorites continued to dominate the court and be the center of gossip. When she heard whispers about them she did not terribly mind, because she had gotten used to it. Still, she was shocked hard when she read a secret report on the vicious remarks against the Two Zhangs by some of her third-generation descendants.

A follow-up investigation exposed a small cabal against the Two Zhangs. At its head was Crown Prince Li Zhe's eldest son Li Chongrun of twenty *sui*. The remaining two members were Chongrun's sister Li Xianhui of seventeen *sui* and her husband Wu Yanji of twenty-three *sui*.

The issue was complicated by the fact that the two young men were actually very high in the line of succession. In the event of Tianhou's abdication or death, her son Li Zhe (Li Xian) would ascend the throne and Li Chongrun would be the first in line to succeed him. Should Tianhou change her mind and decide to place a Wu on the throne after her death, Wu Yanji, as the eldest son of the late Wu Chengsi, would be the second in line to succeed her after Wu Sansi. Li Xianhui, who got along with her husband very well, was the bond that connected the Lis and the Wus.

As for the targets of the cabal, Zhang Changzong and Zhang Yizhi, their very existence and behavior invited scandal. As Tianhou's darlings, they lorded it over Luoyang's residents with immunity. Everyone, from generals to chief ministers, from the Lis to the Wus, had to eat humble pie in front of them. The handsome looks of the two brothers and their immodest ways, combined with their gigolo status, gave rise to wild rumors about them and what they did with Tianhou.

Of course, people had to gossip behind closed doors. This was what the three blue-blooded young people did when they got together in private. Nobody knows what exactly transpired in their conversation on that fateful night. They may have complained about the excessive power the Two Zhangs had or Tianhou's permissiveness. They may have joked about their promiscuous behavior, the white makeup they covered their faces with, or the flashy colors of their garments.

Unfortunately for them, one of the maids who overheard part of the conversation, was an informer in the service of the Two Zhangs.

The moment they received a tip-off from her, they went to see Tianhou with their complaint.

In a burst of rage, she ordered the immediate imprisonment of the three—two grandchildren and one grandson-in-law. An investigation followed that soon yielded a guilty verdict.

What happened next is shrouded in mystery. One source states that the three were taken into the palace and clubbed to death on Tianhou's orders. Another source claims that Tianhou had them delivered to Crown Prince Li Zhe, who for the sake of self-preservation and the preservation of his own family, had the three—a son, a daughter, and a son-in-law—killed by strangulation. The third source records that the unlucky trio took their own lives on Tianhou's orders.[4]

At any rate, on account of the Two Zhangs, Tianhou forfeited the lives of three of her most promising descendants, including two possible successors to the throne. Why? Did she suddenly go berserk and act out of uncontrollable anger? Apparently not. There had been no lack of complaints against the Two Zhangs by court remonstrators and the chief ministers. But these were open and above-board criticisms aimed at behavior that was considered beyond the pale. Although always unpalatable, these criticisms could be tolerated and serve as constraints on the Zhangs' misbehavior.

The attacks against the Zhangs by Tianhou's descendants were different. First, these were underhanded acts that might suggest ill-feelings towards Tianhou herself. Second, precisely because these descendants were possible successors to the throne, their malice towards the Zhangs and, by inference, Tianhou herself was potentially threatening to her political legacy. Tianhou was deeply aware that, as a woman in her late seventies, she did not have long to live. Should power pass into the hands of these rebellious descendants, she was convinced, they would undo her achievements, which had taken a lifetime to accomplish.

***

In the first month of 702, Tianhou issued an edict that introduced a new examination practice called *wuju* (Martial Skills Examination). It read, "Various prefectures in the realm shall offer courses in martial skills. Candidates in this category shall be sent to the capital for their examination, following the examples of the Classicist (*mingjing*) and Advanced Scholar (*jinshi*) categories."

The *wuju* differed from its civil counterpart in its focus on martial skills and military leadership. It consisted of long-distance archery, mounted archery, lancing on horseback, archery on foot, stature and appearance, language, and weightlifting. Passing the examination would pave the way for starting an officer's career in the army. The introduction of the *wuju* was also an important measure Tianhou adopted to reform the examination system. With the Tujue and Tubo threats in the north and northwest unabated, the military welcomed it as a more effective way to meet the growing need for recruiting talented young officers from the populace.

Notes

1 Lord Shun 舜 was the last one of the Five Lords (*wudi* 五帝). He abdicated in favor of Lord Yu 禹. "Lifting the hem of his garment" should be part of a ritual Shun performed as he abdicated the throne.

[2] The Duke of Zhou served as regent of King Cheng of Zhou until the king reached majority.

[3] The prince of Liang 梁王; the prince of Ding 定王; the prince of Henei 河内王; the prince of Jianchang 建昌王.

[4] Some scholars, based on one phrase in Li Huixian's epitaph (*zhutai huiyue* 珠胎毁月, lit. "treasured embryo and waning moon"), assert that, the day after her husband's execution, she was shocked into premature labor, and died in the process. This can only be regarded as a speculation because there exist too many unknowns.

7. The Wei Yuanzhong Affair (702–704)

AFTER THE DEATH of Li Chongrun and his sister and brother-in-law, any criticism of the Two Zhangs was stifled. For a while, it seemed that royals, aristocrats, and top court leaders all vied against one another to curry favor with them. Even the most prominent members of the Li house—Crown Prince Li Zhe, his brother Li Dan, and his sister Princess Taiping—sponsored a joint proposal to enfeoff them as princes in 702. Tianhou, however, knew better. She still remembered the warning by Su Anheng and others against enfeoffing both the Lis and Wus as princes and was in no hurry to create a third princely clan.

***

On a nice autumn day, Di Renjie was riding in the entourage of Tianhou, wearing a kerchief-cap, in a heavily wooded area of the Western Park of Luoyang. The road ahead, covered with fallen foliage, descended into a dell as it was about to cross a bridge. The horse, startled, kicked its forelegs in the air, causing the rider's cap to fly off his head.

Tianhou stuck her head out of her carriage window and shouted at the crown prince riding behind to help. The prince rushed over and seized hold of the reins to calm the horse down. A eunuch picked up the cap and handed it to Di, who put it back on. The prince then placed the reins in Di's hands.

Tianhou waved a eunuch officer over and dictated a rescript while he jotted it down with a graphite pen on a wooden tablet. It ordained, "From this day forward State Elder is no longer required to follow the sovereign on tours."

The next day, Di Renjie handed in his resignation on account of old age and declining health. Tianhou turned it down, saying, "Who can I talk with if State Elder is no longer around?"

A few days later, Tianhou summoned Di Renjie into her study. On seeing Tianhou, by instinct, he fell on his knees with difficulty to make an obeisance. Tianhou rushed forward to stop him. With tears brimming her eyes, she said, "It pains me to see you struggle like this." Turning to her eunuch attendant on duty, she announced, "From now on, President of the Secretariat Di Renjie is exempt from making obeisances. This is a rescript. Understand?"

"Yes, Your Majesty," the attendant answered.

Tianhou went on to waive his obligation to be on duty in office. "He should not be bothered with official business unless it is of great significance to the military and the country."

Now Di Renjie was all but in name retired.

Once Tianhou visited him at home to discuss a whole range of important issues, especially promotions at the highest level. She asked, "Can you recommend a gentleman of extraordinary talent for court service?"

"Yes, Your Majesty. But I need to know what you are looking for in such a gentleman. What Your Majesty wants him to do?"

"To serve as chancellor."

"In that case the first persons that come to mind are Su Weidao and Li Qiao. Both are known for their literary accomplishments. As for a gentleman of extraordinary talent, I can only think of one person: Zhang Jianzhi, chief administrator of Jingzhou."[1]

Two months later, when Di Renjie met Tianhou again, he asked, "Has Your Majesty promoted Zhang Jianzhi already?"

"Yes. He is now assistant prefect (*sima*) of Luozhou.[2] That is a promotion, isn't it?"

"Yes, Your Majesty. The assistant prefect of Luozhou outranks the chief administrator of Jingzhou, because Luozhou is the capital prefecture. But I recommended him for the top job, not the assistant prefect."

The next day, Tianhou raised Zhang Jianzhi to vice president of the Board of Justice.

Thereafter, Tianhou continued to pick his brain for qualified officials to fill key posts. Di Renjie then made a slew of recommendations, all approved by Tianhou, including Huan Yanfan (as vice censor-in-chief), Jing Hui (as right assistant president of the Department of State Affairs),[3] Cui Xuanwei (as de facto chief minister), and Yuan Shuji (as vice chamberlain of the Court for Judicial Review).[4] They would join Zhang Jianzhi in playing a crucial role in bringing about a major political change soon.

***

In early 703, a bad cold left Tianhou in bed for three weeks. When she was too weak to shield the Zhangs from harm, a host of court officials dropped their veneer of politeness to attack them.

They voiced their revulsion at the way the Zhangs were dressed and talked, and their disapproval of the friends they were associated with, especially those bad-mannered, noisy merchants in gaudy silk garments. Had Tianhou not gotten well sooner, the censors would have prosecuted the Zhangs on "moral" grounds for these "vices," and the court leaders would have gone after them on account of abuse of power.

One of their sharpest critics was Chief Minister Wei Yuanzhong, who had made no bones about his animus towards them.

At a time when Wei was chief administrator of Luozhou, Zhang Changyi paid a visit to his prefectural government office on business. As usual, Changyi did not wait in line in the courtyard but went in without his name being called. The moment Wei saw the line-jumper walk through the door, he yelled at him to get out.

Zhang said, "Yuanzhong, it's me, Changzong's brother."

"So what? Everyone has to wait for his turn!"

Changyi turned his heels, slipped out of the room, and went to the end of the line, his head drooping.

On another occasion, Wei Yuanzhong arrested a young bondservant stirring up trouble in a bazaar in the Southern Market of Luoyang. When he was accosted by a group of men in black, demanding the return of the young man to his master Zhang Yizhi, Wei Yuanzhong told them he did not give a fig about who his master was, and had the young man clubbed to death.

When Wei Yuanzhong was vice president of the Phoenix Pavilion (Secretariat), he even had the guts to block the promotion of

Zhang Changqi (another brother of Changzong and Yizhi) to chief administrator of Yongzhou[5] (one of the two capital prefectures).

"Why?" a displeased Tianhou asked.

"When he was prefect of Qizhou,"[6] Wei said, "many of its residents ran away."

"Was that so?"

"I swear that it is true. That is a sign of incompetence or neglect of duty, or both, is it not?"

With reluctance, Tianhou cancelled the promotion.

***

When the Zhangs received reports of Wei Yuanzhong's secret contact with Assistant Chamberlain of the Court of State Sacrifices[7] Gao Jian, they went into panic mode. They feared that a conspiracy against them was in the works, and the involvement of Gao was particularly ominous, since standing behind him was his lover, the overmighty Princess Taiping.

They lost no time in alerting Tianhou to the threat. When Tianhou showed no interest in going after the chief minister, the Zhangs tried to destroy his reputation. They failed time and again until one rumor they spread caught Tianhou's attention. It claimed that Wei Yuanzhong had wished for the crown prince's immediate succession.

Faced with this potential threat to her power, Tianhou was compelled to act and authorized Wei's detention and investigation.

***

Secretariat Drafter[8] Zhang Yue, a brilliant scholar in his mid-thirties, tensed up when Zhang Changzong came to visit him in person, asking him to testify against Wei Yuanzhong while promising a fast-track promotion as his reward. But now in mid-career with a bright future, Zhang Yue showed reluctance to get involved.

"I don't think you want to do that," Zhang Changzong said in a menacing tone. "Don't forget we've got something on you as well."

At work the next day, Zhang Yue sought the advice of his colleagues. To his amazement, a fellow Secretariat drafter called Song Jing gave him an impassioned lecture,

"For a gentleman, what matters most is his integrity. To keep it intact, one has to be true to oneself. Why? Because the ghosts and gods are watching from above and they are hard to deceive. Never side with the wicked and frame the upright in hopes of saving your own neck. If, however, by adhering to the truth, you end up getting banished, you should look upon it as a great honor. Or if, unfortunately, you are condemned, I will go up the basilica steps and knock on the door, asking to die with you. We all dream of becoming a model for ten thousand generations to look up to. The moment to do it is now!"

When Palace Censor Zhang Tinggui came by, he only quoted this Confucian saying, "If I hear the Moral Way in the morning, I am prepared to die without regret in the evening." It was obvious that this colleague did not expect him to come out of the ordeal alive.

Left Historian Liu Zhiji simply said, "Don't leave a stain on the annals of history. If you do, it will affect your descendants for generations!"

Two weeks later, on Tianhou's orders, Wei Yuanzhong and his accuser Zhang Changzong appeared at a special court session to face each other.

Zhang Yue was brought in as the star eyewitness for Zhang Changzong. He had spent days getting ready for this moment. But when he found himself in the presence of Tianhou, Crown Prince Li Zhe, Prince Li Dan, and all the chief ministers, he felt intimidated.

"Zhang Yue," a loud female voice called out. "What do you have to say to Zhang Changzong's accusation against Wei Yuanzhong?"

Before he opened his mouth, he heard a panicky voice shout, "Your Majesty! He has worked hand in glove with Zhang Changzong!"

His face crimson with anger, Zhang Yue responded, "Chief Minister Wei Yuanzhong! How can you talk like a gossip?"

"Zhang Yue, you must keep your promise and testify," Zhang Changzong urged.

Turing to Tianhou, Zhang Yue continued, "Today, standing in front of Your Majesty and the entire court, I must tell the truth, nothing but the truth. I have *never*, *never* heard Wei Yuanzhong say that he wanted the crown prince to take over the reins. It is Zhang Changzong who tries to put those words in my mouth."

"Your Majesty," Zhang Changzong shouted in haste, "now I know why he was reluctant to testify."

"Yes?" Tianhou said.

"He is a member of Wei Yuanzhong's gang!"

"What's the evidence?"

"He once compared Wei Yuanzhong to Yi Yin and the Duke of Zhou. Yi Yin as Shang chancellor exiled his sovereign Taijia; and the Duke of Zhou as regent dominated the court of King Cheng of Zhou. In both cases, the inferior overshadowed the superior. Does it not prove his rebellious intent?"

"I still don't get it," Tianhou said. "If you knew all along Zhang Yue is a member of the gang, why didn't you expose him in the beginning?"

"I beg Your Majesty's pardon. But I was not quite sure whether he is a member until a moment ago. He gave himself away when he mounted a defense of the accused."

"May I say something, Your Majesty?" Zhang Yue asked.

Tianhou waved her hand and he continued, in a raised voice, "Petty men like the Two Zhangs—what do they know about Yi Yin and the Duke of Zhou? Let me explain under what circumstances I talked about them. When Wei Yuanzhong was promoted to a Rank-3 post as chief minister, court officials went to his home to offer felicitations. He then said, 'I'm afraid, I'm promoted without merit. And I feel so ashamed.' I said, 'You are occupying a Rank-3 post. This was the post Yi Yin and the Duke of Zhou once took, and you need not be ashamed.' What I said has been taken out of context. Furthermore, both Yi Yin and the Duke of Zhou were exemplary loyal court leaders. Both gave back power to their sovereigns in due course of time and have been admired since antiquity."

Zhang Yue paused to control his emotions, sighed, and continued, "I know that if I get close to Zhang Changzong and people of his ilk, I will get promoted, and that if I get close to Wei Yuanzhong, I may suffer clan extirpation. However, should Wei die of injustice, his wronged ghost would ascend to Heaven and be watching over us from there. I would then be in fear of him so long as I lived. For that reason alone, I have to tell the truth. That is, Wei Yuanzhong is *not* guilty of the charge."

"Zhang Yue," Tianhou said sharply. "I don't accept your argument. In fact, I find your about-face reprehensible. First, you agreed to testify; then you changed your mind; still later, you agreed to do it again."

With a snap of her fingers, two guards came up to take Zhang Yue into custody.

***

Within days, a stack of paper scrolls were piled up on the long table by the wall in Tianhou's study. Most were memorials backing Zhang Yue and Wei Yuanzhong by the court officials. Shangguan Wan'er selected from them a few she considered important and moved them to the top.

Among these, the most contentious one was by Zhu Jingze, now de facto chief minister. It said, "There is no ground for keeping Wei Yuanzhong and Zhang Yue in custody. If these two men are punished for their 'crimes,' all under Heaven will be disillusioned."

The one by Su Anheng, again submitted to the Bronze Chest, was written in a similar vein, with greater audacity. It said, "At the beginning of the Revolution, Your Majesty was known as 'the sovereign who listened to remonstrances.' But in recent years Your Majesty came to be known as 'the sovereign who enjoys flattery.' Since Wei Yuanzhong's imprisonment, neighborhoods and streets have been in turmoil. All believe that Your Majesty trusts the evil and wicked and turns away the worthy. The loyal and upright sigh at home, but say nothing at court, because they are afraid of offending the Two Zhangs and dying a senseless death. In this day and age, people are already suffering from heavy corvée and tax burdens and bankruptcies. Should they realize that the vicious are holding sway, and reward and punishment are given unjustly, I am afraid, they will become restless, and some of them will even take subversive action, causing trouble inside the Zhuque Gate[9] and seizing power at the Daming Basilica."[10]

For obvious reasons, this memorial stirred up much controversy. After Tianhou passed it around among the court officials for comment, the Two Zhangs suggested that its writer Su Anheng should be hanged for *lèse majesté*. But many officials, led by Secretariat Drafter Huan Yanfan, Chief Minister Zhu Jingze, and Editorial Director[11] Wei Zhigu, rushed to his defense.

"Calling me 'the sovereign who enjoys flattery'—that alone should send him to the gallows," Tianhou said to her advisers

"I agree that the language he uses is foul," her confidante Yidu Neiren concurred. "But the content is not entirely groundless. There are similar sayings going around among the populace. In my humble view, he does not deserve the suggested punishment."

"Do you mean I should let that foul-mouthed codger off the hook?"

"Could Your Majesty do that?"

"Why should I? I just don't get it."

"Well, if Your Majesty sends him to the gallows, it will have a chilling effect on future remonstrators and harm your legacy. If Your Majesty frees him, it will enhance your legacy. At this stage of Your Majesty's career, legacy is what matters most."

Tianhou nodded in agreement as she said, "As I'm getting old, I spend much time thinking about leaving a lasting legacy to posterity. What do you think?"

"In my humble opinion, Your Majesty, there is a good chance you will be able to create a great legacy that will go down in history for generations to come. The situation as it stands today is essentially favorable. Your grip on power has never been so secure. All the chief ministers are loyal subjects recommended by Lou Shide and Di

Renjie, and endorsed by you. Since you made the strategic decision not to appoint a Wu as heir, Crown Prince Li Zhe has returned to favor and remained popular with the masses. Not only that. He now enjoys support from other members of the Li royal house, including his brother Li Dan and his sister Princess Taiping, and is accepted by the Wus. The only major problem now is the rivalry between the Two Zhangs and the court officials. That issue may need to be addressed before long. As for the case of Wei Yuanzhong, as I see it, the Two Zhangs are not well grounded in their charges against him and Zhang Yue at all."

"You really think so?"

"Yes, Your Majesty."

"Do you think they should be set free without consequences?" growled Tianhou.

"No, Your Majesty. They should be punished for attitude, but not for treason."

Two days later, Tianhou handed down her judgment: Wei Yuanzhong was relegated to the very bottom of the bureaucracy as county defender in the far south; and Gao Jian and Zhang Yue were disenrolled and banished to the far south as well. But at least no heads rolled. So long as these banished officials maintained good behavior, there was still a good chance that they would be recalled by the court in a few years.

***

On a fine autumn morning in 703, Wei Yuanzhong was leaving Luoyang for his place of banishment. Eight of his friends—Head of the Livery Service of the Crown Prince[12] Cui Zhenshen and others—went all the way to the southern suburbs to see him off. They held a drinking party on the bank of the Yi River[13] before bidding a tearful farewell to one another at the famous Yi River Bridge. There was nothing extraordinary about this kind of activity, which took place in and around the city many times a day. Except that the departee had just survived an ordeal at the hands of the Two Zhangs, who were keeping a watchful eye on him.

Soon, a court informer called Chai Ming[14] filed a report through Zhang Yizhi to Tianhou. It claimed that at the farewell party Cui Zhenshen and others had discussed a secret plot in collusion with Wei Yuanzhong.

That seemed to have confirmed Tianhou's sneaking suspicion that the former chief minister was guilty after all. She asked Supervising Censor Ma Huaisu to interrogate the accused, saying, "This is based on solid facts. You don't need to spend too much time on it. Just finish the investigation and report back to me."

More than two weeks went by and Tianhou did not heard anything from the censor. She called him in for questioning.

"Why is it taking so long?" she asked.

"Your Majesty," Ma Huaisu answered, "I need to verify a few crucial details with Chai Ming the informer. However, so far I have not been able to locate him."

"I don't know where the heck he is either," answered Tianhou, annoyed. "But you don't need to see him. Just write up the report."

"Your Majesty, the problem is that the informer's account does not always mesh with my findings. None of the accused seems to have the slightest idea about the plot."

Flying into a rage, Tianhou snarled, "Ma Huaisu, do you want to protect them?"

"No, Your Majesty. Pray allow me to explain. After the former Chief Minister Wei Yuanzhong was demoted, his colleagues Cui Zhenshen and others went to say good-bye to him at the Yi River Bridge. But that, in and of itself, is no evidence of a rebellious plot. I just cannot charge them with the crime based on unfounded allegations. In the Han dynasty, when Luan Bu returned from an errand to report to his master Lord Peng Yue, he found Peng had been executed and his head on display on a pike at the city gate. Luan Bu reported to the head instead. That act violated the emperor Liu Bang's edict. So Luan was arrested.[15] But, eventually, Liu Bang let him go without punishment. Wei Yuanzhong's crime is not nearly as serious as Peng Yue's. Wei's friends did not even commit an offense. Still, Your Majesty wants to execute them? Well, so long as I am in charge of the case, I have no choice but to tell the truth."

"You want to exonerate them after all?"

"Pardon my stupidity," said Ma Huaisu as he fell on his knees. "I, your humble subject, have not found a shred of evidence."

Tianhou motioned him to stand up and leave.

Thereafter, the case against Cui Zhenshen and his associates and Wei Yuanzhong was suspended. A few months later, it faded away.

***

After he led his army to withdraw across the Great Desert (698), Mochuo had reorganized his Tujue Empire (699). His brother now served as left shad (*zuo xiangcha*) in charge of the eastern region;

Gudulu's son served as right shad (*you xiangcha*)[16] in charge of the western region. Each had a force of 20,000 men. In addition, Mochuo's son served as minor khan with an army of 40,000.

With a more organized Tujue army under his command, Mochuo had continued to intrude into settled Wu Zhou communities. In early 701, he raided state horse ranches[17] in Longyou (Gansu), seizing more than 10,000 horses.

By then, Wei Yuanzhong had been recalled from banishment and reinstated as chief minister. And Tianhou named him as commander-in-chief[18] of the Lingwu[19] District Expeditionary Army to safeguard the area against future raids.

After a period of lull, Mochuo raided the northern border area again in the eighth month of 701.

In response, Tianhou appointed Prince Li Dan as marshal of a massive expeditionary army to confront him. But before the army was launched, Mochuo retreated.

From spring to autumn in 702, the Tujue raids picked up steam, ravaging Yanzhou, Xiazhou,[20] Bingzhou, Daizhou, and Xinzhou.[21] From Yanzhou and Xiazhou alone, they seized 100,000 horses and sheep.

Then in 703, tensions between Tujue and Wu Zhou eased when a Tujue emissary arrived in Luoyang, requesting on behalf of Mochuo that his daughter be married to one of the sons of the crown prince.

For her part, Tianhou had shown no interest in punishing the Tujue leader for questioning her legitimacy and keeping Wu Yanxiu in captivity. But she still remembered his frequent about-faces in the recent past and was suspicious of his true intentions. Nonetheless, at an audience she granted to the emissary in the Audience Hall, she accepted the request. Present at the evening banquet held in their honor were Li Chongfu and Li Chongjun, two sons of Crown Prince Li Zhe, dressed in splendid attire. It was apparent that Tianhou was hoping to see the proposed union consummated.

Later in the year, Mochuo sent another emissary, bearing precious gifts, including 1,000 horses of good breed, to express thanks to Tianhou for giving permission for a marriage alliance. In another gesture of good will, he released Wu Yanxiu, Wu Chengsi's son, in 704.

In the end, the much-anticipated marriage alliance did not take place after all. Soon relations between the two powers soured again as Mochuo resumed his aggressive tactics towards the Wu Zhou.

***

In the lands of Tubo to the west and southwest, much had taken place following the coup of 698. With the backing of his mother Queen Dowager Molu,[22] the young Zanpu Chidu Songzan had put an end to the dominance of the Gar (Ga'er) clan at court, which had lasted almost half a century. On his orders, their family assets were confiscated, and their supporters eliminated. He had given out generous rewards to those instrumental in crushing the Gars and surrounded himself with loyal supporters.

The Wu Zhou court now provided a safe haven for survivors of the Gar clan and their followers, a fact that did not make the new zanpu and his mother happy. In a show of displeasure, on the zanpu's orders, the Tubo raided Wu Zhou lands in Liangzhou[23] and Maozhou[24] in 700 and 702.

In these areas, Tang Xiujing and Wei Yuanzhong were in charge of military affairs. Both were highly experienced frontier officers. Tang Xiujing, in particular, was known for his thorough knowledge of the vast northern border region from the Shanhai Pass of the east coast to the Four Garrisons of Central Asia.

Under the able management of Guo Yuanzhen, appointed area commander (*dudu*) of Liangzhou (as well as commissioner of the Longyou Armies) in 701, the prefecture of Liang had greatly expanded its territorial holdings. Well supplied with grain, it had now become highly defensible.

The Tubo threat in the meantime had been on the wane. One reason was the unexpected Nanzhao rebellion to the south (in Yunnan)[25] that raised the specter of a two-pronged attack with the Wu Zhou forces invading Qinghai from the north. The Tubo sued for peace in 703 and sent an emissary to Luoyang with 1,000 horses, 2,000 *liang* (ounces) of gold, and a proposal for a marriage alliance.

Having repaired relations with the Wu Zhou, the Zanpu Chidu Songzan led an expedition south against Nanzhao in 704. While on campaign he perished at thirty-five *sui*. Power once again fell into the hands of Molu, now grand queen dowager.

***

De facto Chief Minister Yang Zaisi was throwing an afternoon party in the front yard of the Court of Imperial Sacrifices (*sili si*).[26] The party-goers gathered around the Zhangs, drinking and jesting. One palace attendant (*gongfeng*) made a comment on the legendary beauty of Zhang Changzong, comparing him to a lotus flower.

Yang Zaisi said in mock anger, "How can you say that? Changzong, our dear Sixth Brother, *is* beauty personified. The lotus flower should be compared to *him* instead."

They all gave a hearty laugh.

When the party was halfway through, and everybody was at least somewhat in his cups, Vice Chamberlain of the Court for State Sacrifices[27] Zhang Tongxiu raised his goblet to toast to Yang Zaisi with the casual remark, "President of the Secretariat, you do look like a Koguryŏ man."

Yang Zaisi emptied his goblet in one gulp and staggered away, only to come back a few moments later, with a changed appearance. Wearing his purple robe inside out and a kerchief cap adorned with colorful papercuts, he started making clumsy moves as he impersonated a dancing Koguryŏ geisha. Everybody was amused.[28]

The convivial ambience of the party, however, could not hide a disturbing fact. Yang Zaisi had sent out invitations to all the chief ministers and court favorites. All those who had shown up were members of the Zhang clan and their supporters at court. Apart from Yang Zaisi, all the chief ministers were absent. Some of them could not make it probably because of poor health or old age. But others must have distanced themselves from the Zhangs on purpose.

For the Zhangs, that might be a bad omen, especially for now when Tianhou, sick and old, grew tired of shielding them from harm each time they got into trouble. Perhaps she began to find their scandalous behavior intolerable. Or perhaps she had become less enamored of their company.

The anti-Zhangs people soon picked up on the situation and began to target them. They first went after the three lesser Zhangs: Vice Chamberlain of the Court for State Sacrifices Tongxiu, Prefect of Bianzhou[29] Changqi, and Vice President of the Directorate of Royal Manufactories[30] Changyi. All three were thrown into jail for embezzlement in the seventh month of 704.

Tianhou instructed the Censorate to investigate.

The anti-Zhangs folks then trained their sights on the heavy hitters— Tianhou's lovers Yizhi and Changzong known as the Fifth and Sixth Brothers. Tianhou gave the go-ahead to a request for an investigation. The Court for Judicial Review soon reached a judgment for a fine of twenty catties of copper against Zhang Changzong for acquiring cultivated land by coercive means. Tianhou immediately gave her approval for the ludicrous amount.

Then the investigation of Zhang Tongxiu and his two brothers revealed that they had embezzled more than 4,000 strings of cash. Not a significant amount, but large enough for Censor-in-Chief Li Chengjia and Vice Censor-in-Chief Huan Yanfan to impeach them. For their punishment, the censors recommended dismissal from office.

A follow-up investigation implicated Tianhou's lover Zhang Changzong in a more serious crime—abuse of power. And the censors recommended the same punishment.

Zhang Changzong filed an emergency appeal directly to Tianhou, in which he asserted, "Considering the meritorious service I have rendered for the country, I hope to be spared the punishment."

"Has Changzong performed meritorious service before?" Tianhou asked the chief ministers in a meeting she held in her residential basilica.

Yang Zaisi hastened to reply, "Yes, Your Majesty. Changzong invented the wonder pills. They have proven effective on Your Majesty. Nothing is more meritorious than that."

"Indeed! Thank you for reminding me." Tianhou issued a pardon.

Before the Two Zhangs could breathe a sigh of relief, Chief Minister Wei Anshi filed another charge, against Zhang Yizhi the Fifth Brother. In response, Tianhou ordered a high-level investigation headed by Wei himself and Chief Minister Tang Xiujing. Just as the investigators began to gather evidence, Tianhou removed them from the case before transfering them out—Wei to Yangzhou as concurrent supervising prefect[31] and Tang to Youzhou and Yingzhou as concurrent area commander.[32]

Notes

1 Jingzhou 荊州: prefecture that lay in present-day Jingzhou and others in south Hubei.

2 Luozhou 洛州: capital prefecture with its seat in present-day Luoyang.

3 *Zhongtai youcheng* 中臺右丞.

4 *Sixing shaoqing* 司刑少卿.

5 Yongzhou 雍州: capital prefecture in the Xi'an area, Shaanxi.

6 Qizhou 岐州: prefecture that lay in Fufeng, Baoji, and others, Shaanxi.

7 *Sili cheng* 司禮丞.

8 *Fengge sheren* 鳳閣舍人: a highly important position that dealt with court documents. *See* note in Part 2, Chapter 2.

9 The Zhuque Gate 朱雀門 (Vermilion Bird Gate): the central entrance in the south wall of the Taiji Palace in Chang'an. See *Tang liangjing chengfang kao* 1.9.

10 The Daming/Hanyuan Basilica 大明殿/含元殿: the main structure in the Daming Palace. See *Tang liangjing chengfang kao* 1.19.

11 *Zhuzuo lang* 著作郎.

12 *Taizi pu* 太子僕.

13 The Yi River 伊水 originated from north of Luanchuan in west Henan and coursed northeastward to join the Luoshui 洛水 west of Yanshi.

[14] Chai Ming 柴明.

[15] Luan Bu 欒布 was in the service of Peng Yue 彭越, one of the most powerful local lords, when Peng was killed by Liu Bang 劉邦 (the founder of the Han), who wrongly suspected him of plotting rebellion. See *Shiji* 100, 欒布列傳.

[16] *Zuo/you xiangcha* 左/右廂察.

[17] *Mujian* 牧監.

[18] *Da zongguan* 大總管.

[19] Lingwu 靈武: county northeast of Qingtongxia, Yinchuan.

[20] Yanzhou 鹽州 and Xiazhou 夏州: both prefectures were in north Shaanxi.

[21] Bingzhou 并州, Daizhou 代州, and Xinzhou 忻州 were in central and north Shanxi.

[22] Molu 沒廬.

[23] Liangzhou 涼州. *See* note in Part 2, Chapter 13.

[24] Maozhou 茂州: prefecture that lay in Beichuan, Maoxian, and others, Sichuan.

[25] *Xin Tang shu* 222A, 南詔傳.

[26] *Sili si* 司禮寺 (aka *taichang si* 太常寺): one of the Nine Courts.

[27] *Sili shaoqing* 司禮少卿.

[28] *Tangren yishi huibian* 8.380.

[29] Bianzhou 汴州: prefecture that lay in Kaifeng and others, Henan.

[30] *Shangfang shaojian* 尚方少監 was previously known as *shaofu* 少府.

[31] Yangzhou 揚州 was in south Jiangsu.

[32] Youzhou 幽州 and Yingzhou 營州: two prefectures in north Hebei and Liaoning.

8. Zhang Jianzhi (704–705)

In the Middle East, Caliph Abd al-Malik died after a long reign. He was succeeded by his son Al-Walid I (705), who would preside over the peak of the Umayyad dynasty.

DI RENJIE, WHO had been out of sight at court because of old age for almost two years, caught a bad cold in the autumn of 704. For weeks, he was not able to rise without help. Many friends and colleagues came to see him. Tianhou, who herself was in poor health, sent the best palace physicians to treat him.

One evening, as Di was propped up in bed, taking his meal with the aid of a servant, five top officials—Zhang Jianzhi, Huan Yanfan, Yuan Shuji, Jing Hui, and Cui Xuanwei—filed into his room. After a casual exchange of greetings, Di Renjie fell silent, with tears glinting in his eyes. Two of the five, Jing Hui and Cui Xuanwei, bid him best wishes and departed.

Di Renjie raised his head, tears now rolling down his cheeks, and revealed what was on his mind. "Time is running out. I'm terribly worried what's going to happen after I'm gone. Some people will cause a lot of trouble."

"The Zhang brothers?" asked Zhang Jianzhi, the only one of the five visitors older than Di.

Di waved his hand. His servant withdrew and closed the door on his way out.

"Not really," Di continued. "The favorite courtiers exist at the mercy of Tianhou. When she passes on, they will be toppled from power, no matter what."

"The prince of Liang?"

Di Renjie nodded his head and said in a low voice, "So long as Wu Sansi is in power, none of you are safe. After I'm gone . . ." Di was choked by a lump in his throat. Huan Yanfan helped him to sit up as Zhang Jianzhi patted him several times on the back. When Di resumed a moment later, his voice became raspy. "Remove him at the first opportunity, can you?"

The visitors, teary-eyed by now, all said, "Yes," while nodding their heads.

Two days later Di Renjie passed away.[1]

When the news reached the court, Tianhou broke down crying with abandon. "From now on, the Audience Hall will be empty," she said to herself between sobs.

From then on, whenever the court failed to reach a decision, she would say wistfully, "Heaven took away my State Elder too soon—way too soon!"

***

In early spring, the budding trees and plants added a touch of green to the dreary landscape of the north. With the return of warm weather, Tianhou expected her health to get better as she spent more time away from the hustle and bustle of Luoyang. However, her role as the sole ruler of the extensive empire did not allow her to be absent from the capital for long. So she sojourned again in the conveniently located Sanyang Palace. And yet, as her health continued to decline, even the Sanyang proved too far from the center of power.

It was then that Wu Sansi came up with the idea of building another touring palace even closer to Luoyang. Tianhou was inclined towards it, but a few remonstrators asked some serious questions. "Where is the money to fund this building project?" "Can it improve Her Majesty's image as a benevolent ruler?" "The Sanyang is already an expensive palace to maintain. If the new palace is built, how can the court afford to keep it *and* the Sanyang running at the same time?"

Wu Sansi supplied an ingenious answer: the new palace would replace the old, and the builder would use the timber materials from the Sanyang to reduce cost. After it won Tianhou's approval, the

Xingtai[2] Palace went up west of Shou'an[3] and southwest of Luoyang, and the Sanyang Palace at Mount Song was dismantled.

Some remonstrators complained that the massive labor force mobilized to work on the project for months was a heavy burden on the peasantry. To that Wu Sansi answered, "For the sake of Tianhou's health and the future of the country, it is well worth it."

***

Apart from taking nostrums provided by Shen Nanqiu and other palace physicians, Tianhou kept trying new elixirs formulated by Monk Hu Chao, the Zhang brothers, Daoist adepts from Maoshan, and Buddhist masters from Mount Song. As she fell into longer and longer spells of torpor, she began to entertain the thought of getting ready for the world of transcendents and the Western Paradise. She summoned the abbess of the Linzhi Convent, a learned lady in her early sixties, to her bedside. At her request, the abbess recited sutras to help her cleanse her soul and prepare her for the beyond. In a conversation after a recital, Tianhou asked how to show her profound reverence to the Buddha, the abbess suggested to restore the destroyed statue.

"Here we go again!" Tianhou said to herself. She showed no interest at all. Then, after Wu princes spoke in one voice in favor of the idea, she changed her mind. Thus, despite her misgivings, she issued an edict on a new giant Buddha statue to be set up in the Mang Hills north of Luoyang. It would be of much smaller size, *and* much less costly to build. The project would be funded by a tax on the clergy *and* government sources.

De facto Chief Minister Li Qiao was concerned. He still had fresh memories of the last giant Buddha project. It had been pulled thanks to Di Renjie's opposition in 700. Li Qiao knew very well that he was no Di Renjie. But still, he felt duty-bound to speak out. He submitted a long memorial, in which he said,

> *As of now, there are more than 170 thousand strings of cash set aside for the giant Buddha statue project. In my humble opinion, we should use the money on those poverty-stricken registered households,*[4] *of which there are many. If we give out one string per family, we will help 170,000 families. By so doing, Your Majesty will rescue people from hunger and cold and hard labor and will act in accord with the mercy and compassion of the Buddha and the will of the Sage Sovereign to nourish the masses. Both men and gods will be pleased and Your Majesty's merit will be immeasurable. Setting up the giant Buddha statue in hopes of receiving blessings in the afterlife is not nearly as effective as relieving the masses in need.*

Before Tianhou had time to respond, Supervising Censor Zhang Tinggui added his voice, "From the standpoint of current politics, our focus should be placed on the border area. For that purpose, we should stock up the state storehouses while allowing the people to get rested. From the standpoint of Buddhist teaching, the priority should be given to saving the masses from suffering, eliminating various costly icons and following the practice of non-action. Pray give careful thought to your subject's humble proposal."[5]

Although the message was couched in a mixture of Buddhist and Daoist terms, it at once clicked with Tianhou, who henceforth canceled the project, which had been underway. To show her appreciation, she summoned the remonstrator into her palace and gave him a rich reward.

***

With Wu Yanxiu's return from captivity, the Wu Zhou's relations with Tujue were on the mend. Tianhou seized the opportunity to shore up the northern defense. She appointed Chief Minister Yao Yuanzhi (Yao Chong) as commander-in-chief of the Expeditionary Army of Lingwu District. Yao was not a great general by any measure, having turned down a previous appointment to president of the Board of War. But he was an experienced and trusted administrator. Tianhou granted him a special audience before he left to take up office.

"Can you," she asked, "recommend someone from the Outer Court[6] who has what it takes to be chief minister?"

"Yes," he answered without hesitation. "Zhang Jianzhi is my first choice."

"Di Renjie recommended him as well. But what do you see in him?"

"Well, he is an astute strategist and a decisive leader. The only problem is age. Your Majesty, if you want to use him, you should do so soon."

A couple of weeks later, Zhang Jianzhi, approaching eighty, was given the top job. He made history as the oldest official to have been appointed to the post of chief minister in Tang and Wu Zhou times.

***

Tianhou was taken sick again towards the end of the year (704). The ailment was so severe that she could not get a break for weeks on end, running a constant fever accompanied by chills, coughs, and headaches. On the advice of her physicians and the top ritual scholars, she moved into the Changsheng (Longevity) Basilica in the Luoyang Palace for good luck. During this spell of sickness, when she was bed-ridden all the time, almost no court officials including the chief ministers got to see her. The only exceptions were Zhang Yizhi and Zhang Changzong, who attended on her.

It got Vice President of the Secretariat Cui Xuanwei worried. As soon as Tianhou was well enough to receive guests, he went in to see her. At the end of the meeting, he said, "Pray listen to the advice from me, your humble subject. The world has witnessed the growth and maturation of the crown prince and Prince Li Dan. Both are benevolent, dutiful, and friendly and can do a great job taking care of Your Majesty, attending to your needs, and even administering herbal medicine. Moreover, the forbidden zone of the palace is sacrosanct and should be off limits to nonroyal gigolos."

To that Tianhou only said, "Thank you for your concern," without promising to take action. But neither did she come to the defense of the Two Zhangs. Now it was their turn to get the jitters. They knew deep down that without Tianhou's backing, they were nobodies and could become easy targets for the censors out there to get them. To be sure, the Zhangs still had a coterie of supporters at court. Chief among them was Yang Zaisi, who concurrently held a leadership post in Chang'an. In addition, there were Chief Ministers Wei Chengqing and Fang Rong; Chamberlain of the Court for State Sacrifices Cui Shenqing;[7] and Prince Wu Youyi. But there was no way of knowing whether these were true followers or calculating sycophants. Furthermore, none of them had any military power except for Wu Youyi, who, although a Wu, was only a distant relative of Tianhou.

As a last resort, the Zhangs turned to supernal forces for protection.

At a secret night session, the occultist Li Hongtai, a skinny man in his fifties with a small goatee, studied Zhang Changzong's facial features and bearing and conducted a *Yijing* divination using yarrow stalks. The result was the *qian* hexagram, the one often identified with the Son of Heaven. Staring at the stalks on the table, the occultist declared, "You have the looks of a ruler. That is confirmed by the divination. However, it can cut both ways. If you make it, you will dominate all under Heaven. If you fail, you will be destroyed body and soul."

"How can I avoid failure? And secure my future?" an anxiety-stricken Changzong asked.

" 'To secure' is the right word. You should travel to Dingzhou (meaning, "the prefecture that secures") and patronize a Buddhist monastery there. That will help you secure the hearts and minds of all under Heaven."

Not long afterwards, a lavishly designed monastery began to go up in Dingzhou in a scale and style that violated the ritual code. Before the project was complete, anonymous letters appeared at court and the major crossroads and near the Tianjin Bridge, accusing the Zhangs' involvement in occult practices. To make things still worse for the Zhangs, a well-connected gentleman called Yang Yuansi,[8] after some digging, tracked Changzong down as the man behind the monastery project. After consulting his censor friends, Yang filed a suit against him.

Since the case was too serious to be dismissed, Tianhou, who was often tired and drained of energy but still in control of her senses, appointed a panel of judges to investigate. It consisted of three officials:

Chief Minister Wei Chengqing, Court President Cui Shenqing, and Vice Censor-in-Chief Song Jing. The first two were known toadies to the Zhangs. The last one Song Jing was different. As second-in-command at the Censorate, he was the only high-ranking official the Zhangs feared. It seemed that Tianhou kept him in office on purpose as a countervailing force against them.

Wei Chengqing and Cui Shenqing soon made their recommendation. "By his own account, upon hearing those atrocious claims the occultist Li Hongtai made, Zhang Changzong reported them to Tianhou. And we have no reason to doubt the veracity of the account. In view of the facts, we recommend that Zhang Changzong be pardoned, and Li Hongtai be imprisoned and tried for spreading heresies."

Song Jing and a colleague of his submitted a different opinion. "Despite the great favor he received from the throne, Zhang Changzong defied the law to consult the occultist Li Hongtai. Although he asserted that he had always regarded Li as an evil heretic, his failure to turn him in proves just the opposite. Zhang's claim that he reported Li's evil words to Tianhou does not conceal the fact that he himself harbors sinister intentions. In view of the foregoing, we request his immediate arrest and trial."

A few days later, while still working on the case, Song Jing received a rescript, tasking him with the investigation of two criminal cases in Yangzhou in the south. It was immediately followed by a second rescript, asking him to go up north to Youzhou to look into an embezzlement case. Before Song Jing had time to reply, a third rescript came, ordering him to go to the Long[9] and Shu area in the west to serve as Li Qiao's lieutenant.

"I am awfully sorry, Your Majesty," said Song Jing in his written response, "but I cannot make the trip, either to Yangzhou, Youzhou, or Long and Shu. With due respect, I find it hard to comprehend why I am dispatched to those places in the first place. According to precedent, when a prefectural or county official commits a crime, he should be tried by an attendant censor if his rank is high; or by an investigative censor if his rank is low. The vice censor-in-chief should not go to the provinces to investigate a case unless it involves matters of great importance to the military and the state. None of these cases satisfies even one of the conditions. Therefore, I should not go."

Tianhou had another rescript prepared, which in plain language ordered Song Jing to stop investigating Zhang Changzong. Before she gave it to Shangguan Wan'er for issuance, she saw a pile of memorials on her table. She spent some time browsing through them and found, to her dismay, that most of them censured Zhang Changzong in more severe terms. Vice President of Judicial Review Huan Yanfan, for example, accused him of treason. Cui Xuanwei expressed a similar view. Cui's brother, Vice Chamberlain of the Court of Judicial Review Cui Sheng[10] recommended the death penalty. Tianhou cast a glance at the rescript on her front table, picked it up, and tossed it on to the long table by the wall. She then issued an order to revoke the earlier rescripts to Song Jing.

***

Two days later, Song Jing presented his findings to Tianhou and the chief ministers in her study. At the end of his talk, he concluded that because of his close contact with the occultist Li Hongtai, Zhang Changzong must be arrested and put on trial.

Having worked himself into a pitch of agitation, he continued, addressing Tianhou, "I know that Zhang Changzong is a great favorite of Your Majesty. And what I say now can spell disaster for me later. But this is coming from my heart and is beyond my control. I must say it. Even it costs my life, I will have no regrets."

Yang Zaisi rose from his seat and read out a pre-prepared rescript that ordered Song Jing to leave the room immediately.

Song Jing retorted, "You don't need to do that, Chief Minister. Her Majesty is right here. She can ask me to leave anytime."

When Yang Zaisi was about to open his mouth again, Tianhou stopped him and offered a compromised solution: giving Song permission to prosecute, but not to make arrest.

The next day, Zhang Changzong surrendered himself to the Censorate. As soon as the interrogation was underway, it was cut short by the arrival of a eunuch officer, who announced a special pardon from Her Majesty.

As Zhang Changzong jumped on his horse and rode away, Song Jing snarled, "How I wish I could crush his skull!"

Later, on Tianhou's orders, Zhang Changzong paid a visit to Song Jing to offer apologies. But Song Jing refused to see him.

***

In the early spring of 705, a heavy snowfall blanketed the city of Luoyang. It was followed by clear weather for days. As the snow sitting on rooftops began to melt, the splendid yellow color of the glazed roof tiles reemerged. Hope was raised that, as it got warmer, Tianhou could be carried into the front terrace again to bask under the sun without the fear of catching cold. Then, without warning, she took a turn for the worse. Early one morning, she was found writhing in bed, restless.

With eyes shut, she slurred out words that nobody could understand. Only hours later did she get out of the spell of delirium. She opened her eyes and faintly called out the names of Changzong and Yizhi. The two brothers, apparently their transgressions forgiven, came rushing, knelt by her bedside, and clutched her hands, weeping. They started taking turns to keep watch and became, from then on, her only liaisons with the outside world.

The leading chief minister Zhang Jianzhi was alarmed at Tianhou's reconciliation with the Zhang brothers. "It is now or never!" he shouted at a secret meeting in his home with four other court leaders—Cui Xuanwei, Jing Hui, Huan Yanfan, and Yuan Shuji. All five had been recommended for key positions at the center by Di Renjie before he passed on. They all agreed that time had come for a palace coup to eliminate the Zhang brothers.

Zhang Jianzhi would take the lead. Although pushing eighty, he was as sprightly as ever and soon went about making secret contacts. The first one on the list was Li Duozuo. As general-in-chief of the Right Yulin (Forest of Plumes) Army/Guard, he was responsible for the overall safety of the palace and the throne. The success or failure of the coup rested on his support.

Zhang Jianzhi started the conversation with a serious question, "In all honesty, to whom do you owe your wealth and power?"

Li Duozuo answered without a moment of hesitation, "The Great Emperor Gaozong."

"Today the sons of the Great Emperor are being threatened by the two thugs. Don't you think, General, you should repay His Majesty for his kindness with action?"

"Yes, I do." Li was on the verge of tears. "I will sacrifice my life and the lives of my wife and children for the sake of the country. Chief Minister, just give me the order. I am at your beck and call." He then held up his hand to swear an oath to Heaven and Earth with Zhang Jianzhi as witness.

Next, Zhang Jianzhi went to see his old friend Yang Yuanyan, the second on the list. While he was on his way, he recalled their last meeting a few years before. After he had been ordered to replace Yang as chief administrator of Jingzhou,[11] they had gone on a boat ride together on the Yangzi River. With court spies out of earshot and attendants dismissed, the two best friends had had a talk with no holds barred. It was then that Yang revealed his most cherished dream—restoring Tang rule.

On seeing his old friend again, Zhang Jianzhi found, to his delight, that he had kept his dream alive, and appointed him on the spot general of the Right Yulin Guard.

Going down the list, Zhang Jianzhi made three more appointments in quick succession, raising Huan Yanfan, Jing Hui, and Li Zhan—all members of the anti-Zhang brothers camp—to generals of the Left and Right Yulin Guards, each with his own band of security troops.

These new appointments alarmed Zhang Yizhi and his supporters. To allay their fear, Zhang Jianzhi appointed one of their men, Wu Youyi, as general-in-chief of the Right Yulin Guard, but holding off assigning additional troops to his command.

On the eve of the action, Huan Yanfan, one of the lead conspirators, paid a visit to his elderly mother. He dropped to his knees, full of remorse and self-reproach, and broke into a sob. His mother shook her hand to stop him and said, "My son, don't feel bad. This is one of those moments when you can't have it both ways. You can't be loyal to the throne and filial at the same time. It is the right thing to do to put country before family."

Notes

[1] According to the standard histories, Die Renjie died in 700. However, modern scholars, based on epigraphic sources, date his death to 704.

[2] Xingtai 興泰.

[3] Shou'an 壽安: county in Yiyang, Henan.

[4] Registered households: households registered with the local authorities for taxation purposes. They were the only ones counted in government censuses.

[5] It is interesting to note that his Buddhist argument was couched in Daoist language.

[6] The Outer Court (*waichao* 外朝): the court bureaucracy under the leadership of the formal chancellor with office buildings located outside the palace.

[7] Wei Chengqing 韋承慶, Fang Rong 房融, *sili qing* 司禮卿, and Cui Shenqing 崔神慶.

[8] Yang Yuansi 楊元嗣.

[9] Long 隴 was an area in present-day southeast Gansu. It was named after the Long Mountains that straddled Gansu and Shaanxi.

[10] *Sixing shaoqing* 司刑少卿 Cui Sheng 崔昇.

[11] Jingzhou 荊州. *See* note in Part 3, Chapter 7.

9. Fall from Power (705)

ON FEBRUARY 20, 705, the conspirators with more than 500 troops took a loyalty oath led by Zhang Jianzhi outside the Xuanwu Gate. As soon as the solemn ceremony was over, Generals Li Duozuo and Li Zhan and Wang Tongjiao made their way to the Eastern Palace and found the crown prince already in bed in the bedchamber of his residential basilica.

"The loyal troops are now awaiting Your Highness at the Xuanwu Gate," Li Duozuo pronounced.

"Are . . . are . . ." the prince sputtered. "Are you sure you are ready?"

"Yes, Your Highness," Li Duozuo said. "I believe Huan Yanfan and Jing Hui got your endorsement a few days ago."

"Yes, but I didn't expect . . ."

"Your Highness and my dear father-in-law," Wang Tongjiao said, "Emperor Gaozong entrusted the empire to you before he departed from this world. But you were then thrown into custody, to the indignation of both men and gods. That was twenty-years ago. Today, out of a sense of loyalty, the government and court leaders have come together in an effort to wipe out the evil ones and to restore the rule of the Li house. I am imploring you to join us at the Xuanwu Gate in carrying out this great plan."

"The evil ones should be eliminated," the crown prince said. "But not right now. Her Majesty is in poor health. Can't we wait for a more opportune time?"

"Your Highness," General Li Zhan said, his hand on the hilt of his sword. "The court leaders and generals are putting their and their families' lives on the line. If they stop right now, they will risk being thrown into boiling tripods! Do you really want to see that happen? If not, you had better act now. Only your presence can prevent the tragedy from taking place."

"I have no other alternative?" the prince asked.

"No, Father-in-Law," the hot-tempered Wang Tongjiao answered.

The crown prince gave a grudging nod. With his son-in-law nudging him from behind, he made for the basilica door.

Once outside, the crown prince, almost fifty, waddled towards a waiting horse. Suddenly, his son-in-law seized hold of him from behind, carried his plumpish body for about twenty paces, and lifted it into the saddle. The crown prince was then on his way under a small escort.

Arriving at the Xuanwu Gate a few moments later, the prince on horseback gave a short speech to rally the rebels. Zhang Jianzhi then issued the first attack order. By then, the Xuanwu Gate, the northern main entrance to the palace, had been placed under the firm control of the generals Zhang had appointed.

Pushing south, the rebels stormed the inner gate facing the Xuanwu and broke into the palace grounds and moments later fought their way into the grounds of the Yingxian Palace,[1] a small compound west of the central axis of the Palace City.

About 100 rebel soldiers gathered around the main gate to the Changsheng Basilica.[2] Following a general's order, they stormed the gate after a brief hand-to-hand combat with the gate guards and security troops. A squad of fast-footed rebel soldiers scaled a long flight of marble steps like a whirlwind to disappear into the basilica front terrace.

At the bottom of the steps, Zhang Jianzhi stopped to take a breath and started climbing. The moment he reached the top and gained entry into the terrace, he saw two men, trussed up with rope, dragged out of the basilica door.

Under the upturned eaves of the basilica, the heads of the Two Zhangs fell with thumps on the marble floor.

By then, the Changsheng Basilica had been encircled by two cordons of rebel troops. The lead conspirators, followed by two dozen officers and men, all armored and armed, swarmed into the building, made for the main bedchamber, and barged in.

Tianhou, sitting in her bed against a stack of pillows, asked, "What is the commotion all about?"

"The Two Zhangs were plotting a rebellion," someone answered. "On the crown prince's orders, we already carried out their execution. We apologize for not informing Your Majesty earlier; but we were afraid of disturbing your sleep. We know that bringing weapons into the forbidden zone is unpardonable. We beg Your Majesty's forgiveness."

Tianhou was trying to keep her anger under wraps until she saw Li Zhan among the conspirators. She asked in a sharp voice, "Aren't you the son of Li Yifu?"

"Yes, Your Majesty."

"Haven't I treated both you and your father very well?"

"Undoubtedly, Your Majesty."

"But you are one of the generals who killed Zhang Yizhi and Zhang Changzong? What the heck is going on?"

Li Zhan lowered his head without a word.

"And you?" she asked, addressing Cui Xuanwei. "People usually get promoted on recommendations by other officials. But I personally promoted you. And you are one of them as well?"

"Your Majesty, this is precisely how I repaid you for your kindness," Cui answered.

"Empress Mother," Crown Prince Li Zhe, who had just walked in, called out.

"You too my son?" Tianhou asked. The crown prince fell silent, and she continued, "Now that the two men you were after are dead, you can leave. Get out! All of you!"

"No, we can't leave yet, Your Majesty," Huan Yanfan said. "In the past, the Heavenly Emperor Gaozong entrusted his favorite son to Your Majesty. But, now, despite his maturity, he still resides in the Eastern Palace. The court officials have not forgotten the kindness of Taizong and the Heavenly Emperor. Both Heaven and men are longing for the Li house to return to power. That is why we executed the evil ones today. And we are expecting Your Majesty to *abdicate* in favor of the crown prince, in accord with the aspirations of Heaven and men."

Tianhou closed her eyes as if she had heard nothing.

***

South of the Tianjin Bridge, on a makeshift wooden platform, a row of severed heads on pikes were on display. They belonged to the Zhangs—Changzong and Yizhi, and their lesser-known brothers—Changqi, Tongxiu, and Changyi. The key allies of the Zhangs at court—Wei Chengqing, Fang Rong, and Cui Shenqing—had been taken into custody.

Now Crown Prince Li Zhe, supported by his followers, was firmly in control of the city. On his orders, the Southern Office troops under the command of Prince Li Dan and Yuan Shuji were standing sentry at various structures inside the palace and patrolling the city streets.

On February 21, the crown prince was appointed regent. Yuan Shuji, in his capacity as vice president of the Secretariat and de facto chief minister, sent out ten commissioners to pacify the Ten Circuits throughout the realm.

The following day, Tianhou lost all hope of a rescue and abdicated in favor of the crown prince at the request of the conspirators.

On February 23, the reign of Tianhou came to an official end as Crown Prince Li Zhe (temple name: Zhongzong) ascended the throne. In his inaugural edict, the emperor Li Zhe first granted a grand amnesty to all prison inmates except for those who had committed unpardonable crimes (the Ten Abominations, for example) and those who were allies of the Zhangs. He then ordered to rehabilitate the victims of the Legalist law officers (Suo Yuanli, Zhou Xing, Lai Junchen, and others), alive or posthumously, and free their sons and daughters who had been sent into bondage. He ended the edict with the conferral of titles and the making of appointments, naming his brother Li Dan the state-pacifying prince of Xiang[3] and his sister Princess Taiping the defender of state;[4] and placing descendants of purged royals in high official posts after restoring their status.

***

Tianhou did not show any signs of sorrow in public over the death of Zhang Changzong and Zhang Yizhi, but in private she was grieved beyond words. Her world almost crumbled a few days later when she was told to move out of the Changsheng Basilica, where the Two Zhangs had attended on her as they would their birthmothers until the moment of their death. On the morning when, accompanied by a small retinue, she was making her way on the back of an old eunuch to the Shangyang Palace to the southwest, she hardly said a word, her face contorted with rage, her lips swollen, and her eyes shot with blood.

The army of attendants, eunuchs, and maids had mostly vanished.

In their place were the abbess of the Linzhi Convent and two nuns constantly by her bedside to keep her company. Each day, sometimes under the watchful eye of General Li Zhan, now head of her security detail, the women spent hours reciting the *Great Vows of Ksitigarbha Bodhisattva Sutra*[5] together to help the souls of the Two Zhangs cross over to the next world.

"So, it is all an illusion, isn't it?" Tianhou asked the abbess.

"Yes. As the Buddha says, 'We live in an illusion and the appearance of things.' "

"What then is life for?"

"Life is a preparation."

"For death?"

"Well, you don't really live, and you don't really die. So death is irrelevant."

"Then this life is a preparation for the next life?"

"Well, you can say that. But each life is different as you go up or down the karmic scale. That's what the cycle of rebirth is all about."

"Where does this lead to?"

"In the end, one may be able to break the cycle. But only by avoiding karma, and by following the eightfold path of the Buddha for many lives. Only then can one have hope to end the cycle."

"And then?"

"Then, one will stop living and stop dying and enter a state of permanent bliss. No more suffering."

"Anyone can achieve that?" Tianhou asked, her eyes sparkling. "Even me?"

"Yes, any *creature* can hope to achieve that, eventually." The abbess, bringing her palms together and closing her eyes, murmured to herself, "Amitabha![6] Amitabha!"

Tianhou closed her eyes too; her memory brought her back to her early childhood when Yuan Tiangang made the prediction that she would be the ruler over the realm. Illusion or not, life for her had been a constant struggle against her adversaries, an unending effort to reach the top and stay there. In every fight, she had always emerged victorious until a gang of conspirators had driven her off the throne. Their leader was none other than Zhang Jianzhi. Every trusted adviser around her had recommended the old codger for the top job, including State Elder Di Renjie. She forced a wry smile as she attempted to shut out the unpleasant memory.

Two weeks later, the emperor made an unexpected visit with a large group of court officials. On entering the room, he fell down on his knees to kowtow three times and proclaimed his willingness to atone for his transgression in exchange for her forgiveness. With a vacant look on her face, Tianhou claimed to have gotten over it already and told him not to worry. The emperor then held a ritual ceremony in which he granted her the title of Great Sage Emperor Zetian,[7] in a gesture of reconciliation. From then on, he would visit her once every ten days to show that he was still her filial son even as emperor.

***

In the second month of 705, the dynastic title of Tang was restored. The names of the ritual centers in and around Luoyang, the government agencies, the official titles, and the colors of official banners and robes all reverted to their pre-revolutionary predecessors. The new Wu Zhou characters were replaced with their prototypes with the exception of *zhao*, which was now used exclusively as Tianhou's given name. The Divine Capital Luoyang was once again the Eastern Capital, and the Northern Capital reverted to Bingzhou (in Shanxi). Lord Lao (Laozi) was retitled as the Mysterious and Primordial Emperor,[8] which reflected the elevated status of Daoism.

In the days following Tianhou's fall from power, much of officialdom was in a festive mood. Those instrumental in bringing down the Zhangs and restoring Tang rule were celebrated as heroes. The Li royals were restored to their original status while their supporters regained power.

Yao Yuanzhi was the only court leader who stood apart from the crowd. This chief minister of fifty-six *sui* had been known to be sympathetic to the anti-Zhang brothers camp. He had recommended Zhang Jianzhi as chief minister and thrown his support behind him at the time of the coup. But after Tianhou was ousted from the Changsheng Basilica, Yao went there to bid her good-bye and was the only chief minister to do so.

Later, when talking about the scene, Yao broke into tears and started sobbing. A startled Huan Yanfan said, "What is matter with you, Chief Minister Yao? Choose now of all moments to shed your tears?"

Zhang Jianzhi added with reproach, "If you don't stop right now, you'll get into no end of trouble."

"I can't help it," Yao Yuanzhi said, "I just can't. I served Tianhou for a long time. The sight of her leaving the palace on the back of an old eunuch abandoned by all officialdom filled me with sorrow. Previously,

I supported you in eradicating the evil men around the throne out of a sense of duty to the sovereign. Later, I bid farewell to Tianhou for precisely the same reason. If I get into trouble for this, so be it."

Thanks to his defiant attitude, Yao Yuanzhi indeed got himself into trouble. He was soon demoted and transferred out of the capital to faraway Bozhou.[9]

***

When Consort[10] Wei ascended the throne as Empress Wei in 705, following her husband's enthronement, it did not cause any controversy. Born from a powerful aristocratic family, she had served as empress before in 684 when her husband Li Zhe was placed on the throne for the first time. A woman of forceful character, she called the shots at home and in the palace. It was in response to her demand that Li Zhe, on coming to power, had promoted her father to president of the Chancellery, a move that had triggered an outburst from Tianhou and ended his first reign.

By then Consort Wei had been pregnant for months. On Tianhou's orders, both she and her husband were banished to Fangling,[11] hundreds of miles away down south. On the first day of the journey, the bumpy ride triggered a stabbing pain in her belly. The following day, the pain, attended by cramps and bleeding, became so severe that she could not even sit up and eat. As soon as she was seized with the pangs of labor, the coachman pulled to a stop by the roadside. With the ex-emperor pacing up and down near the carriage, Wei went into labor inside with the help of a maid for hours before giving birth to a premature baby, the future Princess Anle.

While in exile, Consort Wei and her husband Prince Li Zhe were held in virtual detention. Taking their cue from the higher-ups, the local officials were bent on giving them a hard time. Their life would have been miserable had it not been for the help Prefects Zhang Zhijian and Cui Jingsi[12] provided out of sympathy and respect for the royal Li house.

In the wake of the botched Li Jingye and Li Chong rebellions, Consort Wei and Prince Li Zhe went through hell as Tianhou stepped up the campaign to eliminate male members of the Li house. Li Zhe lived with the constant fear of being tortured to death by Tianhou's henchmen—Suo Yuanli, Zhou Xing, Hou Sizhi, Lai Junchen, and others. Each time a eunuch envoy darkened the door of their Fangling home, the prince would be frightened out of his wits. On one such occasion, he almost hanged himself from a white silk band tied to a beam. It was Consort Wei who prevented him from rushing to his death. She said, "One never knows what the future may bring, fortune or misfortune. The worst thing that may happen is death. But it is in the hands of Heaven. Why in such a hurry?" It was such lucidity of mind that persuaded him out of his suicidal angst. Later, as his mood improved, Prince Li Zhe said to her, "My dear wife, I owe you my life. If fortune smiles on me again, I will let you do whatever you want!"

Now, more than twenty years later, Consort Wei was once again Empress Wei. With her husband having her back, she was at the pinnacle of the world. For sure, her husband was still the nominal ruler of the entire realm, but she was the ruler of her husband at home and beyond. With his tacit approval, she got actively involved in government and played a decisive part in selecting the crown prince. When the nomination of the emperor's eldest son Li Chongfu came to her attention, she opposed it on two grounds: his mother was a humble woman, and his wife was a niece of Zhang Yizhi. After Zhang Yizhi's death, she claimed, without proof, that Li Chongfu may have been linked to the death of her own son Li Chongrun. Using that as an excuse, she had him banished to a provincial post. At her insistence, the court then passed him over to appoint his younger brother Li Chongjun as heir.

Empress Wei took as her role model her famous mother-in-law, Tianhou. To be sure, her hands were tainted with the blood of Wei's own children—Prince Li Chongrun and Princess Li Xianhui. But Wei nonetheless admired her success in conquering the world of men and ruling as the first female emperor in history and was determined to tread in her footsteps.

"Why not me?" Empress Wei once asked Shangguan Wan'er, now her confidante. "My moron of a husband can do it. And he is not even half as good as his weak-minded father."

"Indeed, Your Majesty," Shangguan Wan'er said. "You are intelligent and decisive and the only one who can possibly carry on Tianhou's cause."

By then Shangguan Wan'er was already past forty but retained her feminine charm that was often irresistible to middle-aged men. In the last decade of Tianhou's life, Shangguan had become her go-to person. She had gotten to know one of the most powerful Wu princes, Sansi, and ended up becoming his bedmate.

After Tianhou was dethroned, Shangguan stayed on to serve the emperor and his wife, Empress Wei. It was through Shangguan that Empress Wei came to know Wu Sansi. And that marked the beginning of the political alliance between the empress and the prince, reinforced by an intimate physical relationship.

The emperor was probably not aware of the secret liaison between the two. Or perhaps he was but did not really mind. He owed his life to her after all. Besides, he liked to have Sansi around.

So Wu Sansi was given a free pass to visit the emperor and the empress in the forbidden zone, and the emperor, for his part, often traveled incognito to the wards to visit Wu at home. It often happened that when the empress and Prince Wu Sansi played a game of backgammon, the emperor would watch on in good humor and even keep bamboo counters for them.

***

Zhang Jianzhi was dumbfounded by the news that the leader of the Wu clan had cozied up to the emperor and the empress. The mere thought of it sent chills down his spine. He studied the secret report he held in his hands many times before putting it down on the table. He picked up a writing brush and penned a remonstrative memorial to the emperor.

> *Your Majesty, at the time of the Wu Zhou Revolution, members of the Li house were hunted down and almost killed off. By the grace of Heaven and Earth, Your Majesty was restored to power. But now the Wus are still occupying key posts they stole from the court. That is entirely contrary to the will of the people. Please eliminate them or at the minimum reduce their ranks and emoluments in order to appease all under Heaven.*

The next day, a eunuch envoy came to Zhang's home to announce an imperial rescript.

My dear sir, we are already past the time when the Lis and Wus were at loggerheads with one another. For the sake of reconciliation and harmony, I don't think I should do anything that may harm their cordial relations.

With his eyebrows raised into a frown, Zhang Jianzhi knocked his fingers on the table so hard that they started bleeding. He said, "Before the prince of Ying (Li Zhe) gave the impression of a brave man. That was why we eliminated the Zhangs without touching the Wus. We were hoping that he would do it himself. But now it has become clear that it will never happen on his watch. And we will die without even a burial place. Heaven! What can we do?" He let out a deep sigh.

***

The emperor, in truth, was not the figurehead he seemed to be. Initially, when he said he wanted to once and for all do away with unrest in society and restore harmony, he meant business. The first thing he did was reward his staunch supporters, making sure that each of the five conspirators—Zhang Jianzhi, Cui Xuanwei, Jing Hui, Yuan Shuji, and Huan Yanfan—had a chief minister's post, and promoting to key posts other meritorious officers such as Li Duozuo, Wang Tongjiao, and Li Zhan, who had helped restore him to power.

He issued edicts to rehabilitate those families that had been broken because of their association with the Lis and restore hereditary *yin* privileges[13] to their surviving members. He took measures to deprive the Legalist law officers like Zhou Xing and Lai Junchen of their official titles posthumously, if dead; or banish them to hardship places in the far south, if alive.

On the emperor's orders, the original surnames of the late Empress Wang and Consort Xiao, who had been renamed by Tianhou as "Cobra" and "Owl," were restored. Also on his orders, Prince Li Dan was granted the title of defender-in-chief (*taiwei*),[14] and appointed de facto chief minister; after the cautious prince declined both, he was offered the title of "imperial brother," to suggest that he was next in line for the throne. That the prince turned down as well.

Neither did the emperor forget the Wus. He gave Wu Sansi the prestige title of "minister of works" (*sikong*), one of the Three Dukes and among the most prestigious, and appointed him as de facto chief minister; he bestowed on Wu Youji the prestige title of "manager of people" (*situ*), another one of the Three Dukes, and the noble title of "prince of Ding." Likewise, both Sansi and Youji declined the new honors.

At the emperor's request, Wu Youxu, a son of one of Tianhou's cousins, who had been out of sight for years, was recalled from Mount Song to the capital. Having abandoned the desire for worldly power and comfort, he was now committed to a monastic life. As a teenager, he had already shown an intense interest in the hereafter and made a living as a professional diviner in Chang'an's Western Market. His life as a Daoist recluse for years had impacted him in peculiar, mysterious ways. With his face wizened and his eyes emitting a purple light, he possessed a supernatural ability to see the moon and stars in broad daylight. Upon arrival in Luoyang, he was visited by several distinguished guests. He politely exchanged greetings with them but refused to engage in serious conversation. In the end, he declined the emperor's offer of a high official post and returned to the mountains.

So the Wus were not necessarily sticking together in their bid for power. In fact, Wu Sansi was the only one who was really power-hungry. But, at this juncture, every Wu, including Sansi himself, was assuming a low profile, for fear of rubbing the emperor the wrong way.

It was the five anti-Wu (or anti-Zhang brothers) conspirators, especially Jing Hui, leader of the court leaders, who were making aggressive moves to oust the Wus from power. They based their rationale on the same tired argument Zhang Jianzhi had made: demoting, or, better still, eliminating the Wus was in accord with the will of the people.

***

Faced with an onslaught of attack from his enemies, Wu Sansi could hardly hold his own. In the end, help came from two unexpected sources. The first one was a middle-ranking official called Cui Shi, supernumerary attendant in the Bureau of Evaluation[15] in the Board of Personnel.

Initially, Cui was the leading conspirator Jing Hui's man. But he soon discovered that the emperor enjoyed Wu Sansi's company and dreaded the presence of the anti-Wu camp people like Jing Hui in the palace. At a secret meeting he had with Wu Sansi, Cui offered to switch allegiance. Wu was suspicious until Cui presented damning evidence of Jing Hui's underhanded activities—written instructions on spying on his enemies. Soon thereafter, with Wu's help, Cui was appointed Secretariat drafter, a highly important middle-ranking post with access to top state secrets. From then on, while continuing to work for Jing Hui in public, Cui would secretly report on his every move to Wu Sansi.

The second one was Zheng Yin, formerly a minion of the Two Zhangs. After the death of the Zhangs, he had been condemned for embezzlement and banished. He had missed the glamorous life in Luoyang so much that he had risked his life to return. The first man he saw was his old acquaintance Wu Sansi. After he settled himself in a chair he sobbed and cried and then burst out laughing.

"Are you out of your mind?" asked Wu Sansi in puzzlement.

"Great Prince, I cried because I saw a vision in which you will be killed and your entire family extirpated. I laughed because you would acquire the service of somebody to help you avoid that fate."

"You mean yourself?"

"Yes, My Prince."

"The emperor and the empress are having my back. Why should I need your help?"

"Don't forget those five conspirators are still out there. They can get you anytime. All are chief ministers with much civil and military power."

"So?" Wu Sansi did not seem convinced.

"Let me ask you a question. Who was more powerful: Tianhou or you?"

"Without a shadow of a doubt, Tianhou."

"The five conspirators, with extraordinary boldness, deposed Tianhou without making much of an effort at all. Now, not a single night passes without them scheming to devour you alive and exterminate your entire clan. So long as these five men remain in power, you are far from safe. In fact, in my opinion, you are in mortal danger."

Wu Sansi dismissed his servants and invited the guest upstairs, where the conversation continued behind closed doors. Before Zheng Yin took his leave about three hours later, Wu Sansi appointed him as

Secretariat drafter so that he would work alongside Cui Shi as one of Wu's chief advisers.

***

The emperor paid a routine visit to the Shangyang Palace. He was horrified when he saw the face of his mother without makeup for the first time in decades—the furrows on her forehead, the deep wrinkles from the corners of her eyes and mouth, the eye bags, the cadaverous facial color. He broke down in tears.

"My son, don't be startled," Tianhou said. "I wore makeup to cover visible signs of aging, even when I was confined to bed. That made me look decades younger. After the coup, however, I gave up on makeup altogether. And what you see now is the true me. I don't care anymore." She broke into a sob, wiped the tears off her face with trembling fingers, and continued, "Remember, my son: I was the one who summoned you back into the palace from Fangling. And I was the one who handed over to you the power to rule over all under Heaven. But the five traitors have claimed all the credit."

With tears streaming down his cheeks, the emperor flung himself face downward, and blurted out, "Your unfilial son is guilty of the heinous crime and deserves to die ten thousand times!"

"On your feet, my son! I know it is not your fault. And I don't want you to take the blame for others. But if you could demote those five villains, I would die without regrets."

The emperor, sitting up, said emotionally, "Your son will do his utmost to make sure it happens soon."

By the time Tianhou watched the emperor leave, she had calmed down. She knew that what she requested was a nigh-impossible task. But it was comforting to know that he was willing to try.

***

It was a worst-kept secret in and around the palace that Wu Sansi was Empress Wei's lover. Initially, Wu Sansi had disguised himself as a eunuch and slipped into the empress's basilica surreptitiously after dark about four or five times a month. Recently, he had increased the frequency of his visits to two or three times a week in his official attire, before or after dark. Since the emperor often talked about how he owed his life to the empress with great sincerity and gratitude, no censor would risk the imperial wrath by calling attention to her illicit visitor.

When Wu Sansi and the empress were together, apart from having fun, they often talked about politics. A recurring topic was the clique of the five conspirators. He insisted that something must be done about them and convinced her to back him.

On the advice of Cui Shi and Zheng Yin, Wu Sansi broached the subject with the emperor.

"Had it not been for their help," the emperor responded, "I would still be in the Eastern Palace, writhing under the heel of the Zhangs. It is ingratitude to punish them right now or ever."

"Your Majesty, but the issue here is not about punishment, but the clique the five have formed headed by Jing Hui. It dominates court decisions. That is detrimental to Your Majesty's rule and to the country in the long run."

The emperor pondered for a while and said, "You seem to have a point there. Why don't we talk about it when we have more time?" With that, he let Wu Sansi go.

That night, the empress came to the emperor's residential basilica for a routine visit. In the course of their casual chat, the subject of the five conspirators came up again. The empress could sense the quandary the emperor found himself in. While he noticed the threat the five might pose to the court, he did not want to appear ungrateful.

"I fully understand the problem," Empress Wei said. "Perhaps, Your Majesty can work around it."

"What do you mean?"

"For instance, you can raise all five to princes and increase their emoluments, but at the same time take away their chief ministerial power."

Furrowing his brows, the emperor pondered a while before uttering, "Well, I may indeed consider that."

***

A few weeks later an edict went forth that raised the five conspirators to second-tier princes, and grant each with a large fief and numerous feudatory households. One of them, Huan Yanfan was given a new surname, "Wei," so that he and the empress, at least nominally, now belonged to the same extended family. Each prince received very generous gifts as well—gold and silver, silk, good horses, and others. In return, all of them gave up their membership in the emperor's inner circle. Still, they were allowed to continue their residence in Luoyang with the privilege of attending court twice a month.[16] From then on, the five conspirators were known by the prestigious designation of the "Five Princes."

The Five Princes then, through one of their proxies, demanded in a memorial that the Wus drop their current princely titles. Wu Sansi first fought back and had the memorialist banished. But on the advice of Cui Shi and Zheng Yin, he soon relented. So an edict went forth to demote the Wus—Wu Sansi, Wu Youji, and Wu Yizong—to third-tier princes or dukes.

On the surface, the emperor had managed to maintain a balance of power between the Five Princes and the Wus. But the reality was rather different. Although the Five Princes were promoted to higher noble ranks, they were deprived of their ability to influence the court. The Wus, on the other hand, despite their demotions, did not lose an iota of their political power at the center.

With his major political opponents removed, Wu Sansi, for practical purposes, had become the most powerful court leader. He then moved to revive the abolished institutions set up by Tianhou and recall those officials the Five Princes had expelled from the capital. Anyone who refused to go along with these measures were immediately banished or demoted.

***

On the afternoon of December 16, 705, the emperor was in his study mulling over a memorial penned by a country defender. It criticized him for taking part in the annual Water-Sprinkling Festival about two weeks before. That was the time when everyone, rich and poor, royal and common, official and civilian, let down their guard, splashing strangers with buckets of cold water and being splashed by them. The emperor closed his eyes as his thoughts went back to that sunny day. He had first ascended the gatetower of the Luochengmen,[17] the western most entrance in the southern wall of the Palace City. After watching the spectacle from afar for less than an hour, he had decided to join the game in person over the strong protest of the general on duty. He had put on a commoner's outfit, comprised of a kirtle with long sleeves, a pair of baggy trousers, a cloth girdle, and a pair of hemp shoes, and slipped into the city streets incognito. Like everyone else, he had stood around at the crossroads, leaving his naked stumpy torso exposed and waging "water battles" with other semi-naked strangers.

He opened his eyes to examine once more the memorialist's rationales. First, it was a barbarian game, beneath the dignity of a Son of Heaven. Second, even though tight security measures on the ground were in place, the game itself presented an unacceptable level of danger for the emperor. Third, the timing was very inappropriate, considering that Tianhou was seriously ill. As her son, the emperor was expected to abstain from any form of entertainment.

The emperor was not pleased. He felt a strong urge to exile the remonstrator to the far south for life. That was lenient enough. Any judge would have sent him to the gallows for *lèse majesté*. But in reality, the poor fellow had not done anything wrong. As the emperor was agonizing over what to do, a eunuch officer came in to announce the arrival of General Li Zhan.

The moment the emperor saw the visitor, he shouted with reproach, "You should be attending on Tianhou right now! What are you doing here?"

Suddenly, Li Zhan fell on his knees and mumbled between sobs, "The Em . . . Empress Dowager is no more."

The emperor was frozen with shock for a brief moment before he burst out wailing, facing southwest where the Shangyang Palace was.

After Li Zhan took his leave, the emperor unfurled the silk scroll he had left on the table that bore her "Testamentary Edict." It read, "After I depart from this world, my imperial title shall be replaced in all future written documents with 'Zetian the Great Sage Empress.'[18] The clans of former Empress Wang and former Consort Xiao, as well as those of Chu Suiliang, Hann Yuan, and Liŭ Shi are hereby pardoned."

For three days the emperor kept vigil by the coffin in which his mother Tianhou's body lay. Draped in shiny white, the coffin was resting on a bier at the center of the dais in the Hanyuan Basilica.

As the whole country was in mourning, Wei Yuanzhong, the man best-known for his integrity and probity, came out of the woodwork to serve as the ad hoc leader of the court. By a decree Tianhou had issued on her deathbed, he was granted a fief of 100 households. Kneeling down in front of the coffin, Wei held up the decree on silk in both hands, sighed, choked back his tears, and blurted out, "It is all in the past now, Empress Dowager."

Only later was it revealed that Wu Sansi had forged the decree in the hope of softening him up. But as Wu was to find out soon, that was no longer necessary.

Notes

1 The Yingxian Palace 迎仙宮: west of the Hanyuan Basilica, it had as its principal structure the Jixian Basilica 集仙殿.

2 The Changsheng Basilica: all residential basilicas were called "Changsheng" (Longevity). See *Tang liangjing chengfang kao* 5.135. Here it should refer to the Jixian Basilica.

3 Anguo Xiangwang 安國相王.

[4] *Zhenguo* 鎮國.

[5] *Dizang Pusa benyuan jing* 地藏菩薩本願經: this sutra of Mahayana Buddhism tells how Kṣitigarbha became a bodhisattva through rescuing other sentient beings.

[6] Amitabha was a heavenly Buddha in the Mahayana tradition.

[7] Zetian Dasheng Huangdi 則天大聖皇帝.

[8] Xuanyuan Huangdi 玄元皇帝.

[9] Bozhou 亳州: prefecture in north Anhui.

[10] A consort (*fei* 妃) refers to a high-ranking imperial concubine or the wife of a prince.

[11] Fangling 房陵: Fangxian, Hubei.

[12] Zhang Zhijian 張知謇 and Cui Jingsi 崔敬嗣.

[13] The *yin* 蔭 privileges: extended to the top-ranking officials and officers, they allowed some of their descendants to receive official appointments.

[14] Defender-in-chief (*taiwei* 太尉): one the Three Dukes.

[15] Cui Shi's 崔湜 post was *kaogong yuanwai lang* 考功員外郎.

[16] *Zizhi tongjian* 208.6592. Cui Xuanwei was assigned to a provincial post not long afterwards.

[17] Luochengmen 洛城門.

[18] Zetian Dasheng Huanghou 則天大聖皇后.

10. The Chief Ministers (705–706)

EMPRESS WEI WAS now in a position of power very much like that of Tianhou before the passing of Gaozong. At the urging of her confidante Shangguan Wan'er, she wanted to use this new-found power to push her agenda, dealing with such issues as the status of women.

In a 705 memorial, the empress noticed that a mourning rule set by Tianhou had gone by the wayside and requested its revival. It required that the closest relatives of a deceased mother extend their mourning period from one to three years, as was the case for a deceased father. In the same document, she also suggested ways to ease the tax burden of the peasantry.[1] The emperor did not mind the former and liked the latter, so he gave his assent.

In an early 706 memorial, the empress proposed extending a privilege—previously available only to the royal princes—to all the living princesses (Taiping, Changning, Anle, Yicheng, Xindu, Anding, and Jincheng[2]). It would allow them to set up their own administrative offices, complete with staffers and administrators.

The emperor knew that the proposal was a breach of convention but gave his approval anyway. *It can't be too bad since it will make my wife, sister, and daughters happy.*

***

Wu Sansi, for all the power he had, still felt on pins and needles because of the continued presence of his enemies in Luoyang. While two of the Five Princes were now residing in the provinces (Zhang Jianzhi in Xiangzhou[3] and Cui Xuanwei in Liangzhou[4]), the remaining three—Jing Hui, Huan Yuanfan, and Yuan Shuji—were in the capital. Using his power as leader of the court, he managed, with the empress's help, to prevail upon the emperor to have them transferred out to Huazhou, Mingzhou, and Yuzhou.[5]

With the Five Princes out of sight, Wu Sansi now shifted his attention to the the cohort of top leaders still in power. One of them, Yang Zaisi, an erstwhile toady to the Zhangs, had cottoned up to him after the emperor's ascension. As for Wei Anshi, Wei Juyuan,[6] Doulu Qinwang, Tang Xiujing, and Li Huaiyuan,[7] they had stayed aloof from the recent power struggle and were unlikely to back his enemies. However, he was not sure about Wei Yuanzhong, one of the few court leaders who had been bold enough to confront the Zhangs and survived.

***

About this time, Wei Yuanzhong received a letter from a county defender (706), listing what he considered ten major problems plaguing the court and society at large.

> *First, the seat of heir apparent has been vacant for far too long. A crown prince should be set up, and his mentors chosen, as soon as possible.*
> *Second, it is without precedent and a waste of resources to allow the princesses to have their own administrative offices.*
> *Third, veneration of monks has gone too far, which has allowed people in cassock to use the influence of powerful figures to extract donations. Such practice is poisonous to morals.*
> *Fourth, contrary to tradition, base people such as acrobats and other stage performers have arrogated official posts. This runs counter to the fundamental teaching of Confucius on social hierarchy.*
> *Fifth, when government agencies recruit talents, they always seek out those who have paid bribes or are backed by the powerful. This corrupt practice must end.*
> *Sixth, the number of eunuch officers in the palace has swollen to almost one thousand. Sooner or later, they will become a source of trouble.*
> *Seventh, the princes, dukes, and other nobles engage in competitive extravagance. Instead of stopping it in its tracks, the court has continued to shower rich rewards on them.*

Eighth, too many supernumerary official posts have been assigned (often through bribery) at great cost to the masses.
Ninth, palace ladies of the previous reign are allowed to live outside the palace. That has enabled them to consort with outsiders and seek their help, thereby corrupting the ethos of society.
Tenth, scoundrels have stolen many court positions from the emperor. They should be forced to give them back.

The letter ended with: "I am turning to you, Mr. Wei Yuanzhong, because you are a man of moral integrity. If you cannot rectify these problems, who else can?"

Upon reading this scathing indictment against the new regime, Wei Yuanzhong let out a deep sigh. He sent the county defender an apologetic letter but took no action on any of the issues he mentioned. Ever since he came back from banishment, Wei had not submitted a single remonstrative memorial. Either old age or poor health or both had gotten the better of him.

In fact, a common problem with these chief ministers was age. Almost all of them were advanced in years. As they got older, they lost their fighting spirit.

***

The Tang dynasty was a great time for poetry. In its Early Tang phase, the Four Eminences (Wang Bo, Yang Jiong, Lu Zhaolin, and Luo Binwang) dominated the poetic landscape.[8] But the golden age of Tang poetry did not arrive until the High Tang phase with its poetic greats—Li Bai, Du Fu, Wang Wei, and many others.

Between the two phases was the Wu Zhou transition where two poets reigned supreme: Song Zhiwen and Shen Quanqi. The more famous of the two, Song Zhiwen was arguably the greatest master of the five-syllable variety in his day. As a man of letters, Song was less concerned with social issues than with flowers, birds, trees, and landscape. When it came to writing panegyrics in praise of the sovereign and the Wu Zhou regime, he was second to none. As a court favorite, he had received great titles and honors from Tianhou.

Back in the year 700 when Zhang Changzong was editing the voluminous *Sanjiao zhuying* (Essential Pearls of the Three Teachings), Song was one of a team of eminent scholars working under him.

At the time of the Two Zhangs' fall (705), Song was implicated as a close follower and banished with his brother Song Zhixun to the semi-civilized far south.

The Songs were not willing to accept the hand fate had dealt them and stole back into the capital. Song Zhiwen's bosom friend Wang Tongjiao, the husband of Princess Anding, took them in along with Song Zhixun's son Song Tan and nephew Li Quan.[9] They were put up in a small house separate from Wang's mansion to avoid attention.

***

One evening, their host Wang Tongjiao was entertaining friends at home. The younger of the Song brothers Zhixun overheard Wang's rude remarks about the empress and her lover Wu Sansi. No sooner did he rush back to the house he lived in than he started debating with himself about what to do. In the end, he concluded that to continue living in the home of such a rebellious man was dangerous and he must take immediate action.

At Zhixun's request, his son Song Tan and his nephew Li Quan cowrote an accusation letter. What they exposed were not just the inflammatory remarks Wang had made, but his elaborate plot to assassinate Wu Sansi, sack the palace, and topple the empress.

Due to the serious nature of the case, the emperor ordered Censor-in-Chief Li Chengjia[10] to head its investigation, and appointed three chief ministers—Yang Zaisi, Li Qiao, and Wei Juyuan—to conduct its review.

The Censorate's police raided the homes of Wang Tongjiao and his confederates, and arrested them all except for one, who was then out of town. They were put on trial, found guilty, and subsequently beheaded; and their family assets were confiscated.

The confederate who had avoided capture, upon return, made his appearance at the Temple of Bigan,[11] sword in hand. After giving a rousing speech to a large crowd, he struck his neck with the sword and fell. It was obvious that he had chosen to die in this temple on purpose. Bigan, a loyal Shang chief minister, had lost his life while trying to remonstrate with his tyrannical sovereign.

The emperor had not said a word in defense of his son-in-law Wang Tongjiao, obviously because here the empress's life was at stake. In fact, before the case was closed, the emperor had been informed of charges against her illicit behavior. But he had chosen to ignore them. After he learned how the Song Zhixun had exposed the plot and saved the empress from disaster, he showed his appreciation by granting handsome rewards to the Song brothers: forgiving their illegal escape from the far south and promoting both Zhixun and Zhiwen to Rank-5 posts, after rehabilitating them. We must note that Song Zhiwen, who was a court favorite again, had done practically nothing, but benefited from being Zhixun's brother.

***

The sprawling Qianling Tomb Park northwest of Chang'an was built by Tianhou herself after the passing of Gaozong. The site was chosen because it is the point where the Two Forces of yin and yang meet. At its center are the Twin Peaks of Southern Mount Liang. The two tall watchtowers perching on the peaks mark the imperial tomb beneath. The enclosed parkland surrounding the tomb is a miniature replica of the city of Chang'an.[12]

In early 706, the emperor Li Zhe joined Tianhou's cortège to travel from Luoyang all the way to the park near Chang'an. On July 2, her body was laid to rest in the same underground chamber where her husband's bones lay.

As the emperor stood at the opening of a long passageway on the mountain slope leading down to the heart of the mausoleum, he watched on as laborers closed the stone gate some distance down and filled the passageway with stones before sealing it with clay and camouflaging it with grass and shrubbery.

Accompanied by a large entourage, the emperor strolled along the Spirit Path,[13] the north-south central axial avenue that extended south to the southern main entrance, the Zhuque Gate, and beyond. Lining the path were statues of winged horses, ostriches, and court officials and officers. Near the gate stood sixty-four human statues (each with its own inscription), thirty-two on each side of the central road. Sixty-one of them remain today. These were foreign dignitaries who ended up as high-ranking officials at the Tang court, including Peroz,[14] the last king of Sassanian Persia; Nohebo Khan,[15] the last sovereign of Tuyuhun; and Yuchi Jing,[16] king of Yutian.[17]

The emperor, borne in a palanquin by the eunuchs, moved south out of the enclosed area of the imperial tomb. Moments later, he arrived at the tombs of his children nearby, Li Chongrun and Li Xianhui. A whole spectrum of emotions welled up in him as he paid homage and made offerings.

On coming to power, one of the first things he had done was to grant the posthumous titles of Crown Prince Yide and Princess Yongtai[18] to them and have their bones reburied in two accompanying tombs to the imperial tomb to keep company with their grandfather Gaozong and grandmother Tianhou who had ordered their death. Both tombs were built as "mausoleums" on larger-than-usual scales. In fact, Yongtai's tomb is the only mausoleum for a princess in history. For the emperor Li Zhe, this was the best way to honor the memory of his deceased children.

After all the funeral and memorial ceremonies were completed, the emperor made his way back to Luoyang, where he would stay in the Palace City. By the end of the year, he would, accompanied by the court officials, leave Luoyang for Chang'an for good.[19]

***

As the emperor was going through a memorial one evening in the early summer of 706, his face became crimson with fury. In the document, the recluse Wei Yuejiang lashed out at Wu Sansi for having adulterous relations with women in the Rear Palace, and warned against him as a threat to the throne. The emperor took it as a thinly veiled innuendo attack on the empress. He rose from his seat and screamed out his order for the recluse's immediate decapitation.

To his surprise, the Chancellery responded with a request for reviewing the case. With a kerchief-cap on his head and slippers on his feet, the emperor made an unexpected visit to the Chancellery's Office by a side door.

"What's matter with you fellows? Do you think my edict on decapitation is not good enough?" asked the emperor in an angry voice. "I want it done as soon as possible!"

"Your Majesty," Song Jing, vice president of the Chancellery,[20] said calmly, "the recluse is accusing someone in the Rear Palace of having illicit relations with Wu Sansi. It is a very serious charge and should be looked into. If you kill the accuser without an investigation, all under Heaven will ask questions."

"I don't care what you say. This man Wei Yuejiang must die."

Song Jing responded, "If Your Majesty insists on beheading Wei right now, pray cut off my head first! I simply cannot act upon the edict as it stands."

The emperor was stunned speechless. As he stood there, staring down at his slippers, one of Song's colleagues came to the rescue. He offered a compromise: assigning a panel of three judges to review the case in a most expeditious manner. To the emperor, this was enough to help him get out of the quandary he was in, so he gave his nod.

The panel formed to review the case soon reached a judgment that did not challenge the emperor's verdict but put off the execution until mid-autumn as was the custom. But, as it later turned out, the recluse did not get executed in Luoyang after all. After he received a good flogging, he was banished to the far south. Soon his luck ran out after the autumnal equinox. An overzealous prefect carried out his beheading. By then an imperial edict to pardon him was already on its way, but it was too late to save him.

***

Wu Sansi survived the Wang Tongjiao incident stronger than ever. It created for him an opportunity he did not want to see go to waste. With the full backing of Empress Wei, he now went out of his way to further punish the Five Princes. In his capacity as the leading chief minister, Wu submitted no less than half a dozen memorials to the emperor, urging him to take action, and brought up the issue time and again at court when he saw the emperor in person. Empress Wei championed Wu's cause whenever she was alone with the emperor in his residential basilica.

Under pressure from his most powerful minister and domineering wife, the emperor at length gave in, but only to a point. He allowed some light punitive measures to take place. Of the five, Jing Hui, Cui Xuanwei, and Huan Yanfan were relegated to remoter and smaller prefectures by way of demotion. Zhang Jianzhi and Yuan Shuji were left untouched.

Wu Sansi did not like it at all. He sought out the advice of his close associates. One of them, Zheng Yin, then found an ingenious way to link the Wang Tongjiao incident to the Five Princes. Based on this idea, he charged the Five Princes as the behind-the-scenes backers of Wang in a memorial.

The emperor's response was, "But I don't the connection."

The empress countered, "The Five Princes should at least bear some of the blame. They were the immediate superiors of the conspirators before."

The following day, more memorials arrived siding with the empress.

So, the campaign to change the emperor's mind continued. In

the end, exhausted by unrelenting demand from the high-powered individuals and their minions, he gave the go-ahead for additional punitive measures. In consequence, the Five Princes lost all their functional posts, noble titles, and fiefs—everything that counted—and were demoted to supernumerary assistant prefects.

***

As Wu Sansi was busy plotting and scheming to ruin the life of the Five Princes, a new scandal broke that shook the capital.

Someone put up an anonymous poster on the announcement board south of the Tianjin Bridge, in which, it fouled the name of the Empress Wei, calling her a lascivious fornicator, and demanded her immediate removal. The titillating details it offered suggested that the author was an insider with an intimate knowledge of her life.

Censor-in-Chief Li Chengjia took charge of the case under direct orders from an infuriated emperor. By then, Li, who had had an impeccable track record before, had hitched himself to Wu Sansi's wagon. In two weeks' time, he produced a report that fingered the Five Princes as the culprits and suggested the death penalty and clan extirpation as their punishment.[21]

Now the emperor found himself in a bind, torn between wanting to protect his wife's reputation and hoping to keep the Five Princes from unjust punishment. He asked around, and all the advice he got—from Wu Sansi, Princess Anle, Zheng Yin, Cui Shi, and many others—urged him to take firm and immediate action.

The Censorate then produced its own judgment, confirming Li Chengjia's recommendation. That tipped the emperor in favor of the prosecutors until he read a report by a vice censor-in-chief, who warned against rushing to judgment, and called attention to the Iron Certificates they had been issued with. To that the emperor said, "Well, if the Iron Certificates mean anything at all, the five should be spared the death penalty, at least this time."

In the end, the Five Princes were punished with long-distance banishment together with their sons and brothers of fifteen *sui* or older.

***

In Wu Sansi's Luoyang home, a massive palatial mansion, a secret meeting was taking place in his study.

"We did it, didn't we?" Wu Sansi said to his men with a beaming smile on his face.

"Yes, we did it," Zheng Yin said. "However, although Zhang Jianzhi and Cui Xuanwei will die soon, the others are alive and well."

"They are in a no-man's land in the far south thousands of miles away."

"If they keep quiet and don't make trouble," Cui Shi said, "after a couple of years, they can be recalled."

"Besides," Zheng Yin said, "sooner or later, someone will trace the handwriting of the poster to its true author, me."

"What should we do now?" asked Wu Sansi, his smile gone.

"Send an envoy to finish them off," Cui Shi said with decision.

"What do you think?" Wu Sansi asked Zheng Yin.

"Maybe. But on whose authority?" Zheng Yin asked.

"The envoy will carry an edict," Cui Shi said.

"You mean a faked one?" Zheng Yin asked.

"Yes, if we cannot get one from the emperor," Cui Shi said.

"To counterfeit an official document is a capital crime, let alone an edict," Wu Sansi said. "That's way too dangerous. What if we are caught?"

"We may have to do that, Prince," Cui Shi answered. "We really have no choice. If they are allowed to return, they will kill all of us in the same way they killed the Zhang brothers."

Wu Sansi dithered.

"Think of it this way, Prince," Cui Shi said. "These five are the true evil-doers. To rid the world of them is a just cause. For the sake of justice, we should pursue whatever means available."

"Including forging an edict?" Zheng Yin said.

"Yes," Cui Shi said. "This is a typical case where the end justifies the means."

"All right, all right, I'll see if I can get an edict," Wu Sansi said. "But don't reveal it to another soul."

"Of course, I won't," Cui Shi said.

"Neither will I," Zheng Yin said.

***

Zhou Liyong, a rising star among the law officers, was on his way to the far south, bearing a forged edict to execute the traitors. He had a personal reason to be thrilled by his assignment. He had been demoted by the Five Princes' men from a post in the capital to assistant prefect in a remote prefecture. Only recently had he been recalled and appointed attendant censor.

By the time he arrived in the far south, Zhang Jianzhi and Cui Xuanwei had died. Zhou sought out his first quarry, Huan Yanfan now living in Guizhou.[22] On Zhou's orders, his henchmen hogtied Huan to a bamboo raft and tortured him with whips, sticks, and daggers until his bones were exposed. Zhou then clubbed him to death.

Further down south in Qiongzhou,[23] Zhou located Jing Hui, former leader of the court bureaucracy, and personally tried the "death by one thousand cuts" method on him, slicing his flesh, piece by piece, until he breathed no more.

Next Zhou traveled to Huanzhou,[24] where he met his last victim Yuan Shuji. Yuan had just taken a longevity drug made of gold powder and was taking a nap. Zhou's men shook Yuan awake and forced a jar of hemlock drink down his throat. Yuan soon collapsed onto the ground. Zhou watched as Yuan writhed in unbearable pain, clawing the earth so hard that most of his nails came off. Zhou then finished him off with a cudgel.

Thanks to the effective way Zhou Liyong had carried out the executions, upon his return, Wu Sansi promoted him to vice censor-in-chief.

***

Finally, with the death of the Five Princes, Wu Sansi could sleep easy at night. In fact, now at the summit of his power, he enjoyed as much support at court as anyone else. At the very top, the empress as his lover would always have his back. Among the top leaders, he could count on such senior officials as President of the Board of War Zong Chuke, President of the Directorate for the Royal Buildings[25] Zong Jinqing, and Chamberlain of the Court for the State Revenues Ji Chu'ne.[26] At the middle level, he had at his beck and call the five henchmen, known as the "Five Dogs," including Zhou Liyong and Song Zhixun, who were always ready to do his bidding.

Notes

[1] She suggested that the age range of the adult male category (taxed at the highest rate) was reduced from 39 years (21–60 *sui*) to 36 years (23–59 *sui*). See *Zizhi tongjian* 208.6592.

[2] Yicheng 宜城, Xindu 新都, and Anding 安定 were daughters of Zhongzong not born to Empress Wei. Jincheng was Prince Li Shouli's daughter and Zhongzong's adopted daughter.

[3] Xiangzhou 襄州: prefecture that lay in Xiangfan, Yicheng, and others, Hubei.

[4] Liangzhou 梁州: prefecture that lay in Hanzhong and others, Shaanxi.

[5] Huazhou 滑州: prefecture that lay in Huaxian and others, Henan. Mingzhou 洺州: prefecture that lay in Wu'an and others, Hebei. Yuzhou 豫州: prefecture that lay between Luohe and Xinyang, south central Henan.

[6] Wei Juyuan at seventy-five *sui* was a nephew of Wei Anshi, even though the latter at fifty-five *sui* was twenty years his junior.

[7] Li Huaiyuan 李懷遠.

[8] In addition, Li Shimin (Taizong) and Chen Zi'ang should probably be added.

[9] Song Zhixun 宋之遜, Song Tan 宋曇, Li Quan 李悛.

[10] Li Chengjia 李承嘉.

[11] Bigan 比干.

[12] There is a popular belief that the site was selected based on the advice of the two most prominent occultists of the day, Yuan Tiangang and Li Chunfeng, which is not believable. First, Yuan Tiangang died in 645, in the same year when Gaozong

(Li Zhi) was made crown prince and Taizong was still alive. Second, Li Chunfeng died in 670 when Gaozong was still alive and well.

[13] *Shendao* 神道.

[14] Bilusi 卑路斯.

[15] Murong Nuohebo 慕容諾曷鉢.

[16] Yuchi Jing 尉遲璥.

[17] Yutian 于闐: oasis state that lay in Hetian, south Xinjiang.

[18] Crown Prince Yide 懿德太子 and Princess Yongtai 永泰公主.

[19] *Jiu Tang shu* 7.142; *Zizhi tongjian* 208.6606.

[20] *Huangmen shilang* 黃門侍郎.

[21] After the five conspirators had been deprived of their noble titles, they were still referred to as the "Five Princes" out of habit.

[22] Guizhou 貴州: prefecture that lay in Guigang, Guangxi.

[23] Qiongzhou 瓊州: prefecture that lay in Haikou and others, Hainan.

[24] Huanzhou 環州: prefecture that lay in Hechi and Huanjiang, Guangxi.

[25] *Jiangzuo dajiang* 將作大匠.

[26] *Taifu qing* 太府卿; Ji Chu'ne 紀處訥.

11. Li Chongjun (707)

WHEN PRINCESS ANLE came into the world in a carriage by the roadside in 684, her mother was caught unprepared. The maid who delivered the baby had to use some old garments as swaddling clothes. Hence the nickname "Swaddled Baby." The harsh conditions under which Anle was born made her parents feel guilty. And they had spoiled her rotten as she grew up.

Now she had become a ravishing beauty, and a mighty political force at court to boot. She would write her own edicts and request her father to affix his seal. The emperor would happily comply so long as the "edicts" were not too out of line. Rumor had it she even practiced secular simony and sold "get-out-of-jail passes." The emperor did not seem to care.

As the apple of her parents' eye and Wu Sansi's daughter-in-law, Anle enjoyed more power and privilege than anyone of her generation living under the Tang. And yet, she strove for more as she looked up to her famous grandmother Tianhou and set her sights on heirship. For now, the only stumbling block was Crown Prince Li Chongjun, born to a nameless mother of humble birth in the Rear Palace. Princess Anle and her husband Wu Chongxun and his father Wu Sansi had nothing but disdain for the crown prince and often called him "slave" to his face. Under their influence, Empress Wei, who had favored him over his brother Chongfu before, began to have second thoughts.

***

Growing up as a bondmaid in the palace, Shangguan Wan'er had harbored an intense hatred against Tianhou ever since she began to remember things. She knew that Tianhou was the evil person who had taken the lives of Grandfather and Father and sent Mother and herself into bondage. After she entered the service of Tianhou, however, she was surprised to find much in common with her. Her hatred began to dissolve, taken over by a sense of reconciliation, then by gratitude and admiration, which would grow stronger with time.

After Tianhou's death, Shangguan Wan'er even went out of her way to promote her legacy at court. For instance, like Tianhou, she was interested in improving the status of women.

This was something Princess Anle also favored. But she had a far more ambitious agenda. Egged on by Wu Chongxun, her husband, and endorsed by Empress Wei, Princess Anle requested the title of imperial crown princess[1] for herself. In her memorial, she spoke in unambiguous terms that the current crown prince should vacate his seat for her. When Chief Minister Wei Yuanzhong responded with a resounding no, she said, "That country bumpkin from Shandong? What does he know? If Grandmother could ascend the throne as a woman and a Wu, so can I as a woman and a Li."

While the emperor remained undecided over Anle's request, the strongest voice of opposition came from an unexpected source, Shangguan Wan'er. She had sided with Tianhou on issues concerning the status of women. But setting up a female heir to the empire? No! It would never have had Tianhou's endorsement. In fact, it had crossed the line. She filed a passionate memorial, urging the emperor to stop this silly thing in its tracks. The emperor, big-hearted and permissive, did not want to rub the princess the wrong way. So he did nothing.

Soon Princess Anle learned what Shangguan had done. She was white with fury and did everything she could to make Shanghuan's life miserable. When Shangguan could not take it any longer, she put in a request to quit office, which the emperor rejected. Shangguan then asked for permission to renounce the secular life to become a nun, following Tianhou's precedent. The emperor turned that down as well. In despair, she swilled down a bowl of poisoned wine and fell down unconscious.

Terrified to learn what had happened, the emperor thereupon dispatched his personal physicians to treat her while placing a moratorium on the issue of imperial crown princess.

After she regained enough strength several months later, Shangguan, anxious to assume a low-profile for self-protection, submitted a request for her own demotion from Beautiful Visage (Zhaorong) to Fair Lady (Jieyu),[2] which the emperor approved with great reluctance.

To Shangguan, the imperial crown princess incident marked a true turning point in her life. Thereafter, she became an object of hate for Princess Anle and began to move closer to her rival Princess Taiping.

***

Less than a year after the emperor had moved back into Chang'an in the tenth month of 706 with his entire entourage and the central bureaucracy, a traumatic event took place that shook the palace and the city.

On August 7, 707 at dawn, more than 300 rebel riders of the Left Yulin Guard, an elite palace guard force, surrounded a sprawling mansion in the southwest quadrant of Xiuxiang Ward,[3] west of Fuxing Ward[4] and the Palace City. The riders found Wu Sansi and Wu Chongxun, father and son, inside and made short work of them. They went on to kill more than a dozen of their followers. After they combed the property in search of their main target—Wu Chongxun's wife Princess Anle—and failed to find her, they moved east to fall on the Palace City.

Thus began the Li Chongjun incident.

The leaders of the incident—Crown Prince Li Chongjun and General-in-Chief Li Duozuo—had ordered the riders out of their barracks by a forged edict.

The rebels soon reached the outer walls of the Taiji Basilica. They found the gates shut tight and jammed with logs from within and learned from scouts that in the courtyard there were a troop of more than 2,000 men under the command of the loyalists Yang Zaisi, Su Gui, Li Qiao, Zong Chuke, and Ji Chu'ne.

Leaving the basilica alone, the rebels moved northwest. After storming the Suzhang Gate,[5] they made their way to the entrance to the Inner Area[6] of the palace, ready to launch an assault.

***

The moment the emperor learned of Crown Prince Li Chongjun's rebellion, he fled, with the empress and Shangguan Wan'er in tow, from his residential basilica at full pelt north under the escort of the eunuch officers and security guards. He had no time to take a respite until he was hustled into the gatetower of the Xuanwumen, still in loyalists' hands.

As the northern entrance to the Palace City, the Xuanwu Gate opened onto the Forbidden Park to the north. At the south side of the gate, General-in-Chief of the Right Yulin Guard Liu Jingren[7] personally commanded a 100-plus crack cavalry to guard the safety of the emperor.

***

By now the crown prince and General Li Duozuo with a mounted escort had forced their way into the Inner Area and gone as far as the forecourt of the Xuanwu Gate in the northernmost part of the Palace City. Some of their men attempted to ascend the stairs but were stopped by the loyal guardsmen with their swords and spears on the ready.

Riding in circles on their horses, the prince and the general were at a loss what to do next. It seemed that they were hoping that the emperor would come down to listen to their grievances.

All of a sudden, the rebels saw the eunuch officer Yang Sixu charging out of the gate's archway towards them; wielding a broadsword, he lopped off the head of a commandant. Before they could confront him, a voice boomed from above, "My guardsmen, why do you follow the rebel Li Duozuo? If you take him out, I promise, you will be loaded with money and power." They raised their heads and saw a smudge of a figure standing behind an embrasure on the second floor of the gatetower. Although the voice was distant, they could still tell that it belonged to the emperor.

Roused to anger, the rebels on the ground gathered around their commander. After a fierce exchange of words, they raised their swords and spears, unhorsed him and killed him on the spot. Other rebel officers scattered.

The crown prince fled in a frantic rush south, leading more than one hundred riders. Having passed through the Palace City, the Imperial City, and the residential quarters of Chang'an, he galloped in the direction the Zhongnan Mountains beyond the southern suburbs. After losing all but one of his men along the way, he continued to flee until he was thoroughly exhausted. He slipped off his horse to take a rest in a roadside copse when his last soldier companion ran him through from behind with a sword.

***

On the emperor's orders, court business was suspended for five days in mourning for the passing of Wu Sansi and his son Wu Chongxun, a highest honor for nonroyals in death. Some of the most prestigious posthumous titles were granted: defender-in-chief to the father, and de facto chief minister to the son. Princess Anle, who had escaped capture and death by accident, requested that her husband Wu Chongxun be buried in a "mausoleum," a large tomb fit for a sovereign, following a precedent set in the case of Princess Yongtai (Li Xianhui), her sister. But the emperor turned her down, saying, "I can't extend that honor to a non-Li in-law."

On the day of the funeral, the rebel prince Li Chongjun's severed head was first offered to the imperial ancestors at the Ancestral Temple, then placed in front of the coffins of the deceased, and then, after the funeral was over, put on display, hanging from a thick beam in the Audience Hall for days. All known accomplices of the disgraced prince were hunted down and dispatched.

***

In the wake of the Li Chongjun incident, Empress Wei and Princess Anle spearheaded a campaign to ferret out and punish his allies and the empress's opponents. Princess Anle set her sights on the biggest targets: the emperor's younger brother Prince of Xiang Li Dan and his younger sister Princess Taiping. But these had been perennial survivors of court politics and to bring them down would not be easy. Overcautious and self-effacing, Li Dan was on good terms with almost everybody. Even the Wus found it hard to dislike him. Still, Li Dan, who had been emperor once before, could be a serious contender for the throne. So could his brood of princes.

Princess Taiping had lived under the protection of her mother Tianhou. With high intelligence and a strong personality, she would almost surely challenge Empress Wei, should she decide to make a bid for imperial power.

With the backing of her mother Empress Wei, Princess Anle had one of her underlings file a memorial to request the imprisonment of Li Dan and Taiping on account of their close association with Li Chongjun.

The emperor ordered an investigation. To his astonishment, the official in charge of the case, Vice Censor-in-Chief Xiao Zhizhong, broke down sobbing.

"What's matter?" asked the emperor, dumbfounded.

"All under Heaven," Xiao replied, "belong to Your Majesty, and yet, you cannot tolerate your own brother and sister? And want others to frame them? Apart from Princess Xuancheng,[8] who is now in prison, Taiping is your only sister alive. As for Prince Li Dan, he insisted that you should take over the reins and even went on a hunger strike to make his point. Thanks to his persistence Tianhou allowed you to succeed to the throne without incident. How can Your Majesty believe a word of what the accusers say of him?"

This sentiment was echoed by Court Rectifier Wu Jing in his disturbing memorial, which said, "Remember, Your Majesty, you have been on the throne for only a short while, and yet, one of your sons Chongjun was killed in a rebellion, and another Chongfu was banished to a remote place. How many close relatives do you have to lose?"

With tears brimming his eyes, the emperor called off the investigation.

***

To the surprise of many, Right Vice Premier[9] Wei Yuanzhong was now the target of an investigation for his possible entanglement in the Li Chongjun incident.

In their joint memorial, Zhong Chuke and Ji Chu'ne, both Empress Wei's protégés, claimed that, upon hearing the news of Wu Sansi's death, Wei Yuanzhong had said, "The arch-villain is now dead! It is worth it even if it means throwing me into a boiling tripod."

However, although we read these words in a reputable source, they may have been quoted out of context. While it was true that Wei had resented Wu Sansi's dominance, he had lost his mettle by the time of Tianhou's death and remained cautious ever since. How come, in the wake of Wu Sansi's death, all of a sudden, he started talking tough in a way that would almost certainly land him in deep trouble?[10]

Whatever the case, the emperor was floored when he saw the recommended punishment for Wei: execution and extirpation of his Three Clans.

"No! Not Wei Yuanzhong," he exclaimed. "He played a absolutely crucial part in suppressing the Li Jingye rebellion. All these years, Gaozong, Tianhou, and I have respected him." So he did not act on Zong's and Ji's judgment.

Then more charges came in. They cited past cases to argue that Wei Yuanzhong, as a nonroyal with no extraordinary merit, should not escape punishment for his treasonous crime.

While the emperor still refused the request for execution, he in the end agreed to some form of punishment: banishment to the southwest as county defender.

Already at an advanced age and in poor health, Wei had little chance of living to see his day of recall. In fact, while en route to the destination of his banishment, he passed away.

Notes

[1] *Huang tainü* 皇太女.

[2] Jieyu 婕妤.

[3] Xiuxiang Ward 休祥坊.

[4] Fuxing Ward 輔興坊.

[5] Suzhang Gate 肅章門.

[6] The Palace City, like the Daming Palace, was divided into an Inner (north) and an Outer (south) area. The Inner Area was the heavily guarded forbidden zone where the emperor and his women resided.

[7] Liu Jingren 劉景仁.

[8] Xuancheng's husband Wang Xu 王勖 had been killed 691 for involvement in a rebellion. Xuancheng had been in custody ever since.

[9] *You puye* 右僕射.

[10] *Zizhi tongjian* 208.6615.

12. Shangguan Wan'er (706–708)

PALACE INTRIGUES AND upheavals at court in recent years left the north and the west vulnerable to outside attacks. For some reasons, the non-Han peoples living beyond the borders did not take advantage of this situation.

In fact, the Tubo had entered upon a period of political uncertainty after the death of their zanpu Chidu Songzan (704). They failed to get their act together due to an internal power struggle. And, for a long while, the Tang Empire's western and northwestern borders were essentially safe from their intrusions.

In Central Asia (both inside and outside China), the Türgesh (Tuqishi), a Western Tujue people dominant in the Western Regions, were by and large on peaceful terms with the Tang.

In late 706, General Guo Yuanzhen, the Tang top defender of the northwest, at the invitation of the Türgesh, paid a visit to their headquarters camp. As he held a talk with their leader Wuzhile[1] outside his tent, squalls of snow and high wind buffeted the camp. All the while the aging host showed no desire to move the meeting inside. Neither did Guo.

That evening, Wuzhile came down with a bad cold and succumbed soon. His grief-stricken son Suoge[2] vowed to take revenge on the killer of his father.

General Guo turned down advice by his aides to flee and revisited the Türgesh a few days later to pay condolences at the chief's funeral. Under the fierce gaze of Suoge, General Guo dropped down on his knees and cried his eyes out. The deep grief he showed must have softened Suoge's heart. And the Tang continued to enjoy the kind of friendly relations with Türgesh that had existed on his father's watch.

***

About seventeen years after the suicide of Heichi Changzhi, Zhang Renyuan, commander-in-chief of Shuofang,[3] began to emerge as another great frontier general of the north. Thanks to his success in defending the border, he was promoted to de facto chief minister and joined the court leadership. Not given to niceties, he often engaged in rude behavior. Once he wrote up a "call to arms" against Mochuo in vulgar language and had the whole piece inscribed in black ink onto the body of a captured Tujue officer. After having the inscription dried with fire, he handed the officer over to the Tujue. Mochuo was so incensed by the tattoo that he ordered to have the poor man flayed alive.

At a time when Mochuo led the main Tujue force west on a campaign against the Türgesh, Zhang Renyuan marched his troops north to capture large areas north of the Yellow River in south-central Inner Mongolia, against the advice of General Tang Xiujing. He went on to construct three frontier towns (Three Shouxiang Towns[4]) in 708. In a provocative move, he built his "Central Town" (southwest of Baotou) around the Fuyun Shrine,[5] a sacred place where the Tujue had prayed to their god before going on raids to the south. He placed the other two towns about 400 *li* to the east and west of Central Town. All three were located near fords on the northern bank of the Yellow River. In a vast swathe of land between these towns, 800 beacon towers were erected on hilltops to keep a watch on the movement of hostile forces from the north. Over time, these measures had worked as a most effective way to deter Tujue raids.

***

In the early summer of 708, Shangguan Wan'er, who would be promoted to Beautiful Visage[6] again in winter, was tasked by the emperor to revamp the Institute for the Cultivation of Literature,[7] a central government agency in charge of editing and compiling literary and other types of anthologies, in addition to training sons of high-ranking officials. Its four chief academician (*da xueshi*) posts, often filled by chief ministers, were symbolic of the four seasons. Its eight academician-on-duty (*zhi xueshi*) posts and twelve academician posts embodied the Eight Main Solar Terms[8] and the Twelve Chronograms.[9]

Following an established tradition, whenever the emperor toured the Forbidden Park or held a banquet to entertain guests, the academicians would join the entourage.

When an ordinary banquet was held, only a small number of guests were invited. They oftentimes included the leaders of the Secretariat and the Chancellery, princes and dukes, and a few court favorites. Only on the rare occasion of a Grand Banquet was the list of invited guests enlarged to include the Eight Seats,[10] the Nine Chamberlains,[11] and other officials of rank 5 and higher.

On the last day of the first month, the emperor visited the Kunming Pond in the western suburbs, where a Grand Banquet was held. He found himself in a poetic mood, which inspired attending scholars and officials to compose many poems for the occasion.

Shangguan Wan'er sitting under the portico of a basilica was the judge of poetry on duty today. Staring at a nearby building's façade decorated with colorful silk bands, she thought back to a weird dream her mother Lady Zheng had had forty years before when a faceless man gave her a steelyard and said, "Your kid will use this instrument to judge all literati under Heaven." Not long afterwards, Lady Zheng gave birth to a girl. Surprised and disappointed, she asked the baby, "Are you the one to judge all literati under Heaven?" The baby babbled something that sounded like "Yeah, yeah," to the amusement of the mother.

Soon mother and daughter were forced into bondage after Shangguan Wan'er's father and grandfather were executed. But the dream gave Lady Zheng hope that her daughter would not live out her life as a bondwoman.

Now what was prophesied in the dream had become a reality. Shangguan Wan'er was sitting in judgment on some of the greatest poets in the country on behalf of the emperor.

With the arrival of the first batch of poems, she started reviewing them. Each time she finished critiquing a piece, she would fling the scroll of paper into the crowd below on the terrace. And the poets would fall over one another to seize hold of it to find out who the loser was.

In the end, only two pieces were left: one by Shen Quanqi and the other by Song Zhiwen, the two poetic greats of the day. The judge gave the poems one more look and cast out one scroll. A young palace attendant caught it in midair, glimpsed at the name, and handed it to Shen Quanqi.

"Why?" Shen asked.

Shangguan stood up and explained, "Just look at the last couplet of Song Zhiwen's poem: 'No worries that the shiny moon is fading, / The bright pearl will surely arrive.' I like its uplifting vibe." Shen Quanqi stopped complaining. For his rival Song Zhiwen, this victory would not only bring him a generous reward of gold and silk but also earn him the honor of having his poem set to music by a court musician and add to his already stellar literary reputation.

Stories like this fed into the popularity of literature with its focus on florid verbiage, much to the displeasure of scholars devoted to Confucian learning, who felt more and more neglected.

***

In Tang and Wu Zhou times, the emperor and chief ministers were responsible for appointments to posts of Rank-5 and higher; and the Board of Personnel, for appointments to posts of Rank-6 and lower. The official patent of appointment, before it went into effect, had to be endorsed with the character "Rescript"[12] in red brushed by the emperor.

During the reign of the emperor Li Zhe, when a small number

of privileged women proposed certain appointments, they could get around these rules. By using their access to the throne, they could obtain unofficial patents of appointment without going through the approving process. The emperor understood that the practice was inappropriate but found it hard to turn down the requests made by his favorite women, so he endorsed them by brushing the character Rescript in *black*. The appointments approved this way were known as "oblique" appointments.

Those who had made such appointments included Princess Anle, Princess Changning, the state mistress of Cheng[13] (a sister of the empress), Shangguan Wan'er and her mother, and several others. They used these appointments to fill their pockets, charging 300,000 cash per post. At one time, there were as many as several thousand obliquely appointed officials in officialdom.

People complained mightily about them, because the women who proposed them not only made a mockery of proper procedures but also cheapened the appointments by making them available to anyone with money, regardless of social status, including such "base" people as merchants and bondservants, who were normally barred from holding office.

That was not all. Those favorite women also sold Buddhist ordinations at 30,000 cash per person. For a young woman from the country, who, after marriage, would suffer the pangs of childbirth multiple times, pinch and scrape to feed her kids, do family chores, and toil in the field, the prospect of living in a nunnery free of these worries seemed like a pretty good deal. To say nothing of what the religion had to offer: peace, serenity, and hope of deliverance in the next life.

***

After her husband Wu Chongxun's death, Princess Anle took up residence in the palace. Her old home in Xiuxiang Ward was now deemed inauspicious. Soon she acquired a new home to the south of Xiuxiang. It was situated to the north of the Kaishan Nunnery[14] in the southeast quadrant of Jincheng Ward.[15] After taking possession of the property, Anle had it enlarged at the expense of her neighbors and spent a fortune to convert it into a palatial mansion. Upon its completion, with pomp and circumstance, Anle arrived in a fancy carriage from the palace, accompanied by a long procession, with court musicians playing trumpets and beating drums. She then held a largest house-warming party to entertain distinguished guests, including the emperor, the empress, and the top officials.[16]

After settling down in Chang'an, she ranged far and wide in her pursuit of fun activities. She visited the Da Ci'en Monastery in the south of the city to scale its famous pagoda, set sail in the Serpentine River (Qujiang) Pond in the city's southeast corner, and went hunting in the White Deer Plain in the eastern suburbs. Her greatest interest, however, was the Kunming Pond off the Feng River to the west of the city. This was an expansive man-made lake situated inside a royal park. Dug by Emperor Wu of Han about 800 years before, it had been used for naval battle exercises.

The first time Princess Anle paid a visit she fell in love with its beautiful scenery and serene atmosphere.

"Daddy, could I have it, please?" she pleaded.

The emperor said with a smile, "I am afraid you can't, my dear. Thousands of fishermen's livelihood depends on the lake. I can't in good conscience let anyone have it, not even my baby."

She went away in a huff. Several months later, she had her own lake dug, which was much larger than the Kunming Pond. Located to the south of the capital, it extended as far south as the South Mountains and had within its enceinte a range of artificial craggy hills shaped to imitate Mount Hua, and a long winding water channel that symbolized the Milky Way. One of the most precious artifacts installed there was the Treasured Burner, with its bronze body covered with grotesque animals and divine birds in openwork and inlaid with precious cowries and coral pieces. She gave the lake a provocative name, the "Lake That Suppresses Kunming."[17]

In addition, she showed an insatiable desire for grandeur and luxury. The Buddhist monasteries she built were modeled after imposing palace structures and government edifices, with even more elaborate ornamentation. She spared no expense on clothing and jewelry. One famous dress of hers was made from rare bird feathers. Its multicolored floral and animal patterns changed colors when viewed from different angles under the sun. Allegedly worth 100 million cash, it was in the same league with Zhang Changzong's coat of kingfisher feather.

Her interests, however, went far beyond material possessions. With the passing of her father-in-law Wu Sansi, she increasingly stepped in his shoes and played the role of the most powerful figure at court. She had been involved in the appointment of most of the chief ministers and even made a bid for the seat of crown prince, which had triggered the Li Chongjun incident.

Always competing with her for parental favor and bragging rights about who had the most lavish pieces of real estate was her elder sister Princess Changning, who had multiple mansions in both capitals. Take for example her property in Chang'an's Chongren Ward[18] to the east of the Imperial City. It was based on the old home of Gao Shilian, Taizong's adoptive father. Later enlarged to a much greater size, it was dotted with rocky hills, rivulets, and ponds. It had an imposing three-story belvedere as a dominant structure in the neighborhood with a commanding view of the cityscape of Chang'an.

However, what set Princess Changning apart from her more famous sister was her lack of interest in politics.

Notes

[1] Wuzhile 烏質勒.

[2] Suoge 娑葛.

[3] Shuofang 朔方.

[4] *San shouxiangcheng* 三受降城 (three towns where to receive surrender).

[5] Fuyun Shrine 拂雲祠.

[6] Beautiful Visage (*zhaorong* 昭容): one of the Nine Consorts, next in rank only to the empress.

[7] Xiuwen guan 修文館.

[8] There are twenty-four Solar Terms in the Chinese calendar. These eight are considered the most important.

[9] The Twelve Chronograms (*shi'er chen* 十二辰) are the twelve celestial areas from east to west along the zodiac and the celestial equator.

[10] The Eight Seats were the two vice premiers and presidents of the Six Boards.

[11] The Nine Chamberlains were the leaders of the Nine Courts.

[12] *Chi* 敕.

[13] Chengguo furen 郕國夫人.

[14] The Kaishan Nunnery 開善尼寺.

[15] A typical Chang'an ward was divided into four quadrants by two main streets. According to the sources, Anle's residence was north of the nunnery in the southeast corner of Jincheng Ward 金城坊. See *Tang liangjing chengfang kao* 4.116.

[16] *Xin Tang shu* 96.

[17] Lake Dingkun 定昆湖: see *Zizhi tongjian* 209.6623–34.

[18] Chongren Ward 崇仁坊: see *Tang liangjing chengfang kao* 3.54.

13. Türgesh (708)

TROUBLE FLARED UP again on the western frontier. A Türgesh civil war broke out between General Quechuo Ashina Zhongjie[1] and Suoge who had succeeded his father Wuzhile. Before long General Quechuo Zhongjie was trounced and submitted to the Tang. On Guo Yuanzhen's recommendation, he was appointed to a high post. As he was on his way to Chang'an to take up office, he crossed paths with a Tang general, who persuaded him to adopt a different plan, whereby he would stay in the west and use borrowed troops from Tubo to retake Türgesh.

But General Guo Yuanzhen found the plan troubling. It would favor Tubo and endanger the Four Garrisons then still in Tang hands. Guo grew suspicious when he learned that Zong Chuke and Ji Chu'ne, two top chief ministers, who previously had had no particular opinion on the matter, now were strong backers of the plan.

A Türgesh emissary was visiting Chang'an with a tribute of horses at that time. The moment he got wind of Quechuo Zhongjie's plan, he cut short his visit and returned.

Upon learning of the plan from the emissary, Suoge declared himself khan with open hostility towards the Tang in the eleventh month of 708. His troops then intercepted a Tang mission sent by Zhong Chuke, killing the emissary and capturing Quechuo Zhongjie who came to meet him. Suoge then launched a multi-pronged attack on the Four Garrisons. After sacking Qiuci[2] and blocking all roads to the Anxi Protectorate, he sent a letter to Guo Yuanzhen, in which he expressed his desire for a peaceful settlement while laying the blame squarely on Zong Chuke, who, he insisted, was on the take from Quechuo Zhongjie. Guo Yuanzhen forwarded the letter along with his own comments to the court.

Acting on Guo Yuanzhen's advice, the emperor, over Zong Chuke's strong opposition, pardoned Suoge and created him the khan of the Fourteen Clans. A dangerous conflict with the Türgesh was avoided. Once again peace reigned in the Western Regions.

Notes

[1] Quechuo Ashina Zhongjie 闕啜阿史那忠節.
[2] Qiuci 龜茲: oasis state in Kucha, Xinjiang.

14. Zhongzong (709–710)

The Arab general Qutayba ibn Muslim sacked Bukhara and Samarkand (in Uzbekistan) for the Umayyad Caliphate. Various states in the Western Regions appealed to China for assistance (709).
In Japan, the Asuka period came to an end (710), followed by the Nara period when Heijō-kyō (Nara) was made the capital.

AFTER HER HUSBAND Wu Chongxun's murder, Princess Anle sank into a funk she could not get out of for weeks until Wu Yanxiu walked into her life. Anle found it hard to resist his handsome looks. The fact that he could dance the vigorous Whirling Dance[1] and speak the Turkic language like a native added to his appeal.

Having shared her life with him for three months, she asked her father emperor's approval for marriage. It was an audacious move, widely frowned upon, because all marriages were arranged with the help of go-betweens in accord with proper ritual. But to her pleasant surprise, the emperor said, "You have Daddy's blessing."

When the wedding took place on January 6, 709, it was a most spectacular event in Chang'an. The bride rode in the ceremonial carriage loaned from the empress that, under the escort of a long procession, went from the palace to her residence in Jincheng Ward in the northwest section of the city. Both the emperor and the empress mounted the Imperial City's Anfu Gate[2] to view the spectacle. Censor-in-Chief and Chief Administrator of Yongzhou[3] Dou Huaizhen himself served as the master of ceremonies, and half a dozen academicians as the bridegroom's best men. Prince Li Dan, the emperor's dear brother, joined a crowd that "waylaid" the bridal carriage, whooping and hollering. In a gesture of generosity, the princess loaded the waylayers with money, wine, and food, in return for their permission to proceed.

Chang'an residents turned out of their homes in droves to enjoy the festive ambience as the richest among them displayed their generosity by donating vast quantities of money and silk. The entire city was *en fête*.[4]

On the following morning, a grand ceremony was held at the Taiji Basilica in the Palace City. After the stunningly beautiful princess, wearing a cape made of green feathers, emerged from behind the purple stage curtains, she kowtowed twice to the Son of Heaven, and turned around to make a deep bow to the officials and officers, who returned the obeisance.

The sudden advent of Princess Taiping and her husband Wu Youji stole the show as they whirled to the front of the emperor to wish His Majesty longevity.

An ecstatic emperor showered the officials and officers present with overgenerous gifts—hundreds of thousands of bolts of silk, official ranks, and prestige titles. The emperor then proceeded to the Chengtian Gate[5] and mounted the gatetower. From there he announced a general amnesty and a three-day food-and-wine fest as a gift from the throne to the people.

About one and a half months later, on the night of the New Year's Eve (February 13, 709), the emperor, still in a festive mood, gathered an exclusive group of people—the leaders of the Secretariat and Chancellery, academicians, princes, princesses and their husbands, and a few others—to spend the night in the Inner Area of the palace while waiting for the arrival of the New Year. A drinking banquet was held on the spacious front terrace of the Liangyi Basilica, lit up with firebrands, as colorfully dressed court musicians played tunes punctuated with exotic Central Asian rhythms and melodies.

After the party had gone on for a while and everybody was a bit tipsy, the emperor rose to address Censor-in-Chief Dou Huaizhen, "For far too long you have been without a wife. I won't allow it anymore. You know what? On this New Year's Eve, I've found a woman for you! I will see to it that a proper wedding ceremony takes place, right now!"

Completely taken by surprise, Dou Huaizhen responded with a profusion of thanks.

A few moments later, a group of eunuch officers entered the terrace from the west, holding in their hands lanterns, screens, and two large round fans made of silk sewn together with golden threads. Behind the fans walked a tiny figure in ceremonial attire, her hair fastened with floral hairpins in silver. At the emperor's request, she took her seat behind the fans opposite Dou Huaizhen, who was asked to recite a poem on "pulling back the fan."

Abruptly, the eunuchs took the fans away, and the woman removed the hairpins and shed her ceremonial attire. It took the distinguished guests a few moments, by the lantern light, to recognize that the bride-to-be was Empress Wei's old nanny, a barbarian bondwoman. A chorus of raucous laughter erupted. Thereupon, the emperor issued an edict to confer the title the "state mistress of Ju"[6] upon the woman and gave her away in marriage to Dou Huaizhen.

Well, to some she might look like an old hag who had long passed her prime, but Dong greeted her with open arms. It was a distinguished honor to have her as his spouse, because she was related to the empress and gifted by the emperor.[7]

***

Since his accession, the emperor and the court had been guarded by multiple layers of military and security forces. Twelve of the Sixteen Guards under the command of the Southern Command[8] were responsible for the defense of the capital, the Capital Prefecture, and strategic points in surrounding areas and beyond. They constituted the *fubing* (Garrison Militia) forces. The remaining four of the Sixteen Guards were non-*fubing* units that were responsible for guarding the person of the emperor and various gates of the city.

Parallel to these Sixteen Guards were the Left and Right Yulin (Forest of Plumes) Armies,[9] which were stationed at the Xuanwu Gate of the Taiji Palace and near the Daming Palace in the Forbidden Park under the command of the Northern Command.[10] The Yulin Armies were the emperor's Praetorian Guard units directly responsible for the security of the palaces.

With such a strong military presence in and around the palace and the city of Chang'an and with highly restrictive rules governing His Majesty's movement, the emperor felt overprotected. He often looked back on the old days with nostalgia when he was just an ordinary prince living in the residential wards or the provinces. He sometimes felt the urge to have a taste of the everyday life of Chang'an but was frustrated by his inability to do so.

Then a novel idea got into his head that would allow him to have some real fun without breaking the security protocols. On March 17, 709, on the emperor's orders, hundreds of palace maids set up a "bazaar" with dozens of stalls north of the Xuanwu Gate in the Forbidden Park. They would serve as vendors while top court officials would, dressed in commoners' garbs, play the role of traveling merchants. Between the palace maids and the court officials, mock business transactions were carried out as they bickered and haggled over prices.

The emperor and the empress came down from their high horses to mix in with the crowd and enjoy the flavor of an urban marketplace. Accompanied by favorite courtiers, the Imperial Couple also watched with great joy palace maids play games of tug of war.

At the end of the day, when the emperor was about to return to the Palace City, he said to his wife, "I have never had so much fun for a long, long time."

Immediately thereafter, well-meaning censors and remonstrators flooded the court with protests on what had happened north of the Xuanwu Gate under the aegis of the fun-loving emperor. They argued that the barrier between high and low, royal and common, government and trade had been broken in violation of the sacred teachings of the ancients.

The emperor responded to the remonstrances with a sour smile. When a high court official asked if His Majesty would do it again, he replied, "It may be bad form, but my having a bit of fun is not their doggone business." He certainly did not want to issue a self-blaming edict as some of his predecessors had done. But nor did he want to blame the protestors for embarrassing him. He just wanted to do nothing until it blew over.

About the same time, a high-profiled case of abduction got his attention. It involved bondservants who belonged to the households of Princess Anle and Princess Changning. They had carried off underaged sons and daughters of civilian residents and forced them into bondage.

An attendant censor threw the bondservants into jail. The pampered princesses complained. The emperor interceded for them and had the offenders sent back to their masters, much to the chagrin of the censor.

"Your Majesty encourages bondservants to abduct law-abiding residents," the censor protested. "How can that be in accord with justice?"

The emperor accepted the moral reproach with equanimity, and said, "Certainly, it is not the right thing to do, but it involves two of my daughters after all." He took no further action.

Soon the emperor was confronted with something much more serious: a case of treason. At the time of the Türgesh civil war, the Tang had suffered heavy losses after throwing their support behind the rebel general Quechuo Zhongjie. Although Suoge Khan had later made peace with the Tang, the question of what the Tang high command had done wrong had never gone away. Later, intelligence from Türgesh revealed that Zong Chuke and Ji Chu'ne, two decision-making chief ministers, had accepted bribes from Quechuo Zhongjie;

and that seemed to explain why they had sided with him despite Guo Yuanzhen's strong objection.

At a court session, Zong Chuke shrieked and screamed in protest when an investigative censor brought a charge against him. But after the motion to impeach him was announced, Zong went quiet and, as was required by tradition, walked out of the basilica, with his back hunched and his head down, to the Audience Hall, where he would stand still for hours as a punishment.

The emperor pulled the plug on the investigation and took it upon himself to mediate between the censor and the chief minister. At his request, the two attended a ceremony to become sworn brothers. That moment gave rise to a new sobriquet, the "Peace-Maker Emperor."

Zong Chuke, of course, was not an ordinary career bureaucrat, but a protégé of Empress Wei. He was also closely related to the Wus through his mother, who was a cousin of Tianhou.

***

To counter the growing influence of Princess Taiping at court, Princess Anle and her mother recruited their own gang of high-ranking partisans, particularly Wu Sansi's former advisers Cui Shi and Zheng Yin and Empress Wei's cousin Wei Wen. All three were now promoted to de facto chief ministers.

Cui Shi and Zheng Yin had the additional duty to supervise the selection of officials. It could be a lucrative job because it afforded one plenty of opportunity to fatten one's pocket on the side.

Once when a candidate failed to get an appointment he had

been promised, he came to Cui Shi's office to complain, "One of your relatives did not to keep his promise after he took money from me."

"What relative? It is an outrage!" responded Cui Shi in anger. Apparently, he had nothing to do with it. "I can have you clubbed to death!"

"Please don't," the man pleaded. "But I have the proof. The man I was talking about is Cui Yi. Isn't he your relative?"

Cui Shi did not answer, his face turning red, because Cui Yi was his father, a middle-ranking bureaucrat in charge of recruiting young officials.

"Oh well," the man continued, "I have put everything down in this letter of complaint. I will be grateful if you will look into it." He placed a roll of paper on the table and took leave.

The next day Cui Shi arranged to have the man appointed to the post he had requested.

But the case had attracted the attention of two censors. After a bit of digging, they uncovered evidence that not only his father but Cui Shi himself and his colleague Zheng Yin had taken bribes and routinely favored candidates with money or powerful family background. After years of malpractice, things had gotten so bad that there were far more recruits for office than there were vacancies.

An investigation followed. Cui Shi and Zheng Yin expected the empress to come to their rescue, but she did not. The emperor, for his part, saw no reason to let them off the hook, and the two chief ministers went to jail.

The investigative censor assigned to try the case soon suggested decapitation as their punishment, based on the *Tang Code*. It was then that Princess Anle stepped in and, after some arm-twisting, managed to save their necks. In the end, the two offenders were only punished with demotion to provincial posts: Cui Shi as prefect, and Zheng Yin as assistant prefect. It went without saying that both were no longer chief ministers.

***

In 709, a famine had hit Guanzhong hard. As the year wore on, up to 80 to 90 percent of the oxen in the possession of farming households perished due to poor weather. To feed the starving masses, massive quantities of grain were shipped to Guanzhong from Tang Shandong, the Yangzi River valley, and the Huai River valley. Judging from the average grain price (jumping from 1-5 cash to 100 cash per *dou* [peck]), the situation was not desperate. But it exposed a major disadvantage of Guanzhong: it was ill-equipped to cope with the explosive population growth it had experienced in half a century.

A growing number of court officials now favored moving the court to the Eastern Capital Luoyang to tide over this difficult period. While the emperor remained undecided, Empress Wei, a native of Guanzhong,[11] showed no intention of leaving.

At the request of the empress, Peng Junqing,[12] a ghost-seer of formidable reputation, came to the palace on a special visit. After he conducted a survey of the grounds, based on a mixture of yin-yang and Five Phases theory, geomancy, and astrology, he reported to the emperor, "Moving east this year is not auspicious." It was then that the emperor decided to stay.

When some official raised the issue again the emperor responded, "Heck! What do you want people to call me? The 'Food-Chasing Son of

Heaven?' " That finally put the debate to rest. But little did the emperor know, he would never see Luoyang again.

***

At length, some good news arrived from the frontier areas.

First, Türgesh's Suoge sent an emissary out of the blue, offering submission to the authority of the Tang. The elated emperor thereupon granted Suoge another khan title.

Then, the top court leader Shang Zanchuo[13] of Tubo arrived with a delegation of 1,000-plus men to ask for the hand of a Tang princess on behalf of the zanpu Chide Zuzan.[14] At a grand banquet held in the "football" field of the Forbidden Park to entertain Shang and his entourage, the emperor announced the princess of Jincheng[15] as the *heqin* bride. A granddaughter of Prince Zhanghuai (Li Xián), she had been brought up by the emperor in the palace. She would set off early the following year, under the escort of a general-in-chief. It was hoped that her marriage with the zanpu would bring about an era of peace in the annals of Tubo-Tang relations, just as what the marriage of Princess Wencheng[16] had done.

***

After a mild winter, the fear of famine was largely forgotten. By the early spring of 710, everything in Chang'an seemed to have returned to normal.

On the eve of the Lantern Festival (on the fifteenth of the first month), the entire city was lit up by lanterns at night. During a three-day period, the strictly enforced curfew in the wards and markets and on the city streets was lifted. Residents were free to roam after dark from ward to ward and between wards and markets. They would stop in courtyards where lanterns in different colors shaped like frogs, cats, dogs, tigers, lions, and deer were on display. They would enjoy the spectacle while attempting to crack the poetic riddles written on the lanterns or on paper-ribbons hanging from them.

The lanterns in the Palace City were the brightest and the most magnificent. But they were not good enough to hold the attention of the emperor and the empress for long. After midnight, they put on makeup, garbed themselves as common city residents, and slipped into the residential neighborhoods, accompanied by security guards in plain clothes. They wanted to rub shoulders with ordinary Chang'an folks and savor the taste of freedom.

Thousands of palace maids took the opportunity to disappear into the wards and markets. Many failed to return to work the following morning. But this alarmed nobody. It had been the emperor's intention to let them go free so that they would get reunited with their families or married.

In April, the emperor visited the Pear Garden inside the Forbidden Park to the north of Chang'an. The Pear Garden was not only famous for its mouth-watering fruit, but also for its training ground for court performers. But the purpose of this visit was neither to taste fresh pears or to enjoy stage performances by the actors and actresses, but to watch officials of Rank-3 and above, the cream of the court bureaucracy, play "football" and tugs-of-war. It was most amusing to see aging curmudgeons like Tang Xiujing and Wei Juyuan trip and fall minutes into the first game and have a hard time getting back to their feet. The spectators, despite their compassion for the old, held their sides with laughter.

In early May, the emperor ventured further afield into the Fragrant Grove Garden[17] of the Forbidden Park, where large, purple, and red cherries hung in luscious clusters on trees. On the emperor's orders, the leading mandarins—the chief ministers, Board presidents, and other top leaders—shed their ritual attire, pulled on commoners' garments, and threw all etiquette out the window as they picked cherries on horseback. This was his way of building bonds with his subordinates or enhancing camaraderie among them. It was certainly more fun than sitting in a stuffy basilica as sovereign and subjects.

***

By Tang standards, Empress Wei had a rather loose attitude towards sex. Although Tang China was far from being the strait-laced society Song China was to become, Empress Wei's behavior—engaging in sexual relations with multiple partners—had given rise to much condemnation. To some extent, one could explain her lack of moral constraints by the unique position she found herself in. As consort of a Son of Heaven who would pander to her every whim, she came close to becoming the most powerful person in the world. Moreover, she patterned herself after Tianhou, who reduced perfectly functional men to gigolos.

After her coronation, Empress Wei had surrounded herself with men of power. Some of them like Zong Chuke appeared by her side so often that people became convinced that an indecent relationship existed between them.

At her request, Wu Yanxiu attended on her on a regular basis. Soon this Turkic-speaking handsome man became her sex partner. After he started shacking up with her daughter, Princess Anle, and eventually married her, he continued his liaison with the empress. And the three of them lived in a kind of ménage-à-trois arrangement.

Empress Wei also had other lovers. Two recent ones were Mounted Regular Attendant Ma Qinke and Vice Chamberlain for Royal Food Service Yang Jun.[18] Neither was aristocratic by birth. But they had something else to offer apart from their looks and body. The former possessed great medical skills; and the latter was a master of culinary arts.

The grand ambition of the empress, however, did not stop at enjoying male company and indulging in sexual pleasure. Urged on by her daughter Anle, she wanted to follow the example of Tianhou to rule all under Heaven in her own right. As the emperor continued to neglect government and engage in fun-seeking activities, she was getting closer to realizing her dream.

Every now and then, there appeared a whisper about her misbehavior. But each time the emperor ignored it, committed as he was to the belief that it was Empress Wei who gave him a second life.

However, lately, an annoying new trend began to emerge. Memorials critical of her became increasingly audacious. One from Dingzhou[19] predicted in unequivocal language that Empress Wei and Zong Chuke would start a rebellion against the throne. The empress had the memorialist arrested and clubbed to death. The emperor said nothing.

In June, a low-ranking official called Yan Qinrong[20] submitted a memorial through a back channel that gave a stark warning against her. Contrary to his usual hands-off approach, the emperor called him in for questioning. Yan Qinrong stuck to his claim, insisting, "Empress Wei practices promiscuous sex and interferes in court politics. She has formed a sinister clique with Zong Chuke, Princess Anle, and Wu Yanxiu that threatens the very existence of the country." He went on to cite a whole range of evidence to back up his argument. The emperor, instead of rising in anger to defend her honor, sat motionless in his chair and listened.

The audience was over, Yan Qinrong took his leave of the emperor, and was escorted all the way to the entrance to the basilica. He stepped through the heavy front door and walked across the spacious granite terrace alone. When he was descending the steps, he heard the sound of footfall and turned his head. Two musclemen rushed at him and pushed him off his feet. One of them held him under a chokehold and wrung his neck.

"Hurry!" Zong Chuke shouted under his breath from above, his head popping over the balustrade.

***

The emperor's face turned blue when he was told what had happened outside his basilica. As much as he wanted to start an investigation, he did not know how. He was surrounded by her men. Even his dear daughter, Princess Anle, had thrown in her lot with her mother. He then decided to turn to her sister Princess Taiping for help, ordering his most trusted eunuch officer to arrange a secret meeting with her.

For her part, the empress was alarmed by the emperor's apparent displeasure. She was worried about her love affairs being uncovered, her ambition for the throne exposed, and, above all, the murder itself.

On the morning of a piping-hot day, the emperor went into a special room in the Shenlong Basilica,[21] where the temperature was brought down by ice chunks hauled in from an underground ice cellar. At the early afternoon meal, his palace chef served a dozen or so vegetable and meat dishes along with a pita stuffed with lamb. After taking a few bites of the pita, the emperor seemed to choke on a piece of meat and started gasping. Two female attendants rushed over, one holding his back and the other bringing a gold cup of wine to his lips. The emperor, without taking a slip, struggled for air for a few moments before collapsing into the lap of the attendant. It was July 3, 710, one day before the meeting with Taiping was to take place.

At dusk, Empress Wei arrived at the scene. By then the emperor had already breathed his last. Her eyes glinting with nervousness, she assumed in haste the emergency decision-making power of the sovereign and issued a secret order to prevent, under pain of death, the news of the emperor's death from leaking out.

With Zong Chuke by her side, she summoned an urgent meeting of the chief ministers, at which she ordered the deployment of 50,000 additional *fubing* troops in the capital from neighboring areas and appointed members of the Wei clan to command them. One of them was put in charge of patrolling the Six Streets of Chang'an.[22] Three pro-empress men were appointed as de facto chief ministers, Cui Shi, recently recalled, among them.

As an extra precaution, the empress sent a troop of 500 men under General-in-Chief Xue Sijian[23] to Junzhou with the task of keeping a close watch on Prince Li Chongfu, the late emperor's eldest surviving son.

***

Following a previous arrangement, Princess Taiping was to write the Testamentary Edict. At her request, Shangguan Wan'er drafted the first version. It named Li Chongmao, the late emperor's youngest son, as crown prince; and gave the empress broad decision-making power while allowing Prince Li Dan to serve as chief adviser on policy issues.

Both Zong Chuke and Wei Wen disapproved of the last part. Zong argued, "For Prince Li Dan to assume the power of chief adviser is contrary to convention. Moreover, as a brother-in-law of the empress, he is not supposed to have close contact with her. There is no way for him to attend court meetings without violating ritual." Most chief ministers sided with him. In the end, the language that gave Li Dan substantive power was excised.

Notes

[1] *Huxuan wu* 胡旋舞: it originated in Sogdiana. See *Jiu Tang shu* 29, 高昌樂.

[2] The Anfu Gate 安福門 was the northern gate on the west side of the Imperial City.

[3] *Yongzhou zhangshi* 雍州長史: de facto leader of the capital prefecture where Chang'an was.

[4] *Jiu Tang shu* 187.

[5] The Chengtianmen 承天門: the southern main gate of the Palace City. Its gate tower also functioned as a major basilica.

[6] Juguo furen 莒國夫人.

[7] *Xin Tang shu* 122.

[8] The Southern Command (*nanya* 南衙) was located in the Imperial City.

[9] *Zuo you Yulin jun* 左右羽林軍.

[10] The Northern Command (*beiya* 北衙).

[11] According to *Zizhi tongjian* (209.6639), her ancestral home was in Duling 杜陵 (southeast of Xi'an, Shaanxi). Both *Xin Tang shu* (89, 中宗庶人韋氏) and *Jiu Tang shu* (51, 中宗韋庶人) have it in Wannian 萬年 (in Xi'an).

[12] Peng Junqing 彭君卿.

[13] Shang Zanchuo 尚贊咄.

[14] Chide Zuzan 赤德祖贊.

[15] Princess of Jincheng 金城公主.

[16] Princess Wencheng 文成公主 (623–680) was married off to the Zanpu Songzan Ganbu 松贊干布.

[17] Fanglin Garden 芳林園.

[18] *Sanqi changshi* 散騎常侍 Ma Qinke 馬秦客; *guanglu shaoqing* 光祿少卿 Yang Jun 楊均.

[19] Dingzhou 定州.

[20] Yan Qinrong 燕欽融.

[21] The Shenlong 神龍 (Divine Dragon) Basilica was a residential basilica inside the Taiji Palace of Chang'an. It was located to the east of the Ganlu Basilica. See *Tang liangjing chengfang kao* 1.5.

[22] The Six Streets were the three east-west streets that ran through the eastern and western city gates, and the three north-south streets south of the Imperial City that led to the three southern city gates. These streets were crucial to the security of the palace. See Zhang Yonglu 1990, 69.

[23] Xue Sijian 薛思簡.

15. Li Longji (710)

ON JULY 5, 710, the passing of the emperor (temple name: Zhongzong) was announced in the Taiji Basilica to the Hundred Officials. In accord with his Testamentary Edict, Prince Li Chongmao, a boy of sixteen *sui*, sitting in front of the late emperor's coffin on the dais, was crowned emperor; Prince Li Dan, his uncle, was granted the title of defender-in-chief, one of the Three Dukes; five members of the royal Li house were named first-tier princes; and the empress was named the sole regent.

For added security, the empress, already the only true power-holder at court with a firm control of the military, assigned her cousin

Wei Wen to assume ad hoc control of military affairs inside and outside the palace.

***

In the home of Li Dan in the southwest quadrant of Qinren Ward,[1] the prince and his four sons and Princess Taiping were having the first family gathering in the wake of Emperor Zhongzong's death and Li Chongmao's accession. All of them were dressed in mourning vestments of coarse hemp cloth. After three days of fasting, they were partaking of their first meal, consisting of millet porridge and devoid of meat and vegetable, as was dictated by ritual. In low voices, they reminisced about the late emperor and chatted about court politics.

After the gathering was over, the guests began to filter out of the mansion. Princess Taiping pulled Prince of Linzi Li Longji aside to have a private conversation.

"Uncle Li Xián's son Li Shouli was made an imperial prince," said Taiping. Aunt and nephew were sitting in a corner of the spacious banquet hall, now deserted. "So were your elder brother Li Chengqi, and your younger brothers Li Fan and Li Ye."

"So?"

"You are the only one stuck with the title of a 'commandery prince.' "[2]

"Yes, Auntie, I am aware of that," said the third son of Li Dan at twenty-six *sui*. "I am fine with it."

"Not as vice prefect of Luzhou,"[3] asserted Taiping, shaking her head. "But do you know why?"

"Why?" Li Longji did not seem to show much interest.

Taiping leaned over and said under her breath, "They are afraid of you."

"The Weis are?"

"And their cronies."

"Because?"

"Because you are the only one among my brother Li Dan's sons who has both courage and intelligence."

"So?"

"Well, you must have noticed that, to keep your cousin Li Chongfu under surveillance, Empress Wei and Zong Chuke dispatched a force of 500 to the south. We all know that he is not half as bright as you. Still, they consider him a threat. And I have reason to believe that, sooner or later, they will go after you." She paused to wait for a response.

Li Longji remained quiet as a serious look settled on his face. Looking his auntie in the eye, he asked,

"Is there a way out?"

"Yes. But you have to fight to survive."

"How? Wei Wen has assumed command of all the troops inside and outside the palace."

"The Yulin Armies are the key. Aren't some of your buddies Yulin officers?"

"Yes, they belong to the elite Wanqi[4] Division."

"I know for a fact that, after the Weis took charge, they rode roughshod over the riders, using corporal punishment to put them in their place. Everybody hates those upstarts. And I don't think it is farfetched to say that these Wanqi troops are willing to put their lives on the line for the Li house. And . . . are you willing to take the lead?"

Li Longji mulled over his options for a few moments, then said, "I cannot, Auntie. I really cannot do it alone."

"No, no, you won't be alone. I'll give you all the help you need. We, the Lis, are all in this together. Somebody has to step up to the plate, Longji. So far as I know, you are the only one who can do it."

Li Longji paused, his eyes fixed on his aunt's face, then said in a somber tone, "I will do it then."

"Excellent!" the princess exclaimed. "I'll make sure you get in touch with the right people."

***

"I just consulted the grand astrologer," said Zong Chuke at a secret meeting of Empress Wei's inner circle in her home. "This is what he told me: 'Last night, Saturn was shadowed by the Moon. I conducted a divination and the results are: a major figure will die and all under Heaven will lose their sovereign. Regime change will follow.' This is a warning that a world-shaking event will take place soon."

Empress Wei, a worried look on her face, said to Wei Wen, "Cousin Wen, are you prepared for it?"

"Yes, Your Majesty," Wei answered. "We are well positioned to deal with any untoward event. Our men are now in control of the troops at the Southern Office, the city gates, and the palace."

"But," Wu Yanxiu said, "all this may change in a flash."

"I agree," Princess Anle said. "The Emperor Li Chongmao is just a young teenager. We can write him off. But his aunt Taiping is different. She wanted her brother Prince Li Dan to share power as regent. Thank heavens, it did not happen. But we still have to deal with the fact that she hates my guts. The first thing we must do is remove her."

"I think so too," Wu Yanxiu said. "Prince Li Dan seems nice though."

"But his third son, Li Longji," Zong Chuke said, "will probably make trouble."

"Did he leave Chang'an after the funeral?" Empress Wei asked.

"No," Anle said, "he won't leave until all the mourning activities are over."

"What do you suggest?" asked Empress Wei, turning to Zong Chuke.

"In my opinion," Zong said, "you the empress should follow Tianhou's precedent, start another revolution, depose that apology for a sovereign, and rule in your own name."

"I am all in favor," Princess Anle said. "But Taiping and Li Longji stand in the way."

"On the third seventh day after the emperor's passing," Zong Chuke said, "members of the Li house will gather at his tomb for a sacrificial ceremony. Both Taiping and Longji are required to be there by ritual. When they are on their way back after the event, our men can lie in wait on the road and . . ."

"Excellent!" Empress Wei shouted with relief.

***

Cui Riyong, a *jinshi*-degree holder, had been promoted by Zong Chuke to vice president of the Board of War not long before and was now one of a small coterie of trusted followers of Empress Wei privy to Zong Chuke's plan. But he had doubt about the empress gang's control of the military and was troubled by the Wanqi Division's lack of loyalty. And he worried that their animus towards the Weis might spell disaster if the two sides came to blows.

Then from a secret source he received intelligence that a countermove by Prince Li Longji backed by Princess Taiping was already in the works. After many a sleepless night, he decided to switch sides, if only to ease his anxiety. Through the help of a monk friend, he had a secret meeting with Li, and revealed to him the empress gang's scheme.

***

Early the next morning, Li Longji contacted his source at court with access to the astrological records. The moment the source confirmed the accuracy of Cui's account, he felt a chill down his spine as he realized that he was caught in a do-or-die moment and had no alternative but to plunge into action.

The next day was July 21, three days before the scheduled visit by the royal family to the late emperor's tomb. In the late afternoon, Li Longji, disguised as a Yulin officer, was smuggled into the Forbidden Park, escorted by his buddy County Defender Liu Youqiu. They met in secret with Inspector-General of the Royal Parks Zhong Shaojing[5] and Intrepid Commandants of the Wanqi Division Ge Fushun and Li Xianfu.[6] Except for Liu Youqiu, who was left outside to keep watch, all entered Zhong's office in a small bungalow.

Li Longji addressed the gang, "Tonight, we will get rid of the Weis. Do you have any questions?"

Ge Fushun, a tall and gaunt officer in his forties, answered, "Yes, I have got a question about Prince Li Dan: Should we tell him of our plan?"

Li Longji said, "No, we shouldn't. Let me explain. If we tell him now but fail to get his endorsement, our plan will be ruined. If we tell him now and get his endorsement, we will expose him to too much danger. On the other hand, if we pull it off, we can chalk it up to him. If we fail, our action will have nothing to do with him. Do you understand?"

Both commandants nodded their heads.

Sitting down on wooden benches around a rough-hewn table, they drank rice wine provided by Zhong Shaojing as they waited for the signal for action. Every now and then, Li Longji would get off his seat to pace up and down the room or push the door open and stick out his head to check what was going on outside. There was nothing but near complete darkness.

***

On the *zi* double-hour[7] of the night, Liu Youqiu saw in the distance the flicker of a faint watchfire from an embrasure of the gatetower of the Anlimen.[8] All of a sudden, the sky was lit up with meteors raining down like snowflakes.

Liu banged the door open and shouted in nervousness, "Time to go!"

Sword in hand, Ge Fushun, with a band of elite Wanqi troops, stole into the Yulin Army Barracks on foot. Guided by officers they had suborned they made straight for the campaign tents of Wei Rui, Wei Bo, and Gao Song,[9] catching the three top commanding officers in their sleep and lopping off their heads.

In the drilling field lit up by firebrands, Ge Fushun gathered the Wanqi troops and addressed them:

> *Now we know that Empress Wei murdered the emperor with poison prepared by her lover Ma Qinke. By that very act, she has turned into an arch-traitor, hated by both men and gods. Tonight, we are taking action against her and the other treacherous Weis and their close supporters. We will eliminate anyone in their camp taller than a horsewhip. We will give no quarter to those who dare offer resistance and punish them with extirpation of their Three Clans. If we win, I am sure we will, we will crown Prince Li Dan as emperor.*

The crowd cheered.

Under Ge Fushun's command, the Yulin troops moved south and soon afterwards met up with Li Longji and his men consisting of a small detachment of the anti-Wei troops and 200-plus "irregulars"—Zhong Shaojing's craftsmen armed with axes, hammers, and handsaws.

A Yulin officer rode up to the prince, a rattan pannier hanging behind his saddle. He vaulted off his horse and threw the lid open to reveal three blood-stained human heads and hefted them one by one for the prince to have a close look. Despite their distorted features that registered the agony of death, Li Longji could still recognize them under the light of a firebrand as belonging to the three commanding officers of the Yulin Army. Leaning back on his saddle, he drew out his sword to hold over his head and gave out his order in a strident voice: "To the palace!"

Generals Ge Fushun and Li Xianfu marched the bulk of the rebel troops east as far as the east part of the Forbidden Park. Turning south, they poured into the northeast corner of the Taiji Palace through the Anli Gate.

The rebel troops then branched out into two detachments to fall on the Xuande and the Baishou Gates[10] and other inner gates, storming them all. The two bands then merged into one at the Lingyan Pavilion,[11] the Tang hall of fame, and continued to push forward.[12]

Meanwhile under Li Longji's command, a band of Yulin troops and Zhong Shaojing's craftsmen attacked and stormed the heavily guarded Xuanwu Gate and broke into the central section of the palace.

***

In the Taiji Basilica, the security troops under the Southern Office guarding the body of the late emperor were alerted by the commotion from the north and northeast. They put on their armor and picked up their weapons—spears, broadswords, and bows and arrows, only to be told to stay put as their generals negotiated with Li Longji's men. After a deal was struck moments later, the troops on duty, on orders from their commandant, lay down their arms as the rebels took over the iconic building without a single casualty.

Upon fighting their way into the residential palace of the empress, the advance party of the rebels checked every nook and cranny, looking for the empress, but failed to find her.

By then she had given them the slip. Wearing a maid's clothing, she had fled north and sneaked into the Forbidden Park under the cover of darkness. She then turned west and made her way to the Feiqi

(Flying Cavaliers) Barracks. She was probably hoping to organize a counterattack with troops loyal to the Weis. But it would not happen. She was soon recognized and taken into custody.

A high-ranking rebel officer in charge trotted over. On his orders, the soldiers tied the empress up. With a single stroke of his sword, the officer swept off her head. Later he told a subordinate that he had just carried out the order of "giving no quarter."

Princess Anle was in her sleeping gown doing makeup in front of a bronze mirror when the rebel troops barged into the courtyard of her basilica. By the time she changed into her robes, two officers had broken into her bedchamber, swords drawn. Just as she started to scream in terror, one officer dashed forward and lopped off her head.

Her husband Wu Yanxiu had fled on foot, and made it as far as the Suzhang Gate to the west of the Liangyi Basilica before he met his death at the hands of a group of rebel soldiers.

***

When the pale light of dawn began to creep into the palace grounds, the turmoil was practically over. The rebels had taken over the palace and the city.

Shangguan Wan'er led a group of palace maids, holding lit candles to greet the new leaders. The officer who received her was none other than Liu Youqiu, Li Longji's comrade-in-arms. On Li's orders, Liu took Shangguan into custody. With calmness, she produced the draft copy of the Testamentary Edict on silk.

Liu thereupon went to see Li himself, the silk document in hand. "She was not a supporter of Empress Wei after all," he said.

"What do you mean?" Li Longji asked.

"Shangguan should be spared. Just look at the imperial edict she drafted for Taiping. It speaks for itself."

Without a word Li Longji cast a glance at the piece of silk and fell to thinking about his mother who had vanished without a trace after being accused by Tuan'er; his family who had led a precarious existence following his father's dethronement; and many of his cousins, uncles, and aunts who had perished under Tianhou's Reign of Terror at a time when Shangguan Wan'er was her favorite courtier and confidante. With Tianhou's death, Shangguan had become the lover and accomplice of Wu Sansi, who had ridden roughshod over the Lis; and helped cement the alliance between the Wus and the Weis that was behind the killing of the Five Princes. Yes, she did oppose Anle's bid for heirship and perhaps her mother's bid for the throne, but how could she absolve herself of all these abovementioned crimes?

Li Longji turned to his friend and said, his eyes snapping, "I'm sorry, Youqiu, but she has to pay."

The next morning at dawn, Shangguan Wan'er, her face pallid and her hair tousled, was dragged to a flagpole outside the state prison. Under a banner fluttering in the wind, this once-powerful beauty and literary talent, was trussed up, blind-folded, and beheaded.

***

Acting on Princess Taiping's proposal, the boy emperor Li Chongmao abdicated. Prince Li Dan was then called upon to take the throne, but he turned it down, much to the surprise of the royals. He insisted that all he wanted was live out the rest of his life in peace and contentment. It took two of his sons Li Chengqi and Li Longji making an arduous argument about his succession being in accord with the will of the people to cause him to come around and agree to reign as emperor one more time.

The officials and officers came out in droves to show their support for the Second Restoration. None of them would acknowledge having been loyal followers of the late empress and her daughter. Instead, they rushed to sever their ties with them. Take Dou Huaizhen for example. So determined was he to make a clean break with the empress that he cut off the head of his wife, the empress's former nanny, and presented it to the court.

It was obvious that the emperor Li Dan had no trouble winning back the allegiance of the court, but he was soon faced with the thorny issue of crown prince selection. He could not make up his mind between Li Chengqi and Li Longji. Li Chengqi, being the oldest, had the strongest claim to heirship in terms of primogeniture. But Li Longji would be the best choice in terms of merit and personal ability. To say nothing of the vital role he had played in toppling the Weis.

While Li Longji kept quiet, his brother Chengqi spoke out, "When the country is at peace, we may indeed choose an heir based on primogeniture. When the country is at risk, we *must* select an heir by merit. Now the country is still in danger, and I insist that Your Majesty appoint my younger brother as crown prince."

For the emperor, that statement clinched the matter. He forthwith made the appointment as recommended. To his astonishment, Li Longji asked for permission to decline the honor. The emperor had no choice but to put his foot down. With Princess Taiping's backing, he issued an edict to reject the request. Thus, Li Longji became the new crown prince with great reluctance.

However, despite what is documented in the sources, there was a centuries-old practice in which a successor to the throne, in the event of abdication by the reigning emperor, was expected to decline the offer three times before his accession, as had happened to Liu Bang, the founder of the Han dynasty, and Wang Mang, the founder of the Xin dynasty. But the Three Declinations were purely ceremonial.

By contrast, in the case of Li Dan, Li Chengqi, and Li Longji, the efforts to decline the throne or the crown prince's appointment seemed sincere. Li Dan had served as emperor before. That experience had not thrilled him at all. Li Chengqi, self-effacing by nature, was never tempted by the prospect of becoming heir or emperor. Li Longji, self-assured and ambitious, was not daunted by the emperor's job. But still, he wanted to pass up the opportunity in favor of his elder brother, with whom he enjoyed a trusting relationship.

Notes

1 Qinren Ward 親仁坊 was southwest of the Eastern Market. See *Tang liangjing chengfang kao* 3.60.

2 See *Xin Tang shu* 81.3591 (Li Shouli); *see also* "prince" in Glossary.

3 The vice prefect (*biejia* 別駕) ranked second in a prefectural leadership. Luzhou 潞州: prefecture with its seat in Changzhi, Shanxi.

4 Wanqi 萬騎 (Ten Thousand Riders).

5 The inspector-general of the royal parks (*yuan zongjian* 苑總監); Zhong Shaojing 鐘紹京.

6 Ge Fushun 葛福順 and Li Xianfu 李仙鳧 were courageous commandants (*guoyi* or *guoyi duwei* 果毅都尉), upper middle-ranking officers in a *fubing* garrison.

7 Traditionally, a day is divided into twelve time-units or double-hours paired with

the twelve Earthly Branches. The *zi* 子 double-hour starts at 11 PM and ends at 1 AM.

[8] The Anlimen 安禮門 (Anli Gate) was the northern gate of the Palace City east of the Xuanwu Gate.

[9] Wei Rui 韋璿, Wei Bo 韋播, Gao Song 高嵩.

[10] The Xuande Gate 玄德門 and Baishou Gate 白獸門: the precise location of these "inner" gates are unknown.

[11] The Lingyan Pavilion 淩煙閣.

[12] Based on the sources, fighting first started in the northeast corner of the Taiji Palace. The rebels must have entered the palace through the Anli Gate.

Conclusion

After the short-lived episode of ascendancy of the Wus and Weis was over, Tang rule was permanently restored.

By an imperial edict, the posthumous title of Empress Dowager Wu—Zetian the Great Sage Empress[1]—reverted to Tianhou (Heavenly Empress).

With that, we come to the end of Tianhou's story. And it is fitting now to reflect on her legacy.

There have been strong-willed women who have successfully challenged the patriarchal dominance of the political system before and after Tianhou's rise to power. But Tianhou is the only woman in history who actually toppled a powerful dynasty and set up her own for fifteen years.

She set the precedent for attending to state affairs behind a bamboo screen in a court of men before ruling in her own right as emperor.

Thanks to the tradition of male monopoly in politics and the male-centeredness of the education system, only men were appointed to posts in officialdom. Tianhou went out of her way to seek out female literary talents to fill official appointments. One of them, Shangguan Wan'er, served as a senior official to perform a chief minister's duties.

Tianhou tried to advance the cause of women by changing the rule governing the mourning period for the descendants of a deceased mother—extending it from one year to three. In the same vein, she introduced seven female ancestors as objects of worship in the Wu

[1] Zetian Dasheng Huanghou 則天大聖皇后.

Ancestral Temple on a par with their male counterparts. In both cases, in an unprecedented fashion, she placed men and women on the same footing.

Traditionally, it was a given that the emperor should have access to a large harem of consorts and concubines to maximize his chance of producing qualified male issue in order to continue the dynastic line. Tianhou stood it on its head by employing a troop of gigolos who were at the pleasure of the female sovereign.

While readers will not fail to notice Tianhou's cruel streak, they should bear in mind the fact that as a woman trying to rise to power in a man-dominated world, almost insurmountable odds were stacked against her. Reprehensible as it was, she had to be merciless to her rivals and challengers as she fought her way to the top. However, no amount of justification can explain away her brutality towards people who irked her.

Tianhou's political success inspired ambitious women such as Empress Wei and Princess Anle to follow in her footsteps. But their undertaking failed before it got off the ground. One can ascribe the failure to bad luck or poor timing, but perhaps more likely, to their lack of Tianhou's iron will to destroy everyone who stood in her way.

Glossary

- Key names are highlighted in **bold**.
- Pronunciation:

a = a as in f**a**ther

c = zz as in pi**zz**a

ch = ch as in **ch**ina

e or ê = olo as in c**olo**nel without the *r* sound (except after i, u, ü, y, or before i)

e (after i, y, u, ü, or before i) = e as in r**e**d. e.g.: Xue |shü**e**h|

en = en as in **en**d

eng = eng as in l**eng**th (approx.). e.g.: Cheng |ch**êng**|, but Chen |ch**en**|

er = er as in dinn**er** (Am.)

g = g as in **g**irl

i = ee as in d**ee**d (except after sibilants: c, ch, s, sh, z, zh)

i (after sibilants: c, ch, s, sh, z, zh) = the vowelized sound of the consonant. e.g.: Li Zhi |lee jih| ("jih" as in lo**dge**), Heichi |hei-chih| ("chih" not "chee")

j = g as in **g**ee

o = o as in l**o**t (Br.)

q = ch as in **ch**eese (approx.)

u = oo as in f**oo**d (except after j, q, x, y)

u (after j, q, x, y) = ü (Ger. u umlaut). e.g.: Tu**yu**hun |too-**yü**-hoon|

ü = ü (Ger. u umlaut)

x = ch as in i**ch** (Ger.), or *sh* as in **sh**eep (approx.). e.g.: **X**iao |shee'ao|.

y = y as in **y**es

z = ds as in wor**ds**. e.g.: **Z**ong Chuke |**dz**ong chu-kê|

zh = j, as in **J**oe (approx.)

An Jincang 安金藏 (fl. 693): craftsman.

Anle, Princess 安樂公主 |än-lê ~| (684–710): favorite daughter of Zhongzong (Li Zhe) and Empress Wei; married Wu Chongxun (to 707), Wu Yanxiu (to 710); joined Empress Wei in killing Zhongzong; killed by Li Longji (Xuanzong).

Anxi Protectorate (Anxi duhufu 安西都護府 |än-shee ~|): Anxi was a large area that extended from Xinjiang to the Aral Sea.

area command (*dudu fu* 都督府): regional military administration under an area commander (*dudu*) lower than a protectorate in an area that included multiple prefectures often in a border region.

area commander (*dudu* 都督): head of an area command.

Ashide Fengzhi 阿史德奉職 |ä-shih-dê fêng-jih|: Tujue chieftain.

Ashide Wenfu 阿史德溫傅 (–681): Tujue chieftain; defeated by Pei Xingjian; delivered by Ashina Funian to Tang; killed.

Ashina Daozhen 阿史那道真 |~ dao-jen| (fl. 670): Tujue, Tang general.

Ashina Duzhi 阿史那都支 |~ du-jih| (–679): Western Tujue khan of the Ten Tribes.

Ashina Funian 阿史那伏念 (–681): related to Xieli Khan; Tujue khan; defeated by Pei Xingjian; surrendered, bringing Ashide Wenfu as a captive; killed.

Ashina Gudulu 阿史那骨篤祿. *See* Gudulu.

Ashina Helu 阿史那賀魯 (Shaboluo Khan/Qaghan 沙缽羅可汗): Western Tujue leader.

Ashina Huseluo 阿史那斛瑟羅 |~ hu-sê-luo| (fl. 690s): Western Tujue khan.

Ashina Mochuo. *See* Mochuo.

Ashina Nishufu 阿史那泥熟匐 (–680): Tujue khan; killed.

Beautiful Lady (*meiren* 美人): imperial concubine with a rank higher than Talented Lady (*cairen* 才人), but lower than the Nine Concubines (*jiupin* 九嬪).

Bingzhou 并州 |bing-jo|: prefecture in Shanxi with its seat near Taiyuan.

Biographies of Women (*Lienü zhuan* 列女傳): ① by Liu Xiang 劉向 (W. Han). ② compiled during Tianhou's reign.

Biyong 辟雍 (Jade Disc Moat): ritual structure often combined with the Mingtang.

Board (*bu* 部): one of the six powerful central government agencies known as the Six Boards under the Department of State Affairs (*shangshu sheng* 尚書省).

Book of Changes; *Classic of Changes* (*Yijing* 易經): ancient divination manual with interpretations; a Confucian classic.

Book of the Han (*Hanshu* 漢書): history of the Western Han by Ban Gu 班固 (E. Han).

Book of the Later Han (*Hou Han shu* 後漢書): history of the Eastern Han by Fan Ye 范曄 (Liu Song).

Bronze Chest (*tonggui* 銅匭): installed under Empress Wu (Tianhou), it mainly functioned as an accusation letter box.

cash: a round bronze coin with a hole in the center, comparable to a cent, penny, kopeck, sou, etc. Nominally, a string of cash has 1,000 cash (coins).

catty (*jin* 斤): traditional weight measure, slightly less than 600 g (1.32 lb).

Cen Changqian 岑長倩 |tsen ~| (–691): senior official; killed.

censor (*yushi* 御史): powerful middle-ranking official in the Censorate responsible for the surveillance and impeachment of officials.

censor-in-chief (*yushi dafu* 御史大夫; *da sixian* 大司憲): head of the Censorate.

Censorate (*yushi tai* 御史台 |yü-shih-tai|; *suzheng tai* 肅政台): central government agency for the surveillance of officialdom.

Central Plain (Zhongyuan 中原): narrowly, it refers to present-day Henan. More broadly, it refers to the middle and lower valleys of the Yellow River including Henan, Hebei, Shandong, Shanxi, and Shaanxi.

Ceremonies and Rituals (*Yili* 儀禮): a Confucian classic on ritual transmitted in the early Western Han.

chamberlain (*qing* 卿): president of a third-tier central agency called "Court" (*si* 寺).

Chang'an 長安 |chāng-ān|: Western Capital of Tang China in Xi'an, Shaanxi; the largest city in Tang China and the world.

Changle, Grand Princess 常樂長公主 |chāng-lê ~| (–688): Taizong's sister; killed.

Changning, Princess 長寧公主 (fl. early 700s): daughter of Zhongzong and Empress Wei known for her extravagant taste.

Chen Zi'ang 陳子昂 |chen dzih-āng| (661–702): poet.

Cheng Wuting 程務挺 |chêng ~| (–684): top general; son of Cheng Mingzhen 程名振; Pei Xingjian's lieutenant; killed.

Cheng, Emperor 成帝 (51–7 BCE): Western Han emperor.

Cheng, King (Zhou) 周成王 (r. 1042–1020 BCE): second Zhou King.

Chengtang; 成湯; Tang; King Tang: founder of the Shang dynasty.

Chengtianmen 承天門; Chengtian Gate: southern main entrance to the Palace City of Chang'an.

chi 尺 (foot): length unit. In Tang times, one *chi* was approx. 0.31 m, or slightly longer than a foot.

Chidu Songzan 赤都松贊 |chih-du ~| (670–704; r. 676–704) (Qinu Xinong 器弩悉弄; Chidu Song 墀都松): Tubo zanpu (king); seized power from Lun Qinling.

chief minister (*xiang* 相): one of a small group of top court leaders; a de facto chief minister was someone who functioned as a chief minister without going through the official appointment procedure.

Chongren Ward 崇仁坊: residential ward in northeast Chang'an.

choronym (*junwang* 郡望): ancestral native place.

Chu Suiliang 褚遂良 |chu sui-lee'äng| (596–658): top official under Taizong and Gaozong, calligrapher; banished.

Circuit (*dao* 道): local administrative unit at the highest level. Cf. District (*dao* 道).

Classic on Framing (*Luozhi jing* 羅織經): book by Lai Junchen 來俊臣 and Wan Guojun 萬國俊 on how to extort confessions.

commandery (*jun* 郡): defunct local administrative unit equal to or smaller than a prefecture (*zhou*); in Tang and Wu Zhou, it was used as part of aristocratic titles: e.g., commandery prince (*junwang* 郡王), commandery duke (*jungong* 郡公), etc.

commissioner (*shi* 使): suffix to a high-ranking official usually with a specific ad hoc assignment at the center or in the provinces. Later in the Tang, a commissioner could be endowed with long-term substantive power as in the case of *jiedu shi* 節度使 (military commissioner).

Comprehensive Gazetteer (*Kuodi zhi* 括地志): book on administrative geography compiled by Li Tai 李泰.

Confucian Analects (*Lunyu* 論語): a Confucian classic on the words and deeds of Confucius and his disciples.

consort (*fei* 妃): ① one of the highest-ranking imperial concubines, second only to the empress. In the Tang system, there were four types of consorts: Noble Consort (*guifei* 貴妃), Pure Consort (*shufei* 淑妃), Virtuous Consort (*defei* 德妃), and Worthy Consort (*xianfei* 賢妃) — all of the first equivalency rank (*shi yipin* 視一品). (The character *shi* 視 (equivalent to) was usually prefixed to honorific titles.) *See*

Imperial Consort. ② the principal wife of a prince.

counselor of remonstrance (*zhengjian dafu* 正諫大夫): high-ranking official tasked to criticize court policy.

county (*xian* 縣): local administrative unit lower than a prefecture.

Court (*si* 寺): one of the Nine Courts, a third-tier central agency.

Cuan Baobi 爨寶璧 |tsuan ~| (–687): general; killed.

Cui Cha 崔詧 |tsui ~| (–689): senior official; suicide.

Cui Dunli 崔敦禮 |tsui ~| (596–656): senior official under Gaozong.

Cui Shenqing 崔神慶 |tsui shen-ching| (–705 or later): senior official; supporter of Zhang Yizhi; banished.

Cui Shi 崔湜 |tsui shih| (671–713): senior official; attached himself first to Wu Sansi, then to Princess Taiping; suicide.

Cui Xuanli 崔宣禮 |tsui ~| (fl. 692): senior official.

Cui Xuanwei 崔玄暐 |tsui ~| (639–706): senior official; took part in the 705 coup; one of the "Five Princes"; banished.

Cui Yixuan 崔義玄 |tsui ~| (586–656): senior official under Gaozong.

Cui Zhenshen 崔貞慎 |tsui ~| (fl. 703): official; Wei Yuanzhong's friend.

Cuiwei Palace 翠微宮 |tsui-wei ~|: suburban palace on the northern slopes of the Qinling Mountains south of Chang'an.

Daifang Prefecture (*zhou*) 帶方州: prefecture founded by Tang in north Korea after its conquest of Koguryŏ. It functioned more like a protectorate.

Daizhou 代州: prefecture with its seat in Daixian, north Shanxi.

Daming Palace 大明宮 |dä-ming ~|; Penglai Palace 蓬萊宮: palace in the northern suburbs of Chang'an.

Danfengmen 丹鳳門 (Danfeng Gate): main southern entrance to the Daming Palace.

Danyun 大雲 (Great Cloud): Buddhist monasteries in Luoyang and Chang'an.

Department of State Affairs (*shangshu sheng* 尚書省): the top executive branch of the government headed by two vice premiers (*puye* 僕射).

Di Renjie 狄仁傑 |dee ren-ji'eh|; State Elder (*guolao* 國老) (630–704, or –700): top official trusted by Tianhou.

Directorate of Crane-Riders (*konghe jian* 控鶴監): agency for Tianhou's gigolos and male favorites; later renamed Palace Office (*fengchen fu* 奉宸府).

District (*dao* 道): ad hoc district usually associated with an expeditionary army. Cf. Circuit (*dao* 道).

Dou, Consort 竇妃 (–692): Li Dan's (Ruizong) wife, Li Longji's (Xuanzong) mother; killed.

Dou Huaizhen 竇懷貞 (–713): official; attached himself to Empress Wei; suicide.

Doulu Qinwang 豆盧欽望 (624–709): chief minister under Tianhou.

Du He 杜荷 |du hê| (616–643): Du Ruhui's son; killed for taking part a plot against the throne.

Du Jingjian 杜景儉 (–700): senior official.

Du Ruhui 杜如晦 (585–630): top court leader under Taizong.

duke (*gong* 公): in Tang times, the title of duke had three ranks: state duke (*guogong* 國公), commandery duke (*jungong* 郡公), and county duke (*xiangong* 縣公). The first rank, being the highest, was normally reserved for the princes and the most powerful top leaders.

Eastern Palace: residence of the crown prince located to the east of the palace in Chang'an and Luoyang.

Elder Dai's Record of Rites (*Da Dai liji* 大戴禮記): an annotated version of the *Record of Rites* (*Liji*) completed in the Western Han; has near canonical status.

End Gate (Duanmen 端門): southern main entrance to Luoyang's Imperial City.

Fan Yunxian 范雲仙 (–693): senior official; killed.

Fang Rong 房融 (fl. 705): chief minister; supporter of Zhang Yizhi; banished.

Fang Xuanling 房玄齡 (579–648): top official under Taizong; Fang Yi'ai's father.

Fang Yi'ai 房遺愛 (–653): son of Fang Xuanling; husband of the princess of Gaoyang; killed.

Fang Yizhi 房遺直 (–post-653): eldest son of Fang Xuanling. Yi'ai's brother.

Feng Sixu 馮思勗 (fl. 685): censor.

fengshan 封禪: top-level ritual consisting of *feng* sacrifices to Heaven and *shan* sacrifices to Earth, performed on Mount Tai (or Mount Song under Tianhou).

Fengtian Palace 奉天宮: southeast of Luoyang in Henan.

Five Princes: five leaders of the 705 coup: Zhang Jianzhi, Huan Yanfan, Jing Hui, Cui Xuanwei, and Yuan Shuji.

Flying Swallow Zhao (Zhao Feiyan 趙飛燕) (45–1 BCE): dancer; empress of Emperor Cheng (W. Han).

Forbidden Park: royal park immediately north of the Palace City of Chang'an.

Four Eminences of the Early Tang (chu Tang sijie 初唐四傑): Wang Bo 王勃, Yang Jiong 楊炯, Lu Zhaolin 盧照鄰, and Luo Binwang 駱賓王.

Four Garrisons of Anxi 安西四鎮; Four Garrisons: defense command in Xinjiang and beyond in the Western Regions under the Anxi Protectorate.

Four White-Haired Recluses of Mount Shang (Shangshan sihao 商山四皓): four virtuous recluses of late Qin and early Han times.

Fu Youyi 傅遊藝 (629–691): sycophantic senior official; killed (or suicide).

fubing 府兵 (Garrison Militia): military organizational system from

Western Wei to Tang. It constituted the main force of the military.

Fuxing Ward 輔興坊: residential ward in northwest Chang'an.

Gan'ye Nunnery 感業寺: Buddhist institution (where Wu Zetian lived after Taizong's death) in Chang'an's Anye 安業 Ward south of the Imperial City. For an alternative view, *see* Part I, Chapter 2.

Ganlu Basilica 甘露殿: palatial building in the Palace City of Chang'an.

Gao Jian 高戩: official; Princess Taiping's lover.

Gao Rui 高叡 (–698): official; killed by Tujue in Zhaozhou 趙州.

Gao Shilian 高士廉 (577–647): Tang senior official; adoptive father of Zhangsun Wuji and Empress Zhangsun (Taizong's wife).

Gao Zhizhou 高智周 (602–683): senior official.

Gaoshan 高山: palace in Luoyang's Western Park.

Gaoyang, princess of 高陽公主 (–653): Taizong's daughter; Fang Yi'ai's wife; suicide.

Gaozong, Tang 唐高宗 |täng gao-dzong|; Li Zhi 李治 ; Zhinu 雉奴 ; Great Emperor; Heavenly Emperor (Tianhuang 天皇) (628–683; r. 649–683): third Tang emperor, son of Taizong, husband of Tianhou.

Gaozu, Han 漢高祖; Gaozu of Han; Liu Bang 劉邦 (256–195 BCE): founder of the Han dynasty (206 BCE).

Gaozu, Tang 唐高祖 |täng gao-dzu|; Li Yuan 李淵 (556–635; r. 618–626): founding emperor of the Tang dynasty; Gaozong's grandfather; abdicated in favor of Taizong.

Gate of Despair (Lijingmen 例竟門): alternative name for Lijing Gate 麗景門 (the western gate in the wall of the Imperial City).

Ge Fushun 葛福順 (fl. 710): officer of the Yulin Army; took part in the 710 coup.

Ge Fuyuan 格輔元 (–691): senior official; killed.

general-in-chief (*da jiangjun* 大將軍): senior military officer, often head of a Guard.

gongfeng 供奉: palace attendant.

gongshi 貢士: reference to a civil service examination candidate who had passed the local examinations and was eligible to sit for the central examination.

Great Cloud Sutra (*Dayun jing* 大雲經; *Mahāmegha-sūtra*): a Buddhist sutra that prophesies the rise of a female sovereign.

Great Emperor. *See* Tang Gaozong.

Guanzhong 關中: area west of the Hangu Pass, especially the Wei River valley in south Shaanxi with Chang'an as its main urban center.

Guard (*wei* 衛): one of the Sixteen Guards.

Gudulu; Ashina Gudulu 阿史那骨篤祿; Guduolu 骨咄祿 (r. 682–691/694): khan of Later Tujue; elder brother of Mochuo 默啜. [*Zizhi tongjian* (205.6493) dates his death to 694. *Jiu Tang shu* and *Xin Tang shu* differ.]

guerilla general (*youji jiangjun* 游擊將軍): prestige title usually awarded to a military officer.

Guo Daifeng 郭待封: son of Gao Xiaoke 郭孝恪; general under Gaozong; defeated in the 670 campaign against Tubo; faded from history.

Guo Xingzhen 郭行真 (fl. 664): occultist; Daoist.

Guo Yuanzhen 郭元振 (656–713): general, senior officer responsible for guarding the northwestern frontier.

Hall of Heaven (Tiantang 天堂): hall in Luoyang's Palace City for housing a giant Buddha statue.

Hann Yuan 韓瑗 (606–659): senior official under Gaozong.

Hann, state mistress of 韓國夫人 (623–665): Tianhou's elder sister; mother of the state mistress of Wei 魏國夫人 and Helan Minzhi 賀蘭敏之.

Hao Chujun 郝處俊 (607–681): senior official.

Hebei 河北: Tang Circle that encompassed present-day Hebei and southern Manchuria.

Heavenly Pivot (Tianshu 天樞): commemorative column erected south of the End Gate (Duanmen) in Luoyang.

Heichi Changzhi 黑齒常之 |~ chäng-jih|; Hŭkch'i Sangchi (–689): ethnic: Paekche; Tang top general; suicide in prison.

Helan Minzhi 賀蘭敏之; Wu Minzhi 武 - (642–671): son of Tianhou's sister the state mistress of Hann; banished; killed (or died in his place of banishment according to his epitaph).

heqin 和親: marriage alliance.

hexagram: a figure consisting of two trigrams or six (broken and/or unbroken) lines. There are sixty-four hexagrams in the *Book of Changes* with the first one named *qian* 乾 , which is considered the most potent.

Hexi 河西/Hexi Corridor: approx. Gansu.

Honghua, Princess 弘化公主 (623–698): Tang princess; wife of Tuyuhun's Nuohebo.

Hongye 弘業 Ward (Daye 大業 Ward): residential ward in south central Chang'an.

Hou Sizhi 侯思止 |hou sih-jih| (–693): cruel official; killed.

hu 斛; *shi* 石 (bushel) : capacity measure, slightly less than 60 liters in Tang times.

Hu Chao 胡超 (fl. 700): Buddhist monk; tossed a gold tablet for Tianhou on Mount Song.

Hu Yuanfan 胡元範 (–c. 689): court leader; defender of Pei Yan; banished.

Huan Yanfan 桓彥範 (653–706): senior official; took part in the 705 coup; one of the "Five Princes"; killed.

Hundred Officials: court officials collectively.

Huo Xianke 霍獻可 |~ <u>shee'an</u>-kê| (fl. 692): official; nephew of Cui Xuanli.

Imperial City (*huangcheng* 皇城): central government quarter of the capital (Chang'an or Luoyang).

imperial consort (*chenfei* 宸妃): highest ranking consort of the emperor next to the empress. The title was created especially for Wu Zetian in 655.

imperial heir (*huangsi* 皇嗣): title granted to Prince Li Dan in 690.

inner gates: gates within the palace grounds different from outer gates (entrances through which one gained entry into the palace from the outside).

Jasper (Biyu 碧玉) (–691): bondwoman who killed herself for her lover Qiao Zhizhi 喬知之.

Ji Chu'ne 紀處訥 |~nê| (–710): chief minister trusted by Empress Wei; killed after the 710 coup.

Ji Xu 吉頊 |jee shü| (fl. 697–700): official; Tianhou's favorite; demoted.

Jiang Ke 姜恪 |jee'äng kê| (–672): Tang chancellor.

Jianwen, Emperor of Liang 梁簡文帝 (503–551, r. 549–551): strong believer in Buddhism; killed.

Jicui Palace 積翠宮 |jee-tsui ~| (Jadeite Palace): inside the Western Park west of Luoyang.

Jie 桀: bad last sovereign of the Xia.

Jin, Crown Prince 太子晉 (c. 567–549 BCE): son of King Ling of Zhou; immortal.

Jincheng, princess of 金城公主 (698–739): daughter of Li Shouli; Tang *heqin* princess married off to the *zanpu* of Tubo (710).

Jing Hui 敬暉 (–706): senior official; took part in the 705 coup; one of the "Five Princes"; killed.

Jingman 淨滿 (fl. 698): Buddhist monk; savior of Pei Huaigu.

jinshi 進士 (Presented Scholar): the most prestigious degree (and its recipient) with a focus on the study of literature.

Koguryŏ 高句麗: state in north Korea and south Manchuria; conquered by Tang in 668.

Kunming Pond 昆明池: man-made lake west of Chang'an.

Lai Ji 來濟 (610–662): senior official under Gaozong.

Lai Junchen 來俊臣 (651–697): leading cruel official trusted by Tianhou; co-author of the *Classic on Framing* (*see* Wan Guojun); killed.

Lateral Palace (*yeting gong* 掖庭宮): located in the west of the Palace City in Chang'an, it was where disgraced palace women lived.

Left Guard (*zuowei* 左衛): one of the Sixteen Guards.

Legalist (*fajia* 法家): member of an ancient school of thought (known in English as Legalism) that stresses law and punishment and the autocratic power of the sovereign. It originated in the Warring States period and thrived under the First Emperor.

li 里: length unit. One Tang *li* ≈ 558 meters or approx. 1/3 mile.

Li Chengjia 李承嘉 (fl. 706): censor-in-chief under Zhongzong.

Li Chengqi 李成器 |~-chee| (679–742): eldest son of Ruizong; crown prince (684–690).

Li Chong 李沖 (–688): Li Zhen's son, Taizong's grandson; prefect of Bozhou 博州 in Shandong; rebelled; killed.

Li Chong-Li Zhen rebellion (688). *See* Li Chong; Li Zhen.

Li Chongfu 李重福 (680–710): eldest son of Li Zhe (Zhongzong); suicide after a failed coup.

Li Chongjun 李重俊; Crown Prince Jiemin 節愍太子 (683/4–707): third son of Li Zhe (Zhongzong) born to an unknown mother; killed Wu Sansi and Wu Chongxun in a coup; killed.

Li Chongmao 李重茂 (695–714; r. 710): Zhongzong's youngest son; served briefly as emperor.

Li Chongrun 李重潤; Crown Prince Yide 懿德太子 (682–701): eldest son of Li Zhe (Zhongzong); only son of Consort Wei; killed for gossiping about the Zhang brothers.

Li Chunfeng 李淳風 (602–670): famous occultist; astrologer.

Li Dan. *See* Ruizong.

Li Daozong 李道宗 (602–653): Tang royal; general under Taizong.

Li Duozuo 李多祚 (654–707): general of Mohe 靺鞨 descent; played a crucial role the 705 coup; took part in the Li Chongjun incident (707); killed.

Li Fan 李範 (686–726): son of Ruizong.

Li Gui 李規 (–688): Li Zhen's son; suicide.

Li Hong 李弘 (652–675): eldest son of Gaozong and Tianhou; crown prince.

Li Hongtai 李弘泰 (fl. 704): occultist; worked for Zhang Changzong.

Li Ji 李勣 |lee jee|; Li Shiji 李世勣; Xu Shiji 徐世勣 (594–669): leading general under Taizong and Gaozong; grandfather of Li Jingye.

Li Jing 李靖 (571–649): top general under Taizong.

Li Jingchen 李景諶 (fl. 684): senior official.

Li Jingqiu 李敬猷 (–684) (Xu Jingyou 徐敬猷): Li Jingye's brother; killed.

Li Jingxuan 李敬玄 (615–682): senior official.

Li Jingye 李敬業 |lee jing-yeh| (–684) (Xu Jingye 徐敬業): grandson of Li Ji; leader of a rebellion in 684; killed.

Li Jinzhong 李盡忠 (–696): Qidan rebel leader.

Li Jiongxiu 李迥秀 (fl. 697): senior official.

Li Ke 李恪 |lee kê| (619–653): third son of Taizong; killed.

Li Lingkui 李靈夔 (625–688): son of Gaozu; suicide.

Li Longji. *See* Tang Xuanzong.

Li Mi 李密 (582–619): late-Sui rebel leader of aristocratic origin. Li Ji, before joining the Tang, was under his command.

Li Ming 李明 (640–682): younger brother of Gaozong; suicide.

Li Qiao 李嶠 (645–714): senior official.

Li Quan 李悛: Song Zhixun's nephew.

Li Shangjin 李尚金 (–690): Gaozong's son; suicide.

Li Shen 李慎 (–689): Taizong's son; prefect of Beizhou 貝州 in south Hebei and Shandong; banished.

Li Shimin. *See* Tang Taizong.

Li Shouli 李守禮 (672–741): Li Xián's 李賢 son; father of the princess of Jincheng.

Li Si 李斯 |lee sih| (284–208 BCE): Legalist top official of the Qin.

Li Sizhen 李嗣真 |lee sih-jen| (–696): vice censor-in-chief; banished.

Li Sujie 李素節 |lee su-jee'eh|; prince of Yong 雍王 (648–690): son of Gaozong by Xiao Shufei; killed.

Li Tai 李泰 (618–652): Gaozong's elder brother.

Li Xián 李賢; Crown Prince Zhanghuai 章懷太子 (655–684): Gaozong's and Tianhou's son; crown prince (675–680); suspected of rebellion; banished; suicide.

Li Xian 李顯. *See* Zhongzong.

Li Xianfu 李仙凫 (fl. 710): officer of the Yulin Army; took part in the 710 coup.

Li Xianhui 李仙蕙; Princess Yongtai 永泰公主 (685–701): daughter of Li Zhe (Zhongzong) and Consort Wei; Wu Yanji's wife; killed for spreading gossip about the Zhang brothers.

Li Xiaoyi 李孝逸 (fl. 684): Tang royal; general.

Li Ye 李業 (686–734): son of Ruizong.

Li Yifu 李義府 (614–666): top pro-Tianhou official; banished.

Li Yuan. *See* Tang Gaozu.

Li Yuangui 李元軌 (622–688): son of Gaozu; prefect of Qingzhou 青州 in Shandong; banished.

Li Yuanjia 李元嘉 (619–688): son of Gaozu; suicide.

Li Yuanjing 李元景 (618–653): son of Gaozu; suicide.

Li Yuanming 李元名 (–690): son of Gaozu; killed.

Li Zhan 李湛 (fl. 705): son of Li Yifu; took part in the 705 coup.

Li Zhaode 李昭德 |lee jao-dê| (–697): senior official initially trusted by Tianhou; killed.

Li Zhe. *See* Zhongzong.

Li Zhen 李貞 (627–688): Taizong's son; Li Chong's father; prefect of Yuzhou 豫州 in Henan; rebelled; suicide.

Li Zhi. *See* Tang Gaozong.

Li Zhong 李忠; prince of Chen 陳王 (643–665): eldest son of Gaozong; crown prince (652–655).

Li Zhuan 李譔 (–688): Li Yuanjia's son; prefect of Tongzhou 通州 in northeast Sichuan; suicide.

Liangzhou 涼州 |lee'äng-joe|: prefecture that lay in Gansu and Inner Mongolia.

Liangzhou 梁州 |lee'äng-joe|: prefecture with its seat east of Hanzhong, Shaanxi.

Liangyi Basilica (*dian*) 兩儀殿 |lee'äng-yee dee'an|: palatial building in the Palace City of Chang'an.

Liu, Consort 劉妃 (–692): Li Dan's (Ruizong) wife; killed.

Liu Bang. *See* Han Gaozu.

Liu Jingren 劉景仁 (fl. 707): general; leader of a security force.

Liu Jingtong 劉敬同 (fl. 680s): general.

Liu Jingxian 劉景先 (–689): court leader; defender of Pei Yan; banished; suicide.

Liu Rengui 劉仁軌 (601/2–685): top general; conqueror of Paekche.

Liŭ Shi 柳奭 |lee'u shih| (–659): uncle of Empress Wang; court leader under Gaozong; killed.

Liu Sili 劉思禮 |lee'u sih-lee| (–697): senior official; killed.

Liu Xian 劉憲 (655–711): senior official.

Liu Yizhi 劉禕之 (631–687): senior official; suicide.

Liu Youqiu 劉幽求 (655–715): official; took part in the 710 coup led by Li Longji (Xuanzong).

Liu Zhiji 劉知幾 |lee'u jih-jee| (661–721): Wu Zhou and Tang court historian.

loose-rein prefecture (*jimi zhou* 羈縻州): non-Han prefecture with tributary relations with the court.

Lord on High (Haotian Shangdi 昊天上帝): god of Heaven, the highest deity in the pantheon.

Lou Shide 婁師德 |lou shih-dê| (630–699): top official under Wu Zhou trusted by Tianhou.

Lu Dongzan 祿東贊 (–667): top Tubo official.

Lü, Empress 呂后 (–180 BCE): wife of Liu Bang (founder of the Han).

Lun Qinling 論欽陵 |loon cheen-leeng| (–699): Lu Dongzan's son; top Tubo official; attacked by Chidu Songzan; suicide.

Lun Zanpo 論贊婆 |loon dzän-po| (fl. 699): Lun Qinling's brother; top Tubo leader; fled to the Wu Zhou.

Ma Huaisu 馬懷素 (659–718): learned official.

Ma Renjie 麻仁節 (fl. 696): general; captured by Qidan.

Marchmount (*yue* 嶽): one of the five sacred mountains.

meiren 美人. *See* Beautiful Lady.

men 門: gate.

Ming Chongyan 明崇儼 |meeng chong-yän| (–679): occultist trusted by Tianhou; assassinated.

mingjing 明經 (Classicist): degree devoted to the study of the classics and its holder.

Mingtang 明堂 |meeng-täng| (Hall of Brilliance): ritual structure set up by Tianhou in Luoyang.

Mochuo 默啜, Ashina 阿史那 (r. 691/694–716): khan of the Later Tujue; younger brother of Gudulu 骨篤祿.

Molu 沒廬: Tubo queen dowager.

Nanzhao 南詔: one of six non-Han states (known as Liuzhao 六詔) in the southwest (mainly Yunnan).

Narsieh 泥涅師 (fl. 679): Sassanid Persian prince.

Nine Concubines (*jiupin* 九嬪): high-ranking imperial concubines next in rank to the consorts (*fei* 妃).

Nine Courts (*jiusi* 九寺): nine third-tier central government agencies. Their functions often complemented or paralleled those of the Six Boards.

Northern Gate (*beimen* 北門): the Right Yintai Gate 右銀臺門 in the Daming Palace. Northern Gate academicians (*xueshi* 學士) were litterateurs who waited for their summons in a government quarter north of the gate. They performed clerical and literary tasks for the emperor. See *Jiu Tang shu* 43.

Northern Office (*beiya* 北衙): reference to the security forces (Yulin Armies) stationed in the Forbidden Park of Chang'an.

Nuohebo 諾曷缽 (624–688): last sovereign (khan) of Tuyuhun.

Nüwa 女媧: predynastic female sovereign; one of the Three Sovereigns.

Paekche 百濟: state in southwest Korea; conquered by Tang in 660.

Palace City (*gongcheng* 宮城): main palace area inside the capital (Chang'an or Luoyang). In Chang'an, it was also known as the Taiji Palace.

Palace Office (*fengchen fu* 奉宸府): name of the Directorate of Crane Riders (*konghe jian* 控鶴監) from 700.

Pan Haoli 潘好禮 |pän hao-lee| (fl. 696–720s): honest official.

Pan Shizheng 潘師正 |pän shih-jêng| (585–682): Daoist Shangqing school patriarch.

Pang, Lady 龐氏 (fl. 693): Li Dan's (Ruizong) mother-in-law; banished.

Pei Feigong 裴匪躬 (–693): senior official; killed.

Pei Huaigu 裴懷古 (638–712): honest official; savior of Monk Jingman; emissary to Tujue (698).

Pei Xingben 裴行本 |pei sheeng-bên| (fl. 692): senior official; banished.

Pei Xingjian 裴行儉 |pei sheeng-jee'an| (619–682): senior official; leading general in the fight against Western Tujue.

Pei Yan 裴炎 (–684): powerful court leader; executed for offending Tianhou.

Pei Zhen 裴貞 |pei jen| (–690): senior official; killed.

Pei Zhouxian 裴伷先 |pei jou-shee'ǎn| (667–753): Pei Yan's nephew.

Penglai Palace. *See* Daming Palace.

Ping, King 平王: first sovereign of the Eastern Zhou.

Pojang 寶藏 (–682): last Koguryŏ King.

prefect (*cishi* 刺史): governor of a prefecture (*zhou* 州).

prefecture (*zhou* 州): large local administrative unit lower than a Circuit and higher than a county.

prince (*wang* 王): under the Tang and Wu Zhou, the princes fell into two classes: imperial prince (*qinwang* 親王) and commandery prince (*junwang* 郡王). The former's title was composed of two characters: the first one was the place of enfeoffment and the second one means "prince," e.g., Songwang 宋王 (prince of Song). The latter's title was composed three characters: the first two refer to the place of enfeoffment, and the last one means "prince," e.g., Linzi wang 臨淄王 (prince of Linzi).

protectorate (*duhu fu* 都護府): regional military administration under a protector-general (*duhu* 都護) higher than an area command in an extensive area with mostly non-Han residents.

prestige title (*sanguan* 散官): one of a series of ranked honorific titles that carried no substantive power.

puye 僕射. *See* vice premier.

Puyŏ P'ung 扶余豐: last king of Paekche.

Qian Weidao 騫味道 (–689): senior official; killed.

Qianling 乾陵 |chee'än-leeng|: Tomb Park northwest of Chang'an. It is home to the co-burial tomb of Gaozong and Tianhou.

Qianyuan Basilica (*dian*) 乾元殿 |chee'an-yüan dee'an|: principal palatial building in the Palace City of Luoyang; leveled in 688 to make way for the Mingtang.

Qiao Zhizhi 喬知之 |chee'ao jih-jih| (–690): official; lover of Jasper (Biyu 碧玉) (seized by Wu Chengsi); killed. Note: his death is dated to 697 by *Zizhi tongjian*.

Qibi Heli 契苾何力 |chee-bee hê-lee| (–677): Tiele, Tang general.

Qidan 契丹 |chee-dän| (Khitan): non-Han ethnic group active in the Tongliao area in the Xiliao River valley and neighboring areas in Inner Mongolia, with roots going back to the Northern Wei.

Qinghua Ward 清化坊: residential ward east of the palace in Luoyang.

Qiu Shenji 丘神勣 |chee'u shen-jee| (–691): general; cruel official; executed.

Quan Gaisuwen (603–666) |chuän ~| (Ch'ŏn/Yŏn Kaesomun 泉 / 淵蓋蘇文): Koguryŏ power-holder.

Quan Nanjian 泉男建 |chuän ~|: son of Quan Gaisuwen.

Quechuo (Ashina) Zhongjie 闕啜阿史那忠節 (fl. 708): top Türgesh general; rebelled against Suoge; fled to Tang.

ranks: starting in the Cao-Wei (220–265), a nine-rank system was introduced to officialdom. The Northern Wei (386–535) began to use a rank-and-class system, with rank 1 being the highest. Each of the nine ranks was divided into upper and lower (*zheng cong* 正從) classes. From Rank 4 down to Rank 9, every class was further divided into upper and lower (*shang xia* 上下) grades (*jie* 階). In all, there were thirty rungs of the official ladder. The Tang and Wu Zhou used the same system. Roughly, ranks 1 through 5 were senior officials.

Rear Palace (*hougong* 後宮): residential area of the empress, consorts, concubines, and other palace ladies in the palace.

Record of Lineages (*Xingshi lu* 姓氏錄): register that ranks noble clans compiled under the auspices of Tianhou.

Record of Rites (*Liji* 禮記; *Xiao Dai Liji* 小戴禮記); *Classic of Rites*: Western Han Confucian classic on ritual.

Ren Zhigu 任知古 (fl. 691–692): senior official.

rhapsody (*fu* 賦): a type of rhymed prose considered the highest form/genre of literary writing during the Western Han. Stylistically, rhapsody pieces are a cross between prose and poetry.

Rites of Zhou (*Zhouli* 周禮): a Confucian classic.

Ruizong, Tang 唐睿宗 |ruee-dzong, täng|; Li Dan 李旦; prince of Xiang 相王 (662–716; r. 684, 710–712): Gaozong's and Tianhou's son; emperor.

Sanjiao zhuying 三教珠英 (Essential Pearls of the Three Teachings): *leishu* 類書 (encyclopedia) of poetry allegedly edited by Zhang Changzong.

Sanyang Palace 三陽宮 |sän-yäng ~|: built by Tianhou in Mount Song in 700. Here the term *sanying* ("three yang") refers to Wu Sansi, Li Zhe, and Li Dan.

Script Explained and Graphs Explicated (*Shuowen jiezi* 說文解字): lexicon by Xu Shen 許慎 (E. Han).

seat (*zhi* 治): town or city which served as the seat (capital) of a county or prefectural government.

Shandong 山東 |shän-dong|: unless otherwise noted, present-day Shandong province. Note: Tang Shandong referred to the much large area east of the Taihang Mountains, encompassing present-day Hebei, Shandong, and part of Henan.

Shang Zanduo 尚贊咄 (fl. 709–710): Tubo senior official; headed a mission to Tang to fetch the princess of Jincheng.

Shangguan Wan'er 上官婉兒 |shäng-guän wän-êr| (664–710): granddaughter of Shangguan Yi; poet; Tianhou's confidante; Wu Sansi's lover; executed.

Shangguan Yi 上官儀 |shäng-guän yee| (608–665): senior official under Gaozong; Shangguan Wan'er's grandfather; poet; killed.

Shangyang Palace 上陽宮 |shäng-yäng ~|: built in mid–late 670s north of the Luo River in the Western Park and adjacent to the Imperial City in Luoyang.

Shazha Zhongyi 沙吒忠義 |shä-jä jong-yee| (–707): Paekche, Tang general; killed.

Shen Nanqiu 沈南璆 |shen nän-<u>chee'u</u>|: palace physician; Tianhou's lover.

Shen Quanqi 沈全期 |shen chuän-chee| (656–714): leading poet under Tianhou and Zhongzong.

Shi 石 |shih| (Chach): state with its capital in Tashkent, Uzbekistan.

Shouxiangcheng 受降城: one of three towns built by Zhang Renyuan north of the Yellow River and south of the Yin Mountains in south central Inner Mongolia.

Shun 舜 (Lord Shun): predynastic good sovereign.

Shuozhou 朔州: prefecture with its seat in Shuozhou, north Shanxi.

Si of Bao 褒姒 (–771 BCE): femme fatale of the Western Zhou.

Silk Road: the transportation network connecting China, Central Asia, West Asia, and the Mediterranean world. Its starting point in the east was Chang'an or Luoyang. The term was coined in nineteenth-century Europe.

Silla 新羅 |shee-lê|: state in southeast Korea.

Sima Yi 司馬懿 |sih-mä yee| (179–251): Cao-Wei politician; killed his rival Cao Shuang 曹爽; built a power base for the Sima clan.

Six Boards (*liubu* 六部): six second-tier central government agencies under the Department of State Affairs (*shangshu sheng* 尚書省) in charge of personnel, revenue, rites, war, justice, and works.

Song Jing 宋璟 (663–737): top official under Xuanzong.

Song Tan 宋曇: Song Zhixun's son.

Song Zhiwen 宋之問 |song jih-wen| (ca. 656–ca. 712): leading poet known for his panegyric poetry.

Song Zhixun 宋之遜 |song jih-shün|: Song Zhiwen's brother.

Song, Mount 嵩山: north of Dengfeng, Henan; one of the Five Marshmounts (five sacred mountains).

Southern Market: one of the three urban markets of Luoyang.

Southern Office (*nanya* 南牙): office area south of the Palace City in the Imperial City in Chang'an or Luoyang. Not to be confused with *nanya* 南衙 (Southern Command).

Su Anheng 蘇安恆 |soo än-hêng| (–707): commoner memorialist; executed.

Su Dingfang 蘇定方 (592–667): top general under Gaozong.

Su Gui 蘇瓌 (639–710): chief minister under Zhongzong.

Su Haizheng 蘇海政 (fl. 662): general under Gaozong.

Su Liangsi 蘇良嗣 |soo lee'äng-sih| (606–690): senior official.

Su Weidao 蘇味道 (648–705): senior official.

Su Xiang 蘇珦 (635–715): senior official.

sui 歲 (year): the basic unit for indicating a person's age, similar to "year." In the sources, a person at birth was one *sui* old and two *sui* on the first lunar New Year's Day.

successor emperor (*si huangdi* 嗣皇帝 |sih ~|): title invented for Wu

Chengsi.

Suiye 碎葉; Suyab: town in Tokmak, Kyrgyzstan.

Sun Wanrong 孫萬榮 (–697): Qidan rebel leader; killed.

Sunzi 孫子 |soon-dzih| (Master Sun): great strategist; active in the fifth century BCE; author of the *Art of War*.

Suo Yuanli 索元禮 |~ yuän-lee| (–691): non-Han cruel official under Tianhou; Xue Huaiyi's adoptive father; killed.

Suoge 娑葛 |suo-gê| (fl. 706): son of Wuzhile; first Türgesh khan.

Suyu 宿羽 |soo-yü|: palace in Luoyang's Western Park.

Suzhangmen 肅章門 |soo-jäng-mên|; Suzhang Gate: inner gate northwest of the Taiji Basilica in Chang'an's Palace City.

Taiji Basilica 太極殿: principal palatial building in the Taiji Palace in Chang'an.

Taiji Palace 太極宮: main palace area in Chang'an. *See* Palace City.

Taijia 太甲: fifth king of Shang.

Taiping, Princess 太平公主 (ca. 665–713): daughter of Tang Gaozong and Tianhou; suicide.

Taizong, Tang 唐太宗 |täng tai-dzong|; Li Shimin 李世民 (598-649; r. 626-649): second Tang emperor; father of Gaozong.

Talented Lady (*cairen* 才人): imperial concubine with a rank lower than the Nine Concubines.

Tamna (Danluo 耽羅): state on Jeju Island off the south coast of Korea.

Tang Bore 唐般若 |täng bo-rê| (–698): Tang official in Zhaozhou 趙州; traitor; killed.

Tang Xiujing 唐休璟 |täng shee'u-jeeng| (627–712): chief minister under Tianhou, Zhongzong, and Ruizong.

Tang, King. *See* Chengtang.

Tao Yuanming 陶淵明 (365–427): poet.

Three Clans (*sanzu* 三族): the clans of one's father, mother, and wife.

Three Departments (*sansheng* 三省): three first-tier central government agencies: the Secretariat (*zhongshu* 中書), the Chancellery (*menxia* 門下), and the Department of State Affairs (*shangshu* 尚書).

Three Visitors (fl. 694): three occultists who briefly gained Tianhou's confidence: Old Nun 老尼, Old Hu 老胡, and Wei Shifang 韋什方.

Tian Guidao 田歸道 (–706): official; accompanied Yan Zhiwei on a mission to Tujue (697).

Tian Youyan 田游巖: recluse living on Mount Song.

Tianhou 天后 |tee'ăn-hou| (Heavenly Empress); Wu Zetian 武則天 |woo dzê-tee'an|; Lady Wu; Wu Zhao 武曌 |~ jao|; Huagu 華姑 (624–705; r. 690–705): daughter of Wu Shiyue and Lady Yang; Talented Lady (*cairen* 才人) under Taizong; Lady of Majestic Bearing (*zhaoyi* 昭儀); Empress of Gaozong; emperor of Zhou (690–705); mother of Zhongzong, Ruizong, and Princess Taiping.

Tiantang 天堂. *See* Hall of Heaven.

Tiele 鐵勒 |tee'eh-lê|: early Turkic ethnic group.

Treatise on Genealogy (*Shizu zhi* 氏族志): register of noble clans compiled under Taizong.

Tuan'er 團兒 (–693): bondwoman of Tianhou; killed.

Tubo 吐蕃: ancient Tibetan people active in Tibet and Qinghai.

Tujue 突厥: Turkic people active in Mongolia and Central Asia.

Türgesh (Tuqishi 突騎施): ethnic group initially dominated by Western Tujue in Central Asia.

Tuyuhun 吐谷渾 |too-yü-hoon|: ethnic group active mainly in Qinghai and their state, historically hostile to Tubo.

Two Sages (*ersheng* 二聖): Gaozong and Tianhou.

Two Zhangs: Zhang Changzong and Zhang Yizhi.

Uighurs: Turkic people active in Mongolia.

Venerable Documents (*Shangshu* 尚書): collection of ancient documents;

a Confucian classic.

vice premier (*puye* 僕射): one of the two co-president of the Department of State Affairs. The *puye* had been from the start of the Tang one of the two actual heads of the Department, while the president's (*shangshu ling*) post was mostly unfilled after Taizong became emperor.

Wan Guojun 萬國俊 (–693 or later): cruel official; co-author of the *Classic on Framing* (*see* Lai Junchen).

Wang Benli 王本立 (–690): senior official of the Department of State Affairs; dismissed.

Wang Bo 王勃 (650–676): poet; one of the Four Eminences of the Early Tang; early mentor of Prince Li Xián.

Wang Deshou 王德壽 (fl. 692): Lai Junchen's assistant.

Wang Fangyi 王方翼 |wäng fäng-yee| (625–687*): senior official; builder of Suiye 碎葉; banished. *Burial date recorded in his epitaph.

Wang Fusheng 王伏勝 (–665): Tianhou's eunuch officer; killed.

Wang Hongyi 王弘義 |~ hong-yee| (–694): cruel official.

Wang Jishan 王及善 (618–699): senior official.

Wang Mang 王莽 (45 BCE–23 CE; r. 9–23 CE): usurper; founder of the Xin dynasty.

Wang Naxiang 王那相 (fl. 684): co-conspirator and killer of Li Jingye.

Wang Qingzhi 王慶之 |wäng cheeng-jih| (–691): Luoyang resident; advocate for Wu Chengsi's appointment as crown prince; killed.

Wang Tongjiao 王同皎 |wäng tong-jee'ao| (671–706): Zhongzong's son-in-law; took part in the 705 coup; wrongly accused of plotting against Wu Sansi and Empress Wei; killed.

Wang Xiaojie 王孝傑 |~ shee'ao-jee'eh| (–697): general; top official.

Wang Zhaojun 王昭君 (54–19 BCE): Western Han palace lady married to a Xiongnu *chanyu* through *heqin*.

Wang, Empress 王皇后; Lady Wang 王氏 (ca. 628–655): daughter of Wang Renyou 王仁祐; the first empress of Gaozong; deposed; killed.

Wannian County 萬年縣: one of two urban counties of Chang'an.

wei 圍: length unit. One *wei* is the length of an arm span, a bit shorter than a fathom.

Wei Anshi 韋安石 (651–714): chief minister under Tianhou.

Wei Chengqing 韋承慶 (640–706): senior official; supporter of Zhang Yizhi.

Wei Daijia 韋待價 (–689): chief minister; general.

Wei Hongji 韋弘機 |~ hong-jee| (fl. 670s): Tang official, builder.

Wei Jifang 韋季方 (fl. 659): official under Gaozong.

Wei Juyuan 韋巨源 |~ jü-yuän| (631–710): chief minister; killed in the 710 coup.

Wei Suizhong 衛遂忠 (fl. 697): Lai Junchen's friend; roughed up by Lai's men; sought revenge against Lai.

Wei Wen 韋溫 (–710): Empress Wei's brother; chief minister under Zhongzong; killed in the 710 coup.

Wei Xuanzhen 韋玄貞 (–684): Empress Wei's father; banished to Qinzhou 欽州 in Guangxi.

Wei Yuanzhong 魏元忠 |~ yuan-jong| (–707): chief minister under Tianhou; banished; recalled; banished again.

Wei Zhigu 魏知古 |~ jih-goo| (647–715): official; chief minister under Ruizong.

Wei, Empress 韋后; Consort Wei; Lady Wei (–710): empress of Zhongzong; intimate ties with Wu Sansi after 705; responsible for Zhongzong's death; killed in a coup started by Li Longji (Xuanzong).

Wei, Lady 韋氏: ① Zhang Changzong's 張昌宗 mother. ② *see* Empress Wei.

Wei, state mistress of 魏國夫人 (–666): daughter of Tianhou's sister the state mistress of Hann; Helan Minzhi's sister; killed by poison.

Wen, King 文王: father of King Wu (founder of the Western Zhou).

Wenshui 文水: county in Shanxi; ancestral home of Tianhou.

Western Park 西苑: vast royal park west of Luoyang.

Western Regions (*xiyu* 西域 |shee-yü|): Xinjiang and the area to its west.

Wu, Emperor of Liang 梁武帝 (464–549; r. 502–549): pious believer and generous patron of Buddhism; starved to death.

Wu Chengsi 武承嗣 |woo chêng-sih|; state duke of Zhou 周國公 (–698): Wu Yuanshuang's son; Tianhou's nephew; father of Wu Yanji, Wu Yanxiu; died in grief after his effort to become crown prince failed.

Wu Chonggui 武重規 (fl. 698): Tianhou's nephew; one of her paternal cousins; general.

Wu Chongxun 武崇訓 |woo chong-shün| (683–707): son of Wu Sansi; first husband of Princess Anle; killed with his father in the Li Chongjun incident.

Wu Huailiang 武懷亮 (d. early 660s): elder brother of Wu Weiliang and Wu Huaiyun, cousin of Tianhou.

Wu Huaiyun 武懷運 (–666): younger brother of Wu Huailiang and Wu Weiliang; cousin of Tianhou; killed.

Wu Jing 吳兢 (670–749): court historian.

Wu Minzhi 武敏之. *See* Helan Minzhi 賀蘭敏之.

Wu Sansi 武三思 |woo sän-sih|; prince of Liang 梁王 (–707): son of Wu Yuanqing; Tianhou's nephew; Wu Chongxun's father; chief minister; close ties with Empress Wei; killed in the Li Chongjun incident.

Wu Shirang 武士讓: Tianhou's uncle; brother of Wu Shiyue.

Wu Shiyue 武士彠 |~ shih-yüeh| (577–635): Tianhou's father.

Wu Weiliang 武惟良 (–666): elder brother of Wu Huaiyun and younger brother of Wu Huailiang; cousin of Tianhou; killed.

Wu Yanji 武延基 |woo yän-jee| (679–701): son of Wu Chengsi; husband of Li Xianhui; killed for spreading gossip about the Zhang brothers.

Wu Yanxiu 武延秀 (685–710): son of Wu Chengsi; second husband of Princess Anle; killed.

Wu Yizong 武懿宗 |woo yee-dzong|; commandery prince of Henei 河內郡王 (641–706): grandson of Wu Shiyi 武士逸 (Tianhou's uncle; brother of Wu Shiyue); cruel official.

Wu Youji 武攸暨 |woo you-jee| (663–712): grandson of Wu Shirang 武士讓 (Tianhou's uncle; brother of Wu Shiyue); second husband of Princess Taiping.

Wu Youning 武攸寧; Prince Jianchang 建昌王 (–c. 705): grandson of Wu Shirang 武士讓 (Tianhou's uncle; brother of Wu Shiyue).

Wu Youxu 武攸緒 |woo you-shü| (655–723): grandson of Wu Shirang 武士讓 (Tianhou's uncle; brother of Wu Shiyue); Wu Weiliang's son; Tianhou's nephew; Daoist recluse of Mount Song.

Wu Youyi 武攸宜 |woo you-yee| (–705–710): grandson of Wu Shirang 武士讓 (Tianhou's uncle; brother of Wu Shiyue); Wu Weiliang's son; Tianhou's nephew.

Wu Yuanqing 武元慶 |woo yuän-cheeng| (–666 or later): Tianhou's half-brother; brother of Yuanshuang; son of Wu Shiyue and Lady Xiangli; Wu Sansi's father; banished.

Wu Yuanshuang 武元爽 |woo yuän-shuäng| (–666 or later): Tianhou's half-brother; brother of Yuanqing; son of Wu Shiyue and Lady Xiangli; Wu Chengsi's father; banished.

Wu Zetian. *See* Tianhou.

Wu Zhao. *See* Tianhou.

Wu Zhou 武周; Zhou (690–705): the dynasty founded by Tianhou.

Wu, Lady. *See* Tianhou.

Wucheng (Xuanzheng) Basilica 武成 (宣政) 殿: palatial building in Luoyang's Palace City.

wuju 武舉 |woo-jü| (Military Skills Examination): introduced by Tianhou (702).

Wuzhile 烏質勒 |woo-jih-lê| (–706): leader of Türgesh.

Xí 霫: minor non-Han ethnic group active in east Mongolia.

Xi 奚: minor non-Han ethnic group mainly active in Manchuria.

Xiangli, Lady 相里氏 |shee'ang-lee shih|: Wu Shiyue's principal wife; mother of Wu Yuanqing and Wu Yuanshuang.

Xiao Shufei. *See* Consort Xiao.

Xiao Yu 蕭瑀 (575–648): senior official under Taizong.

Xiao Zhizhong 蕭至忠 |shee'ao jih-jong| (–713): chief minister under Zhongzong; attached himself to Princess Taiping; killed.

Xiao, Consort; Xiao Shufei 蕭淑妃 |shee'ao ~|; Pure Consort Xiao (–655): consort of Gaozong; deposed, killed.

Xie You 謝祐 |shee'eh you| (–682): area commander of Qianzhou 黔州都督; assassinated.

Xieli Khan/Qaghan 頡利可汗 |shee'eh-lee ~|; Jieli ~ (–634): Eastern Tujue leader.

Xingning Ward 興寧坊: residential ward in northeast Chang'an.

Xiuxiang Ward 修祥坊: residential ward in northwest Chang'an.

Xizhou 西州: prefecture with its seat in Turfan, Xinjiang.

Xizhou 巂州: prefecture with its seat in Xichang, Sichuan.

Xu Jian 徐堅 (c. 659–729): Tang historian.

Xu Jingzong 許敬宗 |shü jeeng-dzong| (592–672): top pro-Tianhou official under Gaozong.

Xu Yougong 徐有功 |shü ~| (635–702): fair-minded senior official.

Xuancheng, princess of 宣城公主; princess of Gao'an 高安公主 (649–714): daughter of Zhongzong and Xiao Shufei.

Xuanwumen 玄武門 |shüan-woo-mên|; Xuanwu Gate: northern gate of the Palace City in Chang'an or Luoyang.

Xuanyang Ward 宣陽坊: residential ward southeast of the Imperial City, Chang'an.

Xuanzheng Basilica 宣政殿: ① *see* Wucheng Basilica. ② key palatial building in the Daming Palace, Chang'an.

Xuanzong, Tang 唐玄宗 |täng shüan-dzong|; Li Longji 李隆基 |lee long-jee| (685–762; r. 712–756): Ruizong's son; ninth Tang emperor; leader of the 710 coup.

Xue Huaiyi 薛懷義 |shüeh huai-yee|; né Feng Xiaobao 馮小寶 (662–early 695): Tianhou's lover; abbot; builder; killed.

Xue Jichang 薛季昶 |shüeh ~| (–706): senior official.

Xue Rengui 薛仁貴 |shüeh ~| (614–683): leading general under Gaozong.

Xue Shao 薛紹 |shüeh ~| (–688): Princess Taiping's first husband; killed.

Xue Sijian 薛思簡 |shüeh ~| (fl. 710): general.

Xue Sixing 薛思行 |shüeh sih-sheeng| (fl. 705): general; took part in the 705 coup.

Xue Yuanchao 薛元超 |shüeh ~| (622–683): senior official.

Xue Zhongzhang 薛仲璋 |shüeh jong-jäng| (fl. 684): co-conspirator of the Li Jingye rebellion.

Yamato 大和: state based in Japan's Nara-Kyoto area.

Yan Liben 閻立本 |~ lee-bên| (601–673): painter and senior official.

Yan Qinrong 燕欽融 (–710): low-ranking official; killed after charging Empress Wei with conspiracy.

Yan Zhaoyin 閻朝隱 (fl. late 690s–early 710s): scholar, official, one of Tianhou's favorites.

Yan Zhiwei 閻知微 |yän jih-wei| (–698): emissary to Tujue; traitor; killed.

Yang Sixu 楊思勗 (654–740): lead eunuch officer under Zhongzong and Xuanzong.

Yang Yuanyan 楊元琰 |yäng yuän-yän| (640–718): official; took part in the 705 coup.

Yang Zaisi 楊再思 |~ dzai-sih| (634–709): senior official; flatterer; supporter of the Zhang brothers.

Yang Zhirou 楊執柔 |~ jih-rou| (–692): senior official.

Yang, Lady 楊氏 (579–670): state mistress of Rong 榮國夫人, Sui royal, mother of Tianhou.

Yanximen 延喜門 |yän-shee-mên|; Yanxi Gate: northern gate in the east wall of the Imperial City.

Yao Yuanzhi 姚元之; Yao Chong 姚崇 (650–721): chief minister under Tianhou, Ruizong, and Xuanzong.

Yao Shu 姚璹 (632–705): senior official.

Yao 堯: predynastic good sovereign.

Yi Yin 伊尹 |yee yeen| (1649–1550 BCE): chancellor of Shang known for his loyalty.

Yicheng, Princess 宜城公主: daughter of Zhongzong.

Yidu Neiren 宜都內人 |yee-doo ~|: female adviser to Tianhou.

Yijing. See *Book of Changes*.

Yiyang, princess of 義陽公主 |yee-yäng ~| (640–691): daughter of Xiao Shufei.

Yong 雍: capital area in the Wei River valley, south Shaanxi.

You, King of Zhou 周幽王 (–771 BCE): last king of the Western Zhou.

Yu Baojia 魚保家 |yü ~| (–686): inventor of the Bronze Chest; killed.

Yu Shinan 虞世南 |yü shih-nän| (558–638): Early Tang calligrapher, poet, official.

Yu Zhining 于志寧 |yü jih-ning| (588–665): senior official under Taizong and Gaozong.

Yu 禹 |yü| (Lord Yu): predynastic sovereign.

Yuan Gongyu 袁公瑜 |yuän gong-yü| (613–685): senior official under Gaozong.

Yuan Shuji 袁恕己 |yuän shoo-jee| (–706): senior official; took part in the 705 coup; one of the "Five Princes"; killed.

Yuan Tiangang 袁天罡 |yuan tee'än-gäng| (573–645): diviner, astrologist.

Yulin Armies 羽林軍: security forces stationed in the Forbidden Park of Chang'an.

Yun Banqian 員半千 |yün bän-chee'an| (621–714): official; man of letters. Note: 員 is not pronounced *yuan*.

Yuwen Kai 宇文愷 |yü-wên ~| (555–612): Sui builder of Chang'an and Luoyang.

Zang, Lady 臧氏: Zhang Yizhi's 張易之 mother.

zanpu 贊普: Tubo king.

Zhai Rang 翟讓 (d. 617): major late-Sui rebel leader active in the Central Plain.

Zhang Changqi 張昌期 |jäng chäng-chee| (–705): Zhang Yizhi's and Zhang Changzong's elder brother; killed. *Jiu Tang shu* 78, 張易之、張昌宗傳; *Xin Tang shu* 104, 張易之、張昌宗傳. Note: *Zizhi tongjian* (207.6563) records him as Zhang Yizhi's younger brother.

Zhang Changyi 張昌儀 |jäng chäng-yee| (–705): Zhang Yizhi's and Changzong's elder brother; killed. *Jiu Tang shu* 186B, 王旭傳; *Xin Tang shu* 222, 王旭傳.

Zhang Changzong 張昌宗 | jäng chäng-dzong| (–705): Zhang Yizhi's younger half-brother; Tianhou's favorite gigolo; killed.

Zhang Deyu 張德裕 |jäng dê-yü| (fl. 692): senior official.

Zhang Jianzhi 張柬之 |jäng jee'an-jih| (625–706): senior official; leader of the 705 coup; one of the "Five Princes."

Zhang Jiazhen 張嘉貞 |jäng jee'ä-jen| (666–729): chief minister.

Zhang Qianxu 張虔勗 |jäng chee'än-shü| (–691): general-in-chief; killed by Lai Junchen.

Zhang Renyuan 張仁愿 |jäng ren-yuän| (–714): top general; defender the northern border against Tujue; builder of the Three Shouxiang Towns (outposts on the Yellow River).

Zhang Shizhi 張釋之 |jäng shih-jih|: chief law enforcement officer (*tingwei* 廷尉), fair-minded judge under Emperors Wen and Jing of the Western Han.

Zhang Tinggui 張廷珪 |jäng ~| (ca. 662–734): official.

Zhang Tongxiu 張同休 |jäng tong-shee'u|(–705): Zhang Yizhi's and Zhang Changzong's elder brother; killed. *See* Zhang Changqi.

Zhang Xi 張錫 |jäng shee| (–710 or later): corrupt senior official.

Zhang Xuanyu 張玄遇 |jäng shuän-yü| (fl. 696): general; captured by Qidan.

Zhang Yizhi 張易之 |jäng yee-jih| (–705): Zhang Changzong's elder half-brother; Tianhou's favorite gigolo; killed.

Zhang Yue 張說 |jäng ~| (667–731): man of letters; top official under Ruizong and Xuanzong.

Zhangsun, Empress 長孫皇后 (601–536): wife of Taizong; younger sister of Zhangsun Wuji; adopted daughter of Gao Shilian.

Zhangsun Wuji 長孫無忌 |jäng-soon woo-jee| (594–659): elder brother of Empress Zhangsun and adopted son of Gao Shilian; top official under Taizong and Gaozong; uncle of Gaozong; suicide.

Zhao Daosheng 趙道生 |jao ~| (–680): Prince Li Xián's male lover; killed.

Zhao Wenhui 趙文翽 |jao ~| (–696): area commander of Yingzhou 營州 (in Liaoning); killed.

Zhaoling 昭陵 |jao-leeng|: tomb park northwest of Chang'an. It is home to the tomb of Taizong and his wife Empress Zhangsun.

Zheng Yin 鄭愔 |jêng yeen| (–710): poet; chief minister under Zhongzong; attached himself to Wu Sansi; executed.

Zheng, Lady 鄭氏 |jêng ~|: Shangguan Wan'er's mother.

Zhenguan Basilica 貞觀殿: major palatial building in Luoyang's Palace City.

Zhong Shaojing 鐘紹京 |jong ~| (659–746): official; calligrapher; took part in the 710 coup.

Zhongzong, Tang 唐中宗 |täng jong-dzong|; Li Zhe 李哲; Li Xian 李顯; prince of Luling 廬陵王 (656–710; r. 684, 705–710): Gaozong's and Tianhou's son; emperor; poisoned to death.

zhou 州 |jo|: prefecture or prefectural seat, depending on the context; e.g.: Qing*zhou* 青州, Tong*zhou* 通州. *See* prefecture (*zhou* 州).

Zhou Ju 周矩 |jo jü| (fl. 692): official.

Zhou Liyong 周利用 |jo lee-yong| (fl. 706): cruel law officer under Zhongzong.

Zhou Xing 周興 |jo sheeng| (–691): cruel law officer; killed.

Zhou, Duke of 周公 (fl. 1042 BCE): regent of King Cheng.

Zhòu 紂 |jo|: bad last sovereign of the Shang.

Zhu Jingze 朱敬則 |joo jeeng-dzê| (635–709): senior official; historian.

Zhuquemen 朱雀門 |joo-chüeh-mên|; Zhuque Gate: main southern entrance to the Imperial City of Chang'an.

Zichen Basilica (*dian*) 紫宸殿 |dzih-chen dee'an|: palatial building: ① north of the Xuanzheng Basilica in Chang'an's Daming Palace. ② north of Qianyuan Basilica in Luoyang's Palace City.

Zong Chuke 宗楚客 |dzong choo-kê| (–710): son of a female cousin of Tianhou; chief minister trusted by Empress Wei; killed in the 710 coup.

Zong Jinqing 宗晉卿 |dzong jeen-cheeng| (–c. 710): younger brother of Zong Chuke; attached himself to Wu Sansi; killed after the

710 coup.

Zuozhuan 左傳 |dzuo-juän| (Mr. Zuo's Commentary): chronological history of the Spring and Autumn period; Confucian classic of the fourth century BCE.

Bibliography

Note: For official titles, *see* Hucker 1985, Twitchett 1979, and Xiong 2017. For place names, *see* Shi Weile et al. 2005. For additional information on historical figures and other items, *see* Xiong 2017.

Premodern works

Chang'an zhi 長安志 (Gazetteer of Chang'an). By Song Minqiu 宋敏求 (N. Song). *Congshu jicheng chubian* edition.

Henan zhi 河南志 (Gazetteer of Henan). By Xu Song 徐松 (Qing). Beijing: Zhonghua Shuju, 1994.

Jiu Tang shu 舊唐書 (Old Book of the Tang). By Liu Xu 劉昫 et al. (Wudai). Beijing: Zhonghua Shuju, 1975.

Quan Tang shi 全唐詩 (Complete Tang Poetry), 25 vols. Compiled by Peng Dingqiu 彭定求 et al. (Qing). Beijing: Zhonghua Shuju, 1960.

Quan Tang wen 全唐文 (Complete Tang Prose), 11 vols. Compiled by Dong Gao 董誥 et al. (Qing). With Lu Xinyuan 陸心源, comp., *Tangwen shiyi* 唐文拾遺 and *Tangwen xushi* 唐文續拾. Beijing: Zhonghua Shuju, 1983.

Shiji 史記 (Records of the Historian). By Sima Qian 司馬遷 (W. Han). Beijing: Zhonghua Shuju, 1959.

Taiping guangji 太平廣記 (Extensive Gleanings of the Taiping [Xingguo] Period), 10 vols. Compiled by Li Fang 李昉 et al. (N. Song). Beijing: Zhonghua Shuju, 1961.

Taiping yulan 太平御覽 (Imperial Digest of the Taiping [Xingguo] Period), 4 vols. Compiled by Li Fang 李昉 et al. (N. Song). Beijing: Zhonghua Shuju, 1960.

Tang da zhaoling ji 唐大詔令集 (Imperial Edicts of the Tang). Compiled by Song Minqiu 宋敏求 (N. Song). Shanghai: Xuelin Chubanshe, 1992.

Tang huiyao 唐會要 (Tang Compendium of the Essential). Compiled by Wang Pu 王溥 (Wudai and N. Song). Beijing: Zhonghua Shuju, 1990.

Tang kaiyuan zhanjing 唐開元占經 (Divination Classic of the Kaiyuan Reign of the Tang). Compiled by Qutan Xida 瞿曇悉達 (Tang). *Wenyuange Siku quanshu* edition.

Tang liangjing chengfang kao 唐兩京城坊考 (Examination of the City Wards of the Two Tang Capitals). By Xu Song 徐松 (Qing), edited by Fang Yan 方嚴. Beijing: Zhonghua Shuju, 1985.

Tang liudian 唐六典 (Six Codes of the Tang). By Li Linfu 李林甫 et al. (Tang), edited by Chen Zhongfu 陳仲夫. Beijing: Zhonghua Shuju, 1992.

Tangren yishi huibian 唐人軼事彙編 (Collection of Tang Anecdotes), 2 volumes. Edited by Zhou Xunchu 周勛初 et al. Shanghai: Shanghai Shiji Chuban Gufen Youxian Gongsi and Shanghai Guji Chubanshe, 2006.

Xin Tang shu 新唐書 (New Book of the Tang). By Ouyang Xiu 歐陽修 and Song Qi 宋祁 (N. Song). Beijing: Zhonghua Shuju, 1975.

Yonglu 雍錄 (Records of Yong). By Cheng Dachang 程大昌 (S. Song). Beijing, Zhonghua Shuju, 2002.

Zizhi tongjian 資治通鑑 (Comprehensive Mirror for Aid in Government). By Sima Guang 司馬光 et al. (N. Song). Beijing: Zhonghua Shuju, 1956.

Modern works

Chang, Kang-i Sun, and Haun Saussy, eds. 2000. *Women Writers of Traditional China: An Anthology of Poetry and Criticism*. Stanford, CA: Stanford University Press.

Guisso, Richard W. L. 1978. *Wu Tse-T'ien and the Politics of Legitimation in T'ang China*. Bellingham, WA: Center for East Asian Studies, Western Washington University.

Hara Momoyo 原百代. 1985. *Bu Sokuten* 武則天, vols. 1–8. Tokyo: Kodansha.

Hucker, Charles O. 1985. *A Dictionary of Official Titles in Imperial China*. Stanford: Stanford University Press.

Li Jianchao 李健超. 2006. *Zengding liangjing chengfang kao* 增訂兩京城坊考. Xi'an: Sanqin Chubanshe.

Lin Daoxin 林道心 et al. 2003. *Zhongguo gudai wannianli* 中國古代萬年曆. Shijiazhuang: Hebei Renmin Chubanshe.

Minford, John, and Joseph S. M. Lau. 2002. *Classical Chinese Literature: An Anthology of Translations, v. 1: From Antiquity to the Tang Dynasty*. New York: Columbia University Press.

Rothschild, N. Harry. 2007. *Wu Zhao: China's Only Female Emperor*. New York: Pearson Longman.

Rothschild, N. Harry. 2017. *Emperor Wu Zhao and Her Pantheon of Devis, Divinities, and Dynastic Mothers*. New York: Columbia University Press.

Sanders, Graham. 2006. *Words Well Put: Visions of Poetic Competence in the Chinese Tradition*. Boston, MA: Harvard University Asia Center.

Shi Weile 史為樂 et al. 2005. *Zhongguo lishi diming dacidian* 中國歷史地名大辭典. Beijing: Sheke Chubanshe.

Twitchett, Denis C., ed. 1979. *The Cambridge History of China*, volume

3: *Sui and T'ang China*. Cambridge: Cambridge University Press.

Wang Zhenping. 2013. *Tang China in Multi-Polar Asia: A History of Diplomacy and War*. Honolulu, HI: University of Hawai'i Press.

Xiong, Victor Cunrui. 2000. *Sui-Tang Chang'an (583–904): A Study in the Urban History of Medieval China*. Ann Arbor, MI: Center for Chinese Studies, University of Michigan.

Xiong, Victor Cunrui. 2016. *Capital Cities and Urban Form in Pre-modern China: Luoyang, 1038 BCE to 938 CE*. London: Routledge.

Xiong, Victor Cunrui. 2017. *Historical Dictionary of Medieval China*, 2nd edition (2 volumes). Lanham, MD: Rowman & Littlefield Publishers.

Zhang Yonglu 張永祿, ed. 1990. *Tangdai Chang'an cidian* 唐代長安詞典. Xi'an: Shaanxi Renmin Chubanshe.

Heavenly Empress: The Age of Wu Zetian
A Novel of Tang and Wu Zhou China

ISBN: 978-986-6286-80-3
DOI: 10.978.9866286/803
Publishing Date: May 2023
Price: NT$ 650

Author: Victor Cunrui Xiong
Editor-in-Chief: Huei-Chu Chang
Executive Editor: Yi-Chun Liao
Cover Designer: Alan Chang

Publisher: Ainosco Press
General Manager: Chris Chang
18F, No. 80, Sec. 1, Chenggong Rd., Yonghe Dist., New Taipei City 234634, Taiwan
Tel: +886-2-2926-6006
Fax: +886-2-2923-5151
E-mail: press@airiti.com

The publication of this book is supported by the Timothy Light Center for Chinese Studies, Western Michigan University.

Made in the USA
Las Vegas, NV
18 May 2023